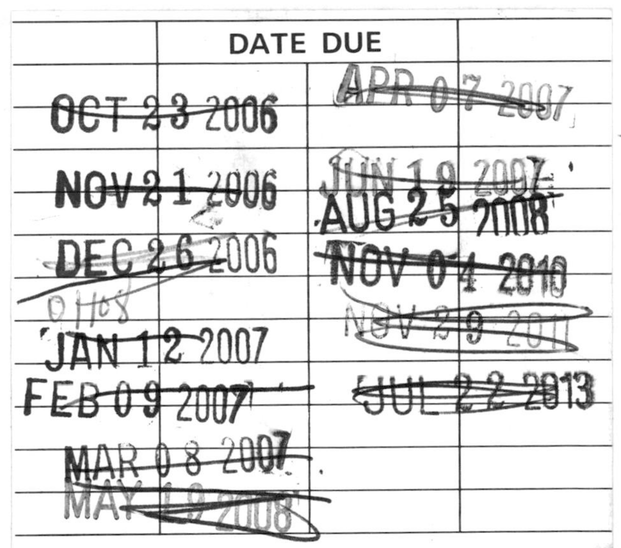
DATE DUE
OCT 23 2006
NOV 21 2006
DEC 26 2006
JAN 12 2007
FEB 09 2007
MAR 08 2007
MAY 19 2008
APR 07 2007
JUN 19 2007
AUG 25 2008
NOV 04 2010
NOV 29 2011
JUL 22 2013

The Leper's Return

A Knights Templar Mystery

MICHAEL JECKS

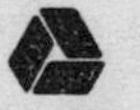

AVON BOOKS
An Imprint of HarperCollins*Publishers*

This is a work of fiction. Names, characters, places, and incidents are products of the author's imagination or are used fictitiously and are not to be construed as real. Any resemblance to actual events, locales, organizations, or persons, living or dead, is entirely coincidental.

AVON BOOKS
An Imprint of HarperCollins*Publishers*
10 East 53rd Street
New York, New York 10022-5299

ISBN-13: 978-0-06-084658-9
ISBN-10: 0-06-084658-5
www.avonmystery.com

First Avon Books paperback printing: September 2006

Printed in the U.S.A.

10 9 8 7 6 5 4 3 2 1

For Marjorie,
a very special friend

But . . .

it has to be dedicated to
Chopsie as well!

Author's Note

It is often difficult to conduct research.

The problem starts with a small area which seems easy enough to resolve, such as: "Did houses in the early fourteenth century have glass in their windows?" but all too often, this start point brings up lots more questions and no answers. As an author, I often find myself becoming so involved in ensuring absolute accuracy that the search widens to an alarming extent. For instance, how did they melt glass? How did they mold it? Was it clear or opaque? How expensive was it? Could anyone under the level of a baron or burgess afford it? It is all very well knowing that deep in the bowels of the new British Library there is a book that tells all, but first one must locate the thing. Sadly, the researcher will probably find that it is hidden in something totally unrelated, such as *Medieval Alchemy and the Search for the Philosopher's Stone, a Feminist View* by Ms. F. Bloggs—and it will take three or four trips to London, spending hours reading irrelevant material, to find that the volume that is needed . . . was destroyed in the Blitz.

However, this is as nothing compared with the problems of editing.

After spending weeks on end living in the British Library, one finally comes upon tons of fascinating data, all rich and absorbing to anyone who is remotely intrigued by how people used to live. If one is fascinated by history, as I am, it is tempting to put it *all* into a story, but it is a depressing truth that readers are not keen on novels of over 1000 pages. Thus much detail has to be discarded. But then, if one cheats, one can put it into an Author's Note!

There are many works which look at lepers and their disease through history. Unfortunate sufferers were looked down upon for centuries as being hideously deformed because God sought to mark them out. The view was, if God felt the need to make them so repellent, he must have had his reasons. Naturally that led to the idea that lepers should be excluded from society—for if God chose to punish them, who could doubt that He was right?

The act of declaring someone a leper was probably quite simple: it seems clear they were often denounced by their neighbors. After the allegation had been made, it would have been difficult for someone to offer any defense, because the evidence was all too clear. Any deformity could be interpreted as leprosy by superstitious and uneducated villagers.

The miserable victim would be hauled off before a board of worthy citizens. Not doctors or surgeons necessarily, because not every village could afford one, but people who were thought honest and religious enough for the task. In some places, over in Lorraine, for example, the suspected leper would have been examined by emissaries of the Bishop and one or two known lepers, presumably on the basis that a leper would know what to look for. The man or woman's blood would be examined and tested with grains of salt, vinegar, and the urine of a young boy, although exactly *how* this was done I haven't had the courage to find out. If the person was found to be clear, letters of absolution would be given to them and read out by the local priests so that no one could be in any doubt as to their being safe.

But sometimes mistakes were made. Several people had to fight their cases vigorously. For example, there was a well-documented case in Britain where a man was accused of having the disease, and he had to go all the way to London to be examined. The learned doctors signed a legal document stating they thought he was safe to live in the community, which the fellow showed to all and sundry. It is also important to note that the doctors could be most assiduous in proving whether someone did or did not have the disease. In a case in Brentwood in Essex in 1468, the doctors looked for more than forty separate distinguishing symptoms before declaring the poor woman in question fit to stay at home.

Taking the example of a male, a medieval man who had been declared leprous would find life instantly changing for the worse. The priest would console him, before making him swear to tell the truth on a number of questions. Was there leprosy in his family? Had he ever had intercourse with lepers? Had he ever eaten with lepers?

There was a long-standing belief that leprosy was in some way related to sex. Either it was sexually transmitted, especially when sleeping with a menstruating woman, or the sins of the father or mother at the time of conception were so great that the child was born with the disease.

After this interrogation, the leper would be hauled off to church to be put through the "Office for the Seclusion of a Leper." Then the poor devil would be given a pep talk, which would go along these lines:

"While you are diseased, you'll not go into any house, inn, forge, mill, bakehouse, or brewery; you'll not drink or wash your hands or laundry at any communal well, fountain, spring, or trough; you'll eat alone or with lepers; you'll enter no church during a service, mingle with no crowd, walk down no small streets or narrow alleys; you'll always stand to leeward of anyone you talk to; you'll always sound your bell or clapper when begging. You'll not go out without your cloak; you'll always wear your gloves; you'll only drink from your own fountain, or from your own stoup, filled from your own fountain; you'll touch no child but your own; you'll always return to your cabin at night."

The leper was then given a box in which to collect alms, and the priest would make the first donation, standing nearby with his eye on all his parishioners to ensure they followed his example.

Others were fortunate enough to find themselves a place in a hospital.

Leper camps, or "lazar" houses, were charitable institutions set up by the wealthy or by the Church. Usually these places provided for twelve or thirteen of the afflicted, and they would live as religious brethren, accepting the same responsibility of looking after the souls of the living and the dead. The brothers would have to pray for themselves, and also for their patrons. Thus at matins the lepers might say twenty-six paternosters; at prime another fourteen; at nones fourteen; at vespers eighteen; at compline fourteen again. In addition each brother would say twenty-five paternosters for his own sins, and as many again for the souls of the benefactors of the hospital.

One must realize that these people weren't in quarantine, but were taking the positive action of caring for souls. Although it may seem strange to us, to say the least, these brothers could be punished by being evicted from their hospital. Usually punishments took the form of a day in the pillory or stocks, but for those who were unusually mischievous, the leper master could order that he be thrown out. The miserable, and obviously lonely, fellow would then be forced to beg his own food and find his own drink. Not easy, when a leper was discouraged from approaching other citizens, and couldn't touch food in the presence of others.

Although all the foregoing refers solely to men, the same comments are, of course, equally applicable to women, but there appear to have been fewer leprous women than men. Whatever the reason for this, convents were available for women, and my researches show that occasionally leper hospitals were designed for both sexes: I understand that the "Maudlin" at Tavistock had spaces for six men and six women.

A leper was defiled, and by touching something else would defile that too. That was why the Church refused to allow lepers to enter enclosed areas, to drink from fountains, or even be buried with ordinary folk. This behavior would have been reasonably effective in preventing the spread of an infectious disease, but ironically it now seems that leprosy is *not* very contagious.

As usual I have tried to be as historically accurate as is possible within the confines of a work of fiction. In 1320 the canonical church of Crediton was only recently completed, and Bishop Stapledon was very generous to it, giving the church two more fairs. Churches liked having fairs: roughly one-tenth of all profits went straight back to the priests, creating a pleasant windfall. In return the precentor of the church, together with his canons and vicars, was bound to celebrate Stapledon's birthday throughout his life, and must solemnize the anniversary of his death. The Bishop also appointed four more young clerks to make sure the services were performed with suitable dignity. Likewise St. Lawrence's Hospital in Crediton did exist, and it was serviced by a monk appointed from the convent at Houndeslow.

However, it is difficult to be accurate when describing real people. The Bishop himself was a highly important man in England. He contributed large sums to Exeter Cathedral, was involved with the Ordainers and helped create the Middle Party, founded Stapledon Hall in Oxford (now Exeter College), and began a grammar school in Exeter. Later he was to become Lord High Treasurer to the King, until murdered by the London mob in 1326. Yet as he appears in these pages his nature and character are entirely my own invention.

One other man in *The Leper's Return* has the advantage of existing, and of being documented. He is Mr. Thomas Orey, a fuller by trade, who was present at one of Bishop Stapledon's services on the Wednesday before August 1 in 1315. The sudden recovery of his sight in the middle of the service led to the events described, although his chance meeting with John of Irelaunde was again the result of my overheated imagination. As for what actually happened to Thomas, I am afraid you must read on . . .

Michael Jecks
South Godstone,
February 1998

The
Leper's
Return

Preface

Walter Stapledon, Bishop of Exeter, watched the sky with a sense of foreboding, trying not to wince as his horse rocked gently beneath him.

"It looks like rain, doesn't it, my Lord?"

The Bishop grunted non-committally. Those few words summed up the animosity with which people viewed the weather. During the disastrous years of 1315 and 1316, the crops had drowned in torrential rain and thousands had died in the ensuing famines. Few families across Europe had been untouched by the misery and even now, in autumn 1320, all feared a repeat of the disaster. Stapledon glanced sympathetically at his companion. "At least this year's harvest was collected safely," he said gravely. "God gave us a respite, whatever He may hold in store for the future."

His companion nodded, but as he surveyed the pewter-colored clouds bunching overhead, his eyes held the expression of one who can see the arrow flying toward him and waits only to see where it will strike. "I pray that God will preserve us in the coming year as well."

Stapledon forbore to comment. God's will was beyond the understanding of ordinary men, and the

Bishop was content to wait and see what He planned. At least this visit should be restful, he thought—away from the circle of devious, mendacious tricksters who surrounded King Edward.

The monk at his side, Ralph of Houndeslow, had arrived in Exeter only a few days before, asking for a room to rest for the night. When he had heard that the Bishop himself was about to depart for the large town of Crediton, northwest of Exeter, he had been delighted to accept Stapledon's offer of a place in his retinue. It was safer to undertake a journey with company in these troubled times, even for a man wearing the tonsure.

Stapledon had found Ralph to be quite unlike previous visitors. Most who asked for hospitality at the Bishop's gates were garrulous, for they were used to travelling, and delighted in talking about their adventures on the road, but Ralph was quiet. He appeared to be holding himself back, as though he was aware of the weighty responsibility that was about to fall upon his shoulders. Stapledon found him reserved and rather dull, a little too introspective, but that was hardly surprising. Ralph's words about the weather demonstrated one line his thoughts were taking, but the prelate knew other things were giving him concern. It was as if a foul atmosphere had polluted the air in this benighted kingdom, and no one was unaware of the poison at work in their midst: treachery!

Stapledon turned in his saddle to survey the men behind. There were fifteen all told: five men-at-arms, four servants and the rest clerics. The troops were all hardened types recently hired to the Bishop's service, and he viewed them askance. Since accepting his high office from the King and Parliament, it had been deemed prudent that he should have some protection, and after persuasion he had agreed to take on a bodyguard. He knew they were necessary for his safety, but that didn't mean he had to enjoy their company. His only satisfaction was that when he studied them he could see they weren't prey to fears for their future. They each knew that a mug of warmed, spiced ale waited for them at the end of their journey, and that was enough to assure their contentment. They were uneducated ruffians, and higher considerations were irrelevant to them. When he cast an eye over his servants, he saw that they weren't plagued with doubts either, for they knew their jobs, and would blindly obey their master. No, it was only when he looked at his monks that he saw the weary anxiety.

Stapledon knew what lay at the bottom of it, and it wasn't only the weather: the clerics, like himself, were aware that civil war was looming.

It was many years since the King's grandfather, Henry III, had engaged Simon de Montfort in battles up and down the kingdom, but the horror of it was known to those who were educated and could read the chronicles. Their trepidation reflected that of all the King's subjects as stories spread of the increasing tension between two of the most powerful men in the land. The Bishop paid no heed to such rumors—he had no need to. He had witnessed at first hand how relations between the King, Edward II, and the Earl of Lancaster had soured.

Earlier in the year, Sir Walter had become the Lord High Treasurer, the man who controlled the kingdom's purse. In theory, the position was one of strength, but it made him feel as safe as a kitten dropped unprotected between two packs of loosed hunting dogs. No matter how he stood, he was constantly having to look to his back. There were many, in both the King's party and the Earl's, who would have liked to see him ruined. Men who had shunned him before now pretended to be his friend so that they could try to destroy him—or subvert him to their cause. Stapledon was used to the twisted and corrupt ways of politics and politicians, for he had been a key mover in the group which had tried to bring King Edward and the Earl of Lancaster to some sort of understanding, but the deceit and falseness of men who were well-born and supposedly chivalrous repelled him.

He had hoped that the Treaty of Leake would end the bitterness, but the underlying rivalries still existed. Stapledon was not the only man in the kingdom to be unpleasantly aware of the rising enmity. Lancaster was behaving with brazen insolence; not attending Parliament when summoned, and recklessly pursuing his own interests at the expense of the King's. Stapledon had no doubt that if the Earl continued to flaunt his contempt for his liege, there would be war. And if that happened, the Bishop knew that the Scots would once more pour over the border. They had agreed to a truce last year, in 1319, but more recently there had been rumblings from the north. Since their success at Bannockburn and their capture of Berwick, the Scots had become more confident. Stapledon was glumly convinced that if the northern devils saw a means of dividing the English, they would seize it.

Stapledon knew that the same thoughts were diverting the monks as they made their way along the road. Leaning over, he patted Ralph's back. "Don't worry, my son, we can set aside all fears for the future of the country while we are here in Devon."

"If war comes, it will reach to every corner of the kingdom."

"True, but it will come here last of all, and there is no need to anticipate it at present. Perhaps there are enough men of good will and good sense to avert it."

"I pray to God that we might be saved from it."

Stapledon peered at Ralph. It was irritating that his sight was so poor now at shorter distances; he could observe things with clarity ten feet away or more, but anything nearer was indistinct, as if seen through a misted glass. "You will find that Crediton will help you forget your fears. It is a happy, bustling town, and the Dean, Peter Clifford, is a good man—and an excellent host."

Ralph of Houndeslow gave a faint smile. Peter Clifford's hospitality was immaterial to him. There were vastly more important things to consider than a dean's generosity to travelling monks and an important prelate—but this was hardly the time for him to raise such matters. He was relieved to see the Bishop revert to silent contemplation of the way ahead.

There was little to see. The rolling hills rose on either side, smothered in ancient trees—oaks, elms, beeches and chestnuts—and here and there a thin column of smoke lifted over the branches until caught by the faint breeze, whereupon it was whipped away like magic. It was good to see that the peasants were industrious here; in so many other places the villeins were surly and lazy. Since the famine, many appeared to resent working for their masters. Here at least the wood was being cut, the coppiced boughs taken for firewood and furniture-making, or being stacked to make charcoal.

But Ralph had heard about this land and couldn't like it. He knew that the further he travelled toward Crediton, the further he was going from civilization. Few desired to go as far to the west as Dartmoor or Cornwall. They were wild lands, with a population that was unchanged, so it was said, from the earliest times when the first men came to these islands. Devon and Cornish men were hard and lawless, as rough and untameable as the moors themselves. Exeter was more or less a haven, a lonely fort on the outskirts of the kingdom, much like the castles of the Welsh or Scottish Marches, an isolated beacon of hope in the wasteland all round.

Just as he thought this, Ralph saw a cart. The sight of so mundane a vehicle made him feel a little foolish after his sour consideration of the land. It was as if God Himself was rebuking him for falling prey to such somber reflections.

Stapledon was still concentrating on the hills ahead. "Look," he said, pointing. "That smoke—that's Crediton."

Ralph followed the direction of his finger. They were descending into a broad valley, the river lying on their left, while on their right the woods were thinning. Beyond them he could see a series of strip fields lying roughly perpendicular to the road. A litter of broken branches and mud bore witness to the flooding of a month before when the rain had swollen every watercourse and the plains had filled with water. Much had been cleared from the road here, but silt remained on the side nearest the water. In front of him he caught a glimpse of a limewashed wall through the trees. He could see that the road curved round to the right and disappeared as it climbed up between two hills, above which he could make out the light haze of woodsmoke. Faintly on the wind came the scent of burning wood from the town's fires.

"Not far now," said the Bishop, wriggling uncomfortably in his saddle.

"No, my Lord," Ralph agreed. He had been told that the Bishop was victim to hemorrhoids, which made any journey on horseback an ordeal. Ralph had never been afflicted with them, but the eye-watering description of the symptoms, which likened the pain to that of sitting upon a sharpened dagger, made him sympathetic, no matter how much some of his servants might snigger behind the Bishop's back.

They were almost upon the cart now. Ralph could see that the driver was a little, hunched figure, elbows resting on his knees, his torso bent, the reins held slackly, as if the driver himself was content to leave the destination to his old pony. Ralph felt his mood lighten at the sight. This was a local peddlar, someone who would buy stocks of bread and beer to trade with households in the near vicinity; hardly the representative of a brutal and ancient race such as the monk had anticipated only a few minutes before. The cleric made a mental note to admit to his foolishness at his next Confession.

"Good morning," he called as he overhauled the carter.

The man idly raised a hand to his old felt hat, lifting the edge of its flopping brim, and Ralph caught a glimpse of shrewd brown eyes, which immediately narrowed in a cheerful grin, and then the hat was swept off with what the priest thought was a counterfeit respect, as if the man was laughing—although not at Ralph himself. It was as though the tranter was sharing a secret joke *with* Ralph, against the whole world. "Your servant, Lord."

"I'm no lord—but you know that well enough!" Ralph retorted, but chuckled when the fellow shrugged good-naturedly. He had seen enough of these wandering salesmen to know that they lived on their wits, persuading dubious farmers or tinminers to part with their hard-earned and jealously guarded money. This man looked capable of selling a broken nag to the King's own grooms, with his frank and honest appearance, easy smile and strong, square face. He gave Ralph a conspiratorial wink, and the cleric felt absurdly honored, as if he had undergone some form of trial and had exceeded the salesman's wildest expectations.

But then Ralph heard the Bishop give a swift intake of breath, and saw him stiffen in his saddle. The monk's pleasure was suddenly shattered as he heard the Bishop gasp: "My God! *You!*"

- 1 -

ir Baldwin Furnshill took another mug of apple juice and sipped. It had taken some years, but Peter Clifford, the Dean of Crediton Church, had finally accepted the fact that Baldwin preferred not to drink alcohol throughout the day, and now, whenever the knight came to visit him, there was usually some form of refreshment on offer which did not threaten him with intoxication.

It was rare for a man to avoid ale and wine, but Baldwin had spent his youth as a Poor Fellow Soldier of Christ and the Temple of Solomon—a Knight Templar. While he had remained a member of the Order he had rigorously avoided strong drink; now he was in his mid-forties, he knew he wasn't capable of consuming the same quantity as others of his age, and thus saved himself embarrassment by sticking to those drinks he knew would not leave him inebriated.

"That must be them," Peter Clifford said as voices were heard in the courtyard. Shortly afterward there was a jingling of harnesses, rumbling of cartwheels and the hollow, metallic clatter of hooves on the cobbles. The Dean stood, emptying his goblet and handing it to the waiting servant. Baldwin set his mug by the fire and trailed after his friend, walking out to welcome the Bishop.

Baldwin had met Stapledon on a few occasions, and had always found him to be an urbane, refined gentleman. Today the knight was somewhat surprised to see the Bishop standing scowling while Peter's stablemen held the horses. The Bishop's men were milling, some pulling chests and boxes from the back of the wagon, others collecting the smaller packages from individual mounts. Their frenetic activity was proof of their own nervousness in the face of their master's anger.

"My Lord Bishop, you are very welcome," Peter said, and Baldwin could hear the doubt in his voice. Peter must also have seen the Bishop's mood. "My Lord, would you like some spiced wine to take the chill off after your journey?"

"My friend, it's good to be here again once more," the Bishop said automatically, though a trifle curtly. "Meet the new master of St. Lawrence's Chapel, Ralph of Houndeslow."

Baldwin had noticed the cleric before he was introduced. To the knight, most young monks looked as if they would benefit from early exercise every morning for several weeks; they invariably had skin that displayed an unhealthy pallor. This one was different. He stood tall and straight, not bent at the shoulder, and from his ruddy color he might have been a laborer. His face was thin, but not weakly. He had a solid, pugnacious-looking chin, and his blue eyes were intelligent, glittering with a prideful confidence beneath a thatch of tawny hair. The monk put Baldwin in mind of some of his dead friends from the Templars.

As they walked back to the Dean's hall, Baldwin noticed that the Bishop did not stride so purposefully as had once been his wont. The prelate had aged in the last year.

Although still tall, he was more stooped than before. It looked as if the burden of his office was becoming too much for him to bear. Baldwin had first met him here in the Dean's house a year before, when Stapledon had pressed him to confirm to whom he owed his allegiance—King or Earl. Then Stapledon had been tall, erect and powerful. But Baldwin knew Stapledon was involved in the politics that surrounded the King, and that the pressure must be crushing. He recalled that twelve months before, they had both been fearful of war. In retrospect this appeared laughable: the situation had not been nearly so fraught with danger as it had now become.

Ralph took a seat a little to the Bishop's left, leaving the older man near the fire. Two balks of oak glowed dully, and as the Bishop dropped down with a grunt, Baldwin gave them a kick, creating a shower of sparks, before tossing split beech logs on top. Peter Clifford chivvied servants to fetch the wine before seating himself opposite their guests, and Baldwin pulled up a stool next to Ralph. As the flames curled upward the monk saw the knight's face in the flickering, lurid orange light, and to judge from the set nature of his expression, his thoughts were not pleasant.

Close to, the knight appeared older than the monk had first thought. Sir Baldwin was a lean-looking man, with the massive shoulders and arms of a swordsman, but where Ralph would have expected to see cruelty and indifference, he was surprised to see rather the opposite. The knight had kindly eyes. They were set in a dark face which was framed by short black hair, frosted with gray at his temples. A well-trimmed beard followed the line of his jaw.

His cheek wore a long scar, which shone in the candlelight. But Ralph could also see that pain marred his features. His forehead was slashed across with deep tracks, and at either side of his mouth were vertical lines that pointed to years of suffering. He gave the impression of a man who had endured, although the cost of surviving was high.

Bishop Stapledon also saw Baldwin's detachment and gave a rueful shrug. "Sir Baldwin, please excuse my shortness. I didn't intend to be rude."

"I am the one who should apologize; my mind was wandering."

"In my case I was reflecting on a chance encounter," said the Bishop.

"Really, my Lord?" asked Dean Peter with interest.

"Yes, Dean. I met a man I had no wish to see again," Stapledon said coldly. He accepted a goblet of mulled wine from the bottler, snuffing the aroma and grunting his approval. "That smells good! It was chilly on the way here; I swear I feel the weight of my years more strongly with each succeeding winter. With age, my flesh grows ever less protective against inclement weather. As a lad I'd have thought the weather today was so mild it only merited a shirt, but now I am old and feeble I have to reach for two tunics, a jerkin, and a thick woollen cloak. Dean Peter, your wine tastes as good as it smells! Thank you—I can feel my good humor returning!"

"But what unsettled you?" Peter persisted, waving at the bottler to top up Bishop Stapledon's goblet.

"That incorrigible little man, John Irelaunde."

"Oh—good God!"

"You don't seem surprised, Dean," the Bishop observed drily. "I am sure I recollect advising he should be banned from the town."

"It was hard to evict him. I'm not responsible for the town's court, as you know."

"You mean to suggest that the good people of this town wouldn't take your recommendation, Dean?"

Ralph heard the Bishop's voice sharpen. The Dean was avoiding Stapledon's keen gaze, and when Ralph glanced at Sir Baldwin he noticed that the knight was once more staring at the flames, but now with a tiny grin touching his mouth as if he was trying to conceal his amusement. Ralph looked back at the Bishop helplessly. "But my Lord Bishop, who was the man? He looked inoffensive to me, just a tranter about his business—why should he irritate you so much?"

The Bishop's features set into a sour mask; the Dean thoughtfully stirred his wine with a finger. It was left to Baldwin to respond. Without turning from his contemplative survey of the logs, he spoke quietly, eyes twinkling merrily in the firelight. "This man John of Irelaunde is well known."

"But why, sir?"

"I'm not the best man to ask. It all happened a long time ago, before I returned here myself. I lived abroad for many years, and it was only when my brother died in an accident that I inherited the estate. All I know is what I have heard."

Baldwin shot Ralph a quick look. The monk saw his features highlighted by a sudden jet of flame, and now he could hear the delight in his voice. So too could the Bishop, for Ralph heard him grunt in a surly manner and shift irritably in his seat.

The knight continued, "John Irelaunde arrived here in 1315—I think in the August, wasn't it, my Lord?" The Bishop gave a short nod. "As I say, I was not myself here in those days, but I have heard the story so often, it almost feels as if I saw it all. But before you hear about Irelaunde, you have to know the background, the tale of the other man, the one whom Irelaunde had met on the road. You see, the Bishop here was holding a service in the church to celebrate a mass . . ."

"It was the mass of St. Peter advincula," Stapledon said quietly. "Orey came here on the Wednesday before the first of August." While Baldwin continued, his voice close to laughter, the Bishop could see the scene in his mind's eye with perfect clarity.

It was a cold and wet August—every month that year and the year following were abysmal—and the congregation was soaked. In the yellow glow of the hundreds of candles, the Bishop could see the steam rising like some strange marsh gas from the clothes of the people standing before him, creating an unwholesome fug. The stench was unimaginable: sodden wool, damp furs, the rank animal scent of badly cured leather, the reek of unwashed bodies—Stapledon had thought they all combined with the burning tallow to create a uniquely repellent atmosphere. He felt it was no way to give praise to God. It was so bad he had to rebuke himself for his lack of concentration.

As he moved on with the mass, chanting the long passages that held such a wealth of meaning for him, submitting himself to the influence of the familiar phrases and soothing cadences, his concentration was shattered by a wild shriek.

It was as if a pig's bladder had been inflated and burst. The noise was so unexpected it was an obscenity in its own right. Stapledon was horrified, thinking at first that the devil himself had polluted the ceremony. Voices called out, some in condemnation, others in praise and while the Bishop stared uncomprehendingly, he saw that a figure was stumbling wide-eyed toward him, shouting, "A miracle, a miracle!"

"What is this? Who dares interrupt a holy meeting?" he demanded, but the crowd had begun to murmur, and he couldn't hear the reply. Holding up his hand, he glowered around waiting for silence.

The man, Orey, had that kind of shabby gentility that was so common among tradesmen of poor birth. He was an unprepossessing fellow; short, grubby, ungainly, fat with too much ale, and flushed. Slack-jawed and apparently nervous, he barged forward and fell on his face on the floor before the altar, lying with his arms outstretched like a penitent imitating crucifixion. A stunned quietness overtook everyone, and Stapledon waited doubtfully, glancing from side to side at the church officials. He could see no help there. They were as confused as he himself.

"My Lord Bishop, I was blind—I came in here with my wife hoping and praying that God in His goodness would grant me a miracle and let me see again, and behold! I can see! It's a miracle, I swear!"

Facing the ground as if scared of seeing the expression on the Bishop's face, Orey's voice was muffled, but enough of the people heard him. A thrill of excitement ran through the crowd. There was a pause, as if the whole congregation was drawing breath, and then the cries came out in a torrent: "Ring the bells!" "Praise God!" "Give thanks to God for a miracle!"

At Orey's side was a woman, thin and careworn, her hair prematurely gray. She held out her hands to the Bishop in supplication. "It's true, my Lord. My husband here went blind weeks ago, and he had a dream that if he could get here to your mass he'd be able to see again. We came as soon as we could, and now he's no longer blind!"

Bishop Stapledon nodded to himself slowly, eyeing

the crowd skeptically before turning to the astounded cleric at his side. "Arrest him."

There had been outrage, the gullible protesting he should be honored, not held like a felon; others, seeing the direction of the Bishop's thoughts, threatened to tear Orey limb from limb for heresy. Stapledon merely motioned the people away from the altar and imperturbably continued with the service.

But all through the rest of the ceremony, he had struggled to control the turbulence that shivered through his body. It was impossible to suppress the hope that this might truly be a miracle, the first he had ever witnessed.

Stapledon gave a heavy sigh as Baldwin finished his story.

Ralph leaned forward, barely controlling his excitement. "But I'd never heard of this! Was he telling the truth?"

Baldwin gave a crooked smile. "Ah, now that is the question. How could the Bishop tell?"

"I couldn't. I *wanted* to believe—of course I did!—but I am too old to take a peasant's word as Gospel truth when he swears to a miracle like that."

"What did you do?"

"I had Orey and his wife questioned. They both deposed that on the Thursday before Easter he had gone to bed perfectly well, and had awoken blind. Orey came from Keynesham, he was the local fuller, and we sent to hear from his neighbors. There were plenty prepared to support his story."

"So the Bishop was left with little choice," Baldwin said.

"No," said Stapledon. "I had to accept their word, especially since all swore on the Gospels. If there had been a shred of doubt I would have had Orey in jail for deception, but as it was, everyone supported his story—

even the local priest, although he was hardly better educated than Orey himself and spent most of his spare time investigating the mysteries held inside ale barrels rather than those in the Bible. No, I had to order the bells to be rung, and held a thanksgiving service for God's mercy in manifesting the illness on Orey, and for giving him his cure."

"And this man Orey is now known as John of Irelaunde?" asked Ralph with confusion.

"No!" laughed Baldwin. "Orey was the man who persuaded John the trickster to come here."

"Orey returned to his business the next January," Stapledon noted drily, glaring at the knight. "It so happened that on his way he met this tranter, John of Irelaunde, and told him of his miraculous cure. Orey was determined to praise God after what he was sure was a miracle, and wherever he went he told people what had happened to him. His wife, I understand, was a most willing witness. But this tranter, this *John,* then changed his direction and came to Crediton. He covered his eyes like a blind man, walked with a stick, and asked everyone he met whether they could lead him to the church. He said he had suddenly been struck blind, but had been sent a dream from God which showed him that he could be cured if he would only come to Crediton and attend a mass."

"He was so transparent," Peter Clifford chortled. "Turning up like that, just a short time after Orey had gone, and all alone on his cart—as if he could have travelled so many miles blind and without a guide! I suppose he never considered how suspicious he would look."

"But why would he bother?" Ralph asked.

Stapledon threw him a patronizing glance. "Ralph, when you have lived as long as I have, you'll realize how gullible people can be. The populace here had showered Orey with money, hoping that by their charity a little of his good fortune would redound to them. No doubt he mentioned this to John. The people wanted to associate themselves with Orey, for after all, God had marked him out as favored. What Irelaunde intended was to visit the church, demonstrate his own marvellous recovery, and be similarly favored by the good burgesses of the town."

"But how can you be certain he wasn't truly blind?"

"In the first place because he could bring forward no witnesses; in the second because his story was too unlikely. God doesn't send miraculous cures by the gross or even the pair; He provides them occasionally as proof of His kindness and power. And then, of course, the fool was seen lifting the bandage from his eyes."

"Our constable has good eyes himself," Baldwin laughed, giving up all attempts to restrain his mirth, "and a deeply suspicious soul. When he sees an apparently blind man lifting one edge of the cloth binding his eyes in order to survey his path before making his way straight to the inn at which, upon arriving, he gives every sign of being quite incapable of seeing anything—the good constable begins to wonder what kind of ocular incapacity he is witness to. The constable kept his own eyes on John, and the next day when John made his entrance in the church, the constable was able to offer some words to the Bishop."

"I doubted the man from the first," Stapledon muttered. "It was too much having a second man with a sudden blindness turn up; miracles aren't that common. No, I had Irelaunde put in the jail, and when he couldn't produce a single witness to support his defense, I said he should be held until he could be tried in court."

"There was no point, my Lord," said Clifford. "He was too obvious. I asked the burgesses what they would do, and relayed your suggestion, but they all seemed to think he was a joke, and only made him spend a morning in the stocks."

"A morning? A *whole* morning? My God, what cruelty!" the Bishop said witheringly.

Baldwin laughed. "Don't be too hard on the town for such generosity. You can imagine how the burgesses would have looked at it: on the one hand they had a fabulous proof of the holiness of their church, an event that had been witnessed by the Bishop himself, and something that would be bound to bring in pilgrims from all over the country—and on the other a simple crook, someone who might, if his case came to be known, ruin the town's reputation. If one man was proven to be a fraud, wouldn't that automatically reflect upon the first miracle? If John of Irelaunde was false, people would wonder whether Orey was as well."

"It hardly demonstrates the correct desire to punish a wrongdoer."

"Oh, I don't know, Bishop. Surely it is better to punish one man leniently than potentially the whole town unfairly," Baldwin said teasingly. "Especially since it might demean a genuine miracle: that of Orey."

Stapledon snorted. "So what has he been up to since? I assume you must be well acquainted with him for you to be able to call him to mind so easily, especially since, as you point out, you didn't even live here when all this took place."

The knight sipped at his juice. "It is true that I have seen something of him." He decided that the most recent rumors he had heard should be withheld. Peter Clifford might know something of them, but there was no need to inform the Bishop when it could only serve to irritate the prelate. "He has been brought before me in my capacity as Keeper of the King's Peace, but never over anything serious: selling underweight loaves of bread, that kind of thing."

"That's bad enough!" exclaimed Ralph. Many poor people depended on their bread for their daily sustenance, and those who short-changed their customers were guilty of trying to starve them, in his view.

"True, but it's not something a man should be hanged for," Baldwin stated easily. He knew how hard some found it to make any kind of a living, and didn't believe in excessive severity against those who only committed offenses to prevent their own starvation.

"So he's hardly a model citizen," the Bishop commented.

"No—but he adds a certain color to the town's life," Baldwin suggested. "He has a bold nerve. I believe he could sell sulfur to the devil—and profit from the exchange!"

"Hardly the sort of comment to endear him to me," Stapledon snapped coldly, but even as Ralph gave a sharp intake of breath at his irreverence, Baldwin could see that Stapledon was concealing his own amusement.

"But it's true enough," Clifford said, with a kind of weary resignation. "Irelaunde has some kind of natural gift with language. Only last week he persuaded me to take some of his cloth. I *know* what he's like, and although I'm quite certain there's no malice in him, I should've known better than to buy from him."

"If there's no malice . . ." Ralph interrupted, confused.

"There doesn't have to be evil intent," Baldwin explained. "John only thinks of the next minute or two, and what he can make. If there's an opportunity for profit, he'll take it. He will trade in anything. It usually won't be something that could hurt—but it wouldn't necessarily match the high expectation the customer had."

"And then," Clifford added gloomily, "he always has a ready explanation, which on the face of it is reasonable, and which inevitably shows that you are somehow at fault. Take my cloth: he let me have it for half the going price—purely, he said, because he had picked up a sizeable quantity cheaply from a retiring weaver, and he'd prefer to see the Church get a bargain than make more money himself or give the benefit to an already fat merchant."

"*That* should have warned you, Peter," said Baldwin, mock-reprovingly. "He actually implied that he would sooner see you gain the advantage of the deal than he himself? What more warning could he have given?"

"He was most convincing."

"He always is! Go on, what was the matter with the cloth? Did it dissolve in the rain? Or perhaps it evaporated in the sun?"

Peter Clifford pursed his lips. "The cloth was for tunics for some of the lay brothers and servants," he admitted after a moment. "Some of them had such threadbare stuff that they were hardly better off than going about naked. But as soon as John's material was washed, it shrank. It had already been made up into clothes by then, and it was all useless."

"And he said it was your fault?"

"He was most apologetic, but he said we should have washed it before cutting and stitching it. I suppose he's right, but you don't expect it to contract to that extent! The shirts were only good for children once they were washed."

"It goes to prove that I was right," the Bishop stated. "He should have been thrown out of the town after his attempted deception."

Baldwin could see that this topic was embarrassing his friend, and changed the subject. "So, Ralph, you are to become the new master of St. Lawrence's? Let me see. That means you come from the Trinity Convent, doesn't it?"

"Yes, sir. From Houndeslow, some few miles from Westminster."

"A good thriving monastery, I hear," Peter Clifford observed approvingly.

Baldwin watched the young monk as he answered the Dean's questions about his House. The knight had known that the little chapel of St. Lawrence's was served by monks from Houndeslow, but he had not realized that old Nicholas, who had died during the previous summer, was to be replaced by someone so young. Baldwin was sure that the lad was no more than twenty, and although that was surely old enough for any man to take up his life's duties, it was disturbing to think that the fellow was taking up such a hazardous role. Ralph had the self-assurance of a much older man, Baldwin noted; perhaps he would be capable of managing the affairs of his little chapel. Observing him, Baldwin was impressed by his stillness; the monk held himself with an almost detached serenity. Unlike so many young men Baldwin saw, Ralph didn't fidget, but sat composedly, his hands resting in his lap.

Baldwin picked up his goblet and took a sip. It was good to see a young man who was determined to serve his God by protecting his charges, but Baldwin was fascinated by what could motivate someone to take on such a job. The inmates of St. Lawrence's Hospital were not ill of broken limbs or cuts. They were not run-of-the-mill patients such as monks commonly looked after. Those who lived in St. Lawrence's were a far more gruesome group.

St. Lawrence's was the leper hospital.

~ 2 ~

nly 200 yards away from where they sat, John of Irelaunde was rattling his way over the unmade road toward his home.

It was rare for him not to smile or wave to those he saw by the side of the road, though it was less common for his greetings to be returned. A young maid at one house glanced at him coolly when he called to her; a little farther along the road a woman hurrying by with her two children reddened and looked away when he whistled and winked. Still, he felt he was adequately compensated for these responses when he came near a group of maids chatting at the corner to an alley. He stood on his board, doffing his scruffy hat and bowing from the waist, and the girls giggled. One met his eye boldly, and he grinned and waved his hat to her.

As he retook his seat, thoughts of the women were rudely cast from his mind. He had caught a glimpse of a man riding toward him. The rider was in his early to middle thirties, with a face overly fleshy from too much rich food and drink, and a thick belly that seemed to rest on his horse's withers. John set his lips and gave a tuneless whistle, letting his head drop so that his face was hidden beneath the brim of his hat. Peering from under this barrier, he saw the legs of the horse approach, then pass by. The carter chortled quietly to himself. "And a good day to you, Master Matthew Coffyn. Glad to see you're on your way. I hope you've left all your valuables safe!"

Soon he was passing Coffyn's house. It was a good-sized place, as befitted the man's status in the town, with fresh paint on the wood, and limewash that was unstained by the weathering that marred a property's appearance. John kept his head down and watched from below his brim as he passed the gates, but he couldn't see Martha Coffyn. The place was quiet, and he nodded to himself. While the master was away, his servants would relax. No doubt most were in the buttery enjoying their master's absence while they simultaneously enjoyed his strongest ale.

After that was a newer building. This one, Godfrey's, was a massive hall, with good moorstone rendered and painted, surrounded by a wall strong enough to deter a mob. John glanced in. A gardener was clearing leaves from the thick clump of cabbages while another spread straw over a patch of vegetables to protect them from frost. They would soon retire as the light faded, John thought to himself contentedly.

As he came level with the gates, his attention was taken by a pair of young women. One was of middle height, with bright blue eyes that held a reserved calmness, as if she had confronted pain and found herself able to cope. Her face was oval, with a tall, wide brow under her little coif. She had the well-rounded body of a mature woman. John knew she was almost twenty-seven, and that was old for a single woman, especially one who was so attractive.

When he saw her glance in his direction, he gave her a happy smile, and nodded his head respectfully. She ignored him, turning on her heel.

"By God, Cecily, you know how to hurt a fellow's pride," he muttered to himself, but then chuckled as he caught the eye of the other woman in the garden, the young maid. She met his gaze unswervingly, with a condescendingly raised eyebrow. It was enough to lift his heart as he rode past the house.

Beyond was a new street. He turned into it and up a steep incline, his pony slowing and hunching in the traces, hauling determinedly. "Come on, girl!"

On his right was the sandstone wall surrounding Godfrey's plot. It had been an expensive undertaking, constructing this barrier, for John knew it enclosed no less than three acres, inside which cows and pigs browsed on the food given to them until they should in their turn feed the household.

John's pony paused a few yards before the next crossroads, at the furthest extremity of Godfrey's wall. Looping the reins loosely around the board that stood by his knee, John sprang down. Crediton was behind him, in front was common land, and on his left stood a wood, but to the right, backing on to Godfrey of London's place, was his own yard.

His small court was hidden behind the fence. Even the wooden gates were covered with boards. John valued privacy in his domain. He unlocked the padlock and released the chain, shoving the gates wide open, the hinges screeching in protest. The noise made him wince, and he made a mental note to grease them again. He led his horse in and slammed the gates, unlimbering her and removing her harness, hanging it from a nail while he wiped her down and brushed her. Leaving her at a newly-filled manger, he went to see to his merchandise. Once that was stored in the lean-to shed at the back of his cottage, he fetched himself a jug of ale and stood at his doorpost, whistling reflectively. He was facing east, but now, as the sun set, he could see the last rays gleaming red and gold on the leaves of the trees opposite.

He was comfortable here. The house was tiny, but then so was the place he had left in Ireland. At least here there were plenty of trees plainly visible. He could sit out here for hours with a quart of ale, just watching the birds and the golden squirrels leaping and playing in and amongst the branches. For most of the year he could tell the season by simply looking over his fence. In the springtime the trees were clad in light green, fresh young leaves; the summer meant a duller verdant tone. Now it was autumn, and the oaks had been licked with a drab ochre as the leaves prepared to fall.

These trees gave him all the wood he needed for heating, and at this time of year he could gather his own food as well. Through the autumn he would store up boxes of nuts: mainly cobs and chestnuts. These last were his favorites. He liked them roasted, eating their fluffy white flesh while still hot, or cooking them in milk and mashing them to make a thick, creamy stew.

John sighed happily. It had been the wish of the townspeople that he should be made to feel excluded from the life of Crediton—and they had been disgusted when they realized he intended staying. The town was united against him; he must be forced to understand how his actions were deplored. That was why they had refused to let him acquire a plot of land nearer Crediton town center. The intention was to punish him for his attempted fraud, but he was grateful that they wanted to alienate him. It had left him with this view up the hill and over the trees—and ensured that he could go about his business without being observed.

And that was sometimes important to him. He stirred himself as the light faded, stretching both arms high over his head. Crossing his yard, he made sure the pony was settled before taking a length of rope from the stable door. Where his plot met Godfrey's, he had not bothered to put up a fence. Godfrey's wall was eight feet high here, enough to deter most unwanted visitors. Now John studied it, sucking his teeth thoughtfully while he fashioned a loop. Ready, he weighed the coil in his hand. A few short feet above him the broken branch of an oak protruded over to his side. He hurled the rope; it encircled the limb, and he tested it a moment before using it to help him clamber to the top. Once there, he unhitched the loop from the branch, whistling absent-mindedly as he cautiously looked out for any watching gardener, then dropped to the ground.

Matthew Coffyn was away again; he often was. And when left to her own devices, his wife, Martha, was prey to boredom.

As soon as he had broken his fast the next morning, Ralph took his leave of both Bishop and Dean and set off to his new position. Ralph had expected to go alone to the lazar house, but Clifford insisted that someone should show him the way. The lepers were to be found at the far side of the town, he pointed out, and it would be easy for Ralph to get himself lost *en route*.

Ralph followed the almoner through the screens to the courtyard and out into the road, the older monk proudly pointing to the imposing new church as they passed it. The bustling little town was already awake, he saw. On every street, people stood hawking wares from baskets. Shops had their windows open. Their shutters were hinged at their lowest edge, so that they could be swung down to rest on trestles, and now they were displaying fresh produce of all kinds. As they walked, Ralph smelled newly-baked bread, cooking pies and stews, fowls roasting, and the clean tang of fish, all of which contended for dominance with the stench from the sewer.

It made him feel foolish after his reservations of the previous afternoon. At Houndeslow, this town was looked upon as a frontier outpost, somewhere so far removed from civilized living that it was a miracle anyone could survive for long, but now he was here, Ralph found it was a thriving, cheerful place. He wondered briefly whether the country further west was as forbidding and wild as he had heard, or whether it would prove to be as friendly as Crediton. Contrary to what he had been told, this was not a border town, not in the same way as Carlisle.

He had heard a lot about the northern marches from older monks at his convent. There, he understood, raiders and thieves were continually attacking from the Scottish side, and it was impossible to live in peace. Carlisle had to be protected by massive curtain walls and a prominent castle, behind whose gates civilians could shelter when the Scottish barbarians came burning and looting on their little ponies. Here at Crediton there wasn't any kind of a wall, yet the people didn't appear to feel its lack.

Further into the town the atmosphere altered. Here was the business center. There were regular squeals from one yard where a pigsticker plied his trade, a butcher standing outside in his leather apron shaving carcasses, while others nearby stoically carved and jointed. One apprentice voided entrails into a little stream, while another knelt downriver rinsing lights and offal ready for sausages. The stench was that of the tanners, an unwholesome odor, and as they walked on, Ralph found himself passing cobblers and cordwainers, fullers and weavers. The town had an enviable busyness.

But the almoner was not taking Ralph to see workers about their business; he was leading the monk to his new post, and they passed through the crowds thronging the streets and out to the other side of the town. As if apologetically, the almoner began to speak of the leper house and the various inmates.

"We have space for twelve, but we rarely have that number. We're not as large as Tavistock, there they always have their places filled." He almost sounded regretful, as if it was an insult to Crediton that the town didn't manage to have a full complement. "Mind, I suppose it means our expenses are lower than theirs."

"It must be costly to keep the lepers."

"Well, yes, it can be. The church looks to the upkeep of the buildings, and not only the Chapel of St. Lawrence's and your lodgings, but the lepers' own rooms—and then there are the pensions as well. We provide two pennies per person per week. That's without thinking of the other charitable works we have to undertake on their behalf—finding cloth for them, extra rations of food during fairs and festivals and so on."

"It must be a drain on your resources," Ralph said. He knew full well that almoners often looked on the money they handed out as their own.

"It is, but not so bad as you might think," the almoner responded, and touched the side of his nose. "The good Bishop has been very generous, and increased our revenues. He's granted the town two more fairs, and we get one-tenth of all tolls, so that makes our finances easier to manage."

"That was good of him."

"I think the Bishop has always had a soft spot for us here. The collegiate church has benefited since our precentor agreed to annually commemorate Bishop Stapledon's birthday. That's on February the first. And when the good Bishop dies, we will solemnize the anniversary of his death each year."

Ralph nodded. "It's only right that a great man like him should have the comfort of the prayers of the canons to assure his entry into heaven."

"Of course. And the Bishop has done so much good work, he surely deserves to be remembered. More than some of our chivalry."

The cold tone of voice warned Ralph that the almoner was one of those who disapproved of modern knights. Too many members of the knightly classes disregarded their duties these days and spent their time in slavish adherence to foppish modern fashions. It had been a shock to many in the country, after the years of austere dress under King Edward I, to find that the new King's courtiers preferred to spend their fortunes on fripperies rather than on more sober items of clothing. Now parti-colored tunics and hose were common, and it was hard to tell a man's position from his apparel. Even peasants could be seen dressing in furs like a lord. Ralph observed quietly, "There should be laws to stop people wearing things that are above their station."

"I agree. Even among our own ranks there are some who go about as if they were simply merchants. I have heard of men in the cities—*brother monks!*—who put on velvet and cloth of gold, and sometimes even go abroad *bearded*! Only last week I was told that in Bristol, monks have been seen without the tonsure!"

Ralph let his companion's scandalized voice carry

on. He too had spoken to travellers who talked of strange goings-on in other parts of the kingdom, but for the most part he was unmoved by the rumors. He had travelled all the way from Houndeslow, and everywhere he had paused he heard tell of other monks or friars who behaved badly, but had seen no evidence of it himself. In any case, he had more important things on his mind. He wanted to see the state of his new chapel.

When they left the town behind the almoner was at last quiet. As they rounded a little hillock, he stopped and pointed. "There it is."

Ralph followed his finger. Ahead of them was a small chapel, a simple rectangle, with no frills or decoration. Nearby was a low terrace of cottages. Like the chapel, they were of simple construction: the monk could see the stones that formed the foundation, while above was smooth cob, limewashed like most other homes in the area, although it was some years since these walls had been painted. The thatch, too, was worn. Ralph could see large holes where birds had nested, and there was little overhang past the walls. As the straw started to rot, the mass of thatch would shrink, and after thirty or forty years the eaves would retreat. That would put the walls in danger: rain trickling down the roof could wash away the top of the wall or soak into it, at best rendering the building uninhabitable, at worst causing its collapse. It was a common problem.

But for all the aura of neglect, the plot given to the lepers covered almost an acre, and was surrounded by a thick hedge, well layered to serve as a defense against wild animals, while a sturdy gate blocked the only entrance. It looked safe enough for the suffering inmates, while giving them space to cultivate their own peas and beans.

The almoner was a kindly man. When he glanced at Ralph, he saw the fixed expression, the intent gaze and tightly pursed lips, and felt a rush of compassion. "It's a hard task, but you'll find you're not short of friends. I'm only a short walk away, and I'll visit often enough to see how you're doing, so if you need any advice . . ."

His well-meaning words trailed off as the younger man looked at him. Ralph felt only irritation that the older monk was keeping him from his duties. He forced a smile to his face. "I'm sure I will be fine, but thank you for your help."

The almoner nodded, said he would drop by to see that Ralph was not in need of anything, and a short while later Ralph was alone. He was about to enter the enclosure when a horse came cantering down the lane to his right, and he waited rather than crossing in front of it.

It was a great black rounsey, gleaming as if oiled. The harness was of the richest, made of well-tooled black leather with silver bells dangling from the reins and harnesses to ease the rider's journey with their music.

The man himself was dressed gorgeously, with a bright blue tunic and hose under a thick woollen jacket, and with a heavy cloak of purple velvet trimmed with fur. From his soft felt hat with its jaunty feathers and trailing liripipe, to the fine supple leather of his riding boots, everything about him proclaimed him a wealthy man.

"Good day, Brother!"

Ralph ducked his head in acknowledgment as the man drew to a standstill in front of him and took off his splendid hat to scratch his head. "A pleasant day for a ride, sir," he replied politely.

The man was middle-aged, with graying hair that had fallen away in imitation of a tonsure. It had retreated from his forehead as well, which only served to emphasize the height of his brow. Shrewd brown eyes smiled down at Ralph, but the monk had the impression that the man would find it as easy to glower. There was a harshness in the little puckering between his eyebrows, and the lips were thin and bloodless. "Aye, Brother. It's good weather for a gallop."

"Have you been far?"

"Over to Bow and back." He appeared a little distracted, and Ralph noticed his attention wavering. Every moment or two his eyes would flit toward the chapel's gates.

"You live here, sir?" Ralph asked, feeling the need to fill the silence.

"Eh? Yes, back your way."

"My way?"

"Back there, near the collegiate church," he said, jerking his head. "I have a house in the street nearby."

"Ah, I see. And you are a merchant?"

"Me? No, I used to be a goldsmith, but that was a long time ago, long before I came here to Crediton. Now I help others . . ."

It was rude to push a man, but Ralph felt sure that the rider wanted to unburden himself of something. For all his evident prosperity, he looked uneasy, as if he had a confession to make. His mien was all too familiar to the monk; men and women would often accost a monk or priest to talk, and the reason was usually some banal misdemeanor which could be dismissed with a minor penance. On such occasions it was always tempting to avoid offering any solace, or to advise a visit to the church rather than waste time listening to foolish stories. He had only met Peter Clifford the once, but Ralph had formed a high opinion of him. The Dean was the vicar of the parishioners, and Ralph was sure that if this stranger needed absolution, Peter Clifford was well able to ease his mind. Yet he must know who his vicar was, so why was he so apparently keen to waylay an unknown monk in the street and engage him in conversation?

"Sir, if you have a need to speak to someone, I am sure the Dean will be pleased to offer you solace, but if you would prefer to discuss things with me . . . ?" He let his voice trail off questioningly.

At his words the man shot him a quick look. "I *should* like to speak with you, if you can spare me a little time, yes, Brother."

Ralph sighed inwardly. The man must be more than twice his age, and here he was, searching for answers. The monk was all too aware of his own unfitness for the task, but he nodded as if content. "You should tell me your name first, then. I am called Ralph."

"My apologies, Brother. My enthusiasm got the better of me. My name is Godfrey—Godfrey of London."

"Good. Well, master, why do you not come into my chapel and I will listen to your problem."

"Your chapel?" Godfrey asked, brows raised in surprise.

Ralph nodded to the little building. "St. Lawrence's."

"You're the *leper* master?"

"Yes, but you have nothing to fear, I—"

"What do *you* know of fear, little monk? You know nothing—*nothing*! You're hardly old enough to grow a beard, for God's sake! You can't know what it's like to have a daughter who . . . Oh, what's the point!" Whipping his mount and digging in his spurs, Godfrey suddenly jerked his horse's head round, and made off along the street, scattering hawkers from his path.

Ralph stood gaping for a long time. It wasn't the rudeness that made him stare along the road; it was the restless passion in Godfrey's outburst. It had not been directed at Ralph—of that the monk was quite convinced. It was the explosion of a man pushed to despair, as if he had seen in Ralph someone who might be able to help him, only to have his hopes dashed.

That made Ralph pause thoughtfully, but he had little time to waste worrying about wealthy burgesses; he had work to begin. He walked to the gate and made himself known to the old leper who guarded it.

Ralph was torn with sympathy for the old man. His face was rotted, the palate gone, and with it his upper teeth, giving him the look more of a brutish animal than a human. In his two-fingered, rough gloves and the coarse material of his hose, jerkin and cloak, he seemed subhuman, just a thing. And that, Ralph knew, was how he would be treated by the people of the town, like a cur to be cursed and kicked, reviled by adults and children alike.

He swallowed the lump that rose in his throat, threatening to choke him. The old leper pointed him to his little room, and Ralph set off, nodding and greeting those of his flock that he met on his way. All were quiet, shuffling their feet and staring down, fearful of meeting his eye until they knew him better, nervous in the presence of their new master, and Ralph had to blink away tears of sympathy at the sight of their deformities: many had stumps where their hands or feet should have been; most had faces disfigured and twisted into nightmarish masks.

Yet when he had opened his door and taken possession of his room, when he stood leaning against the doorpost, arms crossed as he surveyed his estate, he could not help a small frown worrying at his brow. It was not the men around him; his thoughts were not now with the misshapen creatures of the camp.

Ralph was only young, but he had looked after enough ill and dying men in his time to recognize the expression he had seen on Godfrey's face, and that face kept coming back to him: it held a wary sadness—as if Godfrey had been nursing an infinity of despair.

3

Stepping out of the butcher's, John of Irelaunde stood a while leaning against the wall, watching the people pass by. As a young woman caught his eye, he would grin, whether or not she noticed him, and keep his attention fixed on her until she was swallowed up by the crowd. Every so often a girl would realize she was being observed, and it was in order to see how she might react that he stood glancing over the crowd.

There were some, the youngest, who ducked their heads in embarrassment as though seeking sanctuary behind another anonymous person. A few were fetching young women who knew nothing of how to cope with a man's interest, and these he would gaze at longingly—not to offend, but because he wanted to recall their innocence. He knew well that such shy maidenly blushes wouldn't last; all too soon they would inevitably be replaced by knowing smiles.

Then there were the older women who reddened with anger. Often they were married ladies of some status in the town—which was why John assaulted them with his gaze. When he found a woman who haughtily stared back while going crimson with irritation, he would give her a deliberate leer. It was delightful to fan her anger. Women like this had made his life harder, or had tried to, and their impotence in the face of his insultingly lecherous grin was balm to his soul.

He liked the pretty girls, the fresh young women who met his look boldly. They were worth searching for. It was always a delight to assess how much of their confidence was bravado. They offered the potential for delightful speculation, not that he would dare try his luck with them. Even if he didn't already have a woman who had stolen his affection, these were too hazardous; he would be tempting fate, dallying with young women who might have a wealthy father or brother who could wish to seek him out for revenge. Young girls could imagine themselves in love too easily, and were prone to seek satisfaction at the point of a sibling's sword when rejected.

The last category was the other wives—the ones who didn't toss their heads haughtily or purse their lips on seeing him. They were the pretty ladies wedded to older men, women who wanted excitement without risk to their social standing. In a place like Crediton there wasn't an inexhaustible supply of them, but there were enough for those who knew how to look. He monitored them as he surveyed the street, noting them with the eye of an expert cattleman checking stock. These women would meet his glance bravely, brazening him out, whether with their husbands or alone; they wouldn't flush with shame or rage, but would return his pensive stare, and sometimes their eyes made unspoken offers.

That had always been the delight for him, he reflected as he at last pushed away from the wall and made his slow progress to his house, scanning the street for familiar or new faces. It was the thrill of the chase. He knew that the women would have heard of him; it wasn't as if he had hidden himself. John of Irelaunde *liked* women. He enjoyed their company, liked giving them gifts—nothing too expensive, but something that involved thought—and he loved loving them without the risk of financial involvement. That was his reputation.

And that was why so many of them had sought his company. John was safe. He was known to be no threat for a woman who wanted the chance of a fling without her husband finding out. And in an age when many cuckolded men would grab for a sword first and ask questions only once limbs and certain members had been irretrievably lost, that was an important consideration.

At the thought, John's grin widened. He *had* always been careful; he had never let himself get caught. It wasn't arrogance, but the cautious evaluation of dangers that prevented his capture. He always made sure that there was no chance that a husband could catch him. And the benefits had been there for him to take. Women had appreciated him for providing them with the affection they missed in their boring marriages, together with the thrill of the illicit. But no more.

No, for John—the man who had enjoyed the favors of many ladies, the man who was free of the taint of falling in love, who avoided the wily snares of those girls who flaunted themselves at him and laughed at the very notion that he should ever remarry—was smitten. And he knew it must be serious, for he couldn't regret the fact.

When he glanced up, he saw that the sun was sinking. It would soon be getting dark. He paused to smile to himself before hurrying his steps. Coffyn was away again tonight, and that meant John's path was clear once more.

* * *

A week after Ralph's arrival in Crediton, he was told he had a new inmate.

Later he was to remember it as one of those crystal-clear autumn mornings that held the promise of a warm sun and no rain. When he opened the door of his little home, the hospital's grounds lay under a fine coating of frost. He had to pause and inhale deeply, drinking in the view like wine.

The small community was out at the western edge of the town, away from the busy center, and although he could see the smoke rising like columns in the still air, the houses and shops were invisible from here, hidden from view by the sweep of the hill and the trees which covered its side. The only proof of habitation was the clangor of the waking population as they rattled over the roads on wagons, or banged pots and pans together ready for the new day. Doors and shutters slammed, voices were raised as apprentices were called, or cursed for being late.

Ralph smiled. The noise from Crediton was rarely so raucous, but when the morning was as still as this, the sounds drifted down the road so distinctly he could imagine the people were only a few feet away instead of over a quarter of a mile. It removed the sense of isolation that was the occupational hazard of his career.

From the door to his house he could see the whole of his domain. Directly ahead was the gate to the outside world which his inmates simultaneously loathed for its rejection of them, and adored for the freedom—and health—it represented. On his right was the squat little chapel, with its sorry collection of wooden crosses to remember the men who had died here. The lepers themselves lived opposite it. A few, he knew, the most godly, would even now be readying themselves for the first service of the day. Their only possibility of freedom would come from the chapel: either they would enjoy the miracle of returned health through God's kindness, or they would be released. He would mercifully grant them death, and an end to their suffering.

But others would not join him in St. Lawrence's to attend his masses. These were the incorrigible ones, the ones who had already given up. They had succumbed to grief, or had become angry with their God for their living death. Ralph felt he could understand their misery, but could not forgive their loss of faith. They should, he felt, put their trust in Him. It was with a kind of abstract disinterest that he wondered how he himself would react if he became a leper. It was always possible that he might succumb to the malign disease. He only prayed that he could be like the first group, and would relish the opportunity for praising God that its onset would provide—but he wasn't sure.

The message came late in the morning, while he was sweeping the floor in the chapel. Mud and rubbish accumulated in the corners of the old building, and it was a daily task to ensure that God's house was clean. He had almost finished, when Joseph, an old leper much disfigured, caught his attention.

One of the early symptoms of the disease was that the victim found breathing difficult and the voice became hoarse. Poor Joseph had endured his illness for over four years, Ralph had been told, and the monk usually found his speech difficult to understand, but today he quickly understood that he was needed.

At the main gate he found a young woman waiting. She was in her early twenties, plain of face, but with an inner strength that showed in her grave, solemn features. Ralph could see that she was no gentlewoman. Her clothing was clean, but certainly not expensive; the fabric had torn in several places, and had been carefully mended.

As he approached her, Ralph's attention was on her face. The woman was paying him no heed: she was watching Joseph. And unlike everyone else whom he had seen observing a leper, her face held no fear, no horror or disgust, but only an expression of compassion and utter sadness. It made him want to stop and memorize every detail of her as she stood there, radiating kindness like a modern Magdalen. When he came close, he saw that her cheeks were streaked with tears.

"You asked for me?"

"Yes, Brother. I have been sent by the Dean to tell you that another man has got the disease."

"Oh, I see." Ralph closed his eyes briefly. He had five inmates already. Another would be a strain on his resources. The almoner had already hinted that the harvest had not been as good as had been hoped, and that it would be best if the lepers could reduce their demands on the church. He dismissed the thought with a shrug. "I shall come immediately."

Inside Crediton's collegiate church, the candles and sconces threw a dim light compared with the bright sunshine streaming in through the windows. There weren't many people there. It looked as if monks and lay-brothers were almost alone; only a few of the local people were attending. That was no surprise, for nobody wanted to be reminded of the illness. One woman sobbed, and a man at her side held her protectively by the shoulders. Ralph felt certain they were the parents; their grief was so obvious. Not far from them, Ralph was surprised to see the knight, Sir Baldwin, his head bowed in prayer.

The Dean, in his capacity as vicar of the parish, was holding the service as the monk entered. Ralph walked to the altar and knelt, making the sign of the cross and bowing his head in prayer before looking over at this latest victim.

Edmund Quivil felt like a twig that had fallen into a rushing torrent; he was being swept along by a course of procedures he couldn't comprehend. Wrapped in a shroud, he'd been carried in here on a bier as if he was already dead. His movements were mechanical as he obeyed the Dean's instructions. Canons brought forward a pall as he lay down on the ground, and it was draped over him while the requiem mass was chanted. Then Clifford's sonorous voice continued, droning on in the curious international language of the Church.

And then Quivil remembered the significance of the rite.

He almost cried out. It was an effort not to leap up. This was the end of his life. From now on he was dead, to the Church and to the Law.

It had been explained to him the night before, when the Dean had visited him to confirm that he did indeed have leprosy. That was hard enough to accept. Quivil was not yet twenty. He had been courting Mary Cordwainer for six months now, and their banns were to have been read in the little church at Sandford when he had developed the fever. It had come quickly, leaving all his bones aching, and then it was gone. But it had returned, and this time it had brought with it a dull headache that made movement torture, and his nose started bleeding profusely.

The herbarer had been very helpful. When the second attack had struck, the monk had kindly come to visit him, and had given him a powder which had reduced the pains a little, but when this second fever had somewhat abated, the monk had become noticeably anxious. He had seen the little discoloration on Quivil's hand. And soon it was not one, but many. The yellow-brownish lumps multiplied over his face and hands.

That was when Quivil had been brought to the town on a cart and subjected to a detailed examination.

He shuddered, squeezing his eyes tight shut. It was only yesterday, and now his life was ended.

Edmund felt the silent tears trickling down his cheeks. He opened his hands once, to study with disbelief the little nodes on the skin of his wrists; he reached up to touch his face, feeling the faint lumps. It was *impossible* that he should be a leper! He was young and fit, not a mutilated cripple with only a few years to live. It *must* be a mistake! The brother herbarer would come in and rescue him from this living nightmare: it couldn't go on.

But the solemn voice continued its message of doom. No hurrying brother came to rescue him. He lay uncomfortably until the mass was ended, and then there was silence. It was as if his heart had in truth stopped beating.

Ralph rose to his feet. The Dean was kneeling and praying, and as he finished and stood, Ralph could see the tears glistening. The two men stared at each other for a moment, sharing the pain and sadness of the occasion, as if they were accomplices in Quivil's destruction, and then Clifford gave a rasping sigh and walked to the door. Ralph put his hand on the leper's shoulder, and the young man gave a start, looking up at him with desperation. The monk tried to give him an encouraging smile, but Ralph's face felt as if it was going to crack. Uttering a prayer to God for strength, he helped Quivil up, and walked with him to the door.

Outside, Clifford waited with the other brothers near a newly dug grave. The last stage of the rite had to be completed. Quivil found himself being laid down again, and while he stared up at the priest, Clifford sprinkled dust on his head three times. "Edmund Quivil, you are dead to the world. Be alive again to God."

Now Ralph took him by the shoulder once more, and while the monks chanted the *Libera me,* led the leper away to his living purgatory: unalive, though not yet dead.

John saw the pair walking away, and he shook his head sympathetically. Everyone in the town had heard the news about poor Quivil. Gossip of that kind spread quickly.

But the little Irishman didn't have time to dawdle in the street, he had things to do. He walked back toward the church, and was about to turn up his own road when he heard his name being called.

"Yes? Sir Baldwin, how are you this fine day?"

"Well enough, John," Baldwin said. He pulled off his gloves and stuck them in his belt. Truth be told, he wasn't at all content. Witnessing one of his villeins being put through the Office for the Seclusion of a Leper had blunted the pleasure he had felt earlier on seeing what good weather the day promised. "What are you up to, though?"

"Me, Sir Baldwin?"

The knight studied his innocent face. "Yes, John, *you*! I have been hearing rumors about you."

"Ah, surely you'd not listen to villainous talk about me, sir?"

"That would depend on how untrue the talk was, wouldn't it, John?"

"But you know I'm an honest trader, sir. I'd never break the town's laws."

"Really? By the way, did you hear about Isabella Gilbard?"

John forced his voice to sound casual, as if he had not only *not* heard of her, he was sure he wouldn't want to either. "Isabella? No, I don't think so."

"I let her buy her freedom from my manor so she could marry. She was wed in June, but now I hear she has given birth to a bouncing boy—only three months later."

"It's a terrible thing when people behave like that," said John, nodding his head sagely. "Young churls today don't have the manners their grandparents had."

"Quite. It means she was fornicating before she was married; before she bought her freedom. I suppose I shall have to impose the *lairwite* on her."

John pursed his lips. The *lairwite* was the fine imposed on bondwomen who proved to have weaker morals than they should, and who gave birth without first going through the formal and necessary process of marrying. The fine could be enforced when the woman subsequently married in an attempt to conceal her incontinence. And John knew as well as the knight that there was another fine, the *childwite,* for the man who had made her pregnant.

But the fine was imposed on women who were unfree—serfs. It existed to prevent villeins from breeding large numbers of bastards who would then become a drain on an estate. And John was not involved with an unfree woman. He smiled up at the knight confidently. Baldwin seemed to have forgotten his presence for a moment, and was lost in thought, staring over the road at the new church. John was interested despite himself.

"But, Sir Baldwin, surely you wouldn't pursue her now, not when you've already freed her?"

The knight turned slowly and studied him, and suddenly John wanted very much to be somewhere else. Baldwin was known to be kindly and generous, a man who treated all men with respect and courtesy, but now the knight's eye was cold, his voice scornful. "John of Irelaunde, I am the Keeper of the King's Peace. It is impossible for me to condone deliberate flouting of the law—by anyone. How would it look if I were to allow Isabella to commit this crime without punishment? Other criminals might think me an easy touch. Oh no, John. I have my office to consider in her case—and in others."

"Well, Sir Baldwin, I'm glad I've never been guilty of such a crime," John said lightly, but he avoided Baldwin's gaze.

"You've never given birth to a child, you mean? Or do you mean you've never tasted the pleasures of illicit love? Are you so innocent, I wonder?"

John grinned weakly. The knight's words were hitting too close to the mark, and there was a terrible certainty building in him that Baldwin had guessed about his nightly trysts. The direction of this conversation was not to John's liking, especially when another thought struck him: if news had already come to Baldwin, the gossip in the town must have reached a level which could put him—and her—in some little danger.

It was getting late. John made some apology and scurried off homeward, all the way conscious of the knight's stare on his back. It was a relief to slam his gate shut behind him. He rested for a moment with his back to it as if bracing himself against a sudden attack. The knight had unsettled him, that was a fact. "Sodding *bastard*! He was winding me up!"

And back down the hill, as soon as Baldwin saw the little man dart inside his yard, for all the world like a rabbit pelting into its warren at the sound of the hunter and his dogs, the knight's face broke into a smile. He gave a loud guffaw, and had to lean on a fence while he laughed until the tears came.

"And now take the hint and leave the good wives of Crediton alone, you lecherous little git!"

* * *

Sitting before the door to the inn, idly watching the traffic in the street, Jack the smith raised another quart of ale and gulped.

With the slight breeze, he felt refreshingly cool after the searing heat of his smithy, and it was a relief to be able to sit and drink away his thirst, nodding affably to the townspeople as they passed. Few would ignore the smith, for he was an essential part of the town. When tools snapped, he mended them; when horses needed reshoeing, he made them; when cartwheels broke, he had to fit the new steel rims to protect the wood. In all aspects of life, there was little that didn't require his skills at one point or another.

He finished his drink and collected his small barrel, newly refilled with ale, which he installed on his little handcart, and set off home. There were two chains he must repair, taking out links and replacing them with new ones, an old knife that needed a fresh rivet in its hilt, and he must forge a new axehead. It would take time to finish all that, and he hoped his apprentice was stoking the fires and getting the temperature up.

It was when he had only travelled a few yards, while he was reviewing these jobs, that he saw the man sitting huddled at the side of the road, clapper in hand and bowl before him, calling out to all passers-by. "God bless you, lady!" and "God save you, sir!" as the coins were hurriedly tossed to him, while the donors averted their gaze and hurried by.

Jack strode on, his face fixed firmly forward, prognathous features unmoving.

"Sir? Can you spare something for—"

"Not for you, *pervert*!"

"But we need food and drink, same as any man, sir. Couldn't you—"

"Leave me alone! You sickening bastard, you should never have been born. You make me want to vomit—aye, and all others who are normal!"

The leper stared at him, and opened his mouth to speak, but as he did so, the smith reached down and picked up a large cobblestone, weighing it in his hand. The light of a kind of madness was in Jack's eye, and the leper was suddenly afraid. He looked away nervously, certain that at any moment the heavy stone would crack against his head. There came a loud thud, and when he looked to his side, he saw the dent on the wall where the cobble had struck.

"Don't ever talk to me again, or next time I'll smash your skull!" Jack hissed malevolently, and walked on.

Neither he nor the leper noticed the man leaning against the wall of the inn. Neither of them knew he was a guard at Matthew Coffyn's house—nor that he had overheard their argument. At the moment he wasn't greatly interested in what had passed between the leper and the bigot, but if the guard, William, had one conviction, it was that any piece of information might become useful. He had docketed and stored the exchange in his mind before the smith was swallowed up in the crowds.

- 4 -

Thomas Rodde leaned on his staff and rested while he waited. The old man at the gate had refused to let him enter until his master had agreed. It made Rodde give a fleeting smile. As if anyone who was healthy would want to walk into a leper hospital!

The sun was warm on his tattered tunic and robe. It was good to feel the heat. For so many months now he had been living in the north, where the sun was insipid compared to the south.

Thomas could remember hot, balmy days in the southern lands. He had gone there with his father several times when he was apprenticed to the craft, visiting places of pilgrimage in far-flung countries like Castile and Rome. But that was before he had become leprous: that life was over. Sometimes he recalled it with a kind of wonder, like a magical dream in which reality could be suspended for a while, but he tried to avoid thinking about how he had lived. There was no point: he was determined not to torment himself with wondering how things might have been, or how he might have developed. After all, he could easily have died in a foolish accident at any time. It was as likely as his managing to live to a ripe old age.

"There they are."

The old leper pointed along the road. Thomas turned to see Ralph and Quivil approaching. The man with the monk was staggering as if drunk. His eyes held a frantic terror. Thomas had once seen a horse fall after jumping a wall. It had put a fetlock into a rabbit hole. Afterward it had stood shaking, the leg shattered, with eyes rolling in shock and fear. Thomas clenched his teeth. He had seen the same panicked horror in too many eyes over the last years.

Brother Ralph noticed Thomas Rodde, a bowed figure clad in the tattered clothing that denoted another leper, but he had no time to think about him yet, for at the gate Quivil halted, eyes wide, like a horse refusing a jump. The monk spoke gently. "Quivil, come inside. You know you—"

"No! No, I can't! This is all a mistake." He shook his head emphatically, his feet planted firmly.

"You *have* to come in. You know that."

"I . . . I can't. I'm all right now. It's all an accident. I have to go home."

"Edmund!"

Ralph spun to see the same young woman who had summoned him from the chapel. She stood behind them in the road, and the monk realized she had been waiting for them.

"Mary?" Quivil cried, and was about to go to her, when Ralph gripped his arm urgently.

"You mustn't! Quivil, *think,* man. You're a leper: you are defiled—you're already condemned, do you want to ruin her life too?"

"No, it's a mistake, I'm not ill," the leper groaned, but the insistence was gone from his voice.

Mary Cordwainer covered her face with her hands.

Her body was racked with tortured sobs. "I didn't believe it, I thought you'd be all right."

Quivil stood still, as if turned to purest marble. His fists clenched in his despair. When he spoke, he heard his voice rasping with the hurt he had to give her, his woman. "Mary, I'm dead. I'm nothing. You must look after yourself."

Ralph slowly released his grip. Quivil stood shaking, his eyes screwed tightly shut, then they opened with an almost audible snap, and he lurched through the gate and into the grounds of the leper hospital. The girl gave a small cry, and sank to her knees, head bowed, face hidden in her hands. Ralph wanted to go to her and comfort her, but he thought better of it. There was nothing for him to say; no words of sympathy could compensate her. He shook his head, and was about to follow Quivil, when Rodde stepped forward.

"You are the master of the hospital?"

Ralph hesitated, then gave a nod. He already had one extra mouth to feed, and didn't need another.

Thomas Rodde saw the wariness in his eyes and smiled. "I have need of a place to stay, Brother, and would be grateful if I could make use of your hospitality, but I won't be a burden to you. I can pay for what I eat."

"Where are you from?"

Rodde saw the doubt in the man's face and grinned. "I used to live at a hospital in the north, but it was sacked by the Scots. I have a letter here, though." He held out a note. The brother took it warily. It was rare for a leper to move far from his birthplace, and Ralph wasn't sure about this confident man. The letter was from the brother of a small lazar house near Carlisle, and confirmed that his hospital had been destroyed by marauding Scots. It also mentioned Thomas Rodde by name and stated that he was not expelled.

Ralph handed the note back with relief. All too often wandering lepers were those who had been evicted from their old hospitals for disobedience. Their sins had to be extensive for them to suffer the punishment of homelessness and loneliness. "Of course you're welcome. Christ Himself orders us to aid travellers." It wasn't the money that made Ralph make up his mind, it was the edge to the calm voice, as if the stranger was close to the end of his tether. Ralph motioned toward the hospital. Thomas picked up his bundle, swinging it over his shoulder in a practiced movement and walked slowly inside.

"Brother, may I speak with you?"

Ralph was surprised to see that the girl had recovered her composure. The tears still marked her cheeks, but she stood resolutely at his side. He managed to raise a wan smile. "Yes, my sister, of course."

At his home, Matthew Coffyn grunted as he swung down from the saddle. It had been a long journey, and his back and legs ached as if he had walked the whole way. He led his horse to the thatched stables that leaned against the side of his hall, running from the door to the solar block. The window of his bedchamber gave out over the stable roof, and he glanced up hoping to see his wife, or at least the glow of a candle, but there was nothing visible. He watched while his grooms fetched the large trunk from the back of his cart. The light was fading, and he was glad to be back before it was fully dark.

His servants lifted the great box and staggered with it over the threshold and into the hall. They waited while he unlocked the door to his storeroom, then half-dragged, half-carried it inside. Coffyn relocked the door once they were out again, and sent his bottler for a pint of wine.

It had been a good trip. Coffyn disliked travelling, he was happier running his affairs here in Crediton, but for the last four months, through the summer, he had left his home and his wife to sell his cloth at fairs; it was a relief that this was the last of the year. There wouldn't be any more during the winter months.

His business was profitable at long last, and he was determined to make as much gold as he could, and not only to repay his ruinous debts. Rumors were growing of the prospects of war both at home and abroad. Matthew needed the protection that money could provide; money was power, and power was safety. What with the French and the Scots, he found it hard to understand why people wanted to fight each other, but all he heard at the fairs and markets pointed to a battle between the King and Lancaster, and when the soldiers started marching, he wanted to have as large a fund as possible. Sometimes the only defense lay in buying off raiders.

Not that it should come so far south and west, he mused, swallowing a gulp of wine and sitting on the bench before the fire. The two English protagonists would probably slug it out round London and York. They were the wealthy areas, the places where the richest pickings could be had, and any captain of men knew that the best way to ensure loyalty among his army was to pick a field where the best profits were available.

Even if the English themselves didn't go to war, there was always the risk of French pirates or an invasion. The thought was one he had considered several times recently, and once more he resolved to hire some men-at-arms. His eyes went to the locked door. There were dangers inherent in hiring itinerant soldiers, but the advantages outweighed them. He wouldn't be happy until he had some better defense. There were always men at Exeter. He resolved to hire some at the first opportunity.

He wondered where his wife was, and bellowed for his bottler. "Where is my lady?"

"Sir, she went to her bed this afternoon with an upset."

He waved away his bottler impatiently. The bitch was always ill. He slurped wine and belched, and his glower left his face for a moment to be replaced by a hopeful smirk. What if she was pregnant?

Matthew Coffyn was not a particularly cruel or even unkind man. He had been brought up on a farm north and east of Exeter, and had been apprenticed to a cloth merchant at seven because his father was desperate that his son would be able to keep him when he became old. The scheme had failed, though, because his father had died before he completed his apprenticeship.

But Coffyn had thrived, and when he was almost in his twenty-ninth year, he had wooed and wed. Now he was almost thirty-four, and his wife, his beautiful Martha, was just twenty. Yet he had not managed to sire a son, and the lack of children was aggravating. It wasn't right that he should be childless: it wasn't good for a man to go through life without an heir to leave his work to.

He sighed and drained his cup again. It was hard to blame his wife, for as she always pointed out, he was away so much through the summer that it would be a miracle for her to conceive. The optimism that was never far from his cheerful nature rose to the surface: winter was here, and offered unrivalled opportunities for early nights in bed.

The house was silent, and the hiss and crackle of the

fire sounded almost deafening in the absence of all other noise. As Coffyn smiled at his happy thought, he heard a door bang upstairs, and the unmistakable sound of Martha's footsteps in the passage from the solar. He filled his mug quickly and stood, but as the door opened and his wife entered the hall, he was convinced for a second that he heard something else. It was a rustling and a thump, as if someone had cautiously made his way along the thatch of the roof of the stable and down into the yard.

Coffyn's blood ran cold. The pin of jealousy pricked the balloon of his pleasure and suddenly all his trust in his wife exploded in his face.

His cuckold's face.

"Jesus!" John muttered under his breath. He had gained the safety of the tree where his rope was stored, and paused only long enough to throw the coil over his neck before quietly making his way toward the wall and his home.

His ankle was throbbing slowly with a dull intensity. It augured badly for the morning. Nothing was broken, he reckoned, for he could put his weight on it, but he wouldn't forget the sudden stab of pure agony as he climbed silently from the window into the cobbled yard behind. That must be what had done it, he thought, his jaw clenched against the pain. A loose cobble must have moved under his foot.

What a night! That shite Coffyn wasn't supposed to be back yet; he'd told his wife he'd either be late tonight, or more likely wouldn't be home until tomorrow. Why had the stupid sod turned up now? John had been forced to scramble ignominiously from the hall before he could be discovered. The Irishman rested a moment against an apple tree while he enjoyed his bitterness. Then his good temper got the better of him and he grinned to himself.

John wasn't given to introspection: he knew his place in the world, knew what gave him pleasure, and didn't reason or rationalize why things were as they were. But he also had the gift of seeing the ridiculous side of any situation, and at this moment it was tempting to give a guffaw at his own position. Here he was, after a summer of enjoying his woman, complaining because her master had come home early for once. And instead of lying with her in her bed, John was here, in the dark, with a sprained ankle and a damn great wall to surmount.

"Should've taken the knight's advice," he muttered.

Shaking his head at the capricious nature of fate, he haltingly made his way round the wall to his oak. Here he unwound his rope and drew back his arm to catch the broken limb. But as his arm went back, it was suddenly gripped. John stiffened in silent terror as the blade of a long knife shimmered in an arc before him, gleaming evilly in the light of the stars before coming to rest on his Adam's apple.

He swallowed. Carefully. "Ah—it's a fine night for a walk, isn't it, sir?"

It was no surprise that the leper camp was so dark, for there was no need of lighting for the inmates. Their day began with the dawn, and when the darkness stole over the land they went to their beds.

Quivil was used to the dark. In his home, so few miles away, the days were gauged by whether the animals were awake, and at this time of night, all were asleep. Now, he knew, his father would be sitting at his old stool before the fire, occasionally casting an eye at the sheep as they grumbled to themselves, huddled in the corner farthest from him. He would be whittling a stick, sometimes breaking off to whet his blade against the stone by the fire, spitting to lubricate the metal as he honed it to sharpness.

For his whole life Quivil had assumed he would take his place there by the fire. He had thought he would replace his father when the old man died, and then he would sit at the stool and fashion walking sticks and furniture by the firelight until the days grew longer and his every waking hour was filled with other forms of work. He had seen himself growing old and bent, just as his father was, knowing what his responsibilities were, knowing what jobs needed to be done daily. And where his mother sat, near her man, there would Mary sit, her eyes on him, looking to ensure that he was content, just as his mother had always watched his father so lovingly. And now he had nothing to look forward to. His life was over.

A noise came from outside his doorway, and the curtain was pulled aside. Framed against the night sky Quivil saw a darker shape. He muttered to himself, pulled his blanket tighter and rolled away. This room was home to another besides himself, and he assumed this must be his roommate. He had no desire for company, he wanted the peace of solitude.

But it wasn't one man preparing to climb into bed. Quivil heard murmuring voices. They were hoarse from the disease they shared, but it wasn't that which made his blood run chill. It was the cruel delight in them.

"What are you doing? What do you want?" he demanded, turning to face them.

"We want *you.*"

All at once he was grabbed by four pairs of hands, and hauled from his mattress. He could do nothing: his tongue clove to the roof of his mouth, and all he could utter was a whimper of dread.

They dragged him from the hut and out into the black night. The cold penetrated his robe, sending a fresh trickle of ice-cold terror washing down his spine. His mind, which had been in a state of sheer panic for days already, was frozen with horror. He had lost all will. In his blue funk he was certain he was about to die, but after the loss of all his self-respect and the destruction of his life, he had no strength to resist.

He could see them in the miserable light, and to his strained senses they looked like demons: small, misshapen, deformed, swollen with the putrescence of leprosy. Their appearance was that of gibbering fiends, their stench was the reek of the charnel-house. He was transfixed with horror.

They stopped, and he heard one of them give a chuckle. It sounded like the devil himself. Quivil felt his knees weaken, and would have fallen, but felt himself propelled forward, and then he found he was falling. The ground opened into a gaping hole before him, and he screamed, a high, keening noise, as he saw the earth rise up on either side.

Rodde had seen the petrified Quivil being dragged to the chapel's yard as he reentered the grounds. He had slipped into the protection of the building's wall as the group passed by, then followed after. At the sight of the young man being shoved into the newly dug grave, he felt rage choke him. It took but a moment to cover the few yards to the men, and he swung his staff. It caught a leper on the shoulder, then he whirled to stab and thrust at the others. "Leave him, you *bastards*!" he spat, his staff held high over his chest.

"Leave us alone, stranger. It's nothing—we do it to all the new ones," one man whined.

Rodde knew it was true. He had been forced to undergo a similar initiation ceremony when he had first been driven into a camp; the other lepers had thrown him into a grave, then scattered soil on him in obscene imitation of burial; sometimes he had seen other victims squirming while their tormenters urinated over them.

"It stops now." Rodde couldn't prevent his voice from shaking with disgust. He caught sight of a figure hobbling near him, and the stick shot out, catching the man in the chest. "I said it *stops*! Now, leave us."

He stood protectively while the lepers, muttering to themselves, backed away from him and made off toward their huts, and only when they had disappeared did he glance down into the hole. At the bottom, Quivil was kneeling, sobbing, gathering up handfuls of soil and wiping them over his face, smearing blood and tears together into a mask of utter despair.

Quivil's distress was the misery of mankind. Rodde stood quietly by the side of the grave, his staff still held to protect the younger man until Quivil subsided into weeping. Then he cast his prop aside and climbed down to help Edmund out.

A fortnight later the weather had turned. Now each morning the land was frozen, the grass rimed with frost. The ponds and ditches were filled with ice, on top of which the ducks and geese waddled, protesting loudly and with some confusion at the sudden loss of their favorite element. Sir Baldwin Furnshill still found the English weather difficult to cope with, even after so many years back at his estate. His blood had been thinned by his sojourn in the Mediterranean and subsequent soft living in Paris.

He pulled up at his stableyard as twilight fell, shouting for his groom and dropping from his horse. Usually he rode a dainty Arab, but today he had left early, and had chosen his rounsey, a solid beast who jerked his head and pranced skittishly, his breath steaming in the bitter evening air. The knight patted his neck while he waited for his men. "I know, I know—you haven't had enough exercise today. I'll see you're taken out for longer tomorrow. Calm yourself!"

Cold it might be, but Baldwin loved his land. The small estate stood some five or six miles north and east of Crediton, near to Cadbury. It had been his older brother's, but when poor Reynald had fallen from his horse while hunting and broken his neck, the land had come to Baldwin. After wandering for so long with little money and few comforts, the knight was delighted to own so prosperous and fertile a region of Devon—especially with the comfortable house; especially with his recent improvements. He was determined to impress his guests. One of them, anyway, he amended with a small smile.

The sun was already gone and twilight was giving way to nighttime. In the distance he could see a wraith-like streamer of smoke rising over a wood. There, he knew, a tenant of his was settling down with a pint or two of ale, tired after a day of hedging. Baldwin had passed him on the way. Above, the stars were breaking out as the sky dulled and darkened. It was strangely relaxing, as if no harm could come to anyone who appreciated its beauty, and the knight felt some of his earlier trepidation and gloom fade away.

Passing the reins to the groom, Baldwin walked from the yard and strode to his front door. Before he opened it, he looked back over his shoulder. In the time it had taken to reach the threshold, night had fallen. He could make out the faint outlines of the hillsides shining like old pewter in the moonlight. Above him the sky was a deep blue-black, across which silver-rimmed clouds drifted idly.

He opened the door. Instantly there was a scrabbling, and he caught a glimpse of the massive shape.

"Oh, no—God, *no*!"

It launched at him. His eyes widened in shock, then it was on him, and the knight staggered back under the assault. His heel snagged on a step, and he was falling. Even as his shoulder struck the packed earth of the path, he saw the jaws open at his throat, smelled the foul breath, and he shut his eyes against the inevitable.

"Good evening, sir."

Baldwin dared raise one lid, fending off the attack as best he could. A thick gobbet of saliva landed quivering on his cheek and he shuddered. "Edgar, get the brute off me!"

"It wasn't *my* idea to get the monster," Edgar said pointedly. "In fact I remember saying it would be stupid to replace the bitch."

Baldwin felt the weight leave his chest as his servant hauled on the thick leather collar, and rolled stiffly to his side before levering himself up. The mastiff was sitting at Edgar's side now, his hindquarters wriggling as he tried to wag his tail. Slobber dribbled from his huge black jowls, and he was whining excitedly, desperate to greet his master with as much enthusiasm as he could muster. And that, Baldwin knew, was a lot of enthusiasm.

Edgar was right, he reflected, but that hardly eased matters. It had seemed such a good idea at the time, replacing his old mastiff with a new one. Lionors had been his brother's bitch originally, and when the knight arrived after Reynald's death, Lionors had transferred all her affection to him unreservedly. At first it had been stifling, for Baldwin had been used to a hard life of constant travel, and having a creature so dependent upon him was irksome, especially when she took to grabbing whatever she could and chewing it in a demonstration of fervent adoration.

But he had been surprised by his sense of loss when she died. It had happened quite quietly. She had not come to him in the morning when he arose, but had remained lying by the fire. Ben, the brown and black farm dog Baldwin had adopted in days gone by, had stayed at her side, sitting quietly, and gazing at Baldwin with an expression of anxious confusion. When the knight touched her old body, it was still warm, but there was no breath whistling and snorting through her short, age-whitened muzzle, and he suddenly found his eyes brimming at the realization that she would no longer chew his sticks, or dribble on his lap while he ate, or leave a noxious reminder of her presence in the corner of the hall. He found he missed her.

So he had decided to take one of her great-grandchildren to replace her. He had overruled Edgar and gone to the kennels behind the stables, and as soon as he had seen the tawny mass of blubber and fur, he had pointed, and said, "That is the one." And so "Uther" was chosen as the house's guard.

Except Baldwin's servant refused to dignify the animal with such a name. He felt that the monster should be identified by something that reflected the reality. Consequently, due to Edgar's constant repetition, the eight-month-old now answered to "Chops."

"This dog should return to the kennels, sir," Edgar said.

"Uther stays."

"He attacked Cottey this morning."

"Uther st—" Baldwin gave his servant a suspicious look. What do you mean, 'attacked Cottey'?"

"Cottey came to speak to you and the dog scared him almost stupid."

"You mean Uther made him brighter than normal!" he growled.

"It was nothing to laugh about. When I got there, Uther had him up against the table and—"

"The table?" A light glimmered in Baldwin's eye. He asked suavely, "So this was in the hall, was it?"

Edgar waved a hand. "It's irrelevant, the point is the dog terrified the poor—"

"Uther is a guard. Cottey should have known that. If he walked straight into the hall, it's no surprise Uther tried to defend the place. The dog was doing his duty against a draw-latch."

Seeing that he had lost that sally, Edgar ventured a fresh attack. "And what about other guests? What if this mutt should take it into his so-called brain to defend the house against someone staying with you?"

Baldwin's attitude altered subtly. Now there was a degree of shiftiness in his manner as he avoided his servant's gaze. "He just needs a little training. Anyway, he's fine with people he's been introduced to."

"Yesterday Chops was with me all morning. I left the room for a few minutes, and when I came back in he barked at me! I had been gone long enough to draw one quart of ale from the buttery; in that time the mutt had forgotten me, and you seriously suggest he's going to be fine with strangers?"

Baldwin ruffled the dog's ears. At his touch Uther sprang up, and the knight had to avert his face as another gobbet of slobber flew upward. "He's just affectionate," he said gruffly, forcing the dog down again. On his chest two massive, damp paw prints reflected the light from the open doorway.

Edgar stared at them pointedly. "And what about the lady Jeanne?"

The knight hesitated. He had to admit that Edgar had

a point there, as he looked at the fresh mud that spattered his tunic. The widow from Liddinstone was due to visit any day, in the company of Simon Puttock and his wife.

It would be good to see them all. Simon was the bailiff of Lydford Castle, a man with the unenviable task of keeping the tinminers and local landlords apart to prevent bloodshed. He and Baldwin had joined forces several times now to solve unexplained local murders. Simon's wife Margaret had exerted herself on Baldwin's behalf, introducing him to all her more marriageable friends; she had seen his loneliness and had tried to tempt him with women she knew to be available and of the right level in society, yet none had attracted him. None until he met Jeanne, anyway. The slim, grave woman with the red-gold hair. Perhaps . . .

Perhaps it would be better if Uther was elsewhere when Jeanne arrived. He would have to consider it. "Enough! Fetch me wine and water," he commanded, walking into his hall.

As usual, the old black and brown farm dog lay before the hearth, and barely glanced up as the knight crossed to his chair, merely sweeping his tail from side to side and watching without moving his head. Uther forwent the pleasure of the fireside and sat with his back to Baldwin's chair, turning his head to stare at the knight until he submitted to the dog's clear desire and rested his hand on the animal's flank, patting gently.

Edgar walked in with a jug and goblet, setting them by the fire to warm. "So how was the good Bishop?"

The knight shook his head. "He's got too much on his plate."

Testing the watered wine, Edgar poured. "What did he have to say?"

Baldwin had met Edgar in the hell-hole of Acre, when

both were young. Once the city was clearly doomed, the two had been saved by the Knights Templar, who had allowed them space on a ship making for Cyprus. It was as a mark of their gratitude that both had taken the vows of poverty, chastity and obedience and joined the Order. Baldwin became a knight, and Edgar his man-at-arms. More recently, since the Templars had been destroyed by an avaricious French king, Edgar had become Baldwin's servant and trusted seneschal. After so much time, Baldwin knew he could trust his man.

"War is close," he said bluntly. "Stapledon doesn't mince his words. Lancaster has shut himself up in his castle and refuses to meet the King. Stapledon is convinced it's because he doesn't trust the King's new counsellors."

"Stapledon said all this?"

Baldwin nodded gloomily. "Stapledon, from what I can gather, is now one of the few men whose judgment the King *does* trust. Edward knows the Bishop is honest and reliable, while others in the royal household are less committed to the King and more interested in what they can get for themselves. Stapledon thinks the Despenser family in particular have gained too much power recently. They are threatening the peace of the realm, and Lancaster will not tolerate the way their strength is increasing—not for much longer."

His servant watched him with concern. It was rare for the knight to express his thoughts so explicitly, even with him. As Edgar refilled his master's goblet, he considered the implications. War would mean that Baldwin must be called upon to support his lord in battle, and likewise Edgar must go with his master to fight with him. The thought of riding to battle again kindled a spark of excitement in his breast.

But it felt wrong to go to war over such foolishness,

and that fact tempered his delight. King Edward II was too fond of his favorites. Even people here in Crediton had heard the rumors about the King's attraction to other men in preference to his wife, and now that Gaveston had been killed, beheaded by other lords, the Despensers were enthusiastically taking over his place at court. Especially the son, who, from what Edgar had heard, appeared to have designs on the whole of Wales, the way he was acquiring land—and often by illegal means too, if the rumors were true. To support the Despensers and fight Lancaster seemed absurd, yet it was all too likely.

He was about to speak when Uther stiffened and then began to growl, low and insistent. A few moments later the men heard the drumming of hooves, and they stared at each other. It was late for someone to visit, with darkness having fallen, especially since the roads were so icy.

Edgar hurried out, Uther lumbering behind him as far as the doorway. The dog stood there, hackles up, waiting and guarding his domain. Baldwin could hear voices, a tone of surprise in Edgar's, then the speeding steps as his servant returned to the hall.

"Master, you must go back to Crediton. There's been a murder!"

~ 5 ~

It took little time to get the horses ready, and soon Edgar and Baldwin were riding off with the messenger. Baldwin knew that his Arab wanted exercise, but in preference took the rounsey again. The Arab had too much of a mercurial nature, and was dangerous to take out in the dark when it was as chilly and icy as this. Baldwin had made sure that Uther was shut indoors. The dog would want to follow his master if he could.

"Who is dead?" Baldwin demanded when they moved off.

The messenger, a lad barely in his twenties, threw him an anxious look over his shoulder. Baldwin had to give him a reassuring smile. He recognized the symptoms: it was fearsome for a peasant boy or young apprentice to be questioned by the King's highest local official. The lad gave a nervous nod of his head. "Sir, it was the old gold merchant, sir."

"Gold merchant?"

Seeing his bafflement, Edgar interrupted. "I think he means Godfrey of London, sir. He's the only one I can think of."

"Yes, of course."

Baldwin pursed his lips. He had met Godfrey a few times—the Londoner was rich enough to be familiar to someone of Baldwin's status. As he cantered along, mentally cursing the slight breeze that somehow contrived to penetrate his thick tunic and jerkin, Baldwin reviewed what he had heard about the man.

There wasn't much. He had arrived in Crediton some years before Baldwin himself had come home, about seven years ago now. It was hard for a newcomer to find a good plot of land in the town itself, but Godfrey was a foreigner with money, and soon he had the parcel of land he wanted, not too close to the center, so he had his own pasturage for cattle and his pigs. He had a small household, a daughter living with him, bottler, grooms and other servants, as well as various outside workers.

He sighed; there was no point trusting to his memory. It would be better to form his opinion of the matter when he saw the body. There were so many questions at this stage that he might as well wait until they arrived in the town. Besides, with the wind blowing in his face, he was rapidly losing all feeling in his cheeks and mouth. He pulled a grimace and tugged his collar up, trying to sink his head down to protect his neck.

They covered the distance quickly, riding steadily rather than too fast, and luckily none of them encountered ice, but Baldwin was glad when he smelled the smoke from the town. Soon they were riding up the lane that led behind the church, then along the front of it to the main street. It was here that they saw the group.

Baldwin felt a shiver rack his frame. There was a sense of excitement in the huddle of townspeople. He could see the folk whispering in each other's ears, one or two pointing as he and his little entourage clattered up the street.

It was always the same, he knew, but he didn't have

to like it. In a small place like Crediton, murders were a rare occurrence. It was no surprise that when something sensational happened the people wanted to be there to witness it, but these folks weren't here to help in an investigation, they were driven by a ghoulish desire to see the body. He could hear the gleeful, sibilant whispering as he approached and knew that there would be men offering bets as to how the victim died, others speculating on the likely identity of the murderer, many offering their own views as to what the motive could have been. And all would want to witness the arrest of the suspect and the subsequent hanging. In the flickering glare thrown by three torches, he could see the faces, all pale and excited in the presence of violent death—like so many demons. He felt his mouth twist in disgust.

Ignoring them, he rode on, and they parted in deference to his office, leaving a clear path to the gate. Here, preventing them from entering, was the constable.

"Hello, Tanner," Baldwin said, pulling up.

The constable nodded grimly, jerking his head toward the house. "He's in his hall, Sir Baldwin."

"Who found him?"

"His neighbor, Matthew Coffyn."

Baldwin nodded. "Have you sent men to seek the killer?"

"As soon as I heard, I had men chase the main roads, but it's unlikely they'll see anyone this late at night."

"Was there any report of a man riding or running away?"

"No, sir, nothing. As far as I know, no one heard anything."

That was the hardest part of searching for a murderer, the knight knew. It was largely a pointless exercise sending men after a killer when there was no hint as to who could be responsible. Yet if no one was sent, the Coroner would look askance at the constable. And at least the posse would be able to spread the news of the killing, putting remote farmers on their guard against another attack. "Well, perhaps they will be fortunate this time," he murmured. And maybe they won't, he added to himself. Maybe this was a murder committed by someone in the town, someone who bore the goldsmith a grudge and wanted to take his revenge. Who, Baldwin wondered, could have enough of a hatred for the man to want to kill him?

Leaving the messenger holding their horses for them, he and his servant marched on to the hall.

The great studded door stood open, and they entered the black maw of the screens passage. Baldwin hesitated at the door to the hall, through which a little light glimmered, but after a moment strode to the door at the far end of the corridor. He found himself looking out at a large courtyard. Stabling for at least thirty horses was over to the left of the cobbled space, while the kitchen lay on the right, at some short distance from the house itself. Between the hall and the kitchen Baldwin could make out the dividing wall between this place and the next, which meant that this yard was almost completely walled in. Opposite him was a gatehouse set between two large buildings, one of which looked like a barn and storeshed for wagons and equipment, while the other, judging by the gentle lowing emanating from it, was serving as a cattle shed. At this time of day, all was still, and at some windows he could see yellow lights shining.

"Do you want to see the body?" Edgar asked quietly. He wondered why his master was peering out so intently. It wasn't like him to bypass a murder victim like this. To his relief, Baldwin nodded pensively. Edgar led the way back to the hall.

The knight found himself in a room only a shade larger than his own, but with the rich drapery lighted by many candles, it was infinitely more imposing. It was a new house, and no expense had been spared in its construction. The walls were of solid moorstone, and a good fire burned at the hearth in the middle of the floor. Chairs and benches lined the walls; thick tapestries covered the windows; at the far end a raised dais held the lord's table, at the back of which was a curtain which Baldwin knew would conceal another door, one which would lead to the private rooms of the solar block. A building this modern would be sure to have separate sleeping quarters for the master so he could enjoy a little privacy from his servants in the hall. A sideboard with a skewed cloth stood against the wall to the side of the dais, and Baldwin's gaze rested on it for a moment before his attention was drawn to the figure on the floor.

Baldwin had seen many dead men in his life. He had seen corpses by the hundred in Acre when the Egyptians attacked; he'd witnessed his comrades dying in agony on the pyres because they had dared attest to the honor of their Order; and he had seen many victims of murder since becoming Keeper. Like everyone else, he was used to the sight of those who had expired of old age or disease. There were many ways to die.

At least, he thought to himself, this one is straightforward. There could be no doubt as to the reason for Godfrey of London's death. The blood seeping from his crushed skull left little to the imagination.

Baldwin didn't move his eyes from the corpse. "Any weapon?"

There was a thin, dark man with a fearful round face standing by the doorway gripping an oak cudgel. Edgar recognized him as an ostler from the inn. He must have been co-opted to guard the corpse.

"I don't know, sir. Tanner just told me to stay here and make sure no one came in until you arrived."

"Has anyone been in?"

"No, sir."

"Were you here when this man was found?"

"No, sir. Tanner called me here as soon as he arrived, so as to guard the room and see the girl safe."

Baldwin raised an eyebrow. "Girl?"

"Yes, sir. She had been found here unconscious. With the man."

"Man? What man?"

"Putthe, the bottler. He was here too."

Baldwin closed his eyes a moment, then spoke slowly and deliberately. "Go out to the front gate and tell Tanner to get up here now. You stay there and keep people out. You understand?"

Once the ostler had scurried from the room, Baldwin walked to a large candle standing high on a wall sconce. Taking it, he raised it high over his head to light the room more clearly, peering all about him with care.

There was little to see now, but he could discern areas where the rushes had been scuffed and moved. Before going to them, he bent at the side of the dead man.

He was some seven paces from the door, his head pointing toward the nearest window, one which gave out to the yard at the back of the house, near to the kitchen. The figure lay oddly to Baldwin's eyes, but the knight knew that dead men often assumed strange or even bizarre postures. Godfrey's right arm was at his side, while his left was held out, bent at the elbow with the hand up. If he was standing, Baldwin thought, it would look as if he was holding up his hand to tell someone to halt. The strangeness of the pose lay in its very naturalness. If it wasn't for the hideous wound, Baldwin would have thought the man was merely resting.

The knight squatted, the candle held high once more as he surveyed the body and the surrounding floor. He could see no object lying nearby which could have inflicted such a vicious wound. This was no sudden, mad attack, the man clubbed as he walked across the floor, the weapon then dropped as the killer realized with horror what he had done. And yet, the knight reminded himself, there were plenty of cases where a murderer had slain in hot blood and then rushed off still clutching the implement of death.

While Edgar looked on imperturbably, Baldwin set the candle down and performed a quick investigation. He felt the man's skin at the top of his torso. It was still warm. Then the knight sniffed at Godfrey's mouth. There was no sweet, sickly odor of alcohol that he could discern. He probed gently at the quickly clotting wound. Beneath his fingers he could feel the smashed bones moving, and he nodded to himself. He had seen head wounds often enough. This one was certainly adequate to have caused death.

Heaving, he rolled the body over to seek additional wounds, and opened the man's tunic to check there were no stab wounds. It was all too common for a man to inflict an apparently obvious wound on a corpse after committing a murder in an attempt to throw suspicion onto someone else. But there was nothing to be seen.

He had just hauled the body back into its original position when Tanner entered. Baldwin ignored him. Slowly easing himself up from his knees, which cracked as he came upright, he took hold of the candle and walked to the nearest mark in the rushes.

The constable was a steady man, Baldwin knew. As strongly built as a smith, he had the worn, cragged features of a moorman, with black hair that was becoming grizzled. He moved with a deceptive slowness, as though he had to concentrate to achieve the simplest task, but Baldwin had seen him roused, and knew that Tanner had a ponderous strength and, when he needed it, the speed of a striking adder. The constable waited patiently while the knight crouched at the disturbed flooring.

It was close to the door, but although the knight studied the depression with care, he could see no clues; it was merely a scraped mess at the edges of which the straws had been heaped slightly. There was nothing to be learned here. He rose and went to the other disturbed patch of rushes.

Here he paused. This part was nearer an open window. As Baldwin stood looking down, he gauged the distances. It was close to Godfrey's body, and pointed toward the window itself, which made the knight frown. Why should someone have opened the window? He walked over to it and stared out at the dark kitchen block. That at least confirmed one thought: the culprit had presumably escaped from here; rather than fleeing from the front door and risking capture in the street, the killer had made off through the back. In the dark, Crediton's main street wasn't terribly busy, but there were enough people to notice a man running. It would have been safer for the murderer to nip out through the garden unseen.

"Tanner, you found the man just as he is? You didn't see anything moved?"

"No, Sir Baldwin. He was lying just as you see him now. It was obvious he wasn't going to get up again, not with a hole in his head like that."

"Tell me what happened."

"I was at the inn when the neighbor's servant came running for me. Well, not really a servant—Coffyn, the man next door, has been nervous recently, and he's hired some lads to protect his house. They're all hard types, and this was one of them. I came back with him, and found Godfrey here, as he is now." He pointed at the marks near Baldwin. "Just there was where his daughter had been. Feet near the door, head pointed at the window. She'd been thumped as well and was taken to her room before I got here."

"Was she struck on the back of the head like this one?"

"No—punched, I reckon. Her mouth was all bloody. This here," he said, indicating the flattened area nearer the door, "this here was where Putthe the servant was lying. He was unconscious too. He had been struck on the back of the head like his master."

"Was anyone else here when you arrived?"

"Only the neighbor, Coffyn. When he'd seen what had happened, he'd sent his man straight for me, as he should, staying here himself to guard the place."

"Where is this Coffyn now?"

"I let him go home. He was a bit green in the face, sir, and I didn't want him spewing all over the room. It's in enough of a mess as it is."

"And his man?"

"Sent him back too. He's not a local man, and I didn't want a foreigner mucking about in here while I waited for you, sir."

"Good. The two who were hurt, then, the servant and the daughter: are they all right?"

"She should be fine with a rest, sir, and Putthe's got a head like moorstone. Whoever hit him will be lucky if he can use the same club again. Clobbering Putthe hard enough to knock him out would break most cudgels."

Baldwin gave a fleeting grin. "We should leave the girl to recover a little, but what about this bottler: do you think he will be ready to answer some questions? Is he up and about yet?"

"He's come to, sir, but he's pretty confused."

"So would I be if I'd been laid out. Anyway, before we see him . . . That sideboard looks more than a little empty, doesn't it?"

Tanner glanced at it in some surprise and followed the knight as Baldwin walked over to it.

It was an excellent cupboard, Baldwin saw. This was not made of cheap wood knocked together by a carpenter; this was well constructed by a joiner in good elm. There were four shelves, with doors underneath, and Baldwin gazed at it speculatively for some time. He opened the doors and peered inside. Both sides had pewter pots, jugs and plates stacked neatly, but hardly filled the space given. He shut it up again. On the shelves were some plates, of good quality, four on the bottom shelf and three on each of the others. A solitary jug stood next to a drinking horn of silver. Baldwin picked them up one at a time.

"Good silverwork, this," he said.

"What is it, sir?" Tanner asked after glancing at Edgar in some confusion.

"Hmm? Oh, only that Master Godfrey must have been a very wealthy man," stated the knight with sudden resolution. He clapped his hands together. "Now, let's see whether Putthe is ready to answer some questions."

~ 6 ~

The servant was resting on a cot almost hidden behind two massive barrels. He was pale, and opened his eyes with apparent pain, grimacing as he tried to focus on the three men standing in his buttery. The single candle was inadequate, and Baldwin sent Tanner to fetch more.

"Stay there, Putthe, I only want to ask you a few questions," Baldwin said gently, holding up his hand. As he did so, he noticed that the gesture gave him the same pose as Godfrey's body next door. If a man was holding up his hand, he wondered, would he fall to the ground in that same position if he was struck dead in an instant? And if so, could he have been holding up his hand to tell a thief to stop?

Putthe sank back with a grunt. He was a short man, with a grave, round face. Baldwin saw that he had thin lips, which opened and closed as he spoke with a strangely mechanical action that put Baldwin in mind of a helmet's hinged vizor; opening only reluctantly, and snapping shut when allowed to. For such a ruddy complexion, Putthe's eyes were a curiously pale, watery blue, making him look as if he was somehow incomplete; an unfinished mannequin. Above his eyes a band of dirty cloth encircled his brow.

It was this bandage that was giving him the most pain now. His head felt as if it was splitting in half, the top being squeezed off by the pressure. Putthe grimly noted that whoever it was who had belted him hadn't intended him to get up again in a hurry. As his skull touched the cloth of the bolster, he winced and the breath hissed through his teeth. His assailant had succeeded. He would be lying here for quite some time to come. "Sir, how can I help you?"

"You know your master is dead, Putthe—do you know who could have done this?"

"It was that mad Irishman!"

"Did you see him?"

"Tonight, sir, yes. Out in the yard. He's been found here in the garden before. My master saw him there only a few weeks ago. Let him off, at the time, but said if he was ever found here again, he'd be—"

Baldwin held up a hand again. "What were you doing this evening?"

"Me? I was in here."

Baldwin glanced about him. There was the usual paraphernalia of the bottler's place of work: barrels, jugs, pots and tankards. Two stools sat near each other at one cask. Beside them were a pair of large jugs. Glancing at Putthe, Baldwin saw him wince.

Putthe had to close his eyes: the pain was like a dagger thrusting in at his temple. And his head was spinning—the world had gone mad! Godfrey's behavior; the mistress's weird determination to look after a common smith and permit the servants a free evening—and now this! Someone had broken in and the master was dead! Clutching at his head, Putthe moaned.

Baldwin spoke gently. "I am sorry, Putthe, but I have

to ask these questions. I assume you ran from here straight into the hall?"

"That's right." Putthe tried to sit up, but settled himself back against the bolster. A thin dew of moisture shone on his forehead, making it glow in the candlelight. "I hurried along the screens and in through the door, and saw them lying there. I was about to go to them when I was tapped here"—he gingerly indicated his bruised skull—"and down I went. Next thing I know, I'm in here, lying on my palliasse."

"Was there anyone in the room in front of you when you entered? Obviously someone was behind you, but did you see anyone near the window?"

"I ran straight for the hall. As you can see, I had to turn into the screens passage from here, facing the door to the garden, and turn right into the hall itself."

"So what did you see?" Baldwin asked impatiently.

"Sir, as I ran through the passage, I had a clear view of the yard beyond. John of Irelaunde was out there."

"You saw someone out there?" Tanner scoffed, returning with more candles and setting them on barrels. "From how far? Across a darkened courtyard, and at night too? Your brains are addled, man!"

"I know what I saw."

Baldwin studied his obstinate face. "I wonder. How can you be so sure it was him?"

"I know John well enough. He hurt his ankle recently, and this man was limping a bit, but for another, there was light in the yard. The master was nervous about the men from Coffyn's place, like I said, and had a torch burning so no one could get at the horses or equipment without being seen."

"You are seriously suggesting that a weak little fool like John could kill your master?" Baldwin asked, and picked up his cup once more.

Putthe could see that he wasn't convinced. The knight settled back in his chair, peering at him over the top of his drink with a magisterial air. He looked like a benign cleric giving absolution for a minor sin. Shaking his head, Putthe knew he would have to provide the last clue. "Sir, you don't understand: John of Irelaunde was known to my master."

"Speak plainly—I am no mindreader."

"My master found John crossing the garden—*his* garden. He thought John was using it as a covered shortcut through to somewhere else."

Now Putthe could see he had the knight's attention. Baldwin slowly set the cup down again and leaned forward with both elbows on his knees. "Why should he pass through here to another garden?"

"There are rumors about the man's liking for women—especially those who are young and bored," Putthe said, looking away.

"You mean Martha Coffyn?"

The servant nodded. "That's what I think. That's what my master told me."

"I too have heard this," Baldwin murmured, and shook his head. "Why should he come in here and beat you, your mistress and your master? The fact of his adultery is no reason to murder. But you may not be aware of the other thing—did you notice the sideboard tonight?"

Putthe threw him a glance of blank incomprehension. "The *sideboard*? What do I care about that?"

"Putthe, the sideboard looks empty to me," Baldwin explained. "Could you tell me what should be displayed, so that I can verify what is left there."

The bottler grimaced in concentration. He recalled: "On the top shelf there was a pair of silver plates and a drinking horn; on the next was a row of six pewter plates and a silver salt-cellar, shaped like a swan; on the next was another row of six plates, but there were two large flagons as well . . . and on the last shelf was a row of eight smaller plates."

"And you are quite sure of that?"

"Of course I am!"

"Much of it has gone, Putthe."

"What?" The injured man started up from his recumbent position, winced, grabbed at his forehead and slowly eased himself back. "That just proves it, then! It was that miserable Irish bastard. He knocked us out to steal all the stuff, and now he's got clean away!"

"Before we assume anything like that, do you know of anyone else who might have wanted to kill your master?"

"No," said Putthe with conviction. "My master was a quiet man. He only ever helped other people. You speak to anyone, they'll all tell you about Master Godfrey of London."

"Yet you say John *did* hate your master enough to kill him."

"And you are certain it was John you saw out in the yard?" Tanner asked again, dubiously.

"Why don't you ask him! John was found in the back by the master some while ago; John was carrying on with Martha Coffyn; John needs money. If you're right and the plate has gone, you can be sure it's John has got it! And now, if you don't mind, I need to get some rest. My head feels as if it's going to fall off my shoulders!"

"It's too late to see the girl now," Baldwin said as they left the bottler. Tanner, could you go to her and ask if she will talk to us in the morning? Then go next door and tell the neighbor—Coffyn you said his name was, didn't you?—well, say the same to him. And put a man on guard in the room with the body. I'll want to study it again in daylight, in case I missed something. For now, I need to think." He went back along the screens and out through the door to the yard. Tanner and Edgar exchanged a glance before following him.

"What is it, sir?" Edgar asked as he joined his master.

"Hmm? Oh, it's just that I was thinking if someone had killed Godfrey and run away immediately, he would not have gone straight through the front door. There are always too many people out there on the main street. No, I was wondering whether that someone might have come out here, through the back. And the more I stare out this way, the more I feel certain that the killer made off through the garden."

"Ah," said Tanner. "But he's not the sort, Sir Baldwin."

"You think so? He was willing to defraud the people of the town about losing his sight, wasn't he?"

"Oh, that's very different."

"And what if he was trying to steal the plate and got interrupted? He might have knocked Godfrey down without meaning to kill him."

"Do you want me to arrange for someone to keep an eye on him?"

Baldwin grimaced doubtfully, then shook his head. "No. If he was to run away, we'd soon catch him."

"He's no murderer, I'm sure, and I don't think he'd break into a house either."

"Neither do I, but that's not what other people will think, Tanner," Baldwin said softly, still staring out toward the little shack that lay only a few hundred yards up the hill. "Let's just hope no fools take it into their heads to assume the worst of him, eh?"

As the trio turned away, Baldwin and his servant retrieving their horses and making their way home, John sat on his bed rubbing his sprained ankle.

The palliasse was thin now, and the rope mattress beneath was painful through the straw filling, but the little Irishman hardly noticed. In his mind's eye he could still see that room, the two men on the floor, the girl lying near the window.

His heart was still beating furiously. The effort of stealthily making his way home had exhausted him. Especially since all the way he could hear the cries of the men searching for him; the men who would hold him to be hanged because of the sack on his back.

He was very scared; he had to make sure he wasn't searched—not until he had managed to remove the sack of pewter concealed beneath the hay in his little barn and had placed it in a safer cache.

Edgar rose before the dawn, as was his habit. He was a little light-headed from lack of sleep, but he ducked his head in the bucket by the well, puffing and blowing with the cold as he towelled himself dry. Pulling on his tunic, he stood awhile watching the eastern sky as it lightened.

Ever since his time with the Knights Templar, he had enjoyed this early part of the day. It gave him a sense of serenity, as if he was alone in the world, and to enjoy it all the more, he sat on the old oak stump on which the logs were split. From here, by gazing along the length of the house, he could see the sky changing its color, tingeing the clouds with silver and purple, before suffusing them in peach. Almost before he realized, the darkness of the night sky was gone, and in its place was the clear, fresh paleness of the new day.

Only when the sun was beginning to rise above the hill did he stand and make his way into the buttery to prepare his master's meal. Like most houses, Baldwin's had a separate kitchen so as to prevent any accidental fire threatening the hall itself, but Edgar knew his master well: Sir Baldwin would want only cold meats and bread for his first meal.

The servant sought out a good quality loaf, and brought it together with a cold roasted chicken, a large ham and a joint of beef. These he distributed at Baldwin's table in the hall, then he checked the fire. Wat, the cattleman's son, had already been in and blown the embers into flame, stacking a small pile of twigs and tinder above. These were now blazing merrily enough, and Edgar carefully rested split logs on top, squatting beside it to keep an eye on it until the logs should catch. When there was enough heat, he would set the pot above on its stand. The knight might not like too much alcohol, but he enjoyed his cup of weak, warmed and sweetened ale with his breakfast.

While resting, Edgar found his thoughts turning to his master. Baldwin had been a kindly and loyal knight, but all that was about to change. Edgar knew he was looking forward to the visit of Lady Jeanne de Liddinstone, the widow he had met the previous year in Tavistock, and Edgar was convinced that he was set on wooing her. There was no surprise in that—the lady was very attractive, with her red-gold hair and bright blue eyes. Edgar contemplatively nodded his head. She was not the sort of woman he would necessarily select for himself, for he was nervous of women who were too independent, preferring those who were more amenable to his will, but he could understand how his master could become enamored of her.

And a wife about the place would necessarily mean change. She would want to keep an eye on her husband's affairs, would want to ensure that he was properly looked after—and that might not mean in the same way that Edgar had looked after Baldwin for the last few years.

Then there was Cristine at the inn in Crediton. Edgar was aware that his feelings were drawn more and more toward her, although he had no idea why. She was pretty enough, it was true, but she was hardly the compliant, quiet type of woman he had always looked for before. Cristine was strong-willed and powerful, a serving girl with a quick line in repartee, and rather than being irritated and looking upon her as a harpy, Edgar was finding himself attracted to her as an equal. It was an alarming concept.

And if he fulfilled her expectation (and, he suspected, Baldwin's as well), and married her, it would mean a total alteration to his life. Surely Jeanne de Liddinstone would view her with doubt, a courtly lady like herself. She would expect to have a young maiden to see to her sewing and mending, a girl who had been raised quietly, rather than a wench whose education had taken place in the taproom, and whose store of small talk related to raucous jokes told at the inn's hall.

He gave a sigh as he gazed into the flames. When his master married, he would have to leave and start a new life in the town. There were surely going to be many changes soon.

"What's the matter, Edgar? You're mooning at the fire like a lovesick squire!"

"Sir Baldwin, your food is ready, but the fire is still too cool to warm your ale."

Baldwin threw a sour glance at the tiny flames licking up from the wood. "Kick the lad who laid the damned thing and tell him to prepare it better next time, or we'll use *him* as firewood to warm my drinks!"

"Yes, sir," Edgar said, smiling as his master walked to his chair and sat down. Baldwin was one of that rare breed of men: someone who awoke with an easy, light-hearted demeanor. Although he sounded gruff, Edgar knew he was speaking loudly to make sure his voice carried out to the yard behind, where Wat should be stacking logs.

Baldwin made a leisurely breakfast, gratefully accepting a pot of watered wine instead of his ale. As he chewed, his mind was fixed on the body left in the hall of the retired goldsmith, and his ruminations made him glower in concentration. When Wat entered to stack logs by the fire, he noticed the knight's expression, and dropped his load in fear. Under Edgar's stern gaze, he quickly caught up the errant logs, which were rolling over the floor toward his master's feet, and stowed them near the hearth before hurriedly making his way from the room, thankful that his clumsiness had not earned him the whipping he expected.

Edgar turned to his master as the door slammed. "I think he'll be more careful about the fire next time, sir."

Baldwin chuckled, but soon his face took on a faraway look again. He must return to Crediton and continue with his investigation into the killing of Godfrey—Godfrey of London. Baldwin mused over the name. "What sort of a man was he, I wonder?"

"Sir?"

"This quiet goldsmith. What sort of a man was he? Who would have known him best, do you think?"

Edgar scratched his nose thoughtfully. "I know little about him. He wasn't a very sociable man, from what I've heard."

"It might be worth asking at the inn whether anyone knew him," Baldwin said slyly.

Edgar ignored his look. "Perhaps. I could see what I can find out, if you want."

"Very well! When one has a spy ready placed, it's wasteful not to make use of him—or *her*!"

"Quite, master," Edgar said coldly.

"But we need to ask what these others saw as well," Baldwin added, his light-heartedness falling away as he considered the problems ahead. "We have to see this neighbor and his guard, and the dead man's daughter."

"And the Irishman."

"Yes," Baldwin agreed. "And John."

Yet he found it hard to believe that the tranter could have anything to do with it.

They took the ride into Crediton at an easy pace, for there was plenty of ice lying on the flat stretches of road, and where there wasn't, the packed soil of the tracks spelled out another danger: it was all too easy for a horse to slip on a frost-hardened rut and sprain a fetlock; if cantering, a horse could break a leg. Baldwin had no desire to see his rounsey destroyed, so they rode along gently.

He went straight on past the goldsmith's hall, past the little group of excitedly chattering townspeople, and in at the gate of Matthew Coffyn.

The house was set back a few tens of yards from the road, and Baldwin could study it as he approached. It was a new place, one of the most recent in the village, and unlike most of its neighbors, was built of local red stone. That itself boasted of money. The main hall was a broad gray mass facing him, like the long stroke in a capital "T." At the right end was the barred top of the "T," which consisted of storerooms with the solar above. Smoke from over the thatched roof showed the kitchen lay behind.

He and his servant dismounted at the door. Their appearance had been noticed by a burly man who stood at the threshold. He bellowed over his shoulder, and soon a young groom came running, taking their mounts from them and leading them away to be watered.

Baldwin gave a short grunt of disgust. In his youth, men took on their positions with dedication. The old way was for a man to give himself unreservedly to his lord for life, in exchange for which he would receive clothing, equipment, food and lodging, each depending upon his status. As his lord's power waxed or waned, so would his own prospects. The modern vogue for men to sell themselves purely for money made them no better than bankers or lawyers. A man like that was undertaking only a cynical financial transaction with no concept of true duty. He would transfer his allegiance on the promise of more cash.

"Sir?" the man said questioningly.

He put Baldwin in mind of a wandering mercenary. It wasn't the clothing. He was clad like any town-dweller, in simple ochre tunic and linen shirt. There was not even a sword about him, only a long-bladed knife dangling at his hip. He had alert, cheerful eyes, and his mouth seemed on the verge of smiling. His posture was relaxed, his thumbs comfortably stuck in his belt, eyeing the knight with a look of respect—but only that respect due to an equal.

But the negligent pose was itself an act. The man was ready to defend the door against anyone who was foolish enough to attempt to force it. Baldwin could see that in his stillness, and more especially in the way that his attention flitted from Baldwin to someone in the street behind the knight, and back again. That was why Baldwin knew he had been a soldier. He had the warrior's instinct of keeping an eye out for danger.

"I am here to see Matthew Coffyn."

"And your name, sir?"

"You may tell him that the Keeper of the King's Peace is here," Baldwin said easily.

The guard nodded affably, then glanced behind him. "Go and tell your master, and hurry about it! Please come with me, sir."

They followed him along a broad screens passage, and into a wide hall. It was as Baldwin had suspected. Six men, all sitting at tables, were enjoying their first whet of the day, supping ale from large pots and wiping their mouths with the back of their hands, eyeing him suspiciously. For all that it had the charm of a garrison, Baldwin could see that the hall was well-appointed. Above the entrance was a carved minstrel's gallery, and the dais at the far end was deep enough for twenty to sit at table. In the middle of the floor was the hearth, with a cone of timbers smoldering quietly inside a ring of moorstone blocks. He counted seven good-sized tables, apart from the two large ones on the dais.

But even with the tapestries, all of which displayed hunting scenes, there was an atmosphere that belied the apparent homeliness of the scene. The men were plainly not the servants of a prosperous man, they were little more than brigands, and the rolled palliasses and packs against the wall were proof enough that the garrison slept and lived here.

Matthew Coffyn was seated at his table, and Baldwin studied him as he was led to the merchant's presence.

Coffyn was a tall man, Baldwin saw, with a paunch and thick neck that were testaments to his wealth—he could afford as much food as he wanted. For all that, he had a miserable appearance, with a pointed, weakly chin and thin lips under a straight, narrow nose. His eyes were dark, and met the knight's with a curious sadness. Yet there was also a petulance about him, giving the impression of a spoiled child. This was added to by the shock of unkempt, mousy hair, which gave him the look of a youngster, and also by the signs of nervous energy. Although Coffyn was quiet and sat very still in his seat, every now and again his hand would go to his mouth, and he would worry at his nails like a dog seeking to extract the very last vestige of meat from a whitened bone. Báldwin could see thin red marks on two nails where Coffyn had already chewed them to the quick and drawn blood.

Much of this Baldwin came to notice later, as they spoke. His initial thought was, This man is vain and arrogant. Still, Coffyn rose to his feet as Baldwin came to his table, and welcomed him with every sign of respect, begging him to sit at the merchant's side, and pressing him to accept wine. Edgar stood behind his master, while Coffyn waved at the men at the table, and gradually, with an ill humor, they filed out.

"You are here because of the terrible event last night, of course?"

Baldwin inclined his head in assent. "I understand you were the first to find him?"

"That's right. It was a horrible thing to come across. Poor Godfrey! Do you have any idea who could have done it?"

This last was said with a sudden flash of his eyes, and Baldwin was struck with the conviction that the man already had his own suspect filed and catalogued in his mind—and tried and hanged, too. The knight sighed. People were so often willing to allocate blame and condemn on flimsy evidence. All too often, he knew, it came down to prejudice or pure malice for another. "Not yet, sir."

"Fear not, Sir Baldwin. God will show you who was responsible."

"In the meantime, could you tell me what happened last night?"

Coffyn motioned to his bottler, and the man refilled their cups. "I was away yesterday; I had to go to Exeter. It was lucky I came back when I did, because I'd been expecting to stay overnight, but my business was swiftly completed, and I managed to return a little after dark. I had only been home a little while when I heard someone shout from Godfrey's place . . ."

"Could you discern what was said?"

"Oh yes, Sir Baldwin. It was Godfrey, and he shouted, 'So you'd defile my daughter too, would you?' We—that is, my men and I—wouldn't have worried about that—I mean, you hear people having rows even in the best households, and someone shouting may not signify much, but there was something about the tone that made me suspect something was wrong. Anyway, only a short while later there was a loud scream. God!" He wiped a hand over his brow and took a hasty slurp from his cup. "God, it was awful! Now I know it was his soul passing, but at the time, I swear I thought it was the devil! It was a hideous cry, a bellow of anguish—something I'll never forget as long as I live."

Baldwin gave a sympathetic murmur.

"After that," Coffyn resumed, "I got my guard to come with me and we ran round there."

"Hold on! Did you go in by the front or the back of Godfrey's house?"

"By the front, of course! Would you expect me to clamber over his wall?" Coffyn retorted. "We didn't wait to hammer on his door, we went straight in."

"I see. And what did you find?"

"Godfrey: dead. His daughter, little Cecily, unconscious nearby. His servant, that miserable old sod with the crab-apple face, out cold near the door. My God, it was terrible!"

"You saw no one else there in the house?"

"No."

"What about in the street outside when you hurried there?"

"No, there was no one. I'm quite sure of that."

"And you couldn't hear the sound of someone running away or anything?"

"No. But we wouldn't—I mean, we were running so hard . . . If anyone had been there, we'd hardly have noticed."

"That's fine. Now, what was your impression when you first went into the room? Did you think it was a robbery? Or was it a straightforward attack on the man?"

Coffyn gave him a long-suffering glance as if he was convinced that Baldwin was feeble-minded. "I told you what I heard. Does it sound as if someone was robbing the place? I think an intruder was trying to rape Cecily, and her father came upon the bastard. You take my word for it—when you speak to Cecily, you'll find that a man was trying to ravish her."

"I suppose it is one possible explanation," Baldwin agreed.

"Of course it is. The man tried to have his way with her, but was attacked by her father. He struck Godfrey down, and decided to make good his escape, so he knocked out the girl and made off. But he cannot escape God's own justice!"

"What about the servant, Putthe?"

"He came upon the man, and was knocked down too. The assailant slipped out the back, and I arrived there a few minutes later," Coffyn said dismissively.

"No, that's not right. For one thing, Godfrey must have been knocked down as he entered the room . . ."

"Pish! He was heard approaching, so the man hid himself behind the door and clobbered him as he entered."

". . . and yet if Godfrey ran in and shouted, as you say he did, the rapist must have been in front of him in the room. So how was he struck on the back of the head?"

"There must have been something to distract him . . . perhaps he heard Putthe running toward him along the screens, and he turned, and that was when his killer struck."

"I don't think so. If that were the case, I feel sure that Godfrey would have crumpled on the spot, and thus ended up facing the doorway. As it is, he fell the other way, as if he was knocked down a few moments after he came into the room."

"Well, that's for you to sort out. I've told you all I can," Coffyn decided, and made a move as if to get up.

Baldwin sipped reflectively at his wine. "Tell me: are you aware of any enemies that Godfrey might have had? Would there be anyone who loathed him, who was a thorn in his side, or who felt jealous of him?"

"Only one, I suppose," Coffyn said reluctantly. "The Irishman—the two of them never seemed to hit it off. It's hardly surprising, for who could be a friend of a man who was prepared to defraud the Church of money on the basis of trickery? You remember his supposed blindness? Mind you, I think Godfrey disliked him for more mundane reasons. He wanted to buy the plot that John was living on, and John refused to let him have it."

"Why would Godfrey have wanted a run-down little place like that?"

"Godfrey was a rich man. He had his whims. I think

he wanted somewhere else to put his livestock, and he has a growing number of staff—*had,* I should say. That little yard with the cottage would have been ideal, bordering right on his land."

"How does John of Irelaunde strike you? Has he ever shown you aggression?"

Coffyn's lip curled into a sneer. "That little sod? He wouldn't dare! If he had, I would have let my men loose on him, and we'd soon see how disrespectful he would be after that."

"You do have several new fellows here," Baldwin noted dispassionately.

The merchant shot him a look. "Are you insinuating that one or two of them could have been involved in this?" he demanded hotly, but his temper cooled as quickly as it had erupted. "My apologies, Sir Baldwin. I seem only ever to hear of complaints about my men. No, I know that three were here last night before I returned, and the others were with me on my trip. But when I got back here, I had all of them in my yard helping me unload my cart. And none of them could have gone next door between that time and my hearing the call from Godfrey's."

"I see. Tell me, when you heard the shout, where were you?"

"When I got home, I had the wagon pull up in the yard, and immediately went inside to seek my wife. She wasn't in the hall, so I told all the guards there to help unload the goods and went to see her in my solar. I . . . I had thought I heard someone in my private chambers, so I had a good look around. I even called up the guards to help me. That was when I heard the shout—while I was in my bedchamber."

"And you didn't go straight out when you heard the cry?"

"Well, no. No, I had the impression that someone was here, you see. It was only when I heard the scream that I realized something was dreadfully wrong at Godfrey's house, and I ran there with one of my men."

"Leaving the other guards . . . ?"

"I left them looking still."

"For whoever might have been in your private rooms." Baldwin nodded; he need ask no more. The merchant's face had become flushed, but not with anger, and now he avoided Baldwin's eye. It was clear enough that Coffyn had expected to find someone there, and that he had been unwilling to give up his search. That was why he had left most of his men there when he eventually decided to find out what was going on next door. He was still hoping that they might catch the man. "Tell me, which guard did you take with you? He might have noticed something you did not."

Coffyn shrugged and bellowed, "*William!* Come here a minute."

The guard from the door appeared a few moments later. There was something unsettling about him, something that grated, and the knight tried to isolate what it could be. Generally, the man looked happy and calm, with an easy demeanor, and a relaxed attitude: he still had his thumbs hooked into his belt. His mouth was fixed in a perpetual half-grin, but there was nothing sneering about it, it merely made him look as if he knew that meeting someone new was bound to be interesting and rewarding. His eyes too looked frank and cheerful, with little crow's feet at the corners, as if he was ready in an instant to burst into laughter. He gave one the feeling that he would be good company over a jug of ale.

But there was still that hint of readiness about him. Baldwin had lived among soldiers for the greater part of his life, had trained with them, and seen them in action, and this guard had the same aura of danger. His dark eyes were almost bovine, but they were also steady and intelligent; his hands hardly moved from his belt, but that meant they were always close to his dagger's hilt; he stood easily, his legs a short distance apart, but he was also braced as if prepared to repel an attack at any moment.

"I believe you went with your master yesterday to the house next door, and you found Godfrey's body with him?"

"That's right, sir. We went straight in as soon as we heard the scream, and found all three of 'em on the floor."

"Your master then sent you to find the constable and raise the Hue?"

"Yes, sir. He remained to prevent anyone else from breaking in and stealing anything."

"Did anyone come in?" Baldwin asked Coffyn.

"Only the maid. Almost as soon as we got there, she came down. She had been too scared to come down before, but when I called for help, she ran in quickly enough and helped us carry Lady Cecily up to her bedchamber. William and I left the two of them there, and that was when I sent him to fetch the constable. Not long after that, the constable arrived, and he said we could leave."

"You saw no one else in the house?" Baldwin asked, turning once more to the soldier.

"I saw only the three people on the floor and the maid."

"And there was no sign of anything being moved or stolen, as far as you saw?"

"No, sir. But I'd never been in there before, so how could I?"

"I hope you have some reason for asking all these

questions, Sir Baldwin, because I have plenty to be getting on with, and surely you have enough other people to question," Coffyn interrupted irritably.

"There are others I need to speak to, yes," said Baldwin, rising. "I thank you both for your help."

"At least you know no one escaped from the front of the house; he must have gone out by the back. And it seems as if he was trying to rape Godfrey's daughter. That appears plain."

"Does it?" Baldwin peered at the merchant. There was an eagerness in his face, an almost greedy look, like a dog which expects its reward after performing its trick. Baldwin felt only revulsion for the man.

~ 7 ~

"It is later than I had thought," Baldwin said once they had retrieved their horses. He climbed the step and mounted, turning the beast toward the road and setting off at an easy walk. At the gate he hesitated, torn with indecision. He knew he should go to study the body again, see if he could speak to the girl Cecily and, from what he had heard, talk to John of Irelaunde, as well as seeking out other suspects, but he could only sit staring at the road, wondering what to do for the best.

This confusion was a novelty. Usually Baldwin was certain of the path he must take, no matter what the issues which confused the way. If he was involved in a judicial matter, he could find a logical solution; if he investigated a robbery or murder, he would be able to decide upon an appropriate course of enquiry—after all, most killings were committed in the heat of an argument, and premeditated murder was a rarity. But whenever he had embarked upon solving a crime of this kind, he had always had the assistance of his friend Simon Puttock. This time, Simon was not around, and Baldwin found his absence to be a constant niggling emptiness. The knight had never before thought of Simon as essential to his function as a servant of the King, but now that there was a serious crime to consider, he realized that he needed the bailiff, not only in his capacity as a sounding board, but also because his friend was apt to think of points that the knight, with all his education and experience, would never have considered. "Where are you, old friend?" he muttered.

"Sir?"

"Nothing. Let's get something to eat before we see the girl."

Thomas Rodde sat resting against an oak near the western edge of the town and dozed. The sun was warm on his face, the thick grass of the roadside was as soft as the finest down beneath him, and for a few minutes he could forget the horror of his disease and cling to a memory of what life used to be like before he became ill.

Now he was twenty-nine those far-off days of his youth seemed to be suffused with a rosy glow. Nothing bad or evil ever seemed to interrupt their easy flow. The weather, as now he remembered it, was always balmy—and when it did rain, it was always gentle showers, never harsh, bitter drops that felt as if they had been frozen before falling.

These reflections made him give a small smile, his eyes still closed against the brightness of the sun. He knew, logically, that the rain *had* been bitterly cold on occasion, just as he knew he had seen thunderstorms, had suffered biting winds while riding through the winter, and had more than once felt frozen to the core when he had been out in snowstorms—yet it was hard now to bring them to mind. It was as if his memory was separated into two parts: that before his illness, the happy life, and that after, the living death. All that happened in his early years was splendid: it was as if his childhood was a perfect dream in which even the elements had conspired to ensure his memories were delightful—and now, since developing leprosy, his entire existence had been blighted.

Whenever he thought about the winter, it was the desolate plains of the northern marches which sprang into his mind. The misery—of being constantly damp, of having the rain driven into his face by a wind that felt so cold it froze the blood in his veins; of walking through puddles and rivulets that might have been composed of pure, liquid ice, that penetrated his cheap shoes in an instant; the pain while his feet at first went cold, then became vessels of pure fire before losing all sensation, followed by the torture of recovery. It often seemed to him that he would be better off staying out and allowing the life to leave his freezing body. Once he had attempted this, remaining in the open air as the ground around him hardened and his breath misted before his eyes. But his will to live was too deeply ingrained in his soul, and he had returned, half unwillingly, to the protection of the fire at the leper camp.

That was all he could recall of the bleak wasteland of Northumbria. He had loathed the climate, the country and the people. It had been a refuge of sorts, somewhere for him to escape to, far from the disgust he saw in the eyes of his friends and family, but, like any place of sanctuary, it was no substitute for home, especially when his mild antipathy to the area developed into fierce repugnance.

This was partly due to the apparent slowness of his disease. The suddenness of his affliction had been hard to accept, but if he had continued to slide steadily toward death, he would have been able to cope with his burden. It wouldn't give him that satisfaction. For some reason, while he had remained in the north, he had enjoyed a period of remission, and it had left him nursing a perverse, bitter fury against God. Thomas could have borne the trials of death, but knowing that he must stay away from contact with society, was excluded from all the pursuits and pleasures which made life bearable, while remaining fit enough in body and mind, was unendurable.

He had stayed there for six years, six long, intolerable years, living in the closed community of lepers, watching others suffering, becoming hideously disfigured, dying. And at last he was forced to leave. The Scots poured over the border in one of their periodic raids, and his little refuge was wasted. There was nothing to keep him there. To him the very air was foul, the climate worse, and he had made his way by easy stages down to the south.

And now it was almost possible to forget some of the pain and hardship. He opened his eyes and gazed up into the cornflower-blue sky, enjoying a moment's serenity. The tree above him stood solid and unmoving, there was a scent of thyme and wild garlic in the air, and his contentment was enhanced by a small bird high overhead, which sang with a clear, liquid tone. Closing his eyes again, he could imagine himself back in the fields of his old country home in the flat lands of Stepney in the county of Middlesex.

His mental meanderings were called to an abrupt halt. "Thomas? Are you awake?"

Sighing, Rodde slowly eased himself upright. "Hello, Edmund."

Quivil was tired, Rodde saw. His face was pale from lack of sleep, his eyes red-rimmed and hollow. Rodde had heard him at night cursing and muttering to himself. It was irritating. Since the abortive initiation ceremony, Rodde and he had shared a hut, so when Quivil couldn't sleep, often Rodde couldn't either. But it was impossible for Rodde to snap at him. Perhaps it was that Quivil's incomprehension of the injustice of his illness was so similar to his own. Whatever the reason, Rodde found himself warming to the farmer's son, and in return Quivil appeared to look on him with near slavish devotion.

"You look like you need a rest more than me," Rodde observed.

"I didn't sleep well."

"No." Further comment was unnecessary. All the lepers knew how the depression came on with increased force at night, especially for those most recently consigned to the human midden that was the hospital. Rodde's voice was sympathetic. "What do you want?"

"I'm going into town to collect food from the church," Edmund said, waving toward his little handcart. "Will you help?"

Rodde stood. Although Quivil hadn't said as much, Rodde knew that the lad would be desperate for company. "I'll come."

The street was quieter now, as the townspeople sat in their homes and ate their midday meals from good bread trenchers or wooden bowls. In his mind's eye, Rodde could picture them: comfortable, prosperous traders with their wives and servants all around them, children running and playing among the rushes, the fires glowing and adding to the thick atmosphere as servants ladled stews, panters cut hunks of bread, bottlers topped up mugs and cups, and all about dogs sat and scratched or waited, watching hopefully. Even poor homes would have a good quart of ale and loaf for the master of the house, he knew.

And he was going with Quivil to the church to collect what gracious charity the almoner thought fit for them. It made Thomas' anger rise again, and it was only with an effort that he could force it down, reminding himself that it was not the fault of the people of Crediton that he was struck down with this disease—it was merely a twist of fate: *luck*.

They were at the top of the main street in a few moments, and could gaze down the wide thoroughfare. As soon as they appeared, walking slowly with the little cart, Rodde's bell sounding its doleful tone, the area before them cleared. It was so shocking, Quivil halted for a minute.

He had himself abhorred lepers all his life, but now that he was afflicted, he found the urgency of other people to avoid him to be terrible, as if he was damned. Feeling Rodde take hold of his upper arm, he moved off again, his head hanging with self-disgust and loathing of the people around him.

A child stood watching them approach with horror-filled eyes, only to be scooped up by its mother at the last minute before they came too close; a little group of youngsters ran ahead of them, chanting, "*Le*-pers! *Le*-pers! Stinking, rotting *le*-pers!"

Quivil shuffled on, avoiding the eyes of any who might be watching him. These were the people he had grown up with, and now he hated to think that anyone he knew could see him.

He wasn't sure which he feared most: expressions of revulsion from those whom he had called friends, or looks of sympathy from them. If he had any choice, he would have turned tail and fled back to the lazar house, but Rodde's hand remained gripping his upper arm, and there was enough strength in that hold to firm his resolve. He had promised Ralph that he would fetch the alms from the church, and with Rodde's help, he would do so.

Rodde was a support to him—the only one he had. The tall, quiet stranger exuded a calm self-confidence which was proof against any brats' taunts, and stiffened Quivil's own nerve. He seemed to be saying, *I am stronger than you. Look upon me if you dare.* The steady tap . . . tap . . . tap of his staff on the cobbles was proof against the contempt and disgust of the whole world. He walked as if he was sneering at all about him.

Quivil was soothed by the presence of his companion. With Rodde beside him, he knew he need fear no one—his rescue from the attack on his first night had been proof of that. Quivil had been raised in the simple environment of a peasant, knowing that he must obey his father's wishes, and his lord's, and the commands of the Church. In the space of a few moments all that had been reversed, and now he knew loyalty only to his new friend.

It wouldn't have been so difficult for him if there had been any stable friendships he could have relied upon, but there were none. His friends now shunned him. He had tried to talk to the butcher's apprentice, a lad he had known since his childhood, whose face he had pushed into puddles, who had brought him to the ground when they had played camp-ball and forced him into a muddy ditch, who had vied with him for the love of the local girls as they grew, and with whom he had drunk many hundreds of pints of ale—and Quivil had been distraught when his old friend had shied away from him. The last girl for whose charms they had competed was Mary Cordwainer; that victory, which at the time had been so vital, so crucial to his well-being, which seemed to have guaranteed his life's pleasure, was now hollow. He could never touch her, never kiss her, never know her body. All his future was barren, his life utterly meaningless. It might as well have ended.

He could have wept with the thought. Oh, for only a kiss—even a smile or a grin of acknowledgment from her. Just the simple touch of the girl's hand would ease his soul. And his curse was, he knew it was impossible.

As they came level with the inn, Edmund heard horses. Looking up, he saw a couple of men riding toward them, and automatically drew to one side. He saw that it was Sir Baldwin and his servant, and waited for them to pass, when he heard the knight rein in his horse and speak.

"Friends, if you ever want for anything at the hospital, tell Brother Ralph to send for me, and I will try to help. Edmund Quivil, I am sorry this has happened to you. Let me know if there is anything you need."

"Thank you, sir. What could a poor leper ask for?"

Baldwin ignored the petulance in his voice. "I will be making sure that your parents do not want for help on their land, Quivil. They will be under my protection now."

Quivil nodded ungraciously, and began to move away again. After a short pause, he heard the clatter of hooves as the knight and his man carried on. In some way he felt easier in his mind that Sir Baldwin was gone. His sympathy was all too plain, and Quivil wanted no one's sympathy. He wanted cure.

"Who was that?" Rodde asked quietly.

"He's the Keeper of the King's Peace for this town."

Rodde glanced at his friend. For someone who had just received a warm expression of kindness from a knight, his shortness was at best ungrateful. "Why was he so willing to offer his help?"

"I used to be one of his men. My father is one of his bondmen, as I would have been, had I not . . ."

There was no need for him to continue, and soon they had other matters to distract them.

The wheel of the cart squeaked, an irritating, insistent little noise that came and went, and drew more attention to them; and yet there was one group which didn't turn and stare as they came closer. It was the men and women huddled round Godfrey's gate. They were all staring fixedly at Godfrey's house, ignoring all about them, and even the banal jeering of the boys, who kept their distance up ahead, went unnoticed.

"What are they all staring at?" Quivil heard Rodde mutter.

"Lepers!"

This came from a young maiden who, about to enter the street, narrowly avoided walking straight into Rodde. She winced and drew her apron over her mouth to protect her from the foul vapors that everyone knew lepers exhaled. Anyone who breathed in their noxious fumes could become infected. She drew away. The call was enough to make the crowd pull back, and one man jerked his head at them. "Off with you, scum! Keep away from good healthy folk."

"I'm sorry, Arthur," Quivil said. "We meant no harm."

"Edmund?" asked the man. He was a pompous little fellow who had always reminded Quivil of a gamecock, strutting and preening himself in the vicinity of any women, and invariably lambasting anybody weaker than himself. Now he peered, and blew out his breath in an expression of disgust. "Come on, walk round! You don't want your sins to infect others, do you? That would be as good as murder, and we don't need another."

"Another what?" asked Rodde.

"Murder, leper. Haven't you heard? A man was killed here last night."

Quivil felt his friend's grasp on his arm tighten. Rodde snapped, "Here? You mean Godfrey of London is *dead*?"

Baldwin couldn't help staring back down the street once he had dropped from his horse. An ostler scurried forward to take the reins from him and lead the rounsey to the back of the inn, where it could be fed and watered, and he handed them over absentmindedly.

Seeing Quivil again was a shock. It was some weeks now since that dreadful service in the church where the poor man had been outcast from society, and with so many other things to take up his time, Baldwin had not spared many thoughts for the peasant's son from his estate. The sight of the lad looking so crushed while the people of the town avoided him tore at Baldwin's breast. Even as he stood, shaking his head, he heard a catcall, and then a group of gutter-urchins dashed past, all shouting abuse at the lepers. Caught with a quick anger, Baldwin bellowed at them to be silent, and they hurried off, some gaping with dismay, but others grinning. It was only fun to them, Baldwin reminded himself. Only those who were fit, healthy, and strong were safe in this country. The thought made him sigh, and he turned into the inn with a heavy heart, which was not eased by the reflection that he had not decided how to progress with his investigation.

But as he entered the hall, and heard the laughter, his mood altered.

"Jeanne!—Er . . . and Margaret and Simon! Welcome, all of you, I am delighted to see you here!"

* * *

John of Irelaunde eased the gate shut and clambered onto his cart, grunting with relief once he was safely seated on his plank. Thrusting his bad leg out before him to rest atop the footboard, he clucked his tongue and snapped the reins.

That at least was one less problem for him to consider, he thought as the wagon rattled and clattered down the track toward the main thoroughfare from Crediton to Tedburn. The sack was safely hidden at the mill's outhouse. Old Sam the miller had rented it out to John some months before, and now it appeared in the Irishman's eyes as God-sent, perfect for the purpose of concealing those things that the Keeper of the King's Peace should not be troubling himself over.

As the horse leaned forward in the traces to drag the cart up the hill toward the town center, John winced with every jolt and thud. There were too many ruts and holes in this road; it was always so busy with traffic from Exeter. Each and every one of them made his ankle bang against the wooden footboard. He was glad it was beginning to mend. Now it felt only as if it was badly bruised.

In the town, he soon saw the crowd waiting at Godfrey's gate. Some men were arguing with Tanner, no doubt trying to gain access to the hall to see the body, but Tanner was resolute. No one would enter until the Keeper had told him they could, and it didn't matter how much money they offered. John averted his eyes so as to avoid being brought into any discussion, but he did wonder whether there could be potential in this latest twist: perhaps he could offer people the chance of getting in over Godfrey's wall from his yard—for a small fee, of course. This delightful prospect kept him speculating as he carried on up the hill.

At his yard, he hobbled to the gate and opened it

leading the horse inside, but as he turned to close the gate, a figure sidled along and into the yard behind him.

"What do you want?" John grumbled irritably.

"Me, John?" Putthe asked slyly, his eyes roving all over the yard as if seeking the missing plate. "All I want is to give you some help—if you'll let me, that is."

~ 8 ~

aldwin waved to the nearest serving-girl as he walked in, his face smiling as proof of his pleasure. The hall was a large one, with tables scattered haphazardly around the floor, and Baldwin and his servant were forced to take a circuitous route to the one where his friends were sitting.

It was over six months since Baldwin had seen Simon Puttock, the bailiff of Lydford, and longer since he had met Simon's wife, Margaret, but neither was surprised when the knight offered them only a perfunctory greeting. They both knew he had not spoken to Jeanne de Liddinstone for twelve months, not since the affair of the murders at Tavistock Fair.

Jeanne had not changed over the interval, and to Baldwin she was beautiful. She was tall and strongly built, with long limbs and a slim figure. Her face was regular, with a wide mouth whose upper lip was a little over-full, giving her a slightly stubborn look, but her nose gave the opposite impression, being both short and slightly tip-tilted. Most important to Baldwin, though, were her eyes: bright and clear blue, intelligent, and almost without exception, smiling.

She was wearing a long riding cloak trimmed with gray fur, over a deep blue tunic embroidered with flowers at hem and throat. On her head was a simple coif, which gave the knight a tantalizing glimpse of the red-gold hair plaited and pinned beneath. He took her hand and bowed, and she gave him a mocking curtsey in return.

"Is that enough now, Sir Baldwin? My very bones ache after riding all the way here, and you force me to bend to you?"

"My lady, please . . . I mean, please be seated," he said, flustered in case he might have given offense.

To Edgar, the scene carried more than a faint feeling of *déjà vu*. His master had wooed this woman when they had last met, he knew, and had achieved only moderate success. In Edgar's view it was in large measure due to the knight's nervousness and anxiety about hurting the lady's feelings that he had not won her. Now he saw her smile more kindly on Baldwin, and to his relief, his master relaxed slightly and sat with her.

"So, Baldwin, should we leave immediately?" Margaret's tone was playful, but there was an undercurrent of asperity.

"My lady, I am confused and blinded by the beauty of two such perfect women. How could a poor knight like me ever dream of being honored by the presence of both of you at the same time? It is as if the sun itself has fallen into the room, I feel so utterly . . ."

"All right, Baldwin," Simon interrupted hastily. "You've satisfied the greed of these two for compliments—now, if you wouldn't mind, I'd like a cup of good strong wine to take away the taste of all the dust I've swallowed on the way here!"

"It is ordered, I think," Baldwin said, peering over his friend's shoulder toward the buttery. "Edgar, see if you

can hurry them along, will you? I think today I will cel
ebrate with wine as well."

Nothing loath, Edgar went off, for this was the in
where his Cristine served, and he had the hope that h
might be able to corner her for his own purposes for
few minutes.

It was Margaret who broke the short silence. "An
how are affairs in Crediton?"

Her words brought Baldwin up with a jolt. He ha
been watching Jeanne and wondering when he woul
be able to speak to her privately, but Margaret had un
thinkingly reminded him of Godfrey's body. "Not good
I fear. There has been a murder."

Instantly Simon leaned forward. He was a strong, hard
man in his middle thirties with brown hair, slightly griz
zled. Four years ago he had been a young, ambitious baili
on his way up; then his face had been free of any wrinkles
but since the death of his little son Peterkin the previou
year, he had lost much of his aura of youth. Now he wor
deep creases at his brow, like the battle scars of life.

The bailiff waited while Cristine doled out cups an
wine, quickly hurrying back to the buttery, then jerke
his head in a gesture of interest. "Come along, tell us a
about it."

It took little time for Baldwin to describe the scene h
had found the night before, or to summarize the evi
dence he had been given by the bottler and first finder.

When he was finished, Simon took a long gulp c
wine and sucked his teeth thoughtfully. "So you haven'
done too much yet. You've only spoken to one neighbo
and a wounded servant. There's still this other neigh
bor . . . who is it? Anyone I know?"

Baldwin grinned. Simon had lived in Crediton an
the surrounding area for many years before moving ou
to Lydford with his new job. "It was Irelaunde."

"*That* little bastard!"

"Simon!"

"What, Meg? Oh—I'm sorry, Jeanne. But Christ's Blood, Baldwin, if he lives close, he's the first man you should question. You know what sort of a character he is!"

Baldwin leaned back with a beatific smile. "It is a wonderful relief to have you here, Simon. Up until now I hadn't realized how much I relied on your judgment and fair-mindedness. I was thrashing around and going through the motions without thinking about the crime itself."

"So you'll go and see him immediately?"

"No. I'll go and speak to the man's daughter. You've just told me how the locals will all think, and I'd better get my hands on the real killer before some fool decides to take the law into his own hands and lynches the wrong man!"

Simon gave a short laugh. He knew that he was often prone to leap to conclusions, and overall he was content with the trait. In the main, while he worked out on the moors, settling disputes between miners and landowners, it was a useful ability, to be able to see who was the most likely culprit, or who was probably at fault. With simple arguments, such as who should be permitted to change the flow of a stream, or whether a tenement-holder had the rights of pasturage over a particular plot, there was little analysis required. It was more a case of applying common sense and maintaining an attitude of fair play. For that, Simon's brand of quick intuition often saved a lot of time.

"I'm glad you're here, Simon," Baldwin continued more seriously, and Simon felt his smile broaden. The knight's words carried too much sincerity for him to be doubted.

"So when are you to go and speak to this young woman?" Jeanne asked. "Is there time for us to get to your house first?"

"With your permission, lady, I will send you off with my servant. Simon, you have brought Hugh with you?" The bailiff nodded. "Then, Jeanne, you will have two good men to protect you on your way."

"Jeanne has better protection than you realize, Baldwin," said Margaret lightly.

The knight threw her a baffled glance, but had no time to ask what she meant, for there was a sudden commotion from the buttery. Muttering under his breath, Baldwin rose to his feet, but before he could discover the cause, the cause discovered him.

Edgar fell back from the doorway, his arm round Cristine's waist, staring at the door with a smile of sheer delight. There was a short silence, then Baldwin watched with astonishment as Simon's servant, Hugh, hurtled out, slipping on a patch of wet rushes and falling over. He sat up, rubbing a sore elbow and glowering ferociously as a massive shape filled the doorway.

"I said you've had enough!" the shape boomed. "That means you won't have any more ale. I'll not have a drunk escorting my lady."

"Baldwin," Jeanne said sweetly, "my maid didn't join me at Tavistock, so you haven't met her, have you? This is Emma."

Ralph crossed the small yard to the chapel, and stood at the entrance, wiping a hand over his forehead. The night before he had sat up with one of the older inmates while he slowly faded, dying just before dawn. The monk sighed. It was a hard duty that he had taken up. The only certainty was that his flock would diminish faster than any other.

Opening the door, he walked inside, and was about to reach for his broom when he heard the regular sweeping. It brought a tired smile to his lips. "Mary?"

"Oh, Brother Ralph, I didn't worry you, I hope?"

He could see her face now, vaguely anxious, as if her taking on the cleaning could be construed as an insult to his own cleanliness. "No, my dear. No, I am very happy that you should help me, but . . . Surely you have other things you could be doing?"

"No, sir," she said, leaning on her broom-handle and speaking with a calm certainty. "I want to help the men here."

"Mary, you are young. You will find another man to marry. It's not right that you should stay here, among all this disease."

"I know my man has always been a good soul. It was my intention to marry him, and if I can't, I won't marry at all. Anyway, I can do more good here, for you, for your lepers, and for my soul, than I could by becoming a farmer's wife. No, I was prepared to wed Edmund Quivil, and if he's going to die, then at least I can see he dies easy in his heart. He'll know that I've always been loyal to him."

Ralph sat at a stool, and gestured for her to follow suit. "But perhaps your presence is not so beneficial?"

"What do you mean, sir?"

"Well, you see, he can watch you every day here, and that must be unsettling for him. He was to marry you, as you say. If he loves you, how would he feel knowing you are here with all the other lepers?" He held up a hand to prevent interruption. "Your being here, near him, must always be a sore temptation."

At this she laughed. "Oh, Brother! You think he might rape me? My Edmund?"

"You may find it hard to believe, but worse things

have happened to young women in lazar houses. And even if he doesn't, don't you think it might be cruel to remind him of what he is missing?"

"Like letting the bull see the heifers but keeping him fenced off?"

"Well, er, yes. Something like that."

"I suppose it's possible. But I think my Edmund would prefer to see me here and know I care for him still than wonder what I was doing outside. And if you've heard the talk, I don't care what people say!"

This last was said with a sudden passion, and Ralph nodded slowly. "The people of the town can be very cruel, but try to forgive them. They don't understand—all they know is, they're scared of the disease that we hold in here."

"Saying I'm no better than a *whore*!" she declared hotly. "They ought to know better."

"Well," he sighed, "some misguided people believe that leprosy is an evil brought about by lust. They think it's transmitted by intimate relations, and therefore lepers are especially libidinous."

"You don't?"

"No, Mary, and even if they were, that would be no reflection on you. I think my charges have more important things on their minds than fornication. They have their eyes firmly fixed on the life to come, or on how their poor, tortured bodies will be eaten up and destroyed by their disease. Anyway, I don't believe that leprosy is sexually transmitted. It's a gift from God, and the sufferers should be honored. I agree with St. Hugh of Lincoln, that the more deformed they are, the more they suffer here on earth, the more brightly their souls will shine in Heaven. They have been sent their diseases to teach us all how we shall be tormented with pain in Purgatory. Their Purgatory is here, now!"

"Yes, Brother. But if it is a gift from God, then maybe He intends honoring *me* too."

"We should never presume to look for such things from God," he said sententiously. "Whatever He decides for you, you must accept it."

"But it cannot be wrong for me to want to help look after His own selected people."

"No," he said uncertainly. It was considered that women were capable of looking after others in certain circumstances, he knew. "Except I really do think you should be considering starting a new life without Quivil. He's lost to you now."

"So he is, but that's no reason why I shouldn't help you, is it? Especially since by so doing I'll be helping those whom God Himself has chosen to be a sign to us all."

"Well . . . I suppose so."

"Then I'd better get on with the sweeping."

Ralph watched her move down the little aisle, rhythmically swaying as she moved the broom. She was the picture of a rough, untutored peasant girl, with heavy body and coarse, grubby hands, and yet she was demonstrating more generosity of spirit and kindliness than many of his brother-priests. The thought made him sigh, but it also gave him a spark of satisfaction. He walked forward and bent at the altar, offering up a short prayer for her and her doomed lover, before leaving the chapel. He might as well go and see to laying out the body of the dead leper.

After all, he reasoned, what harm could come from letting Mary work in the lazar house?

"My God! Simon," Baldwin gasped. "How could Jeanne have allied herself with *that*?"

"It can't have been her fault. She must have been stuck with the woman from an early age," Simon said.

They were standing at the entrance to the inn, watching the small cavalcade disappear down the street. Edgar was leading the way, Hugh keeping the rear with the packhorse, although from the way he kept throwing appealing glances back at his master, he would have preferred to remain. Baldwin couldn't blame him.

"She's a bear, Simon, a ravening, insane beast! How could a frail thing like Jeanne stand to live with something like that?"

As they made their way along the road toward Godfrey's hall, Simon laughed. "She's not so bad as she looks, Baldwin. She can even tell jokes."

"Jokes? I daresay she could, but not the sort I'd want a soldier to hear! And did you see the warts on her chin? And her arms are more strongly muscled than my own, I swear."

"Baldwin, you can't deny that she's eminently capable of protecting her mistress, can you?"

That, Baldwin agreed silently, was the whole point. With a fearsome guard like Emma he would find it very hard to get Jeanne on her own, if the display with Hugh was anything to go by. He had no objection to Jeanne being safe from footpads and felons, but that was very different to her being carefully fenced in from him by her maid. And he had no doubt that Emma would be a most resolute guardian. He had seen it in her eyes as she was introduced to him—cold, astute eyes that seemed to read him with terrifying ease. Little, brown eyes, they were, but without any of that gentle, bovine softness that Baldwin had always associated with the color. Emma's were sharp and angry, like a small hog's.

The rest of her bore out the analogy. She was short, but with a massive frame that made her look almost perfectly round. Her chest was carried like some kind of armored buttress—or maybe like the curtain wall of a castle, Baldwin amended, recalling the awesome immensity of her bosom. An army, he felt, could batter itself to death against such a vast obstacle.

Seeing his self-absorption, Simon laughed. "Forget her. You have a murder to solve. So tell me, whom are we to see now?"

"The daughter of the man who was killed. Her name is Cecily, and she was discovered in the same room as her father's corpse. She was knocked senseless."

They were soon at the house. Clearly most of the townspeople had accepted the fact that Tanner was not going to be bribed into allowing them to view the corpse or the place where Godfrey was killed, and had left to get on with their work. Tanner stood aside for them to go in, and Simon led the way, but not before Baldwin had caught a glimpse of the men standing well back, almost in the alleyway opposite. It made him frown for a moment, seeing the lepers there, but then he shrugged. Why should he assume that lepers, by mere virtue of their disease, should be uninterested in the fate of others? He knew that old men were always keen to hear of the demise of their peers, or of those younger than themselves. There was a greedy fascination with death among those who were likely to experience it for themselves in the near future, and lepers surely fell into that category.

Yet when he glanced over his shoulder, he was surprised to see how keenly one of the rag-clothed figures was following his progress to the door. It was the new man, the one he had seen with Quivil earlier, and Baldwin made a mental note to ask the leper master about the stranger when he had a chance.

The door was open, and just inside, seated on a stool from which he could see both front and back doors, was a watchman. He stood and nodded to Baldwin, and let the two pass into the hall itself.

"Ugh! You could have warned me, Baldwin!"

"Squeamish, Simon? I had thought you would have been cured of that after looking into so many murders."

"It's one thing to become used to the sight of dead men, but quite another to suddenly get presented with a corpse, especially when the stench is so strong!"

The knight had to agree with that. Someone had been in and fuelled the fire, and the room was close, the atmosphere heavy with the sweetness of death. As he moved toward the body, he grimaced. The crushed skull was already feeding the flies. Waving them away as best he could, he crouched down to repeat his investigation of the night before.

Godfrey had been an older man, certainly over fifty, and his hair was thin and gray. From the size of the damaged area, one conclusion seemed obvious. "He can't have known anything about it." Something caught Baldwin's notice as he spoke. The man's nose was scratched, and as Baldwin peered closer, he saw a series of short, but deep marks on the chin, and more on his left cheekbone. The wound on the back of the head itself was on the right side, a little above the point where it joined the neck. "Yes, we can be quite sure that as soon as this blow struck, he was dead," he said musingly.

"Fine—you enjoy yourself, and I'll get some fresh air while you carry on."

Suiting his action to his words, Simon went to the nearest window, the one toward which the body was pointing. Soon he had thrown open the shutters, and could breathe in deep, satisfying lungfuls. There was something about Baldwin's eagerness to examine the victims of violent death that had always repelled the bailiff. He took a little too much pleasure in his work.

Today was no exception. Even now, Baldwin turned the body to and fro in his search for other wounds, opening the dead man's shirt and checking the torso, feeling the chilly flesh for the onset of rigor mortis, before prying the lips apart to gaze in at the mouth.

Simon looked away. It was too morbid for his taste. When a body was dead, that was an end to it as far as he was concerned. Simon's interest lay in people's motives for killing, and that meant questioning all those concerned; Baldwin's conviction was that any body could tell how it died, and that might give clues as to who the attacker was. It was a view which Simon had seen demonstrated often enough for him not to dispute the fact, but he was enormously grateful that Baldwin was always keen to take on that part of the investigation himself, and didn't require Simon's help. In fact, Simon knew full well that his friend was glad to be left to study any clues alone.

The window was quite low. This place was not designed for defense like so many others. Standing here, Simon could see the stableyard to his left. In front was the edge of the kitchen's wall, which stretched on to the right, out as far as the wall between Godfrey's and Coffyn's.

If someone was to try to rob the place, they wouldn't try to escape through any of the windows at the front of the place. Only a fool would run away through a busy street, surely—but then many felons *were* fools, he reminded himself. Intelligent men rarely turned to crime. But if that was the case, and if plates *had* been stolen, then the best escape route was through the back, and perhaps over one of the walls.

The idea caught his imagination. From what Baldwin had said, Godfrey had shouted at someone trying to defile his daughter. That implied the drawlatch was at the window. Why else should Godfrey have tried to cross over to this window? Yet if the thief was inside, and Godfrey thought he was trying to rape or harm his daughter, did that mean the man had taken the plate with the woman's agreement? Or had he struck her down and then removed it—in which case, what on earth had Godfrey meant when, according to Coffyn, he had shouted: "So you'd defile my daughter too, would you?"

"Baldwin," he said, "tell me again where the three bodies were."

"Hmm? Godfrey was here, as you can see. Arm held up, as though he was instantly killed by the blow to his head. I think that is quite likely—the blood flowed freely, as you'd expect, and although there was a light spray under his arm, the main flow of the blood followed the line of his arm. This other arm is interesting, though. Very!"

"Come on, tell me where the bodies were."

"You see, the knuckles of his hand have been barked, as if he managed to thump one of the men before he was killed."

"That is not a surprise."

"No, but at least we know that one assailant might have been wounded. It might help. Oh, very well, Simon, don't fret! The servant was there, nearer the door, as if he was going to his master or Cecily."

"The girl?"

"She was here," said the knight, getting to his feet with a groan and cracking of bones. "Here, Tanner said, between the body and the window. Why?"

"I wonder what she was wearing."

"Simon, what *are* you talking about?" Baldwin demanded.

In answer, the bailiff pointed. At the side of the window,

where the shutter met the wall, was a splinter of wood, and on the splinter was a torn piece of blue material.

"So? Anyone could have snagged their tunic on that," Baldwin said dismissively.

"True enough," Simon agreed, pulling it gently. "But it looks very fresh. The cloth hasn't been here for a long time—if it had, it would have faded. This window faces south, it catches the sun all day, but this stuff has kept its bright color."

Baldwin held his head to one side, gazing at his friend. He took the scrap from him and turned it over in his hand. "It does look new," he admitted. "I wonder if it is Cecily's or the thief's."

"Let's ask her."

~ 9 ~

The guard fetched a maid, a pretty young girl with dark flowing hair named Alison, who was, they were told, Mistress Cecily's servant. She took them back through the hall and into a warm parlor. Here they were told to wait, and she slipped out through a door. A few minutes later Cecily was with them.

Simon placed her at some twenty-five years old, perhaps a little more, but she had the natural grace and the elegance of a much older woman. She entered softly, seeming to float over the ground. The bailiff couldn't help comparing her with the gorgon accompanying Jeanne de Liddinstone. Emma and Cecily were of about the same height, but that was where the similarity ended. Cecily had large, luminous eyes of a peculiarly intense shade of blue, and a fine, pale complexion that looked almost transparent. Her features were oval and regular, and there was a pleasing regularity in the high cheekbones, small mouth, and delicately arched eyebrows.

But that wasn't what Baldwin noticed about her. It was her sadness that struck him. Her high brow should have been unmarked in a woman born to wealth, but the lines were etched harshly across her forehead like parallel scars, her cheeks were sunken, her lips swollen and bloody from being punched, her eyes red-rimmed from sleeplessness and weeping. Her whole demeanor was that of a beaten cur, worn down by constant ill-use, and the livid pink and mauve bruise that marked her chin and cheek only served to emphasize her distracted misery.

"Please, take a seat," the knight said quietly. "We shall be as quick as we may be."

She went to a seat near the fire, all the way her head hanging, the picture of grief. But just for a moment, after she had settled herself and arranged her tunic to her satisfaction, she met his gaze, and he could swear that he recognized a cynical, measuring look in her eye. It was only fleeting, and was immediately replaced by every appearance of sober misery, as he would have expected from a dutiful daughter when her father has been killed, but the impact of that swift glimpse into her mind wouldn't leave him. Although he wanted to believe her, he couldn't forget it.

"You are here to ask me what happened last night?" she asked softly, mumbling slightly as she tried to move her mouth as little as possible.

"Yes, if it will not upset you too much. I am the—"

"I know you. You're the Keeper."

"Yes, and this is a friend of mine, who is helping me to try to find your father's killer. Simon Puttock, bailiff to the Warden of the Stannaries at Lydford. Can you remember what happened to you last night?"

"As if it was burned on my soul!" she declared, and gave a sudden shiver.

That, at least, Baldwin thought, looked genuine. "Please tell us all you can."

"I was up in my room when it became dark, and

walked downstairs. When I came to the hall, I noticed that a tapestry over one of the windows was loose. So I drew it back over the window, and was about to leave the room to look for my father or one of the servants, when I heard a noise behind me. I turned, and was hit." She touched the tender bruise at her mouth.

"You fell unconscious immediately?"

"Yes."

"And so far as you could see, your father wasn't there then?"

"No. Father had the habit of going and walking the boundaries of the garden each evening, and I think he must still have been out when I was attacked."

"What next do you remember?"

"Nothing. When I came to, I was in my chamber, and my maid was with me."

"This man who hit you," Simon asked, "what did he look like?"

She shot him a glance. "I don't know. It was dark, and I think he had his face covered with a strip of cloth or something."

"Was he taller than you? Than your father? Fat or thin? Muscled or weak?"

"I feel he might have been taller than me, but really, anything more than that I couldn't say."

Baldwin leaned forward. "We have heard that your father gave a loud cry. That must have been as he was struck. You heard nothing?"

She closed her eyes for a moment. "If I had heard him, I would have said."

Baldwin bit back a sharp retort, reminding himself that the girl had suffered an attack herself. Taking a deep breath, he said, "Please try to concentrate. I know it must be very difficult, but if we are to find your father's killer we shall need something, even the most trivial-seeming detail . . ."

"You think I don't know my father's dead?" she burst out. "Good God in Heaven, if I could tell you who it was, I *would*!"

"Then, lady, think hard. Did you see what he was wearing?"

"It was all dark clothing, I think he had a rich scarlet tunic, and a heavy cloak."

"What color was the cloak?" Baldwin pressed.

"It was dark—one color looks like another!"

Baldwin sat back and threw a harassed glance at his friend. Simon shook his head. It was plain enough that they would get nowhere with Mistress Cecily, not unless she recalled some more hard facts they could deal with. Baldwin nodded to himself, then leaned forward, his elbows resting on his knees.

"There is another thing we have been told," he said hesitantly. He was reluctant to bring the matter up, for it smacked of prurience. "My apologies again if it is distasteful, but I have been told that your father was heard to shout at your attacker. He bellowed, 'So you'd defile my daughter too, would you?' You didn't hear anything like that?"

She looked up at him, and he could see a tear moving slowly down her cheek as she shook her head. Her mouth moved slightly, as if to frame the word "No," but no sound came.

"Putthe thought you were missing some plate. Have you checked it all?"

Cecily clutched for the arm of her chair. "The plate? You expect me to count up all my poor father's silver when he's lying in there dead? I neither know nor care whether someone might have taken it!"

Simon stirred. "Baldwin, I really think we should leave the lady alone now, she's told us all she can."

"Yes, of course. Lady, I am grateful to you, you have been most helpful, and I am terribly sorry to have had to bring it all back to you. If you could ask your servant to show us out."

Simon glanced at him with faint surprise. Baldwin was not usually so keen to stick to formalities. The young woman called sharply, and they heard a pattering of light footsteps, then Alison was with them. Baldwin stood, bowed, and walked back into the hall with the maid, leaving Simon to mutter his own farewell and trot after them.

He found the knight by the body once more. Baldwin had paused, as if caught by a sudden thought. "Tell me, Alison. Your mistress—the last time I saw her, she was wearing a new blue tunic, I think. Very dark. Isn't that what she was wearing last night?"

"Why . . . Yes, sir, she was."

"Tell us what *you* heard, and what *you* found when you came in here and discovered your mistress."

"Well, sir, I don't know that I should. I—"

"Come along! You have already told all the gardeners and grooms, haven't you? And your friends, so it is already all over the town," Baldwin grinned.

"He wouldn't—I mean . . ." She stopped, flustered.

"Do you want me to have to question each and every other servant until I discover who your sweetheart is?" the knight chuckled. "Come, I am not asking from some perverted motive. I have to try to find your master's murderer."

She gave him a quick look from the corner of her eye, then ducked her head. "All right, sir. I was upstairs with my mistress in the early evening, but when it got dark, she came downstairs. She told me to wait."

"Was it usual for her to leave you up in her chamber while she went to fetch something for herself?"

"Mistress Cecily is a very gentle and kind lady. If I'm busy she'll often help me, and yes, sometimes she does run her own errands."

"So you were busy last night?"

"Not particularly. I was making up her bed and sorting through some of her clothes, that's all."

"And her father was out, she's told us. That was normal?"

"Recently, yes. What with the . . ."

"Yes?" Baldwin prompted gently.

She gave a little sigh, and a shrug. "Well, since Master Coffyn next door got in these soldiers of his, the master was nervous. He argued with Master Coffyn several times over them."

"You heard them argue?"

"It was hard to miss them, they were shouting so loud."

"Where was this?" Simon asked.

"Why, in the hall here."

"So Coffyn used to come here often enough?" Simon pressed.

"Oh yes, sir. My master had invested a lot of money in Master Coffyn's business over the last few months. He often used to come here to tell my master how the business was doing."

Baldwin pulled her back to his own theme. "But your master thought Coffyn's men might rob this house?"

"Yes, sir. Not that I saw any of them near, but you know what stories there are about wandering soldiers like them. None of them owe any loyalty but that which they give for money."

Baldwin nodded. He was perfectly well aware of the increasing public concern about such people, but he had no desire to be caught up in a debate on their morals with a serving-girl. “And is anything missing? Could Coffyn or his man have taken anything?”

She gave him a quick look, then studied the sideboard. When she faced him again, she met his gaze with what looked like defiance. “No, sir. Nothing is missing.”

He peered at her, nodding slowly. “Very well. What happened when your mistress left you and came in here?”

“Well, sir, she was gone some little while when I heard her father. He was shouting something about her being defiled. I didn’t know what to do. I was just going to go downstairs, when I heard something else. It froze the blood in my veins, sir, it really did. It was her father. He gave a great roar, and I swear I never want to hear a noise like that again as long as I live!” She shivered at the memory, and wiped her eyes on her sleeve before continuing. “I was scared out of my wits, not knowing what to do. The only way out of the solar block is through the main hall, and if there was a madman killing people there, I didn’t want to go! But then, when things had been quiet for some time, I thought I should steal down. I was about to go when I heard another scream, and—”

“*Another* scream?”

“Yes, sir, not so deep as the master’s, more like a kind of shrill cry, it was.”

“Could it have been Putthe?” Simon asked.

“I suppose so. Anyway, after that, I heard footsteps running away, and—”

“In which direction?”

“Hmm? Oh, out at the back . . . but not straight away. I am quite certain that the man went out along the house. I think he must have gone to the wall to the side of the house, and out over the wall into the little street."

"The street that leads up to John's house?"

"Yes, sir—but if it had been John of Irelaunde, he'd have run through the garden and over the wall without going into the road."

Baldwin nodded. It was a logical enough inference. "How much time was there between the cry and the running feet?"

"Oh, I don't know, sir. Only a few minutes."

"It wasn't immediate, then? Another point, how many footsteps did you hear running away?"

"How many, sir?" For the first time Alison appeared confused. She bit her lower lip, as though concentrating, but her face reddened as if embarrassed.

The knight smiled to calm her. "It doesn't matter that much if you don't know. Please, carry on."

"There's not much more to tell you, sir. Soon after I heard the man running away, I heard other men down here, and I recognized Mr. Coffyn's voice. I thought I'd better come down; with Mr. Coffyn and his men, I should be safe enough, I reckoned. I found Mistress here, not far from the window, her father there where you can see him, and Putthe by the door. Mr. Coffyn was standing and staring at them all."

"What then?"

She gave a shy smile. "I screamed at them to call the watch and the constable, told them to wake up. Master Coffyn and his man helped get my mistress upstairs for me, and then Master Coffyn sent his man to fetch Tanner. When the constable arrived, he and Master Coffyn's man carried Putthe out to his room, while Master Coffyn went home again."

Baldwin nodded and was about to walk from the

room, when Simon said, "But why didn't any of the servants come in? They must have heard the shouting and screams if Coffyn did. Why did all the servants, apart from Putthe, stay away? If they heard a fight going on in here, and their master being attacked, what were they thinking of?"

"Oh, they weren't here, sir. Mistress had sent them all to the inn."

"What?" Baldwin burst out.

"It was a treat for them. She even gave them money."

Margaret smiled at Jeanne as they slowly made their way up the hill on the Cadbury road heading toward Baldwin's home. "You'll like his place. It's not new like some, but he tells us he's had a lot added this year. He's built a new solar and kitchen."

"Are you trying to sell it to me?" asked Jeanne lightly.

Margaret laughed and wisely decided to change the subject. "I thought Baldwin looked anxious. I hope this murder won't take up too much of his time."

"I think it a great insult that he should be spending his time looking into some horrible killing when he should be entertaining *you*, my lady."

"Now, Emma," said Jeanne, with what Margaret thought was a trace of coldness. "He has his duties to attend to. We cannot expect him to forget his responsibilities just because we happen to arrive as a man is killed."

"I should have thought an important knight, a Keeper of the King's Peace, no less, should have had enough minions to look into it, while he saw to his responsibility to *you*," her maid responded sharply. "It's not as if you're some ordinary guest, you're—"

"Enough, Emma! It is not your place to decide where his duty lies."

It interested Margaret that the maid was so forthright in her views. Of course, many servants were, because they were commonly the closest friends and advisers to their masters or mistresses, and often a servant's opinion would rate higher in a man's estimation than that of a doctor or a lawyer, who were, after all, merely mercenaries after a man's wealth. Still, for someone in Emma's position to criticize her mistress' host did show an extreme arrogance.

And what a maid she was! Where Jeanne was slim and elegant as a well-bred Arab mare, Emma was large and clumsy. Her face was harsh, and Margaret thought her small, deep-set eyes stared at the world with a vindictive distrust. That she enjoyed the confidence of her mistress, Margaret couldn't doubt, but *why* was a different matter, and she found herself wondering how Jeanne could have kept such a maid by her side.

The bailiff's wife found herself looking at Emma askance. After hearing her comments on Baldwin, Margaret felt that the maid was prepared to seek out any fault and emphasize it to Baldwin's disadvantage.

"Is it very much further? It seems like an age since we left the town, and years since we saw a decent road," Emma demanded some little while later.

Edgar was some distance in front now. In Margaret's jaundiced opinion, he was trying to leave as much space as possible between himself and Emma. It would be difficult to question him. "What do you think, Hugh?" Margaret asked, glancing at him.

Hugh rode along uncomfortably, gripping the reins of the packhorse in his fist. He was one of those moormen who seemed to have held on to more of his Celtic past than most of his contemporaries. He was lithe and short, with a shock of untidy dark hair over his morose features. The man had been in Simon's service for many years, and the bailiff swore that with Hugh at his side he need fear neither footpad nor trail bastion, for Hugh's expression was such that those upon whom he glowered would be certain to be turned to stone.

He now looked up at the sun, then at the road ahead, at the trees on either side and the icy mud at his horse's hooves. "It's about another league."

"You can tell that by looking at the sky and the trees? Hah! I suppose it might be double that, or treble, for all you know. And my poor lady tired out there after coming all this way, too! Surely the knight could have arranged for a room at the inn so we could break our journey a little."

Margaret listened with frank astonishment, then nodded to her man. "Hugh? Tell her how you know it's one league."

"That oak with the broken branch," he pointed. "Lost that branch in the bad winter of '15, and it was down when me and the master were riding back from Tiverton. I know it from the elm opposite, that one that's got the sort of fork in its upper branches there. See? It's quite odd. Don't know another one like it. And that holly, up ahead there, is where I once saw a pair of thrushes attacking a magpie that was trying to get into their nest. It didn't, though."

"Was it scared off by the thrushes?" asked Jeanne, interested despite herself.

"No," he said simply. "I killed it with my slingshot."

"That was kind," she smiled.

"Not really," he grunted, scowling at his horse's neck. "I was trying to get the thrushes. Make a good pie, do two thrushes."

Emma was studying him with ill-concealed disgust,

and on hearing this gave a little exclamation. "My lady adores little birds that sing. And you kill them for food? I hadn't realized this area was so poor that peasants and bondsmen ate songbirds."

Margaret saw Hugh's expression become even more somber as he sullenly surveyed their path ahead. She quickly interrupted his thoughts before he could express his feelings, which she was sure were colored already by Emma's eviction of him from the inn's buttery. "I think you'll find that the people living here are better off than your folk in Liddinstone, Emma. Your mistress no doubt has a flourishing estate, but the land here is most fertile. All farming prospers in Baldwin's fields. And then again, he is known for his kindness and generosity to those who cannot support themselves."

"That's the trouble with so many knights nowadays. They have no idea how to treat their people. If they're hungry, it's because they're idle. They need the whip more than they need largesse."

On hearing this, Margaret surrendered in the unequal battle. The maid was plainly incorrigible, and Margaret preferred to ignore her rather than hear her friend the knight being slandered. She was surprised that Jeanne did not defend him, and shot her a glance. Jeanne exhibited every sign of anger. Her mouth was compressed into a thin line, and she stared ahead fixedly without blinking.

Margaret was content. Emma would be lashed by her mistress' tongue later.

As they came to the top of a long rising slope, Edgar turned off into a rough track that led away to the right, and they set off after him.

Jeanne allowed her fury to fade away. There was no point in raging at the stupid woman, not once she had made up her mind. Jeanne knew Emma too well. The maid had already decided that Baldwin was no good for her. Emma thought that someone who lived so far from what she called "civilization" was likely to be a boor.

But Jeanne was also aware that Emma's antipathy to Baldwin was not caused solely by concern for the welfare of her mistress. Emma liked running her own household. She enjoyed a good life at Liddinstone, the other servants all went in fear of her, and she could get her own way with ease. If she were to move with her mistress to live at Furnshill, there was no telling how the new servants would react to her.

It made Jeanne sigh. Emma had been with her from very early on—indeed, that was partly why her respect for her maid bordered on fear. When Jeanne had been orphaned, her uncle had taken her in to live with his household in Bordeaux, and had set Emma the task of being her maid. For a farmer's daughter from Devon the rules and conventions of polite society in such an important town were mind-boggling, but under Emma's rough tuition, Jeanne had avoided some of the worst and most embarrassing *faux pas*. While she grew to womanhood, Emma had been the constant reminder of the debt of honor and fidelity Jeanne owed to her uncle. Whenever she put a foot wrong, Emma snapped at her in correction; when Jeanne made a foolish comment, it was Emma who criticized. Even when she had married and returned to Devon as the mistress of Liddinstone, it had seemed impossible to discard Emma, and the maid had remained with her.

But her presence was not relaxing, and now, after so many years, the bonds of obedience to her uncle, the ties of loyalty and, if she was honest, of habit, were beginning to chafe at her. Jeanne was no child now, and her automatic deference to her tutor was increasingly difficult to sustain.

Jeanne knew her maid was unhappy at the thought that she might be about to remarry, but her maid's fears were not, she felt, sufficient reason for her to reject Baldwin. She had enjoyed her time with him when they had last met, and the way that he had smiled at her at the inn had made her heart leap. She would reserve her judgment, but of one thing she was determined: no matter what Emma's feelings, Jeanne would make up her own mind whether or not to wed Baldwin, and that decision would be taken in her own interest—not her maid's.

Jeanne nodded to herself with determination, and gave herself up to studying the countryside.

From here she could see for miles in the clear winter air. Before them were woods dropping away to river beds. Over the sound of their hooves she could hear the rushing water. Right, though, the land undulated gently, falling in ripples and small hills, until it climbed again many miles to the south. And there, south and west, she could see the blue-black hills of the moors. "What a perfect view."

"It is lovely, isn't it?" Margaret agreed softly. "So much more beautiful here than Dartmoor, with its blasted and dingy commons. This area is the most delightful I know."

For once Emma was still, and they carried on along the track, which fell into a valley between two tree-covered hills, then wound around the side of another little hillock, until at last Hugh pointed. "There it is!"

Jeanne was enthralled. A large whitewashed house lay before them, long and low, built for comfort, not defense, for here there was little need to fear attack. The ground rose up to it, with a great sweep of pastureland before it on which some sheep grazed, while on the other three sides the property was enclosed by trees. She opened her mouth to express her joy on seeing it.

Emma beat her. "Ugh! It's tiny, isn't it?"

- 10 -

Simon and Baldwin walked from the hall and only when they were in the open air again did they exchange a glance.

"Baldwin, you know what I'm thinking, don't you?"

"It does seem suspicious that she should have sent the servants away," Baldwin admitted cautiously. "But there might be a perfectly sound reason for her to have done so. There is a little evidence pointing to her, but no proof. And no motive, so far as we know, for her to want to have her father killed."

"Perhaps not—*yet*! But if what we have heard is true and she sent all the servants away, it was she who gave the killer a clear run at her father."

"Why should a girl want her own father dead?"

"There are many possibilities. To take one: perhaps he didn't approve of her lover."

"Her lover?"

"We know she was at the window. You yourself confirmed that she was wearing the tunic that left the threads at the window. Who should she be speaking to except a lover?"

"There *are* other possibilities, Simon," Baldwin

pointed out dryly. "But let us treat your proposition seriously for a moment. If you are right, why should she give us a description of his clothing, when she could more usefully give us her lover's name? And why tell us that the man wore a scarlet tunic when she declares that she couldn't see what kind of cloak he had on? If she could see the one distinctly, she could also see the other, so she was lying for some reason—although *why* I cannot think. And as far as the piece of blue tunic goes, we haven't seen the dress she wore last night, so we cannot be certain that the scrap came from it. We have, in reality, learned very little."

"Baldwin, you can raise objections like that for as long as you like, but—"

"And what were Putthe and the maid doing here?"

"Eh?"

"Come, Simon. If Mistress Cecily was so keen to get rid of any dangerous witnesses, why didn't she go the whole hog? Why let two remain?"

"I suppose the maid Alison could be entirely trusted, so Cecily allowed her to remain; while Putthe was her father's most loyal employee, and was expected to guard the place. Presumably someone had to stay with her to chaperone her. Even if the chaperones weren't as competent as Jeanne's appears to be!"

Baldwin ignored the dig. "Also, what was her father shouting about? Why say 'defile' her—why not just say 'rape'?" he mused.

"That's one thing you'll probably never know. You can't ask him now," said Simon callously.

"No," Baldwin agreed thoughtfully. "And another thing: I don't understand what is happening regarding the plate. Why should Putthe describe a load of stuff which doesn't exist?"

"It was the knock on his head."

"No. I've known men lose their memories, but I've never known a man invent things after a bang. I am certain he was describing the plate when I saw him last night. You weren't there—he was absolutely convincing. Yet it's not there, and Alison denies anything is amiss."

"For now, the theft, if there was one, must play second string to the murder," Simon said decisively, and looked upward. "And we'd better make our way back. It's late, and I don't want to have to ride all the way to your house in the dark."

"Hmm, I suppose you're right," Baldwin said. He nodded to Tanner at the gate as they passed, and the two turned back up the street toward the inn to collect their horses.

The grooms came running as soon as Jeanne and Margaret turned into the yard. Simon's wife remained on her horse while all the travellers' bags and boxes were untied from their packhorse, before springing down and leading Jeanne to the front door.

Jeanne stood for a moment and surveyed the country. From this slightly prominent position, she found she was looking down a shaft of greensward between trees standing like walls on either side. The sky was almost perfectly clear, and the sun shone with cold brilliance on the rich grassland where the sheep browsed. She drew in a deep breath and let it slowly sigh out. "It's beautiful!"

"Isn't it? You have no idea how jealous I am of Baldwin having this view to look at each day, when all I have is the sight of those bleak moors," said Margaret at her side. It wasn't strictly true, since their little house was at the western edge of Lydford, and their view was of farmland and woods like this, but Margaret was peeved by Emma's words on the journey and intended to ensure that Jeanne appreciated Baldwin's assets. "Shall we go inside?"

Jeanne shivered suddenly. "Oh, yes! It's amazing how quickly one feels the cold once one has stopped riding, isn't it? I was fine all the way here, and now I am quite frozen. Let's find a fire!"

Hugh appeared, carrying a large and apparently very heavy strongbox, while Emma chivvied him. Jeanne, seeing his strained features, called sharply, "Emma, open the door for him! He can't carry that and operate the latch."

"Oh, very well, but why on earth the knight hasn't got enough servants, I don't like to think. You'd have thought a man to open the door wouldn't be too—"

At this point Emma had reached the door. She put her hand to the latch. Her thumb pressed the lever. She pushed the door wide.

Margaret was surprised. She'd expected Edgar to be there to open up the place to guests. She caught a glimpse of him, heard a growl from somewhere and saw the expectation on his face. She wondered why for a moment.

Then Wat gave a loud scream, which was drowned by Emma's, as the growl became a roar and Uther burst forth.

Thomas Rodde hesitated. It was tempting to go after the two men and try to listen to what they were saying, but that kind of spying was easier for the able-bodied. In his leper's clothes it was impossible to be discreet, and if he was to approach too close, especially now that the wind had changed direction, he would be shouted at. He knew the law: lepers must always stay downwind of other people so that their contagion couldn't be passed on the corrupt air that emanated from their leprous flesh.

The crowd had all left the gate, and there was only the constable left. Making a quick decision, Rodde left Quivil, stepping forward, his clapper sounding its knell as he walked. "Constable, sir," he called.

Tanner turned sharply on hearing himself hailed, but seeing who it was, he curled his lip. "Keep away, sinner."

"I'm sorry, constable, if I alarmed you," Rodde said, standing at a decent distance. "But I've been watching, and I wondered whether there was any idea who was the murderer of poor Master Godfrey?"

"If we knew that we'd have arrested him," Tanner said shortly. He was not a cruel man by nature, but he detested the sight of lepers. They reminded him that no matter how strong he himself was, one day he would also suffer illness and perish. He shivered at the thought.

"Sir, it's only that I wondered who could want to kill a man like him."

"You're right there," Tanner said, glancing over his shoulder at the great dark building behind him. "I mean, he was rich, respected, and didn't have any enemies that I know of."

"So there is no obvious suspect?"

Tanner stirred himself and gave the leper a sharp look. "Why, do you know anything about all this?"

"No, sir, nothing. I'm not even a local man. But when you have to wear this dress and toll your clapper to warn others to keep away, any news is interesting."

The constable watched as the leper made his way off along the street, collecting the other on his way, their little wooden bells sounding at regular intervals. Tanner leaned back against the wall. It was a relief to see them go: it was unsettling having them nearby, their hungry eyes fixed on him as if needing not only food but something more simple: mere human company.

And that thought made him shiver again as it gave him a glimpse of the worst punishment that leprosy inflicted upon its victims: that of utter loneliness. He looked up the street, tempted to offer the two men a drink at his expense, or the price of a loaf of bread, but they had disappeared.

Bugger them, he thought. But he crossed himself nonetheless as he offered up a short prayer for a speedy death, and no lingering anguish such as he had seen in Rodde's eyes.

All the way home, Baldwin was curiously silent. Simon had expected passing comments about the murder, or perhaps words reflecting his nervousness about seeing Jeanne again, but the knight said nothing.

Unknown to the bailiff, his friend was repeating certain phrases in his mind, then editing them with cold brutality. They were none of them very imaginative, for Baldwin had never before felt the need to try out expressions of love. It took him five miles of riding to give up the attempt and erase from his memory all the hard effort. All he could do was pray that she would be content with his obvious devotion. It was all he felt capable of relying on—he certainly couldn't trust to his tongue.

The house was quiet—ominously so—when Simon and Baldwin arrived. Their horses left with the groom, they made their way to the front door. Simon almost laughed out loud to see how Baldwin dawdled.

Baldwin sensed impending doom. The glimpse of Jeanne at the inn had been as refreshing as he had hoped. She was as attractive as he remembered, and his decision to try to win her hand was strongly reinforced—but such a decision was hard to put into action. From all he had heard from others, it was a simple case of asking the question, gaining the required acquiescence after a moderate show of unwillingness, and then "hey for the priest." But with Jeanne it was not so straightforward. He had already asked her once, the year before, and although she had not firmly rejected him, neither had she promised that a repetition of his offer would receive a different response. The only favorable sign she had given was her suggestion that she should visit him here; in effect, as he had so often told himself, viewing her prospective husband's resources before committing herself.

"Come on, Baldwin! Anyone'd think you were nervous!"

"Most amusing! I was just thinking about this murder, that is all."

"Of course, Baldwin. Naturally. But won't your guests be wondering why their host is lurking out here in the cold as darkness falls?"

The knight gave him a look of such pained confusion that the bailiff was tempted to suggest he should immediately resaddle his horse and make for the Cornish border. Instead Simon clapped him on the back.

"Let's get inside. You look as if you need a good hot mug of wine."

"You know I don't like too much alcohol, Simon."

"Remember your lady's maidservant?"

"Perhaps tonight *could* be an exception!"

At the door, Baldwin steeled himself and crossed over his threshold resolutely. He was about to enter his hall when he heard a strange noise. Frowning, he crossed to the opposite door, and peered out. In the yard, stacking logs with determined stoicism, was Wat.

"What is that noise for?" Baldwin demanded.

Wat wiped his eyes, clearing them of tears, and incidentally wiping green muck from the logs all over his face. This was his master, the man he held in the highest esteem. "Sir, I'm sorry."

"What is it? What have you done?" demanded the mystified knight. It was odd enough to see young Wat crying, without hearing him apologizing as well. Neither was in character for the tough youngster.

"It was Chops, sir. I had him with me in the hall like normal, and then this woman walks straight in. I tried to hold him, sir, but I couldn't, and she hit me so hard, sir . . ."

As his voice trailed off into snivels, Baldwin held up his hands helplessly. "Well, I'm sure you couldn't help it, Wat. Now stop your sniffing and finish tidying up those logs, all right?"

Leaving his servant, Baldwin wandered back into the screens, where Simon waited, and thence into the hall.

"We were wondering where you could have got to."

It was Margaret, and as Baldwin walked in, she set aside some needlework which she had been using to while away the time, and rose to greet him. The knight nodded edgily, his attention wavering from Margaret even as he welcomed her once more to his home.

And the source of his unease stood gravely. "Good day again, Sir Baldwin."

"I . . . er. You are most welcome, my lady. I hope my servant has seen to your comfort?"

"Oh, he has been most attentive. However, I fear my servant is out of temper with your dog!"

Baldwin threw a glance at Edgar, who stood near the fire, a large jug of wine held in his hands. "Hippocras, Sir Baldwin?"

The knight blinked. "Er . . . yes, thank you." It was many years since his man had bothered to behave so formally with him, even in public. Simon nudged his elbow as if accidentally as he passed, muttering under his breath, "Go on, man!" and he nodded dumbly.

"Simon, could you come and help me? I need to prepare for our meal," said Margaret sweetly.

Jeanne watched them leave the room with a faint smile. "Edgar, I think I would like a little more wine. This tastes a little too watery. Could you fetch me some more?"

"My lady, of course," the servant said suavely, and bowed himself from the room.

Watching him leave from lowered brows, Baldwin was almost jealous. He had been waiting for a year to be alone with Jeanne, and now he was, he was numb with shyness.

"Er . . . What did the dog do?"

"It was nothing," she said happily. "He gave her a fright, that's all. It would be different if he had attacked." Jeanne could see Baldwin's embarrassment, and was touched by his shyness. "Sir? I am pleased to have come here at last."

"You honor me by being here," he said.

The stiffness of his words was belied by the pinkness of his cheeks. Jeanne wanted to laugh out loud at his discomfort, but instead asked teasingly, "So have you invited many widows alone to your hall?"

"No!" he exclaimed hotly, and then gave a shamefaced grin. "Jeanne, you are the very first woman who has been in here with me alone. I have never known Edgar to trust me before."

"He appears most trusting today, sir!"

"Yes. Don't worry, I am sure it will not last. But tell me, what about you? Is this the first hall in which you have been alone with a dangerous bachelor?"

"Dangerous? How interesting! But yes. My dear maid

only rarely permits me the opportunity to commit an indiscretion."

"How kind of her to risk my safety."

She laughed then, quietly so as not to attract the attention of their servants or friends. Serious in an instant, she looked him full in the face. "I am sorry I could not come earlier. It feels like more than a year since we last met."

"I had hoped you would have been able to come before."

"I know. But it was impossible, what with the problems and the harvest."

Baldwin nodded. Jeanne de Liddinstone was a tenant of the Abbot of Tavistock, and it was important to her that she should be seen to be no less efficient than any of the others who lived on his lands. She had accepted Baldwin's offer of a visit early last spring, but since then her estate had suffered from a succession of disasters. Early in the year rain had devastated the young crops, which had then been subject to a freak storm just before harvest, and she had lost her largest barn in a fire. "I hope the good Abbot was able to help you?"

"Abbot Champeaux has done everything he possibly could," she said. "He's sent men and provided me with materials for a new barn. But I did have to stay."

"Yes, of course. And the important thing is, you are here now."

"I am glad to be."

And Baldwin felt quite certain, when he looked into her eyes, that she was in earnest. "Perhaps we could—"

"Mistress? Mistress, this man has been keeping me from you! I informed him that you'd need me, but he wouldn't listen."

Jeanne turned discreetly, thereby moving herself to a less compromising distance from the knight, who kept the emotion from his face with an effort as Emma lumbered into the room like a belligerent war-horse.

Baldwin kept his mouth shut with difficulty. At that moment the maid was the epitome of everything he loathed. Because of her, his attempts to get closer to Jeanne had all come to naught. All the endearments he had rehearsed in his mind were wasted. He could not understand how Jeanne could have been so careless as to have associated herself with such a monster. With that in mind, he gave the maidservant a cold glare before turning to Jeanne once more, and it was with a feeling of relief that he saw a similar anger glittering in her eyes.

As soon as it was dark, he slipped over the low fence into the Coffyns' back yard. It wasn't large, not on the same scale as Godfrey's, and he had to tread warily to ensure he was unobserved. The moon was a gleam of silver behind the fast-moving clouds, and with the freshening breeze he was confident that there was another storm brewing. It suited his purposes to have the weather deteriorate, for it was hardly likely that any sensible man or woman would be out on such a wild night.

He skirted the garden, keeping to the additional cover offered by the trees and bushes at the boundary, all the time warily watching the house. He could hear voices, and at one point there was the unmistakable sound of a woman sobbing. It made him pause and listen, but he had business of his own, and he shrugged his shoulders and continued on his way.

The wall was a barrier of darkness in the night, seemingly as insubstantial as a shadow, but his native caution served him well. Before approaching it, he slowly dropped to a crouch, and listened intently. There was nothing to be seen, but he trusted to his instincts, and they screamed out to him to be cautious. Something before him was out of place.

It was some minutes before he could see it, but then, as the moon was released from its heavenly captivity for a few moments, and the area was lighted by a sudden white glare, he saw a man leaning against a large tree.

The guard stood silently, his attention apparently fixed on the wall. It seemed that he was prepared to stay there the whole night, and the crouching figure behind him calculated quickly whether there was another route for him to take, but none sprang into his mind. He was about to turn and go back the way he had come, when the guard shifted. With a soft grunt, he turned away from the wall. There was a quiet trickling.

Grinning, and hoping that urinating would take all of his concentration, if only for a moment or two, the trespasser hurried to a section of wall some distance away and silently climbed up. Once there, he lay on top a while, peering back the way he had come. The man by the tree gave a little gasp, settled himself, and leaned back to renew his solitary watch.

Seeing he had noticed nothing, the shadow rolled off the wall into Godfrey's land. He fell automatically into a crouch, his eyes darting hither and thither, seeking any new dangers, but he could see nothing to cause him alarm, and soon he was stealthily making his way to the window he knew so well. He never saw the second shape drop from the wall behind him and steadfastly follow in his tracks.

But after the murder he wasn't so foolish as to walk straight up to it as before. There could be a trap waiting for him. He moved slowly from the wall to a great elm, and paused, then on to a holly a little nearer, then up to the shelter offered by a laurel almost at the hall's wall, each time waiting, listening, and staring on all sides. The danger here was almost tangible, and he wasn't prepared to put his life at risk for no reason.

At last he was content. He edged forward, until he was at the building, and tiptoed to the window. The shutter was closed, the tapestry drawn, and only a dull glimmer of light escaped. He reached up and scratched softly at the wood of the shutter, making a faint rasp as if a mouse were gnawing.

He had to repeat the signal three times before he heard Cecily call out, "Go and prepare my chamber. And see to it that my bed is properly warmed. I feel frozen to my very marrow."

For a few moments there was nothing, but then the corner of the tapestry was lifted, and he could see her sweet face. "Thomas, are you there?"

- 11 -

The guard almost jumped out of his skin when William dropped lightly from the wall in front of him. He grabbed for his sword and would have swept it out, if William hadn't snarled quietly, "Leave that block of metal in its seat if you don't want me to use it to beat some sense into your thick skull."

Leaving the astonished guard, William walked pensively back to the hall. He had learned much tonight, and some of it might well be useful in the future, but he wasn't sure that it was any business of his master, and William had a firm belief in information: when it was useful, it held value. Coffyn had hired William to be the officer of his men and to guard the house, not to be his informer, but he might still be prepared to cough up for something as juicy as this.

William went through to the private solar and knocked. Coffyn was awake still, his angry, unblinking eyes pouchy and red-rimmed from lack of sleep. As usual, his wife was nowhere to be seen. If William hadn't heard her weeping earlier, he might have wondered whether she was still alive—but he didn't believe in speculating on matters like that, not where they affected his master.

"Well?"

"Someone's been trespassing over your land."

"What? Who?" Coffyn leaned forward, peering closely, his swollen and bleary eyes screwing up with concentration. He chewed his nails, and William looked away.

It was ever the way, the guard thought, that men would be fooled by their women into trusting them too much, only to find that they had been deceived. He could only feel sympathy for his master.

"Tell me! It was the Irishman, wasn't it?"

His words were spat out with as much virulence as if they had been a noxious draft, and it gave William a certain perverse pleasure to be able to shake his head. "Oh no, sir. It wasn't him. It was a leper."

"A leper!" Coffyn sank back in his seat, horrified. "A leper," he breathed.

Fifteen minutes later William left the solar and made his way to the buttery to fetch a quart of ale. All in all it was shaping up to be a profitable night for him, and he smiled as he poured his drink.

Baldwin left his hall not long after Jeanne had departed to change from her travelling clothes. For the duration of her visit, Baldwin had given up his own bedchamber. It was the newest room in the place, and seemed to remain the warmest. The other upstairs room, the one at the opposite end of the hall above the buttery, he had allocated to Simon and Margaret. That left the undercroft beneath his bedchamber. It was to this little room that he now repaired, and as he entered, he found his servant sitting on his chest and watching Uther, who, on hearing his master, instantly left his bowl of food to leap at him.

"Down, you brute! Edgar, how *could* you—"

"Yes, Sir Baldwin, I'd think so," Edgar said quickly, and strode from the room.

"I . . . Edgar?" Baldwin felt his mouth fall open at his servant's behavior, and hared after him. He found Edgar outside in the little plot that Baldwin had optimistically termed his orchard. "Edgar, what in God's name are you doing, walking away from me when I—"

In answer, Edgar glanced back at the building. "I could hear almost everything that Lady Jeanne said to her maid in the room above."

"But I . . ." The knight fell silent. Two possibilities were suddenly opened before him: one was that his servant had just saved him from shaming himself by insulting Jeanne's maid in full hearing of both women, something which, no matter what Jeanne's private thoughts about Emma, must surely offend her to some extent; the second was that Edgar had, no doubt unintentionally, become privy to Jeanne's views on her maid as well as, possibly, Baldwin himself.

"I hope you didn't try to listen to their conversation. That would be quite shameful," he said cautiously as Uther appeared at the door and sat down for a scratch.

"No, sir, I was careful not to listen," Edgar said.

His response irrationally irritated Baldwin. He was of a mind to be insulted—not for any failing on Edgar's part but because of Emma's interruption of what Baldwin was already thinking of as his first attempt at romance. The fact that Emma had necessarily made it an abortive attempt made the knight want to share out his bitterness. "I should hope so too!" Uther shook himself, sending a small gobbet of drool flying against the wall. "And Uther—how could you have let

Emma get to the door first like that? You know Uther is a guard."

"I'd have expected Wat to leave Chopsie tied up. I wasn't to know the dog would be free. Anyway, since then I've had the hound locked up in your room."

Some women liked dogs, and Baldwin had no reason to think that Jeanne herself didn't but there was a great difference between a little lapdog and Uther. There was a brash, confident slobbering enthusiasm about him that was entirely lacking in a gentlewoman's small pet. Some dogs could subtly work their way into a household without being noticed. One moment there was a space in front of the fire, and the next a small mongrel had filled it. It was that way with old Ben, Baldwin's farm dog. One day there had been space before the fire, the next the little mutt had inveigled his way in, and it was as if he had always been there.

Uther, on the other hand, was incapable of insinuating himself into a small gap. If there was a small gap, it soon became Uther-sized as he shoved his way through. When Uther was present, it was impossible to miss him. It wasn't only the fact that a creature weighing over six stones was hard to ignore, nor the smell of three-week-old damp rags that he invariably carried with him wherever he went. No, it lay more in the fact that Uther had about him a variety of canine devotion that was touching to someone who liked dogs, and intensely repulsive to someone who didn't.

But Baldwin wasn't going to admit that in front of his servant. "This is nonsense!" he snapped. "Uther is my dog, and he always stays in the hall. How else can he protect the place? You'll give him the run of the hall again immediately."

Edgar raised an eyebrow, and opened his mouth as if

to argue, but Baldwin held up his hand. "That is my decision. Is that clear?"

"Yes, Sir Baldwin," Edgar said again with that irritating servility that felt like condescension. "If that is what you wish, I will see to it."

"Good."

"But . . ."

Baldwin glared. "What?"

"I was thinking, sir, that it might be best if we kept Uther from the hall while you're eating. He might unsettle Emma—or Lady Jeanne."

It was a sensible suggestion. Baldwin nodded, absently patted the dog on the head, and began to walk back to his new room. "And now fetch me water and a bowl. I need to wash."

The meal was not an unqualified success. Edgar remained on his best behavior, which meant he cultivated an air of suave competence, responding to any orders with a distant politeness. His demeanor left Baldwin disgruntled; he would have enjoyed being able to order his man about, to demonstrate he knew how to keep his servant on his toes.

Jeanne could see that Simon and his wife were more interested in her and their host than their food, and that was enough to make her maintain a calm reserve. It was easier than trying to make polite conversation in which every subject was analyzed for a possible second meaning.

Yet she was struck with the knight's property. The house was a great old cob and thatch longhouse, generously proportioned, but Baldwin had made several improvements, according to Simon and his wife. When they had first visited him here, it had been merely a single-storied hall with a small dairy at the back, a buttery and pantry to one side. Now each end contained upper rooms, areas of privacy from the servants and bondsmen who messed and slept in the hall. That was not all, for the new red sandstone block attached to the rear of the house was Baldwin's new buttery, where all his brewing equipment was stored. It meant that he now regularly had too much ale for his own people and could sell off his excess. The old buttery was still in use, but like the undercroft was used more as a storeroom than a working area.

"That stew was excellent," she commented as Edgar placed a fresh bread trencher before her.

"I am glad you enjoyed it," Baldwin said. "It wasn't so easy before with the old kitchen."

"When did you have the new one built?" asked Margaret.

"During the summer. The old one caught fire. I must admit, I'd been thinking about doing something about it for some time already, though. It was too small for my purposes. I used the quarry over at Cadbury for the stone, and now I have a kitchen large enough to feed an earl, should it be necessary!"

"Do you look for advancement, then?" Margaret asked.

"Christ's Blood, no!" said Baldwin, sincerely shocked. "What benefit would I gain from banneret's rank or higher? All it would mean would be that I would have to fund more men to no advantage."

"Come on, Baldwin," Simon said reasonably. "Largesse is a key attribute for a knight; you should be happy to have more men so you can show your generosity."

"That may be a good principle for a wealthy duke or prince, but it's cold comfort to a poor local knight who each year spends all his income feeding the mouths he already has living on his estates."

"You tell us that you are impecunious, Sir Baldwin? With your new kitchen, solars and brewery?" asked Jeanne teasingly.

"Perhaps not impecunious, but not rich. The brewery is for my workers, for they need the sustenance. My kitchen had to be rebuilt anyway, and it made more sense to have something worthwhile, rather than a cookhouse that was too small for my retinue. But if I was to seek higher rank I would immediately have to find men to flock to my banner in time of war, and they would be extra mouths to feed."

"Some knights would think that a small price to pay for their elevation," grunted Emma through a mouthful of stew.

"Some no doubt would," Baldwin agreed, eyeing her with distaste. "But I consider my first duty to be to protect the poor on my lands, and those who cannot feed themselves. Worldly positions matter little compared with that."

"I think so too," said Jeanne, and Baldwin was pleased to see that she gave her maid a look of cold disapproval.

After they had finished their meal, and while Edgar chivvied servants to clear away the mess, Baldwin and his guests moved nearer the fire. While it was not yet deep winter, the nights were cold enough, and the flames offered some defense. The doors had large gaps which let in the drafts, and the tapestries which covered the shuttered but unglazed windows were only partially effective, but for all that, Jeanne felt as comfortable here as if she had spent her childhood in the house. It had a warmth and serenity that was missing in her own.

It was perhaps because she had been orphaned while very young. Her parents had been the victims of a gang of trail bastons, a group of murderous thugs who robbed, murdered and looted wherever they could. Her father had been murdered, and her mother raped and killed. Jeanne herself, although only a child, had been struck with an axe, but the killer had been drunk and had missed his mark.

Jeanne had been saved and taken to Bordeaux, where relations protected her until she met Ralph de Liddinstone and agreed to marry him. But she had found life with him to be a nightmare. He had abused her, beaten her, insulted her before his friends, and finally taken to whipping her. It was a relief when he contracted a fever and died.

It was already well over a year since his death—he died in the summer before she had met Baldwin—and in that time, although the estate had suffered from near-catastrophic disasters, she was happier now than she had been for many years. The only event which had shaken her initial resolve to remain free and uncontracted to any man had been her meeting Sir Baldwin de Furnshill.

Glancing over at him, she felt her face soften at the sight. The knight sat, clearly at his ease, his eyelids drooping with the somnolence induced by a heavy meal, his drink tilting at a dangerous angle in his hand as he tried to fight sleep. Simon had already given up the battle, and was snoring gently, arms folded, head resting against the fireplace, Margaret nodding at his side. They looked comfortable together, and Jeanne felt a quick jealousy. She had never known such companionship with a man, and it seemed unfair that Margaret should have found happiness with the first man she had married.

Baldwin appeared kind, she thought. He had eyes that were keen to smile, rather than scold; his temperament was geared to protecting others rather than taking for himself. The talk about self-advancement they had held over the table had confirmed that, and she could recall conversations with him in Tavistock when he had evinced compassion for the innocent when accused, and for those who were unable to defend themselves. It made her certain that he would make a good husband.

He had asked her to marry him then, but she had temporized. It was not solely because she felt it was too soon after her husband's death to be seemly, for the Abbot would have married them, and no one would have dared gainsay *him;* it was more due to her own doubts. After suffering unhappily in one marriage she had no desire to repeat the experience.

And that was her sole remaining source of uncertainty. Was Baldwin pleasant only to her face, and a brute in private? That was how her husband had been: he had been civility and generosity itself while courting her, and it was only when she wed him that she realized his true colors. But there was no denying the fact that she was lonely.

While she contemplated his dozing figure, she heard a soft pattering of paws, which suddenly increased their speed.

Uther had been shut away in the undercroft for the previous two hours while his master ate, not that Uther knew that was the reason. To his simple mind, all that mattered was that he had been away from Baldwin's side for a long time, and that, he knew, only happened when he had misbehaved. Now he was released, he knew he must make his apologies to his master for whatever he might have done. On entering the hall at a gentle trot, he saw the familiar shape in the chair at the fireside, and launched himself forward.

It was a pleasant dream into which Baldwin had slipped. He was walking once more with Jeanne in the Abbot's garden at Tavistock, building up to asking her the crucial question, and as he asked, she turned her sweet face to him, and he saw her smiling lips open . . . and she butted him in the stomach.

"Jeanne!"

He opened his eyes to a mask of horror. Massive brown eyes met his, jowls quivered with saliva which dropped on his chest, and then the jaws opened like the maw of hell, and he saw the tongue flicking forward before he managed to snap his eyes shut.

Only later, long after the disgraced mastiff had been ejected, after the abundant apologies from Edgar, after the pint of strong wine which he had felt entirely justified in drinking to calm his shattered nerves, only then did Baldwin remember the gales of laughter pouring from Jeanne.

But still later, when he was lying in his bed, he recalled with overwhelming horror what he had cried out loud as his dream was shattered by that blasted hound.

In the morning, Simon was annoyed to be woken before daylight. Someone was gently shaking his shoulder, and the bailiff had to stop himself from cursing as he recognized his servant. "Hugh? What is it?"

"Sir Baldwin's getting ready to go into town, sir. He thought you'd want to join him."

"He did, did he?"

The disgruntled bailiff dressed himself and went down to the hall. There he found the knight sitting in his chair by the fire, which had only recently been made up and was making more smoke than flame. Wat was on his knees blowing enthusiastically at the feeble embers.

"You're in a hurry to be off today," Simon observed suspiciously.

"Sorry, Simon, but I have a murder to solve, and there are many people to speak to."

The bailiff watched him don a thick coat and cloak. "So it's got nothing to do with nervousness about seeing Jeanne as soon as she wakes?"

"Nervousness? What have I got to be nervous about?"

"Oh, nothing, nothing. How's your dog today?"

Baldwin glowered at him scornfully. When Edgar appeared and announced that their horses were ready, the knight walked past the bailiff with an air of absolute disdain. Uncrushed, Simon trailed after him, still fastening his cloak, whistling tunelessly and grinning broadly.

The town, when the three men rode in, was just stirring. Dogs barked, cockerels squawked their welcome to the new day, shutters slammed open, men and women cursed or bellowed, and over it all there was a general hubbub of pots and pans banging as meals were prepared. They rode past shopkeepers dropping their shutters onto trestles and setting goods on display. Some recognized Simon from the time when he had lived here—was it really four years since he had left for Lydford?—and gave him a good-natured nod of the head, or a doubtful frown, depending upon their experience of him. It made him feel good to be alive. He hadn't realized how much he had missed the town.

"Where to first, Baldwin?"

"Up to see our old friend John of Irelaunde. He'd be the first man to be suspected by the average townsman, and I'd rather have a chance to speak to him before someone tries to dangle him from a rope."

They were soon at the road that led up the hill to the Irishman's. On the corner stood Godfrey's house. Baldwin carried on toward John's property, but Simon called to him. "There's someone trying to attract your attention, Baldwin. Is that Putthe?"

Without answering, Baldwin trotted his horse

through the gate and up to the front door. "Putthe? You've had second thoughts?"

"Me?" Putthe, his bandage even grimier now, looked up as if surprised at the question. "No, sir. When I saw you the other night I was still half-concussed, and fearfully upset, what with the strain of losing my master. I forgot to tell you something."

Baldwin and the others dismounted and followed the servant into the buttery. Here he had a small copper pot heating over a brazier. The scent from it made Simon salivate. It was the smell of sugared wine, mulled with sweet, aromatic herbs. After the journey, it was the tonic he needed.

Even Baldwin couldn't refuse a mug, and he sighed with gratitude as he felt his first gulp sear a glowing path down his gullet. "Come on, Putthe. What stunning news do you have for us?"

It was hard, but now Putthe knew he had been wrong at first, and he had to ensure that John was protected. He didn't need any more trouble, and his mistress could make his life a misery if he didn't protect the Irishman.

"Master, my memory was weak after I was hit. Otherwise I'd have told you when you were here before."

"Never mind the excuses, what wonderful clues do you now remember?"

"On the night my master was murdered, I was out here. I didn't say before, because I didn't think it mattered, but I had someone with me . . ."

"Who?" Simon demanded immediately. "We already know that your lady had allowed all the servants to go to the inn apart from you and her maid. Who was here with you?"

Puuhe lowered his eyes for a moment. "It was Jack, the blacksmith. He was often round here to see to the master's horses."

"And you shared your master's best ale with him?"

"I was asked to, sir. It wasn't as if there was any problem with it. Jack had been here to see to Mistress Cecily's mare—it had cast a shoe, and he had to fit i back."

"What really happened, Putthe?" Baldwin asked, setting his pot on the floor.

"As I told you, sir, I got such a knock on the head tha I couldn't remember everything all at once," Putthe sai reproachfully. "Soon as I recalled it, I wanted to let yo know. What happened was this: Jack was here in th late afternoon, and the mare was skittish, didn't wan any part of having the shoe refitted, so Jack got quit hot and thirsty. Mistress Cecily asked me to invite hin in here. I wouldn't normally, he's a bit rough and ready if you follow me, but after he'd spent so long here wit the mare, I suppose the mistress thought it was only polite to give him an ale when he was done.

"The master came in after a while, and shared drink. He was in an excellent mood, and went out jus as dark was falling. It was his way to go out whe Coffyn was away. He didn't trust Coffyn's hired men— thought they could rob the house. Master Godfrey wa worried they might decide to take some of his tools o steal a pig or something. You never can trust their type

"What with one thing and another, it had been a har day for me and for Jack. We had a few quarts togethe One man came, asking for the master, but he went whe I said he wasn't here . . ."

"Who was that?" asked Baldwin sharply.

"Only one of Coffyn's men. He said he wanted t pass on some news about Coffyn's business."

"Was it normal for Coffyn's men to come round lik that?"

"Not really," shrugged Putthe, "but they came ove

sometimes. My master had some interest in helping Matthew Coffyn, and had been for several months."

"And what happened then?"

"After he'd gone, Jack and I had a little more to drink, and then he left. I put my feet up with another pint or two. I suppose I must have dozed. I don't know what stirred me. All of a sudden I was wide awake. It took me a minute to get my bearings, as it were. I couldn't hear anything, not even a mouse, so I just put it down to some noise from the street. You get that sometimes, from carts hitting potholes and suchlike. But then I heard this terrible scream!"

Putthe stopped and turned to Baldwin. He knew that the Keeper was the more important of the two men, and it was the knight whom he must convince. That cry was a sound he'd never forget, not if he lived another thousand years. The pain in it was too great. As soon as he heard it, Putthe had recognized it as his master's.

"I knew it was the master. I couldn't miss his voice—but, Sir Baldwin, it was as if he'd concentrated his whole soul in that one bellow. It was awful—the agony of it. God's Blood! I hope I never hear anything like it again!"

Baldwin eyed him with a cool detachment. There was little doubt in his mind that the servant was honest in his horror at remembering his master's shout, but that begged the question: had he concealed hearing it before? The knight had known head injuries of many kinds—both at first-hand from practicing warfare, and from watching tournaments where others were buffeted and struck down. It was not uncommon for a man to waken from such a blow having forgotten things, but he was convinced Putthe had intentionally kept this hidden. "And?"

Sighing, Putthe topped up his copper and set it to rest

upon the brazier once more. "It was impossible for John to have killed him. I was there too quickly. He didn't have time to get out before I was there."

"So now you think John wasn't involved?"

"No, sir. He couldn't have been."

"But John hated your master because Godfrey found him in the garden?"

"Well, I don't know, sir," said Putthe thoughtfully. "Maybe I was wrong and my master disliked John more than the other way around, if you take my meaning. I think Martha Coffyn reminded the master of his own wife, and perhaps he didn't want to think of someone like John . . . well, you know."

"Godfrey's wife is dead, isn't she? How did she die?"

"A cart in the street. The horse bolted, and she was caught by a wheel. Didn't look as if it had touched her, but she was bedridden almost at once, and just faded away over the next couple of days."

"How long ago was that?"

"Eight or nine years, sir." Putthe stirred the drink with his wooden spoon. Eight years! It hardly felt that long. It seemed as if it was almost yesterday when Godfrey had come out of the bedchamber with his face working like he was going to burst out sobbing. "It was after that my master decided to leave London forever and retire to the country."

"What has he been doing since he came down here?"

"He has a small estate toward Exeter, sir, and that brings in enough money for his household. Then he also had stocks of gold and silver. I might as well tell you, he was helping people here in Crediton. He lent his money to people who needed it, people like Coffyn. He didn't really need to keep himself overly busy. I think he was content."

"And you said he found John in his garden and realized the Irishman was carrying on an affair with Mrs. Coffyn?"

"Yes, sir. It's no surprise—the little git's known for messing about with the women of the town."

"I know," Baldwin said dryly. "I've spoken to him about it before."

Simon shook his head with a look of consternation. "It doesn't make sense. If he thought John was making merry with another man's wife—his *neighbor's* wife, for God's sake!—why didn't he just tell the neighbor and let him sort it out?"

"Because he could never do that, sir. My master loved his wife, as I said, and I think Mrs. Coffyn reminded him of her, just a little, and he didn't want to hear her being beaten or whipped, let alone killed. No, he thought it was better to stop John. Well, that was why he was out there each evening, to make sure the little sod didn't get up to his old tricks."

~ 12 ~

Matthew Coffyn stood at his table and glowered out over the fields behind his garden. The view from here was stunning, for now, in the middle of the morning, the sun was low over the hill, and every tree and bush stood out in relief against the green fields, each with a stark shadow like a warped copy of itself, creeping slowly across the landscape as the sun traversed the sky.

William's news of the night before had kept him from sleep as effectively as his distrust of his wife. The idea that lepers could have invaded his land—could have polluted it with their obscene presence—made him feel physically sick. It wasn't only that strangers had been into his garden, it was the fact that they were lepers.

Coffyn knew much about the disease. He sold cloth at every major market in the south of England, and often supplied bolts of cheaper material to priests and monks for them to give to lepers and other more worthy beneficiaries. It was while he had been staying at Winchester that he had heard from the almoner there how people contracted leprosy.

He was hazy about the details—he was no physician

or priest—but the main principle he understood only too clearly. Lepers were afflicted because of their moral degeneracy; it was a physical manifestation of the sufferer's wickedness. And that meant they were all evil.

Coffyn had spent his life unaffected by significant hardship. Throughout his apprenticeship he had enjoyed a good relationship with his master. When he had qualified and started out on his own, he already had enough expertise to be able to hold his own against almost all his competitors, and had never known want, not even when the famine had struck. Food had cost more than before, but he had not suffered as badly as some; he had merely to borrow more money. Although it was true that it was a *lot* more.

Many men who enjoyed such ease were prone to look on their poorer counterparts with sympathy and attempt to mitigate their worst hardships, but Coffyn was not of that stamp.

Just as someone who has never known want of food cannot comprehend starvation, Coffyn, who had never experienced a day's illness, could not believe that those who were struck low with so debilitating a disease hadn't brought it upon themselves. Life was God-given, and the condition of a man's life was a reflection of the way he lived: someone with disease had committed a sin. To deny that would be to allow that God could make an error—and that was unthinkable.

No, someone who was so evil that God had smitten him with this most appalling punishment must be deserving of it.

With the righteousness of the frustrated, law-abiding citizen, he punched a fist into his hand. He knew it was wrong that lepers should be provided for. If they were evil, then why should they receive charity? It was nonsensical! They ought to be evicted; turfed out of the town and forced to wander somewhere else. All the time they remained in Crediton they must blight the town. How could God look favorably on a place where His chosen victims were harbored?

His eyes slitting with the intensity of his concentration, he slowly eased himself into his chair, and gradually a smile spread over his face.

"What do you think, Baldwin?" asked Simon as they left Godfrey's hall. Edgar had already been dispatched to the inn to see what his charming spy could tell him, and the two were alone as they made their way up the hill toward John's house on foot, leading their mounts by the reins.

"I don't know what to think, quite frankly. It seems strange that Putthe should be so keen to transfer our attention from John to the smith, but I must admit I find it hard to believe the Irishman could have murdered Godfrey."

"It was strange that Putthe should want to bring Jack into it," Simon mused.

"That struck you too, did it? Yes, Putthe might have seen John out in the yard, as he first said, but if he did, someone had already knocked out Cecily and killed Godfrey. It could have been the smith, Jack, of course, but equally it could have been John. What I don't understand is why John should have stepped back in to strike down Putthe if he had already knocked down the other two and was about to make his escape."

"Maybe John didn't realize Putthe had seen him? Or maybe he thought it was the only way to silence Putthe so he could run off."

"But he hasn't run off, he is still here," Baldwin pointed out, stopping near the Irishman's open gate. Inside they could see the man sitting comfortably on a stool with his back to the wall, sipping from a great jug of ale. "So why should a man attack someone like Putthe unnecessarily, and then not make a run for it?"

"He didn't realize he would get found out," Simon offered.

"After a murder, I tend to find most men prefer not to gamble on a thing like that—not when the stake is their own neck," Baldwin said caustically. "A killer would have bolted. This man hasn't."

"By the same token, neither has anyone else from the town, have they?" pointed out Simon reasonably. "What's good logic for John is surely good for another as well."

"I take your point: whoever *was* responsible *is* brazening it out—and of all the people in this town, I can think of none better qualified than him. He lives by deceiving people."

"You almost sound as if you admire him, Baldwin."

The knight threw him a quizzical glance. "Do I sound so? I suppose I do, really. He is gloriously unashamed. All he does, he does to please himself, without embarrassment. Yet such a hedonistic attitude can be dangerous, especially in a small town like this. It's too easy to make enemies."

"As he appears to have done."

"Yes, although I confess I believe that most of his detractors are inclined that way more as a matter of principle than from any genuine dislike for him. He just isn't unpleasant enough to upset many people, and in fact most people like him precisely because he is cheeky and irreverential. There is something attractive about a man who treats you as an equal when you both know he is not."

As they watched, John lifted his jug in salute, as if offering them a drink. Baldwin groaned. "Ah well, we might as well hear what he's got to say for himself."

* * *

John watched the two approach with a fixed smile on his face. There was no point being nervous, he knew, for any officer of the law would be likely to construe that as a sign of guilt. John had not survived the last few years by being incautious. He treated danger with great respect; it was just that his variety of respect was sometimes regarded by others as excessive flippancy.

"Sirs, I'm your servant. How can I help you, now? Are you thinking about buying something from me?"

"I think you know well enough why we are here, John," Baldwin said mildly.

"Now, there I suppose you're right. So could I tempt the pair of you to a little ale, gentlemen? You're on my property, after all, and I consider hospitality to be one of the cardinal virtues."

He was not surprised when the Keeper refused his offer; Baldwin's views on alcohol were odd enough to have become a minor talking point in Crediton. Hearing Simon's approval, John walked inside and was soon back with a small bench for the two of them, another jug in his free hand. "I'll admit it wasn't made by my own hand, sir, but you'll not reject it on that account, I'm sure. It was made by a delightful widow over at Tedburn, who was grateful that I'd take away her surplus in exchange for some little favors I had on me at the time."

Baldwin nodded sourly. He had no wish to hear what kind of favors had been so happily received.

John grinned, seeing his expression. "Only old clothes, Sir Baldwin. Nothing else."

"It was about Godfrey's death we wanted to see you."

"Ah yes, a terribly sad thing, for a man to die like that in his own house."

"You know how he died?" Simon cut in quickly.

John smiled gently, as if apologetic that a potential snare had been carelessly evaded. "And doesn't all the town know by now? The man's groom has told everyone at the inn, and that means there can be no secret about any part of it. He was found on his belly, his head stove in like a crushed egg, his servant on one side of him, his daughter on the other, and no sign of another person in the house except the girl's young maid."

"Were you there that night, John?"

The Irishman paused, the jug almost at his lips. Shrewd eyes met the knight's. "Why would I be up there?" he asked innocently.

"As to that, you might have been trying to see Mrs. Coffyn, knowing her husband was away again; or perhaps you were trying to see someone else? Or hoping to remove Godfrey's plate?"

While he took a long draft of ale, John recalculated quickly. Somehow the Keeper had guessed a great deal in a short time, but he obviously couldn't have arrived at the truth or he'd not be asking such indirect questions. He carefully set the jug at his side and folded his hands over his belly. "Well now, you seem to have unearthed some things I'd have preferred to have kept quiet, but I'll not blame you for that. No, I wasn't on my way to see Mrs. Coffyn. She's not my sort of woman. Even if she was, I'd not have tried to get to see her, not with all those damned guard chappies to protect her. I wouldn't want to meet them on a dark night! Nor was I on my way to rob Godfrey. I'm no thief, and if I was, I wouldn't be stupid enough to steal from my own neighbor."

"Why were you there, then? You were seen."

"Me?" John raised his hands, palms uppermost, in a gesture of frank unconcern. "Who could have seen me?"

"Two men, John," Simon lied blandly. "Not all Godfrey's servants were allowed out for the night. Two men stayed put."

"Come along, now," John said, but the bailiffs assertion had thrown him. He knew Putthe had caught a glimpse of him through the open door to the yard; the bottler had warned him that he'd already told the knight as much—but another? John upended his jug and waited, curbing his impatience.

"John, I know you were there for some reason," Baldwin declared. "If you don't tell me why, I'll have to assume the worst. Perhaps I might wonder whether you *were* trying to see Mrs. Coffyn, you understand? The only way I could verify that, if you won't talk, would be to see Matthew Coffyn and ask him whether he knew you were out that way that night, and could you have got up to his wife's room without his knowing. And then, I suppose, he might decide to come here and have a talk to you himself."

"I do understand your drift, Keeper." John grinned mischievously. "Could you warn me before you see him, though?"

"John, this is no laughing matter. I must know what you were doing there."

The smile didn't leave the Irishman's face, but it became hard, like a statue's, and his voice was cold as he said, "You have come here suspecting me of murder, and threatening me with exposure as an adulterer, something that would get me killed, and then say I have no right to behave as I will?" Then, as suddenly as it had appeared, his anger left him. "Let me tell you a little story about an Irishman before I answer your other questions, Sir Baldwin. Then you'll understand why I make light of anything that happens to me.

"There was this Irishman, Sir Baldwin, who was as merry a little fellow as any who lived on that lovely island. He had everything he wanted: he had a beautiful wife who had been his own since they were both fifteen years old, and as fine a little family as you could hope to see. Three boys there were, and two girls, and this little man had his own farm, with livestock of all sorts thriving happily. Oh, but he was a happy fellow!

"And then, Sir Baldwin, there came a day when this man's lord said, 'Little fellow, our country has been invaded. Our homes are threatened by monsters from over the sea, and we must protect our farms and our women. Come and help me, because I find I need an army,' and the little fellow went to the blacksmith and bought himself a good long knife, which he thought might be good for cutting the hedges when he got back, and a leather hat to protect the little brain in his little head, and he went off to join his lord as a soldier. And he was lucky, Sir Baldwin, because the little fellow didn't die with his lord. No, he managed to escape the lunatics who tried to kill him just because he was wearing the wrong badge, and got home again."

John was silent for a short space, and he stared out over the wall as if far in the distance he could see the scene. Continuing, he gripped his jug as if for support, but now his voice was less light-hearted. There was a low, angry tone to it.

"Only when he got back, Sir Baldwin, he found there wasn't a home to come home *to,* if you take my meaning. His little farm was wasted. All the cattle and animals were dead, or taken. His little family was still in the little house, and the little house had been burned, Sir Baldwin. And the little wife, Sir Baldwin, she was very little, for the soldiers had not left much of her once they had finished their playing with her."

John stood, without looking at either of them, and went inside. When he returned, his jug was filled again.

"So this little fellow, he thinks to himself, Well, I've been a good fellow all these years, and there's nothing to show for it. I worked hard to raise my little family, and now there's none left; I did all I could to protect my wife, but she was murdered; I built up my farm, and now it's gone. Maybe I'll try to enjoy myself instead. No more hard slogging to make the land produce my food for me; in future I'll take an easier occupation. And whatever happens, I'll make light of it, because there's nothing left for me to worry about. You see, Sir Baldwin, when you've already lost everything, there's nothing seems that serious any more."

Simon glanced at his friend. The knight was frowning hard at his boot, but he looked up at John's last words. "I am sorry. My words were thoughtless. If I seemed hard, you have my apologies. I can understand your feeling of loss."

To the bailiff, it seemed as though the two men, the knight and the Irishman, had a perfect understanding. They stared at each other for a moment with a kind of weary, mutual comprehension. Baldwin, Simon knew, had seen many of his friends burned at the stake after the French King had succeeded in persuading the Pope to condemn his most loyal troops, the Knights Templar, the body of which Baldwin had been a part. Both men had lost everything. It made Simon feel oddly apart—and it was something he was fervently glad of.

"So you came here afterward?" Baldwin asked softly.

"Oh, after many interesting exploits and adventures, the little Irish fellow arrived in this pleasant little town, yes. And settled as well he could, for the people generally are a nice sort of folk. They like their pleasures, and they aren't too worried about a fellow's foibles." He gave the Keeper a glance from the corner of his eye, and there was a glint in it. "Even when a fellow is tempted to recover his sight, perfectly justifiably, in the middle of a church service."

"What of the night when Godfrey died?"

"Well, I said I might speak after you'd heard my story, and you've been patient enough," John said, and stretched his leg out. It still hurt, but only intermittently. "Sir, I was there, although how those buggers saw me is more than I could say. I had been going to see someone. Someone, a friend, who needed a little help and advice. But on my way, I suddenly heard all this shouting and bellowing from Matthew Coffyn's place. It occurred to me that all this row could bring Godfrey's household out, so I dodged back carefully, and in so doing almost came across two gentlemen. It made me think to myself, courage is all very well, but maybe discretion is a useful trait as well—which is something a soldier tends to learn very early on in his career, unless his propensity for learning is curtailed by a sword. So I dodged back toward the house, there being nowhere else for me to go."

"Hold on! You say these men were in *Godfrey's* garden?"

"Yes. And it seemed to me then that they were looking for someone—but maybe they weren't. It's possible that they were themselves hiding from pursuit."

Baldwin scratched his beard. "So you went into Godfrey's back courtyard?"

"Yes, and saw with some delight that it was quiet, and that there were places for me to hide myself."

"So why go to the open door?"

"Ah, now. It was the crack. It was so loud, I wondered what it could be."

"A noise like someone striking another over the head?" Simon demanded.

"It's possible, but Bailiff, I've not heard a sound like that for many a long year. It wasn't as if as soon as I heard this noise, I thought to myself, Oh, so a man's just been clobbered over the nut! I'm a peaceable fellow, me. I don't think of such things."

"You say," Baldwin continued, "that you were trying to avoid all these men, and yet you went back to Godfrey's hall, away from your own house, and finally went into the hall. Why go inside?"

"Excuse me for being inquisitive, but if you're walking past a great hall like Godfrey's, and you see no one, no stablemen, no maids, nothing, but a great number of torches lighting the place, and a door wide open, and then you hear a loud crack from inside, now wouldn't you be a bit intrigued? Surely you'd want to glance in at the door, wouldn't you?"

"So you saw the bodies there, and did nothing?" Simon demanded. "You saw the girl unconscious, and the servant, and left them there? You were the first finder of Godfrey's body and didn't raise the Hue and Cry?"

John gave him a very old-fashioned look. "Now let's just suppose I *was* in there, and let's suppose I was about to report I'd found these three people on the floor, when I heard someone's men running toward me. And let's suppose I knew there were rumors in the town that I was an adulterer with the neighbor's wife, and let's suppose I had every reason to believe this neighbor might want to see exactly how my body fitted together by taking it apart piece by piece. Now, do you suppose I'd sit there politely, waiting for him and his men, with all those bodies lying around me? I know people here don't have a great respect for the intelligence of my folk, but I can promise you, when men are running my way with swords in their hands, I can be very thoughtful, very quickly."

Baldwin chuckled. "So you escaped out through the back of the house before Coffyn arrived?"

"As he ran in, I hopped out. There was a window open, and I went through it. It was tight, but I managed it."

"If this is all true," Simon asked slowly, "didn't you hear the scream Godfrey gave as he died? We've been told it was very loud. It was what caused Coffyn to rush round."

"He told you he came immediately? I think he must have been exaggerating," John replied primly, as if offended that another might try to mislead the Keeper. "I could hear him and his men going through his house as if they were looking for someone as I arrived in Godfrey's garden. I did hear something, and it might have been Godfrey, for all I know, but at the time Coffyn and his lads were shouting, and I wasn't concentrating on who was saying what, or where they were. I was mindful of my own affairs."

"These two men," Baldwin said, "the two who drove you back to Godfrey's house. Who were they? Did you get a clear look?"

"Well, now. I did—and I didn't. I saw them, but I couldn't swear to their faces."

"Why not?"

"Sir, it was dark. And I wasn't going to wait to ask them who they were. Like I say, there was plenty of noise from Coffyn's place, and it seemed to be getting closer. I wasn't of a mind to hang around."

"Did the two you saw in Godfrey's garden shout?"

"No, sir. From the way they behaved, I thought they were trying to ambush me."

"Whereabouts were they?" Simon asked.

"Up at this end of the garden, near the wall here," John said, jerking his head toward it. "There are some bushes, and these chaps were taking cover near them. It looked like they were waiting for someone, and what with the noise behind me, and these two waiting for me, I considered the other direction safer."

"They weren't there when you passed by on your way out?" Baldwin mused.

"Not that I saw. I don't think so. And I was looking pretty carefully."

"Why *did* you go through Godfrey's garden? Surely you had no need to trespass?"

"There are some things I don't like to do—and one is advertise my business, especially when I am protecting another's honor. Anyway, I thought it should be safe enough. I knew Coffyn was supposed to be away, and what the devil he meant by coming home so early, God only knows!"

"What was your mission?"

"That I cannot tell you."

Baldwin eyed him dubiously. The man had an easy air, as if he was truly apologetic about being able to say no more, but there was also resolution in the set of his chin. "Very well," he conceded. "But tell us what you know about Godfrey. What sort of a man was he?"

"He was the sort of man who'd steal your wallet to see how you'd survive with nothing, and then laugh when he saw you begging."

Simon raised his brows. "He was well considered in the town."

"So? What does that mean to me? You asked me for *my* opinion of him. The people of Crediton liked him because he had money, not for his character. Oh, Godfrey had a lot of money, and he was useful to some. Coffyn himself borrowed money from him, so I've been told, but . . ."

Baldwin peered at him. "Why should Coffyn ask Godfrey for money? Coffyn surely has enough and to spare."

"He's had troubles for the last three years, so I understand. Well, four months ago he had sunk to the level whereby he couldn't afford any new stock. He had to borrow, and the first man who offered to help him was his kindly neighbor, Master Godfrey of London."

"How can you know this?" Simon demanded. "You're inventing it."

"I have no need to invent, Bailiff. My information comes from an unimpeachable source."

Baldwin was aware of a fleeting sympathy for Matthew Coffyn. John was surely hinting that he knew of Coffyn's business affairs—and Baldwin suspected that he might have learned it from his adulterous affair with the man's wife. Others in the town would laugh at the expense of the husband if they were to hear.

"John, we have already heard rumors that you were having an affair with Martha Coffyn. You have also been accused of trying to rape Cecily. What have you to say about that?"

John stared a moment, then roared with laughter. "Me? With one of them? Dear Jesus! Well, Sir Baldwin, perhaps you should ask them what *they* think about such allegations!"

• •

~ 13 ~

The two men left him shortly after. Making their way to the inn to collect Edgar, Baldwin paused outside the gate to Godfrey's house. Simon glanced at his frowning expression.

"There is enough to suggest that John of Irelaunde could be the killer," he suggested.

"It is suspicious that he was there at the time, that he didn't deny being seen by Putthe. He was in the garden, certainly, and admits going into the house."

"And he could have killed Godfrey, punched Cecily, nipped out through the window, realized he'd been seen by Putthe and gone back inside to knock him out as well."

"True enough, but I find it hard to accept that Cecily wouldn't have recognized him."

"Come now, Baldwin, it was dark! She said herself that she couldn't see anything of the man."

"Except the rich scarlet of his tunic," Baldwin mused, turning from the place and strolling on pensively. "But if you caught a glimpse of someone you knew very well, wouldn't you recognize him?"

"She's a well brought-up girl," Simon reminded him.

"She probably doesn't give any thoughts to her servants, let alone an impoverished neighbor. Why should she? She is as far above them as a lioness is above a vixen. If it was Irelaunde in the room that night, she would have been so transfixed with terror at finding someone there that she wouldn't have been able to swear it was even a man!"

"A good point." Baldwin nodded. "When one catches sight of something strange, it is all too easy to let the imagination run riot."

"Yes, so if she *did* say she recognized someone, her evidence couldn't be trusted."

They were at the Coffyn house now, and Baldwin looked in. At the main door, lounging comfortably, was William, who gave the knight an affable nod.

"Now look at him," Baldwin mused, "he's about the right size and build. If he was smothered in a cloak, with something to conceal his face, he could look like John, couldn't he?"

"Only because he's short. Apart from that, there's not much to make him look like John," said Simon dismissively.

"Yes, even after a short acquaintance you'd find it hard to get confused between them, wouldn't you? And yet you're seriously suggesting that Cecily, who probably sees John almost every day, could fail to recognize him."

"In the heat of the moment—in her fear of finding someone in her house she wasn't expecting, she might have missed any clues as to who it was. And anyway, you know what women are like. They aren't like men. You or I would merely have hit the man as an intruder—but women are flighty. They work on feelings, not facts."

Baldwin winced. "Simon, you have yourself a good wife—do you honestly mean to tell me that you wouldn't trust Margaret's word compared to a man's just because she is female?"

"Oh no, that's different! She's my wife."

"Yes, but she is still a woman. No, Simon, your argument is illogical. If something happened to Cecily, you may be assured she would note it as well as you or I. Especially if she was raped."

"You are thinking of what Putthe and Coffyn said?"

"Yes. Both tried to imply that John was so lascivious in his desires that he could have tried to rape her. I cannot believe that."

"No. After talking to him, he does appear too ordinary to try to rape a wealthy girl in her father's hall."

"I didn't mean that—I was thinking about *her.* She wasn't raped! If she had been, she would have demanded that the culprit be captured. She had enough evidence, after all, with that blow to her face. No, she wasn't sexually attacked." The knight recalled the look he had caught a glimpse of in her eye. "But if she wanted to conceal something, she would be perfectly capable."

"What do you mean?" Simon asked, but his friend remained silent and thoughtful. To draw him out a little, Simon considered a new topic. "Did you know what John was talking about when he said he was taken to be a soldier?"

"The invasion, of course."

"*Which* invasion?"

Baldwin gave a faint smile. "I sometimes forget that your interests lie so firmly rooted in Devon. Let me give you a short lesson in recent history:

"The Scottish have always been quick to exploit any weakness on our part. Bannockburn gave their leaders cause to hope that they might be able to drive us from the north of our country, but it also gave them pause for thought. If they could defeat our King in open battle, why should they not take some of his other possessions for themselves? It would be costly to try to steal over to France to invade the English territories, but King Edward has other lands under him. And the Bruces were well acquainted with one.

"Edward Bruce landed in Ireland on Lady Day in 1315, at a place called Larne. He had thousands of battle-hardened men with him, veterans of Bannockburn and other fights, and the poor Irish were no match for them. Our people there had no experience of serious fighting, and had to depend on feudal levies; everywhere they met the Scots, they were rolled up. By May of 1316, Edward Bruce had conquered most of the place, and had himself crowned King."

"But John was here before that!"

"Yes, it appears he was one of the levies, and saw the destruction of his farm and family early on. After that, it's no surprise he left the country."

"What happened to Edward Bruce? Isn't he dead?" Simon frowned. He recalled hearing something of the affair in church, but it was just as he was taking over his new post as bailiff, and his interest in affairs so far away was not as important as sorting out the tinners on the moors.

"Yes, he is dead. Like so many who aspire to great things, he sought to take what he wanted ever more quickly. At the end of 1316 his brother Robert joined him. Just think, two brothers, and both pretending to different thrones! Robert brought with him a new army, and they rode out over Ireland, devastating the land. And this at the time when Ireland and England were both already laid waste by the famine."

"How did Edward Bruce die?"

"He told the Irish that he wanted to throw out the English and return the land to the ancient Kings of

Ireland. Fine words, but he insisted that he would be the new High King. Many weren't convinced he would be a good monarch—and though the Irish are poor, and often complain about losing their language and laws, for all that, they are a proud race, and have a true determination to keep their freedoms. After months of seeing how a Scottish army could trample all underfoot—you heard what John said about his farm—many chose to support the English in ridding their country of the invaders. Dublin fought and beat the Scots back when they laid siege to the city; loyal subjects in Connaught defeated them too, and soon a new army arrived—an English one, determined to throw the brothers out of Ireland forever. Robert Bruce withdrew to Scotland, and his brother was left alone. In 1318 he was beaten, and he died in the battle."

"I see," said Simon quietly. "It makes it easier to understand how John could have got to be as he is today, learning about his past. God knows how I would react to finding my home destroyed, my family dead. The poor devil!"

"Yes," Baldwin agreed. "It does make sense, once you realize how the shock must have affected him. His devil-may-care cheeriness and relaxed attitude is more understandable."

The bailiff walked on a short distance, and then stopped dead.

"What is it, Simon?"

"Baldwin, I was just thinking, if a man like John lost his wife, surely the first thing he'd want to do would be to take revenge."

"Ah, but when it's a matter of warfare, Simon, things . . ."

"No, you miss my point. If that's so, then in the same way, a man who finds his wife has been committing adultery would also want vengeance." Simon gazed back along the road toward the two houses. "And it seems everyone knows John was seeing Coffyn's wife. Surely Coffyn himself must have heard—so why the hell didn't he take a dagger to John himself?"

They meandered along the street, and hitched their horses to the rail outside the inn. Inside they found Edgar seated on his own at a table near the door. Baldwin sat at his side. "Well?"

Before his servant could speak, Cristine appeared and strode to them. "Do you want wine, Sir Baldwin?"

He smiled up at her, and she returned it brightly. As she would, he reminded himself wrily. She was no fool, and seeing how Edgar had become ensnared by her attractions, it was only sensible for her to try to similarly win over Edgar's master.

But for all his cynicism, it was hard to view her harshly. Cristine was a buxom, cheerful girl of thirty. She was remarkably unscarred by her life as a servant to travellers through Crediton, and her features carried no signs of starvation or cruelty at her broad forehead. A little over average height, she had dimples at either cheek that gave her a happy, if slightly vacuous look.

But that look was a carefully fabricated mask to conceal a sharp mind, Baldwin knew, and he motioned toward a bench, waiting until she was seated before he spoke.

"Cristine, I know that Edgar will have mentioned that I want to ask you some questions. Tell me first what you know about Godfrey."

She glanced at Edgar, but then held the knight's eyes as she spoke. "I didn't know him well, Sir Baldwin. He only rarely came in here, and then he was with someone else. It was not common for him to be here alone, so all

I do know is what I have picked up from others talking about him in here."

When he nodded, she continued. "He came to Crediton some years ago, before I began to work here myself. His household was himself, his daughter, and a few servants. Putthe is the only one left; the others have all gone now. Putthe comes here sometimes, usually with the head groom from Godfrey's house, but they rarely talk about their master. I get the impression Putthe is a close, cautious sort of man.

"What I have heard is, Godfrey was free enough with his money when it came to his horses, but other people could whistle—although he was known to lend money for interest."

"What was his temper like?" Simon asked. "Was he the sort to get involved in fights?"

"Not that I'd ever heard, sir. I had the impression he was a bitter, angry sort of a man. He snapped at us in here when we were held up and he wanted his drink, and used vicious language sometimes. I've heard he used to beat his daughter, too, but none of that means he'd pick a fight with other men."

"You mean he was a bully," Simon summed up for her.

"Yet he was apparently getting into a fight with thieves or others when he was killed," Baldwin pointed out. Then, "Tell us what you know about his daughter."

"Mistress Cecily is even more rarely seen in here than her father was, sir," Cristine protested. "She's too much of a lady to come into a lowly hovel like our little inn!"

"Yet you must have heard something of her," Baldwin pressed. "Has she any admirers? Are there rumors about her with men in the town?"

"Not that I know of. From what I've heard she's a quiet girl, keeps herself to herself. She's known to be kind, though. I caught sight of her in the street only ten days ago, or thereabouts; she saw a leper, and opened her purse to give him money. When he said something, she thought again, and emptied the whole purse into his bowl."

"Exceptionally generous," Simon murmured.

"That's what I thought too, sir. She looked quite pale afterward, and I thought she might have breathed in some of his smell, so I offered her wine, but she refused and went off home."

"What do other people say of her?" Baldwin asked.

The girl set her head to one side as if listening to the echoes of voices which might have spoken of Godfrey's daughter.

It was hard to recall all the things she had heard of the girl. Cristine had to listen and make polite conversation with all the people of the town, and usually her contribution was no more than apparent interest while her mind whirled on over other matters. It was nothing to her what a farmer might think of the neighbor's pig-breeding techniques, nor what a tanner felt about a butcher's ability to flay a calf efficiently. But some things *did* come to her.

Who was it? she wondered. It was two or three weeks ago she had heard someone talking . . .

"The leper master!"

Baldwin blinked. "What of him?"

"I heard him talking to another monk last week. It was on that really warm day, you remember?" she appealed to Edgar, who grinned in acknowledgment. "The leper master and the almoner were here, and the two of them shared a drink out in the garden. I had to serve them, and I did hear them talking about her."

"What could they have wanted to discuss her for?" asked Baldwin with frank astonishment.

"I think she had spoken to the leper master to ask

him about his charges and offer to help him—with money, I believe. Not like some."

"Who do you mean?"

"There is a girl there already. There are all sorts of rumors about her."

"Oh, you mean Mary Cordwainer?"

"Yes, poor girl. She's lost her man, young Edmund Quivil. Lost her husband-to-be; lost her whole future, if you know what I mean. And some people here are putting a horrible slant on her motives. No, I think Cecily wanted to help with money. The master was asking the almoner about her, trying to find out what he could, but I doubt whether the almoner could have told him much."

There was no need for her to explain her words. They all knew as well as she that he went about the town to distribute alms and often entered shops to purchase items needed by the poor, but the houses he entered were those of the poverty-struck, never the wealthy. In the same way, he could hardly meet Cecily while shopping. The places from which he would buy cloth, shoes or food weren't the sort that a young lady of Cecily's class would willingly go into. The almoner lived in a different sphere of the town to her.

But as Cristine considered this, another thought struck her, and she shot a glance at Edgar, wondering whether to tell him so he could bring it to his master's attention. Even as he caught a glimpse of her expression, Baldwin rumbled, "Yes? Out with it, Cristine."

She smiled again, her head lowering as she met his gaze full on. "I am sorry, Sir Baldwin, but I was thinking: if you wanted to find out what you could about Cecily, surely you'd be better off talking to the Dean, to Peter Clifford. He's the priest for the town, and he'd be more likely to know her, wouldn't he?"

* * *

William entered the hall with the careless mien of a man who knows his own position is safe enough. Whatever the reason for his urgent summons, William's conscience was easy.

He glanced about him as he walked in. Two men were playing merrils near the door, and they nodded to him as he passed. Apart from them there was only one other person in the room—Matthew Coffyn.

William ran through his dispositions: there was the man at the front door, one at Mrs. Coffyn's private room, and the last two in the stableyard. He had looked to them all a few moments before he was called, and was sure there was nothing for him to be concerned about with them, so he was curious as to why his presence had been demanded. "Sir?"

"Come with me, William."

William allowed his eyebrows to rise as he followed his master through the door behind the dais. This was the first time he had been permitted to have a view of the special strong room where Coffyn kept his money and plate.

It was a small rectangular cell. A tiny, slit-like window set high in the wall allowed in a gloomy light, and by it William could see that the place was filled. Two large chests sat on the floor, both solid and metal-bound. At each wall were shelves, and on these lay a selection of some of the best cloths William had seen. But that wasn't all. There was also some silver and pewter, although not as much as William would have expected. His fingers itched to fondle it, but now he was here, he was sure this was a test, and he forced his hands to his thick leather belt, hooking his thumbs over. He daren't appear too interested. It was more difficult to control his eyes, which sauntered over the plates, goblets and bowls with an almost salacious desire.

"You see all this?"

Coffyn's voice brought him back to the present with a snap. Fortunately, the merchant had his back to him, and hadn't noticed his expression. Carefully, William ventured the word, "Yes?"

"Used to have more. Had to hawk it like a peasant to pay a debt. It's usually Jews who fleece us, isn't it? But now it's Florentines, Genoese or other Englishmen as well! There's always someone prepared to make a profit from somebody else's misfortune."

He spun round on his heel, scowling. William maintained his disinterested stance, but he was intrigued despite himself. He wanted to know what was behind this interview.

"I was talking to one of your men today, William. He told me you're only a short while back from France. Is that right?"

The guard walked to a chest and sat upon it before giving the question his attention. Reviewing in his mind the fights he had been involved in, he couldn't see how any of his past offenses or victims could have come to haunt him here in England. He hadn't done anything wrong here, he was convinced of that. "Yes?" he said again, questioningly.

"Is it true about the peasants? Have they revolted?"

"Oh, yes!" William shrugged. He couldn't believe that Coffyn had asked him into this room simply to ask about affairs in far-off France.

"Tell me about it."

"I know little about it, sir. It's been going on for a couple of years. This time it was a group of peasants marching from the north, heading southward. They claimed that the nobles were thieves and worse, taxing the peasants too highly, that sort of thing. Said what a peasant produced in a year would be consumed in an nour by a knight. Normal rubbish you hear from the poor." William had a simplistic attitude to the pastoral folk of France. They had useful food and wine, but rarely any means of defense, and could be looked upon as a handy source of free meals.

"And what when they reached the south?"

There was a note to Coffyn's voice that made William pick his words carefully. "They stormed castles, re-eased prisoners from jails, killed bailiffs and soldiers, burned town halls and record offices—all the things you expect of a rabble."

"And the Jews?"

"Oh, *them*! Well, they set upon them, of course. Massacred them whenever they could. That wasn't a surprise. Jews hold all the money, don't they?" It wasn't something to trouble William. After all, even the Eng-ish King had eventually thrown all the Jews out of his country. The French had expelled them in 1306, and many people had applauded the action, thinking that all heir debts would be wiped out, but then the French King's son, Louis X, had let them back, with terms that meant he was a two-thirds partner in all their efforts to recover their debts.

So the peasants were repaying theirs the only way hey knew how: at the points of pitchforks and lances.

Coffyn nodded at the sentiment, but for him there was a different reason to applaud the actions.

He was a keenly religious man. That was something hat had been carefully instilled in him by his master when he was still apprenticed, and the thought that lepers might be endangering the town by their existence had taken hold. His face was flushed with excitement as he sat opposite William.

"Others were attacked as well?"

William shrugged. There was a greediness in Coffyn's

stance, almost as if he was discussing food. It was a look the soldier had seen before in the faces of zealots. "Almost anyone with a position of power, or those with money."

His master made an irritable click of his tongue and snapped his fingers in a gesture of contempt. "What of them? They hardly matter. When they are gone, God will recognize His own. Those whom He ignores won't be missed. The good will go to Heaven and should be grateful for their death for releasing them from this life of toil! No, it's the others: there was a group stoned and hanged along with the Jews, wasn't there? The lepers. Why were they also killed?"

"They were accused of being in league with the Jews," William agreed. "It was said that the lepers had agreed to a pact with the Jews in which they would be given any women they wanted from the towns, and in return they were poisoning the wells."

"It is as I thought!"

"Master, these were the ravings of peasants," William pointed out reasonably.

"You are a soldier, William; you can't understand how these things happen," said Coffyn confidently. "But you must have heard the priests talking about lepers. Their every mark and sign of disease is a divine punishment for their sins."

"What sins?" asked William, casting his mind back to a friend from an army in Spain who had developed the disease.

"Concupiscence and pride."

"Oh." Yes, he thought. That would describe his Spanish comrade well enough—randy and arrogant. Then William shifted uneasily on his seat, wondering whether he should make a visit to the church himself.

"And it is the duty of good Christians to throw these loathsome dregs from our town," Coffyn stated.

"Isn't that illegal?"

"Their monstrous sins are made visible by God in the shape of their hideous deformities."

"But they're under the protection of the Church."

"That needn't prevent citizens from helping us rid the town of them."

"How would you persuade people to help chuck them out?"

Coffyn lowered his head and grinned. "You heard what I said? These people are foul and driven by uncontrollable lust. Look at that poor Mary Cordwainer, going there every day. Can there be any doubt that the inmates of the lazar house have forced her to their will?"

"You mean they're . . . ?" William's lip curled in revulsion.

"Yes. They have polluted her, and bound her to them by their depraved behavior. I have heard it from your friend the smith."

William pursed his lips. "What'll you do?"

"It's more what I want *you* to do."

- 14 -

Baldwin and Simon waited while Edgar fetched his horse from the yard behind the inn, then all three rode to the Dean's house.

When they arrived, the place was in a flutter of activity, with servants rushing around and getting into each other's way as they cleared up after a meal. The smells from the kitchen made Simon's mouth water, and it was only then that he realized how hungry he was. He hadn't eaten all morning.

Peter Clifford was seated in his hall. Bishop Stapledon was visiting once more, and sat at his side. Baldwin and Simon took their places on a bench nearby while the Dean finished washing and drying his hands. The bailiff couldn't help giving a platter of bread a longing glance. Clifford saw the direction of his gaze and smilingly ordered the panter to bring fresh loaves and wine and set them before the bailiff. As the others spoke, Simon listened as best he could, chewing hungrily.

"The Bishop and I were just discussing the choir," Clifford said. "He was concerned that it wasn't being performed with the right degree of solemnity."

"It's important to ensure that the services are conducted with the uttermost dignity," Stapledon nodded. "They exist to praise Our Lord, and if they fail to impress someone as poor and ignorant as myself, how can we hope to please Him?"

"So what has been decided?" asked Baldwin.

"I have agreed to appoint four young clerks to assist—one to see to the sacristy, books and the ornaments under the tutelage of the Treasurer; one to be responsible for the bells; a third to attend to offerings at the high altar; and a last who will instruct the others, and inspect their morals."

Baldwin glanced at Clifford, who studiously avoided his eyes. It struck the knight that the Bishop had agreed to invest in a not inconsiderable number of new clerks for the church, while the Dean was to be the main beneficiary. Baldwin told himself not to be cynical, but he could see that the Bishop appeared tired, and wondered whether his friend Clifford might have taken advantage.

"By the way, Dean, about these fairs . . ."

Baldwin settled and resigned himself to waiting until the two priests had finished their business. Now they were talking about the two fairs Stapledon had granted the town. He was alarmed at the drop-off in tolls. This involved a great deal of poring over old parchments and rolls of figures, each of which had to be brought in by troops of monks and canons, until Baldwin was becoming thoroughly irritable. He waved to the panter for food, and soon had a large mug of watered wine and a plate of cold meats.

It was half an hour before Stapledon motioned his clerks away and peered at Baldwin. His eyesight had been failing for some years, and he needed to use spectacles now, which gave him something of the appearance of a bemused owl. "You've been very patient with us, Sir Baldwin. My apologies for keeping you waiting so long, but it's so much better to get these things out of the way when one can. My time isn't my own any more."

Baldwin dismissed the apology as unnecessary. "My Lord Bishop, we should apologize for turning up unexpectedly."

"What can I do for you, Sir Baldwin?" Clifford asked.

"Peter, I wanted to ask you about a girl in the town," he said. "It's Cecily, the daughter of the dead man. I understand she's very generous to the poor, including the lepers."

"Yes, I believe she has assisted with a few good works. Why?"

"Since her father has been killed, we have been trying to find a reason for his murder, but it's possible it was only a robbery that went wrong. I am fairly certain that a lot of Godfrey's plate has gone missing. Similarly, I have to wonder about the dead man's last words."

"What were they?"

"Apparently, 'So you'd defile my daughter, would you?' "

"What has she to say about this?"

"She says nothing. She is adamant that she was struck down by a man at the window, and knew nothing of her father's death."

Stapledon sipped his wine. "And you do not believe her."

"I wouldn't say that, my Lord—I simply don't know. But it does seem odd to me that she should walk into her hall and be instantly attacked. Most thieves would run away on hearing someone approach. And those words—they allow for some intriguing speculation."

"Obviously he came upon someone trying to rape the poor girl," said Clifford.

Simon stole a morsel of Baldwin's meat. "That's what it *sounds* like."

"What do you mean?" asked the Dean.

"If it was a simple attack of that nature, why say 'defile'? If it were a rape, wouldn't he have said just that? 'So you'd rape my daughter, would you?' Surely it's the form of words that would come most easily to a man?"

"I'm not so sure," said Stapledon. "One hears such stories nowadays: of nuns being raped in their convents, women being taken from their homes, their husbands murdered or tortured to show where their valuables are stored. These villains are bestial. If this poor man came into his hall and found these men had knocked his daughter down, and were trying to rape her, perhaps he used the first words which sprang into his mind. Defile is a very strong word, but when used against some of the footpads I have seen in my own court . . ."

Baldwin gave a slow nod. He too had seen some of the very dregs of society before him when the court was in session. How, he wondered, would he have reacted to seeing one of them pawing *his* daughter? If he had a daughter he would adore her, he felt, just as surely as Simon doted on his; and if he ever found a scruffy, degenerate, drawlatch of a man fondling her youthful body while she lay unconscious, punched in the face by her attacker, Baldwin was sure he would use stronger language than "rape." But then he would probably have used stronger language than "defile" too. In fact, he thought, he probably wouldn't have used any language at all: he would have grabbed for his sword or a club, and expressed his feelings more forcefully.

"So what do you want from me, Sir Baldwin?" the Dean enquired.

"Anything you can tell me about her, about her father, or anyone else who might have a bearing on this horrible murder."

"Well . . ." The Dean gazed into the middle distance thoughtfully. "Her father was quite a strong character, I always thought. He wasn't very forthcoming, and not particularly popular, but he always struck me as a resolute man."

"When you say he wasn't very popular, in what way?"

"Oh, he upset quite a few folk. Used to refuse to give alms to certain people. He was quite cruel toward lepers. Insulted them and once even threw stones at one who stood too close to his gate. But nothing serious, the leper wasn't hurt. Still, his attitude to those who weren't as healthy or wealthy as he, was quite off-putting."

"Did he often lose his temper?"

Clifford glanced at the knight. "He did on occasion, but usually only when it was something that bore on his daughter. I think that was why he was so harsh toward lepers, because he feared that one of them might attack her."

"Why should he think that?" Simon interrupted.

It was Baldwin who answered. "Because many people think that lepers have an insatiable appetite for sex."

"Yes," Clifford nodded. "Some think leprosy is a sexual disease, acquired by those with abnormal lusts, and shows the nature of the soul within. Others think it's caused by perverted parents, and is actually the proof of some kind of moral deviance. I think Godfrey thought so, and wanted to keep such people from his daughter."

"And stop them defiling her," Simon mused.

"It's possible," Baldwin agreed. "And what of her, Cecily?"

"Oh, she's a treasure. Where her father was hard and unswerving, she seems generous to a fault. She shows every sign of compassion and tolerance. I have tried to broadcast St. Hugh's opinion: that lepers are here to show us all the way to redemption, demonstrating by their worldly suffering what is to come; they are set before us by God as a reminder, so that we may always tread the right path. That was St. Hugh's view, and I believe in my heart that it's the correct one. Mistress Cecily is one of the few people of the town who has taken my words to heart."

"God be praised," murmured the Bishop.

"And how does she evince this care for the ill?" Baldwin probed.

"She's spoken to the master of the lepers about making a small but regular donation to assist the house, and also to offer a chantry."

Simon stared, his mouth falling open. "She wants to pay for regular mass in the lepers' chapel?"

"Yes. She won't stretch to a new altar for them, but she said she will be pleased to give them money annually if they will celebrate a mass in memory of her father, both on his birthday and on the anniversary of his death."

"That is extremely interesting," Baldwin noted. The rich often endowed a chantry on their favorite church so that they might be remembered and prayed for while they remained in Purgatory, but the knight had never known it to be paid to a lepers' place of worship. "Why should she ask for that, I wonder?"

"Because she wanted to save his soul, Sir Baldwin," Clifford said sharply.

The knight gave him a half-apologetic grin, for the Dean knew that he had little faith in the Church as an institution; after the betrayal of his Order by the Pope, his trust had been shattered. "No, Peter, I think you miss my meaning. It appears highly curious to me that she should endow this little chapel with funds, specifically to pray for her father, when she must have known how he felt about lepers. It is almost a studied insult to do so, surely? Why not give you the money to hold masses in the canonical church here, rather than at the lazar house?"

"Sometimes, Baldwin, you can be too suspicious! I am quite sure she wanted to help the poor victims of St. Lawrence's, that's all. And why shouldn't she? If she is a true believer, she should want to use her money to save as many souls as she can."

"No doubt you are right, Peter," Baldwin said soothingly. He had upset the priest, he saw, and spoke more carefully now to mollify him. "Tell me, I have also heard of Edmund Quivil's woman, young Mary. Is it true that she is working there to help your leper master?"

"Yes, it's so. She too has a strong conviction and faith. I would be glad if more people in this town demonstrated half the goodness of those two young women." His face darkened. "And I would be glad if some of those who try to smear the girl could do something useful themselves rather than slandering her."

Baldwin's eyebrows rose in his astonishment. "I am sorry, Peter, I didn't mean—"

"Not *you*! It's the others. Some people will go about casting slurs on those who don't deserve it. Young Mary Cordwainer has been insulted in the street by some who should know better. I even heard this morning that someone has been saying she is only going there for—well, saving Your Lordship's presence—for the gratification of her passionate desires."

Baldwin had to cough to stifle his laughter. It was novel to hear Peter Clifford speaking in so refined a manner. Baldwin knew that two weeks ago he had berated a drunken farmer in language the knight had only before heard on a Cinq Ports trader, because the poor fellow had dropped a cask of the priest's Bordeaux wine. Then a thought struck him. "Who did you hear speaking of this?"

"The smith, Jack, out on the Exeter road. Could you talk to him and get him to stop making such comments?"

"I think so. At the least we should go and see why he passes such gossip on," said Baldwin.

The smithy was a low, one-story shed at the eastern edge of the town, set some way back from the traffic. It was a convenient site, Baldwin knew. This road was the busiest one west of Exeter, and the smith had the custom not only of all the farmers and peasants in the town, but also all the passing travellers who might need a wheel remade, or a horse shod.

There was a large yard before the smithy, and when Baldwin, Simon and Edgar arrived, the place was alive with the ringing of steel. As was usual, the doors were thrown wide—even in midwinter the smith was often too hot to have them closed—and the three men could see a sweating figure hammering at a bolt of glowing metal. Baldwin strode to the door and entered, the other two behind him. The percussion of the metal being struck with the hammer, the ringing of the anvil, was an awful cacophony. It made Baldwin feel as if his head was being pounded, and he was tempted to cover his ears with his hands.

The smith turned, and beyond a curt nod expressed no surprise that someone had walked in. Shoving the still-glowing metal into a barrel, he scratched at his chest. Steam rose while the water spat and crackled angrily. Wiping an arm over his brow, Jack looked at them enquiringly before drinking from a huge jar of ale.

To Simon he looked like any other smith. He wasn't

particularly tall, but he made up for his lack of height by his breadth. His torso was almost as well developed as that of a man-at-arms, and was almost hairless. At either side of the bib of his heavy leather apron there were a number of welts and scars, evidence of mistakes or errors in his trade, and he had lost two fingers of his left hand.

But it was the man's face that caught the bailiffs attention. He had a low, sloping forehead which made him look as if he was thrusting his head forward aggressively, with heavy brows, a thick nose and small, widely spaced eyes.

All of this the knight took in at a glance, but there was something else that Baldwin noted, and that was that the smith avoided meeting his eye. There were few traits that Baldwin had learned over the years to distrust, but this was one. "Are you Jack?"

"Yes," he grunted, lowering the drink for a moment, then replacing it. When it was emptied, he set it down near a small barrel and stood with his arms akimbo. "Well? Is it a horse, or a cart or what?"

"It's to find out why you have been saying villainous things about a girl in the town."

"What do you mean?"

Baldwin watched him as he took a step closer. The smith's eyes were focused somewhere around the knight's left ear. "I hear you have alleged that a girl who spends her time trying to ease the pain of people afflicted with leprosy is herself no more than a harlot."

"Whoever said that was a liar. Who says it? Eh? Who accuses me?"

This was addressed to Baldwin's right ear. Apparently emotion caused his attention to wander. The knight moved to meet the man's eye, but it moved with him, and Baldwin gave up the attempt.

"You were overheard by priests. They have told me what you said. What I would like to know is, what evidence do you have for your allegation?"

"I don't need any proof."

"You do, because without it, your comments are vile slanders. And you could be forced into court for that. Do you have any proof?"

The smith's interest had moved on to the cobbles at his feet. He stood perusing them for several minutes, before giving a short shake of his head.

"What was it you said about her? That she was a wanton?"

"You know so much, why ask me?" His tone was sulky, and now a boot scraped its way over a patch of dust, sweeping it away, then moving it all back again. From his behavior, Baldwin would have assumed him to be a young apprentice, not a smith of some twenty-eight summers.

"Jack, why did you say such things about her?"

"She's only young. It's not right for her to be up there, not with that lot." He spat accurately out through the doors. The forge was cooling without attention, and he cast it a lackluster glance before going to the doors and pulling them to.

"You must say nothing more about them, Jack. If you do, I can have you amerced for slander. You understand me? I can have you fined for telling people villainous things; things which you know are untrue."

"*I* don't know they're untrue. What if it's right?"

"If there is any truth in it, you show me the proof, all right? For Christ's sake, man, think what you are doing!" Baldwin let the sea of his frustration break through the dam of his self-control. "There she is, trying to help mitigate the worst pain those poor devils are suffering, and while she's there doing God only knows what to help soothe the agony of their disease, here you are inciting people against her! It must stop."

The smith walked to his barrel and refilled his mug. Adopting an air of unconcern, he met the stare of Baldwin's right shoulder. "Is that all?"

"No! What were you doing up at Godfrey's house on the night he was murdered?"

"What? I was only there for a while . . ."

"When did you get there?"

"I was there late afternoon. There was a mare had lost a shoe, and I had to—"

Simon cut him off. "How long did it take?"

"All I had to do was nail it back on, it was hardly anything . . ."

"Did you come straight back here?" Baldwin shot.

"No! No, I went into Putthe's buttery."

"Why?"

"To take a drink with him. It's not illegal!"

"How long for?"

"I don't know. It was after dark, that's all I—"

"How many ales did you drink?" Baldwin rasped.

"I don't know—ask Putthe, he can tell you."

Simon gave Baldwin a scarcely perceptible glance with a faint shrug.

The knight fixed his eye on the smith again. "So you say you went to the hall in the late afternoon, made a new shoe . . ."

"No, all I did was refit the old one."

"So you nailed it back on, went through to the buttery—was it dark by then?"

"Oh, no. It was a good hour before nightfall."

"And in the buttery you drank quarts of ale with Putthe. Did he leave you alone while he got on with his duties?"

"No, he said there was nothing for him to do."

"But you didn't leave until night?"

"That's right. I can remember it quite clearly: it was so black outside I tripped over a loose cobble in the road, and I thought to myself, If this was daylight, I'd not have missed that."

"And you left Putthe asleep?" Simon interrupted again. "Did you hear a man shouting? A scream, anything like that?"

"No, sir. If I had, I'd have gone back immediately. No, if I'd thought poor Master Godfrey would be dead so soon after I was drinking his health with him and—"

"He was with you in the buttery?" Baldwin asked. "For how long?"

"Not long. He walked in before checking his fencing. Looked surprised to see me there, but he had a drop of ale with me and Putthe before he went out."

"Did you see anyone else in there? Did Mistress Cecily come in?"

"No, sir. No one 'cepting the master himself."

"Which way did you come home?"

"Along the main road, through the town, past the church, and down the hill to here."

"Did you see anyone else on your way?"

"No, sir, it was empty. But it was quite late."

"Is there anything else you *can* tell us about that night? Anything you feel could help us find the murderer?"

For the first time the smith let his eyes fleetingly meet the knight's, and Baldwin saw he was debating whether to mention something, seeking reassurance from the Keeper before raising it. "Yes?"

"It's nothing, I daresay, but as I left the place, I could have sworn I heard voices in the hall itself. A man and a girl."

"Did she scream, or cry out in some way?"

"You asked me that," Jack said peevishly. "I told you, no one screamed or anything while I was there, but I was fairly sure I heard these two voices. Just talking low, almost whispering. There was one thing, though: the girl sounded sad, I reckon. Really sad."

- 15 -

Riding from the little smithy, Baldwin turned to Simon and held out his hands in a gesture of bafflement. “So what do *you* make of all this? I tell you now, I feel that the more people I speak to, the more confusing it becomes.”

Simon tilted his head on one side. “You know as well as I do that often these crimes are utterly incomprehensible until you have all the facts laid out, and then the whole picture locks together. At least we know the people who were present, which means we can isolate who might have had a motive to crush Godfrey’s skull.”

“I suppose so, but I wish I knew who the two were in Godfrey’s garden.”

“If John was telling the truth and wasn’t simply confused by seeing two bushes in the dark, you mean?” Simon chuckled. “Come on, Baldwin, don’t look so glum! You’re on your way to meet your Lady.”

“Oh, shut up!”

Simon laughed. They made their way into the outer fringe of the town, then on up to the church. Here they were about to turn right to head up to the north, when the bailiff saw Cecily’s maid at her gate. “Baldwin?”

Following his friend's gaze, the knight gave a low whistle.

At the entrance to Godfrey's house, hidden from the road by the wall, and only visible from this angle because the gate was ajar, Alison stood laughing and chatting to John of Irelaunde. As Baldwin watched, he saw John tweak a curl from her wimple and chuck her under the chin.

"That bloody Irishman," Simon grumbled. "Look at him!"

"He certainly appears to take his pleasures where he can," Baldwin chuckled. "Ah, and who's this?"

Riding toward them was William. He smiled broadly to them, and jogged off back the way they had come. The knight stared after him. "I wonder where *he's* off to?"

Jack wiped his hands on his heavy leather apron, and stood contemplating the view bitterly. The questioning by the Keeper had unsettled him. The smith was a man of few words normally, and now he felt as if he had been forced into giving away too much—something he could regret later. Jack was all too well aware of the risks of telling law officers too much. It often led to a man being arrested and hanged.

There was a scuttling noise near the forge, and he turned to see his cat lying, tail twitching, watching a large rat scrabbling for a crumb. Jack let out a curse, and swung his boot at the cat, who, realizing her master was not of a mind to scratch her ears, flattened them against her skull before pelting off to a dark corner where she judged she should be safe enough.

Jack turned back and supped ale, disconsolately studying the sweep of the river. He was still standing there, his great mug in his fist, when he was hailed.

Entering his yard was a cheerful-looking man on a

decent palfrey. "Smith? Can you make me a shoe? My fellow here has cast one."

Jack looked up into William's face and grunted.

"I'm very glad to find you here," said William with feeling, falling from his saddle and strolling to a bench while Jack set to pumping the bellows. The guard held his hands to the fire, a small frown creasing his brow. He had also seen John and the maid in the road, and it had interested him a great deal. He decided he would have to tell his master as soon as he returned to Coffyn's house. For now, though, he had another task to perform.

He grinned up at the smith. "Smiths always hear all the gossip before anyone else. But I suppose you need a tale in exchange, yes? Have you heard what the lepers are up to?"

•

Baldwin walked into his hall and threw his gloves onto the table. Margaret was there, sitting at the fire as she unpicked stitches from a tapestry. When Simon walked in, she stood to greet him, and he glanced down at her work.

"But you never make mistakes with your needlework!"

"Sometimes even the best seamstress must have a bad day," she said. "How has yours been?"

Baldwin bellowed for Wat and sank down into his chair. His boots were too tight, and after wearing them all day, his feet felt as if they had swollen so much he would never be able to get them off. "Where is that blasted lad? WAT!"

"Don't shout at him, Baldwin," Margaret said urgently. "You're not the only one to have had a bad day."

Baldwin and Simon exchanged a glance as the boy came in, snivelling. Immediately behind him was Emma.

To the knight she looked as threatening as a warhorse pawing at the ground, and he flinched as he felt her eyes flit over him, registering his mud-bespattered hose and tunic, the hair lying lankly where he had been wearing his hat, and his booted feet.

"That dog of yours," she stated firmly, "ought to be killed."

Emma was disgruntled. This place was so far from anywhere important, she was seriously alarmed her mistress might choose to marry the knight and move here permanently. Here! So far from any decent town or city.

It had been bad enough when she had been told she was to join Jeanne when her charge was wedded the first time, to Ralph of Liddinstone. That was very hard, when she was so fond of the shops of Bordeaux, the little pie shops and sweetmeat stalls where she could purchase whatever she wanted while escorting Jeanne around, but she had accepted that it was necessary for her mistress to be married, and had finally agreed to stay with her.

But for little Jeanne to consider coming to a benighted spot like this was intolerable! The road—hah, it was what passed for a road here, at any rate—was little more than a quagmire. At the moment it was frozen into reddish muddy ruts, each of which threatened to snap the bones of a horse's leg, but the nearest town was miles away, either northward up to Tiverton, or south to Crediton or Exeter. There was *literally* nothing in between, just a few hamlets filled with grubby peasants and their ragamuffin brats. How could poor Jeanne consider living in a place like this?

Crediton wasn't so bad, she'd grudgingly agreed that yesterday when Jeanne had asked. But that was when they had only just entered the town, and soon Emma's attitude had changed. In its favor, at least Crediton had some cobbles, and there were walkways so that ladies and gentlemen did not have to trail their finery in the filth of the sewer, or in the horse dung that lay all over . . . or in the feces from dogs and cats, goats and sheep, steers and heifers. In real towns, she had reminded her mistress scathingly, such wastes were found only in the market area where butchers and tanners plied their trade, but Crediton was such a one-road place that the animals got everywhere.

This farm, where the "noble" knight lived, was hardly good reason to want to live here. Emma could only gaze around her with scorn. There were no fine paintings on the walls, no elaborate carvings; it was just somewhere where a wealthy peasant wouldn't have looked out of place. She glanced around the hall. A large table for Sir Baldwin and his guests lay at the far end, and the rest of the rush-strewn floor held other benches and tables—for the most part trestles that could easily be cleared away. There was no grace or elegance about it whatever.

And then there was the dog.

"Killed?" Baldwin repeated with horror. "But why? Uther's always so gentle."

"Gentle? I suppose you think when the monster knocks you flat on your back and stands slavering at your throat, he's being playful?" Emma's lip curled into a sneer. Her logic was unanswerable, she knew. She had always had a detestation for dogs of all sorts. Their slavish obedience, their fawning displays of affection and the filth they would eat, made her stomach churn. As if that wasn't enough, she had a horror of the huge teeth. They looked too much like those of a wolf. "That dog should be killed," she said again, with emphasis on the last word.

"But my dear woman, I really must say that I think Uther was only—"

"Why you should think my mistress would consider living in a hovel running with flea-bitten, mangy runts like that, I don't know. As if it wasn't enough that she should be killed by your hounds while she's asleep, I expect she'll scarcely get any rest, what with the fleas and other things. A fine place! The only way to get this household fit for a lady like her is to have the dogs out where they belong, in their kennels."

With that, having confirmed that Baldwin's face was as shocked as she had hoped, Emma rotated her massive bulk and steered a course through the door and out.

Baldwin passed a hand weakly over his forehead. "Is it true that she really has gone?" he asked. "I swear, if I'd had a javelin here, I would have hurled it at her, whatever the consequences!"

"Don't worry, Baldwin," Margaret said sympathetically. "I'm sure she's not as bad as all that once you get to know her. Maybe it's just that she's some way from home and feels a little uncertain."

"I rather think she has too many certainties for my liking," Baldwin pointed out acidly. "And what in the name of God has got into *you*, Wat my lad?"

For answer, the boy began to weep, and covered his face with his hands.

"God's Blood!" muttered the knight. "I really believe this household has gone mad in the last day. Wat, calm yourself—and if you can't, go out to the buttery and fill yourself with strong ale. Ah! Hugh—what the hell has been going on in here? What's the matter with *him*?"

Hugh watched the lad shuffle out, and set his jaw. "It was *her*," he said contemptuously. "She said the fire in her lady's room wasn't hot enough, and when Wat tried to make it burn better, he dropped an ember on her cloak and burned a hole. She clouted his ear for it."

"He'll have to learn to be more careful," said Baldwin.

To Hugh he looked very pensive, and it wasn't due to the murder, Hugh thought. Simon's servant had known the knight for several years now, and Hugh had seen him investigating enough other crimes to know some of his moods, but he had never yet seen Baldwin in so irascible a temper.

No, the trouble was that Baldwin was so keen on this woman, Jeanne. It was as plain as a black sheep in a white flock that he wanted her. But he was terrified of the woman's servant.

That was a position that Hugh could understand. As far as he was concerned, the bitch was mad. She had slapped Hugh's mug from his hand at the inn, wasting over a pint of ale, just because she thought he'd had enough—as if she could tell. He'd only drunk two quarts, and that was nothing for him. Especially after a long ride like the one they'd had to get to Crediton. She'd come up, slapped his wrist and sent the lot flying. It had shocked him so much, he'd not been able to make any complaint, not even when she grabbed him by the nape of his tunic and hurled him out into the hall. Landing on the floor like that had been humiliating. And Hugh didn't like being humiliated.

He also didn't like people who disliked dogs. Hugh was a farmer's son from the old moor hamlet of Drewsteignton, and had grown up on the open land around there, spending much of his time as a youth protecting the flocks. He knew dogs as well as any who spent their life with only a pair of sheepdogs as companions: he knew their strengths and their few weaknesses, and anybody who could want to condemn a dog to death for no reason was no friend to Hugh.

A moorman learns early on to value self-reliance. When a man lives out in the moors, he has to shift for himself. But a shepherd develops other skills: how to be devious, how to trap and destroy many wild things by stealth. Hugh stood grim and silent as Edgar walked in, holding Uther by the collar, watched as Baldwin laid a hand on his head and stared the dog full in the face contemplatively. Hugh's expression darkened, and the room was quiet as they all waited expectantly.

"Baldwin, you can't," said Margaret quietly.

The knight held his mastiff's head in both hands and stared into his eyes. "Uther, old friend, I don't know what to do."

"Sir, surely you should just lock him away in the stable or something," said Edgar.

"What? You don't want him put to the sword straight away?"

Edgar shifted from one foot to another, almost embarrassed. "It would be a great pity to kill the brute just because a maid doesn't choose to like him. Poor old Chopsie isn't vicious. I'd stake my life on it!"

"Chopsie?" asked Margaret.

"Don't ask! Lock him up, then," said Baldwin, and stood. "And now I am going to change out of these clothes. Excuse me, Margaret."

He left the room without a backward glance, which looked to Hugh like a determined effort to appear blasé. But Hugh knew how much Baldwin's dog meant to him, and at that moment his mind began to scheme and invent methods of avenging Uther.

William waited while the hoof was cleaned and rasped into shape, and while the new shoe was forged and fitted. Only when the new one was nailed in place, did he offer to buy the smith an ale.

It took more than William had expected. The smith appeared to have an insatiable thirst, and yet managed to remain upright. It was not long before William found himself having to pretend to drink in order to prevent himself getting too drunk to continue with his careful prompting.

His task was made the easier by the presence of a man, Arthur, whom William had noticed about the street but to whom he had never spoken. Arthur, he learned, was a fishmonger, and Arthur was possibly even more bigoted than Jack. For some reason, Arthur was convinced that the sole reason for his sales having fallen off was that lepers were allowed into the town.

"I mean, why should they be let in, eh? What good do they do? And all the time they're leching after our wives and daughters."

"They're an offense in the sight of God," William offered sanctimoniously.

"Of course they are. Just look at the way they go around whining and begging. If they really wanted to get better, they'd go to their chapel and pray—that's what I'd do! I wouldn't sit around whinging, demanding money from strangers all the time. No, I'd get off my arse and pray to God, that's what I'd do."

"But you hear stories about them," said William, dropping his voice to a low whisper.

Arthur nodded emphatically. "That's right. The bastards. They're in league with heretics and Jews. They've all agreed to attack us, and take all our property."

"And our women," added Jack, taking another swig of ale. "And what then? That's what I'd like to know. They're all such dirty bastards. God knows what they're doing to poor Mary Cordwainer. She's going up there every day. Helping them, she says. Cleaning up and such. Who believes her? *I* don't, I can tell you. No, they have her doing something else for them, that's what I reckon," he said, and made an emphatic gesture.

"You think so?" asked Arthur. "That's disgusting,

that is! I've known little Mary all my life, and I'd never have thought—"

"Well, she was going to get engaged to Edmund wasn't she? It's no surprise she went up there at first but to be still going there every day? No, she's been perverted into their ways, that's what's happened. Poor girl."

Jack stared angrily at his jug. William almost said something to prompt him on, but then decided against it. The smith had the look of a man who took time to come to his conclusions, but with the inevitability of molten metal slowly pouring from a clay vessel into a channel, once he had started on a theme, he would follow along the track until he came to a solution which satisfied him.

When William left the inn, tugging his thick green velvet cloak about him against the frosty air, he felt well pleased with himself.

In the leper camp, Ralph finished his work and leaned back on his stool, his eyes shut as he allowed them a moment's rest before packing up for the night. Day had ended long ago, and he was writing with the help of a small candle, whose flame was almost unequal to the task of shedding a little light on his parchment. Yet he was grateful for the meager amount it gave. He knew that it was provided by the kindness of others who had no need to supply him with anything.

It was frustrating to write up his accounts in this way late at night when he was already exhausted, but there was so much to do during the day. He had the small garden to help cultivate, the chapel to keep spotless, the services to hold in order to protect his little flock, and the never-ending round of helping the inmates to change their bandages and apply ointments.

Many of them were showing the onset of the more serious symptoms, and their pain was all too evident. It was a hard cross to bear for Ralph, but he had no idea what he could do, other than clean their sores, wrap up the worst of the weeping wounds, and try, by his own example, to show how they might each hope to gain entrance into Heaven.

Three were showing no signs of accepting their fate. It was a cause of constant worry to Ralph, for his most urgent and pressing duty was to ensure that they all reached that state of grace whereby they might die at peace with God and the world. Alleviation of their pain was, when all was said and done, only a short-term issue. Their souls were the important thing.

And of them, one was most pressing of all. The other two, Thomas Rodde and Edmund Quivil, had plenty of time to learn the error of their ways and come to thank God. No, the real problem lay with old Bernard.

His speech was difficult for the monk to understand, but Ralph had learned that his life had been full of hardship, for he had once been an important soldier in the service of the King, fighting away on the Welsh Marches, before he had caught this evil canker. Now the body that had been strong and vital, which had held its own in a hundred bloody campaigns, was falling apart, eaten away from within.

Bernard had been struggling against his fate for long enough now, and he was almost ready to surrender, but not easily, and not willingly. To Bernard, life itself was the sacred essential—he simply couldn't, or wouldn't, understand Ralph's insistence that he should give himself up to God with enthusiasm. The old warrior wanted to contest every step, as if taking part in a rearguard action. But his enemy was as implacable as himself, with greater resources and powers. As Bernard failed and gradually sank, Ralph was ever more aware of Death waiting at the side of the mattress.

If only Ralph could have persuaded him to confess his sins, he would have felt that he had achieved something, but the hunched, wretched figure refused. It had now come to pass that he permitted the cleric to dress his wounds, but made it clear that he preferred the company of Rodde and Quivil at his bedside. The three of them had some kind of compact in which they all accepted their status as outcast. It was as if their very difference from the society that shunned them was itself a badge to be worn with pride.

He found it profoundly hard to talk to them and explain how dangerous their actions were. If they wanted to enjoy any peace in the afterlife, they must reject their fixation with the secular world, and prepare for Heaven. Only the week before he had suggested it to Rodde. The stranger had laughed, with a quiet, distracted air. "Look at me, Brother. Look at these sores and wounds. Do you really think that me saying to God, 'I am sorry for whatever I might have done,' will win me a place in Heaven? I don't even know what I'm supposed to have done to offend Him!"

"My son, His will is not for us to understand," Ralph had answered, but he knew he was fighting the wrong battle, for he didn't believe it himself. He wanted to; he wanted to think that the passport to Heaven was the simple acceptance of guilt, but his logical, educated brain couldn't quite adopt it as a principle. If God Himself had chosen to cause this disease, and had selected these men to make this cruel example, Ralph had a sneaking suspicion that it was not they who should be demanding forgiveness.

Even without the certainty of conviction, Ralph carried on: "Look at all the good people around here. They

ll pray for you, so that you may save yourself, for they
ll know that a single soul saved is an unending delight
› God and the angels. They want you to admit your
ns to God so you can be taken to Him. They are all
illing you on, for your own good. They pray for you.
an't you confess? It would make you a great deal more
omfortable."

"You think these people are all keen to see me saved?"
t that, Rodde began to laugh. "I hope, Brother, that
ou manage to keep your naïvety. But don't be too de-
ressed when you're let down, will you?"

Ralph bit the end of his quill at the memory. He stared
ıto the distance with a wrinkled brow before throwing
ıe feather down with a gesture of impatience. The sad,
urt and vulnerable expression on Rodde's face had
ıade him want to fall at his feet and pray for him on the
ɔot. More than other lepers, Rodde seemed to feel the
ideous reality of his doom. Ralph had noticed before
ıe signs of education, the marks of a man brought up in
higher station, and he was given to reflect how much
ıore terrible it must be for a man who had a bright fu-
ıre to accept God's judgment in this way, rather than a
ull serf who could only expect hard work and a short
fe. It made Ralph even more sympathetic.

And Rodde's difference was what attracted others to
im. It was his learning that made Bernard ask for him.
he two would whisper together about strange lands
ıd peoples that Ralph had never heard of. They were
curious pair, the old dying man on his mattress, the
ɔunger one kneeling, gripping his ever-present staff.

Edmund Quivil was similar, in that he too couldn't
elieve that he would soon be gone. He too stood apart
om the other lepers in the camp, and feeling himself a
bel, naturally attached himself to Rodde and Bernard.
hese three comprised the incorrigibles—the ones who

would never conform. Except there were only the two now. Poor Bernard had died as night fell, and soon Ralph must go and prepare the body.

He sighed. Next, he knew, it would be Joseph's turn.

There was some kind of commotion outside, and it was intruding on his thoughts. Muttering to himself Ralph carefully snuffed the candle—such lights were too valuable to waste—and made his way to the door.

As soon as he opened it he realized it was more serious than he had thought. Torches burned, and by their light he saw little groups of lepers standing fearfully staring toward the gate. As Ralph gaped, he saw Rodde stumble in, falling to his knees just inside the compound. What Ralph had taken to be some kind of sack rolled from Rodde's back, and grunted as it hit the ground. Only then did he recognize it as Edmund Quivil.

Running over, he knelt beside the two. Touching Rodde's shoulder, he murmured softly, "Who did this to you, my son? Who would dare?"

The eyes opened, and Rodde gave a twisted grin. "Our friends the townspeople. You remember—the ones who pray for us, and will us to find peace with God. It was them, Ralph. They found us in the street and chose to welcome us by throwing cobbles at us. They are good friends, Brother. No doubt they will pray for us at the next mass they attend."

- 16 -

Margaret entered the hall at her husband's side, and as soon as she was through the door she peered at the main table, seeking Jeanne. There was no sign of her, and Margaret hesitated when she realized Jeanne had not yet come. She was half-tempted to go and fetch the guest of honor. Simon's grip reminded her that she couldn't. Not in front of all these people.

Baldwin had arranged a feast to celebrate Jeanne's visit, and had insisted on having his servants and reainers in his hall to dine with him. The place was filled. Baldwin's table at the top, on the low dais he had recently installed, was set out, and Baldwin had his seat in he middle, his sideboard with its two shelves filled with his most elegant and costly plate. It was all of pewter, and Margaret was sure that none of it would be of a superior enough quality to impress Jeanne, but the fact hat he had set it out made a statement. Jeanne already knew that Baldwin lived the life of a rural gentleman, and the fact that he had ordered his best and most costly goods to be displayed could only impress her with the mportance he attributed to her.

However, Margaret was worried. She knew all too

well how much Baldwin had looked forward to the young widow's arrival. Although he had spent but a short time with Jeanne, when all of them had been staying with the Abbot of Tavistock, he had soon become smitten with the elegant lady from Liddinstone; Margaret had quickly agreed with Baldwin's early opinion that she would make a suitable wife for him. It was saddening for her to see how this visit, which Baldwin had arranged with the intention of asking Jeanne for her hand, was so quickly becoming a disaster. If she could, she would have counselled Jeanne to send her maid away immediately, for Emma was the problem.

But for now, Margaret had thoughts only for the knight. He sat at his old table, waving her and her husband on with every indication of pleasure. The servants were waiting, one with the bowl of water and towel, the panter with his loaves of good white bread, Edgar with his jugs and bottles, Wat waiting anxiously to run to the kitchen and tell them to bring the food to table as soon as the last of the guests should appear. But there was no sign of Jeanne.

"Margaret, my dear, please sit here. Simon, you take your place at her side." Baldwin peered toward the door, and noticed Hugh sidling in and seating himself beside one of Baldwin's cattlemen. That was all, then, apart from Jeanne.

Then he heard a whispered comment, and a light step, and suddenly the door behind him that led to his solar opened, and in came Jeanne.

He had never seen her look more lovely. Her face was framed by her red-gold hair, which was plaited and coiled under a light veil, setting off her regular, if slightly round features. She had a pale complexion, and this was perfectly complemented by the fine scarlet tunic she wore, with simple white embroidery at the neck and hem. Her face, with its mouth looking wide and stubborn, the upper lip more prominent, was at first glance grim, and Baldwin felt a quick tug at his heart, as if at a premonition, but then, when her clear blue eyes met his, and she recognized his appreciative wonder, her face broke into a smile.

Margaret, watching them closely, felt a rush of elation at the way that Baldwin quietly led his guest to her chair and sat her down. It was as if he was walking in a dream, entranced by his guest's loveliness, and she almost wished there were musicians to play some light, airy and above all cheery tunes. It would be a fitting accompaniment.

But the scene was ruined as Emma came out and glowered at the assembly. She took in the seated men at their benches with a sneer, before studying the upper table. All at once the light of battle shone in her eye.

Edgar went to her side and was about to escort her to a seat near the dais, when she froze him with a look. Instead, she went to her mistress and stood at her side, where she could not be ignored. "My lady, I understand I am to be seated at the common mess there. Was this your wish?"

Jeanne threw a harassed glance at the indicated seat. "What is the matter with it, Emma? It is near me here in case I need—"

"It is not for me to sit with common farmers and serfs!" she whispered furiously, bringing her mouth close to Jeanne's.

"I do not see any threat to you by sitting there, Emma. Go to your place and eat!"

"Very well. But no good can come from it. Remember, Mistress, that I warned you and it was you yourself who insisted I should sit there," the woman said, and swept down off the dais to her seat.

Baldwin noticed that the exchange and her common neighbors didn't affect her appetite. Emma set to with gusto, carefully selecting the best lumps of meat from the stew, the best slices from the cuts presented. Such behavior showed an appalling lack of manners and would have been frowned upon in the meanest household. To his way of thinking, Jeanne was perfect in every way—she was his ideal woman—but now he found that while he wanted a marriage contract with her, when he conjured up in his mind the scene of domestic bliss that she represented, he couldn't leave out of the delightful prospect the human contagion that was Emma. Where there was peace, she would bring enmity; where there was calm, she would bring strife; where there was comfort and ease, she would inevitably poison it.

Baldwin wanted Jeanne, but he most categorically *did not* want Emma into the bargain.

Edgar had done well, he saw. The best available meats and fowls were laid out and steadily consumed. And yet Baldwin found he didn't have an appetite.

In the town, William arrived at the hall wearing a pensive frown. He had done the best he could, and he was reasonably satisfied. It hadn't taken much to wind up the smith into a vindictive rage against lepers in general and as William had walked home, he had seen two of them limping and shuffling back toward their lazar house. He had felt agreeably confident that they would meet Jack and his friend and had halted, listening. Sure enough, soon he heard the sneers and taunts, then the cries as stones were hurled.

Now, leaning at the door and staring back the way he had come, he could see that there were few fires or candles burning. It was late enough, and most people were ılready in their beds, but here and there a stray beam ightened the gloom. His own master was not yet abed, or if he was, wasn't asleep, for the shutters of the bed-chamber in the private block were showing clearly, out-ined by the yellow glow, and William could hear voices: his a low rumble; hers a malevolent whisper. A door slammed, and William heard Coffyn stride through the hall. Glancing over his shoulder, he saw his master at the screens. Matthew ignored his guard and walked out o the garden.

William shook his head. It was not good to see a cou-ple so bitter toward each other. God knew it happened often enough, but that didn't make it any better. His master couldn't control his wife, and that was wrong.

Turning, he walked through the screens to the hall and peered inside. Two of his men were drinking and playing dice, while another was rolled in a heavy cloak and lay asleep on a bench. Glancing at the dice players, William guessed they must be playing Raffle. It was the only game the heavily bearded Welshman, who was even now groaning as he counted his score, knew the rules for.

Grinning at the curses hurled at the dice, William walked on along the passage and out into the yard after his master. Something, he didn't know what, was setting his nerves on edge. Standing on the threshold, he leaned against the doorpost.

There was another light, this one from the house next door. It was broad, like a partly opened window, and as he watched, he saw it darken and become smothered, then blaze again. It looked as if someone was standing before an open shutter—or climbing through the window, hiding for a moment the bright candlelight inside. Intrigued, he stepped quietly along the path until he came to the stone wall that separated the two properties.

Godfrey had built his wall highest at the road. Here, at the boundary of his own and Matthew's properties, it was only some five feet high, and William could just peep over. At first he could see nothing, but William was experienced in warfare, and a man who has mounted guard over encampments learns how to watch and listen. He stood, his mouth slightly open, staring at nothing, but waiting for a sound or movement to catch his attention. Soon he heard it.

It was a faint rustle, then the snap of a twig. A man was stealthily making his way round from Godfrey's hall toward the kitchen. As William concentrated, he could just make out the muffled and cloaked shape of someone crouched low, someone stepping cautiously along near the hall's wall. As soon as he was away from the yard area, which, although it was dark and unlighted, must have felt threatening by virtue of its being a large, open space, the figure came upright, apparently staring back the way he had come. As William watched, he saw the man—for he was sure it was a man—raise one hand and hold it to his face for a moment before letting it fall.

That was when William decided to make his presence known, and he pursed his lips to give a piercing whistle.

The man dropped his hand, gave a short bleat as if of terror and bolted away, behind the kitchen, up over the enclosing yard wall, and off.

William was still laughing as he shut the door behind him and returned to the hall.

The food all done, Baldwin washed his hands again in the bowl of warm, scented water, and dried them.

Jeanne watched him with renewed interest. She had begun her meal feeling irritable with her maid, but once Emma had been removed, and the food began to arrive she had lost her annoyance, and with the knight beside ıer trying so hard to make sure she was at ease, she had ound herself succumbing to that warm, pleasurable ensation of being desired and pampered.

There were conventions, of course, and Baldwin was crupulously polite and charming, although at certain noments she caught a gleam in his eye, as if he was naintaining the outward aspect of gentility with diffi-ulty, and would prefer to take her outside, away from ll these eager eyes, to a place where they might talk and augh together without restraint.

It was like that first meal they had eaten, a year ago n Tavistock: on that occasion they had been placed to-ether, and then observed closely by the Abbot as well s Simon's wife, Jeanne recalled. The whole time she ad felt Margaret's gaze on her, as if watching for the lightest indication that Baldwin and she might be pre-ared to pledge their vows. It had been aggravating, and ad caused the same reaction in both, that neither vanted to speak to the other. It was only later, as they vere leaving the room, that Baldwin had tentatively sked her to join him in a quiet walk, away from the iew of people whose sole desire was to see them en-aged, and whose enthusiasm for the alliance was so verwhelming that it threatened to prevent it.

Servants and bondsmen were rising from the tables nd standing talking, but she saw that their attention vas focused on her and their master. There was a neasuring quality in their looks, as if they were as-essing what sort of a mistress she might be to them: vhether she would be harsh and might order them vhipped for being late with her food or logs for her re; or whether she would be kindly, a gentle lady who vould show them compassion, who would tend to neir wants, who would see to it that those who were n need would get help.

They could not know that Jeanne herself had not ha
an easy life. Her first husband was dead, God b
praised! When he died of that sudden fever which ha
struck him down, she had sworn that she would b
careful in her selection of a new husband if she was eve
to remarry, and she had vowed never to show a servan
needless cruelty.

There was nothing she could do that would convinc
any of these people as to the quality of her tempera
ment; she would only win them over once she was mis
tress here—*if* she ever was, she added to herself.

"Jeanne . . ."

She turned to face him, and was surprised to see tha
his expression was quite blank, as if he was keeping hi
own feelings hidden behind an emotionless mask. "Ye
Sir Baldwin?"

"Some people can be fearful about dogs, I know. I
fact, I know some ladies hate them."

"I cannot understand why."

"But some hounds . . . like my mastiff, for exam
ple . . . can be rather fierce-looking. And some ladie
even those who are well-bred and noble, can feel re
volted by such ugly brutes."

"Sir Baldwin," she said softly, trying to suppress
smile, "if you are asking whether I am scared of you
dog, I am not; if you feel that I think him ugly, I do no
if you fear that I would not have such a hound in m
house, all I can say is, I would feel safer with a dog suc
as he in my house than with ten men-at-arms, becaus
Uther is loyal by nature, not by purchase."

The knight gave a heartfelt smile of relief and grat
tude. They had all eaten their fill, and the last of th
wine and ale had been consumed. At length he stoo
and all those remaining at the tables rose to their fee
Baldwin was about to leave the room when he realize

that Jeanne hadn't moved. She was watching him with a raised eyebrow, and on catching her glance, he gave an apologetic smile and held out his hand to help her up. "Would you like me to have the fire remade, Lady? I would be happy to sit with you. There is much I would like to talk to you about."

Jeanne seemed pensive. "You remember that walk we took last year?"

"Of course! That was where we saw the monk running from the girl."

"I was thinking," she said caustically, "of the pleasantness of walking with you. Not of the fact that it led you to finding a murderer."

"I know," he chuckled. "In fact, so was I. Would you like to walk around my grounds tonight?"

"Why, Sir Baldwin, I fear I would feel the cold."

It was with those same words that she had refused him at first a year ago. Then he had been devastated, thinking that she was refusing him any opportunity of speaking with her in private. Now he bowed, mock-seriously, and inclined his head toward the door. "But if you were to have your cloak brought down, you would be fine, wouldn't you?"

Her face was transformed. To Baldwin it looked as wonderful as watching the sunlight flooding over the land on a clear summer's morning. The reserved, almost cold expression she had worn through the meal became a bright, delighted smile. She jerked her head to Emma, and the maid, glowering, slammed through the door to the solar. Within a few minutes she was back, a heavy woollen cloak trimmed with fur over her arm. And a thick jacket on her back. Out of the corner of his eye, Baldwin noticed Hugh quietly leave the room.

Jeanne took the cloak and clasped it at her throat,

nodding at the coat. "There's no need for you to come as well, Emma."

"Oh yes there is, Mistress. I cannot let you go out on your own," said the maid with a distrustful stare at Baldwin, who stood nearby, appalled at the thought that his attempts at subtle wooing could be conducted under the baleful gaze of the maid whom he now thought of as the "Harpy from Hell."

"I think not. You will stay here."

"I would prefer to go with you, Lady," Emma stated resolutely.

Baldwin was brimming with frustration. He loathed the sight of Emma, yet he couldn't be rude to her. She wasn't his servant, and he had no idea how much regard Jeanne had for her. Until he knew Jeanne's thoughts, he dared not risk upsetting her by insulting her maid.

At that moment Hugh reappeared and marched up to him. "Sir Baldwin? I thought I saw someone walking out near the road, so I let Uther out. If there's a trespasser, he will soon find them."

"You let him out?" Baldwin repeated. "You shouldn't have, you know he—"

"That beast? My lady, you mustn't go out, not while that mad dog is free. You've seen how it attacked me when we first got here! You cannot go out."

"Oh, I don't fear Uther. And Baldwin will wear his sword, won't you?"

"Eh?" Baldwin had the impression that the look that passed between Hugh and Jeanne contained more than a simple exchange of greetings. "Oh yes, of course. Well, a dagger, anyway."

Hugh said, "Edgar told me to be careful, after the way Uther attacked that man recently. Cottey, wasn't it?"

"You see, Mistress? That creature will eat us alive! I

said it should be destroyed! It's worse than a ravening wolf."

"Emma, silence! I am going out, and you are staying in." Jeanne swept around, her cloak whipping out regally, and strode to the door. Baldwin had to break into a trot to catch up with her. In the screens were several of Baldwin's workers, and Jeanne and he had to slow down in their rush while the men all moved out of the way.

It was noticeable that none of the men seemed scared of their master. Jeanne, who had been married to a knight who had struck terror into the hearts of his peasants, was forced to take stock.

There was something awesome in a man who could instill such loyalty in his servants. Her husband had whipped and beaten his people into submission. That was the only way to make them behave, he had always asserted. Otherwise they would lapse into indolence and laziness.

Yet this strange country knight had managed a productive manor efficiently, without driving his peasants into utter submission. As Baldwin walked past, they nodded or grinned; not cowering, but meeting his look almost as equals. And Baldwin had a word for most of them, recalling all their names, asking after wives, children, or sweethearts. One man he made a detour to speak to, a ragged, worn-looking older man, with a drawn and wan face. Jeanne couldn't hear his words, but she saw Baldwin pull some coins from his purse and press them into the other man's hand.

She also saw the way that the people glanced at her, and was again aware of their cautious assessment, but now she was as certain as she could be that the man with whom she walked was as unlike her first husband as was possible. As they approached the door, she found herself being forced nearer to him, for the press of people was thicker here, and as they walked out into the clear evening air, she was close at his side.

"Who was that old man you were talking to?"

"The farmer? Quivil. He and his wife live out toward Crediton."

"You spoke to him for some little while."

"His son has developed leprosy," Baldwin explained. "I wanted to make sure he was all right, and to offer any help I could."

"It must be awful to lose a son like that."

"Indeed. To see your child condemned to years of disease is somehow worse than a simple death, after a short illness."

"Yes, for how could you look your child in the face, knowing that you live and prosper while the child dies so slowly and horribly?"

"Ah, but it's not just that, is it? It's not only the guilt of failing to help one's child to grow healthily," Baldwin said, pausing.

The scene was all silver and gray, under an almost full moon. By its clear light Jeanne could see the view rolling away into the distance between the trees. Something in Baldwin's voice made her look at his face, and under the benevolent, if cold, glimmer, she could see he was worried.

"It's not only the fact that the parent can see the son or daughter slip further and further from life," he went on slowly, "it's also seeing the jealousy and rage in the child, knowing their confusion, wanting to give them comfort and not being able to. I wonder how poor Edmund feels now."

"He is Quivil's son?"

"Yes. And a happier, lustier, more comely fellow you couldn't hope to see plowing a field or reaping the corn. Poor Edmund! He was about to wed."

"Perhaps it is fortunate that he was found out before he could marry."

"Yes. But it seems so unfair, so unjust, that a man should be taken away into confinement just as he was about to enjoy the companionship of his woman. Even as he was preparing to enter into marriage, with the knowledge that he would henceforth have the comfort of a partner in life, that succor is stolen from him."

"You sound as though you have considered this at length, Sir Baldwin."

He gave a dry smile. "I have. I have sometimes seen myself as a kind of social leper."

"That's a terrible thing to say."

"As a Keeper, and a knight, it's difficult. I am often cut off from other people because of my position."

"You are denied companionship?"

"I sometimes feel I'm denied the companionship of a woman who understands me."

"Perhaps you might discover such a woman after all."

"My lady, I have."

She walked on a short way, gripping the cloak tightly around her body, her hands crossed over her breast. The knight remained where he was, and she had to turn to face him. His expression was one of mistrust—almost of suspicion. But there was a gentleness too. Jeanne knew that he had been badly hurt when she had refused his offer of marriage before, and knew that he wanted to ask again whether she would accept his hand, yet was fearful that she might reject him; he was unsure whether he could rely on her giving him the answer he craved.

"Jeanne, you know me. You have seen my land, my home, my life. Is there anything you could not grow to be comfortable with?"

She felt her breath catch. For some reason, this offer, which she had anticipated for over a year, which she had expected and mused over since she had first arrived, was now a surprise. She hadn't thought that he could spring it on her so suddenly. "I . . . I don't know!"

"Is it your last husband, Lady? Is that what makes you hesitate?"

"How can I be sure what *you* are like? He seemed so kind and generous before we married. How can I be sure you will not change when I marry you?"

"*Me?* Change? This, *this* is me!" he cried, and held both arms out, embracing the country before, behind, to either side, the sky above, the silver clouds chasing across it, the moon and the stars. He smiled up, his eyes fixed on the unfathomable distances, and slowly let his arms fall, and let his face drop to hers. "You know all about me. I know what I need to know about you. I am no courtly knight, and God willing, I never will be. I am the King's officer here, and that is enough for me. Could I be enough for you?"

"I don't know, Baldwin. I don't know."

Simon left his wife in their room, and walked downstairs. In the buttery he found Hugh, who was morosely filling a jug from a large barrel. As his master entered, Hugh nodded. "Ale, sir?"

"Yes, a pint would round off the evening."

Taking another mug from the shelf, Hugh took the jug and wandered out through the screens to the hall. Following, and burping softly, Simon was surprised to find Edgar waiting with the boy, Wat. The lad looked at the bailiff with an unfocused stare, grinning foolishly, but Edgar motioned toward the door.

"Sir, please shut it."

Surprised, Simon did as he was bid. Only then did Edgar rise and open the door to the solar. Instantly Uther bounded out and looked about, seeking his master.

"What's *he* doing here? I thought he was out seeing trespassers!"

"Ah, he must have decided to come back," said Hugh stantly.

"But, you said to Baldwin that he was patrolling the nd to keep someone at bay."

"Yes, Master."

As Simon frowned with incomprehension, he was re he could hear a querulous voice. He was about to alk to the solar, from where the sound appeared to ue, when Edgar put out a hand to stop him.

"Sir, you don't want to go through there."

"But can't you hear someone?"

"Sir, I think it's the wind."

"I can hear someone—it's Emma! She's calling for lp!"

"Surely, if she *wanted* help, she'd come down to ask r it."

"She would, sir," Hugh confirmed. "She would only ve to open her chamber door and walk down here, ouldn't she?"

Simon looked at his servant, then at Baldwin's. Both oided his gaze, studying their ales carefully. The iliff looked at Uther, who seemed to share his confu-on, and scratched an ear thoughtfully. Then Simon oked at the doorway, and slowly a smile creased his atures. "Do you think Uther is protecting his master ell even now?"

"I think his master would be delighted to know how ell his dog is keeping unwanted folks away from n," observed Hugh, and belched.

hn got back to the wall and stood, panting as quietly he could, nervously studying his surroundings as he ught any sign of a waiting guard.

The same sky which Baldwin was standing under few miles away was becoming congested with clou that looked as if they were composed of finest spu silver threads. Only now and again was the moon vi ble. For the most part it was obscured by the clouds they grew ever larger.

It was some consolation to John, as he hesitated the wall, that the land was not under so bright a light before. When he had set out earlier, the sack on his ba filled with the hollowly clanking pewter, he had felt if he had been under constant scrutiny from every m and woman who lived in the town. It had seemed th every tree and bush had intentionally dropped twi and branches to try to trip him and make the sack r tle ever more loudly, or to ensure that the ground its crackled and crunched with every footstep to show p cisely where he was. The journey to the hall had be one of terror for him, each step another pace towa possible ruin. When he was almost halfway to t opened window, a screech owl had given its rauco shriek, and he had thought he might end up at the t of the oak beside him, so high did he jump at the une pected noise. Every hair on his head stood upright sympathy with his pounding heart.

Thankfully the sack had been passed over without cident, and John could stand out in the yard in the da ened shadow of a tree while it was hauled inside a stored. After a few whispered words, John had turn and set off home again, and it was then that he h heard that awful whistle.

While the owl had set his heart thudding with sudd fear, the whistle had made that organ attempt the posite feat. He had uttered a shocked gasp, his he filled with every combination of ghoul, ghost, fai goblin and devilish story he had ever heard. Then th

'ere superseded by the memory of the soldiers billeted
: Coffyn's house, and he took to his heels.

It was fortunate that he could remember the way
ack to his wall, especially as his path took him by the
nost circuitous route he could devise. Scorning the di-
:ct way, he had rushed toward the road, doubled back
ırough some trees, squirmed his way under a thicket,
ıt his hands on brambles in the process, shoved him-
:lf between the bars at the window of the stables, mak-
ıg soothing noises to the intrigued horses within, and
:uttled forth from the darkest opening at the furthest
›rner from the house, only to wait, desperately scan-
ing the ground ahead for pursuers, before making his
ainstaking way back to his tree and safety.

He watched carefully, his eyes screwed to mere slits as
: tried to observe the faintest hint of movement, but
›uld see nothing, and at last he was satisfied. Stepping
ith a high gait, testing the ground before trusting his
eight on it, he made his infinitely slow and cautious
:ogress to the wall. His rope was quickly off his shoul-
:r, and he took one last glance behind him. He had no
ish to be snared as he had been the last time. Then he
ırew. It caught, he yanked twice, it held, and he scram-
.ed up. On the wall, he unhooked it, and let himself
ll at the other side, giving a sigh of relief.

Coiling the rope, he glanced up. The sky was filling
ıickly with fresh clouds, and he stared a moment in
›preciation. Going to the stable door, he tossed the
›pe over its nail, patted the mare, and made his way to
e house. After the excitement of the evening, he felt
.e need of a good two quarts of ale. Thrusting the door
ide, he went to the little fire and kicked the embers to-
:ther, throwing a handful of tinder on top, and setting
log over all, then crouched to blow it into life.

"So, Irishman, you feel the cold?"

He froze. "You wouldn't hit a man on the grounc
would you, sir?"

His answer was a blow on the side of his skull thа
felled him. He grunted, while the pain exploded, both i
his head and at the top of his neck. It was as if he ha
fallen from a height and crunched the bones. It was aş
onizing, and he was so stunned he couldn't shout c
scream, but could only lie dully, unable to reach up an
feel the wound.

He could see the second blow approach. It was
club, he noted, and he saw the heavy wood rise slowl
hesitate, and then sweep down.

"No, please—"

It struck, and his last conscious thought as the cudg
met his skull was how strange it was that he couldn
hear it strike. But then the pain returned, and ove
whelmed him. He was unaware of the hand gripping h
leg, lifting it gently, while the club swooped down
shatter John's knee.

~ 17 ~

dgar winced at the sight of the fire in the hall. There was not enough dried timber to make a flame. It had burned through in the night, and no one had tended it yet his morning. He could fetch Wat, indeed he *should* kick he lazy devil from his palliasse in the kitchen, but when he glanced in, he guessed that waking the lad wouldn't help much.

Instead, he marched to the logpile. Dropping an armul carelessly on the floor, he fetched the sack of kinlling. Soon he was kneeling, flint and his dagger critching and clattering together as he tried to bring a park to the tinder. Blowing, he managed to produce a iny whisp of smoke, and fed it with dried leaves and rasses before adding small twigs left over from the learances of the previous summer. Each year as trees vere felled for firewood or coppiced for fencing, furniure and charcoal, the smaller, useless branches were aved for this function.

When he had produced a healthy flame, and had set wo logs side-by-side over it, he settled back on his heels o watch it suspiciously for a while.

"You could have been quieter, if you'd wanted."

Edgar grinned at Hugh's sullen tone. "True!"

Hugh was lying on a heavy bench, like two or three other guests of Baldwin's from the night before, and he groaned to himself as he hauled himself upright to rest on an elbow, scowling at Edgar. He grabbed at his rough blanket before it could slip off. "Where's Wat? I thought *he* had to make up the fire."

"Someone got him drunk last night. I think he'll be late to rise today."

Hugh chuckled quietly. "He seemed to enjoy his beer."

"You shouldn't have kept feeding him that strong ale, though. He doesn't know how much he can take."

"It happened to us all when we were young. I thought he coped well."

"Until he got outside," Edgar agreed. As soon as the wobbling boy had got to the back door and taken in his first deep breath of cool night air, he had hiccuped once, then started walking up and down the yard with increasing speed. Edgar and another had gone to watch and make sure he was safe, for it was all too common for a youngster to fall asleep and drown in his own vomit, but Wat had seemed fine—except he had refused to acknowledge any of the pleasantries hurled in his direction. And then he had been sick. Edgar had been quite surprised at the volume emanating from such a slight figure.

Wat had been carried to the trough and forced to swill his mouth and wash before being sent off to his bed. There was a maid who usually slept by the fire in the kitchen, and she took it upon herself to watch over him for the night.

"He'll have to clear up all his puke before anything else," Edgar noted. "But he slept all right. He looks very pale, though. I thought it would be kinder to him to let him rest a little longer. Anyway, he looked as though he was liable to throw up again when I looked in on him just now. I didn't fancy getting him to try to blow the fire into light, not if he was going to spew all over it."

"I suppose we'd better wake our masters," Hugh grunted, stretching luxuriously. He set his feet on the ground, then winced at the pain in his head.

Cocking an eyebrow at him, Edgar grinned. "Wat wasn't the only one had too much last night."

He set the pan, ready filled with water, over the flames, and wandered through to the solar where Baldwin lay sleeping. Opening the door quietly, he was welcomed by a low grumbling. When he clicked his tongue, the noise stopped and the tawny dog padded over the floor on his massive paws, his tail wagging berserkly. It caught at the top of a chest as he passed, and swept a dagger, Baldwin's purse, and a goblet clattering onto the floor.

"Christ's Blood!"

"Good morning, Sir Baldwin," said Edgar suavely. "I am glad Chops managed to waken you so quickly."

Baldwin peered at him wearily. "There are times, Edgar, when I wonder why I don't look for a new steward of my household."

"It's morning, sir, and you asked to be woken early so that you could get back to Crediton."

"Oh!" Baldwin clutched at his head as he sat up. He closed his eyes, then daringly opened one into a slit. "I think I drank more wine than usual last night."

"I think that is a fair comment, sir."

"I remember now why I prefer not to drink too much," Baldwin muttered as he came to his feet.

"But the evening went very well," said Edgar, spreading out the knight's tunic and inspecting it doubtfully. "This is torn."

"The dog caught it last night."

Edgar left his master to dress himself. Out in the hall once more, he saw that the fire was blossoming flames, and set more logs alongside to dry thoroughly. Returning from the log store, he met Hugh coming through after waking his own master, and the pair of them entered the hall to find Emma leaving it.

She glowered at them. There was no proof, but she was convinced that these men were responsible for her confinement the previous night. That dog had been left outside her room to prevent her protecting her mistress.

Emma was not interested in her mistress' attraction to Sir Baldwin. To the maid, one man was pretty much the same as any other, although she had respected and felt sympathy for Sir Ralph de Liddinstone. It was the comparison between the two that made her feel such disgust for the knight of Furnshill. Ralph would never have invited all his bondsmen and freeholders to a feast such as Baldwin had held the night before; the idea was laughable. No, Sir Ralph was a real nobleman, in Emma's eye. He was strong, and demonstrated his strength by imposing his will on his tenants, whereas the feeble Furnshill knight thought it better to pander to them.

In truth, the virulence of her loathing for Baldwin was based on the simple conviction that once her mistress had enjoyed a true, honorable, powerful knight, she would demean the memory of the man by wedding herself to a weakly article like Baldwin. That was why Emma was determined to prevent any possibility of a match between the two; and why she was seized with rage at having been effectively locked in her room the night before, with that slavering hound wandering outside her door. It had stopped her from walking with her mistress and protecting her from Sir Baldwin's pathetic attempts at courtly lovemaking.

It was the first time in a long while that Emma had been so effectively thwarted, and she was furious that these two uncultured, common peasants could have succeeded. And now she had to bring the reward to the knight. It made her gorge rise.

Hugh quailed under her piercing gaze, and dropped back so that Edgar was a little in front and shielding him. She looked Edgar up and down contemptuously. In her hand was a rough bundle. After a moment's silence, she thrust it into his hands.

He looked at it with some surprise. "What's this?"

"It's for your master. From my lady. She asked me to tell you to give it to him."

Edgar took the light package straight to his master. Baldwin was about to leave his room, and gave his servant a surprised glance when he appeared.

"What?"

"This, sir. It's for you, apparently."

Baldwin frowned at it, then motioned Edgar into his room. The servant took it to the bed and untied the cord that bound it. Inside, he found a bright crimson cloth. Shaking it out, he stared.

"A new tunic?"

Baldwin felt the fine woollen cloth. "Do you remember? She said she would make me a new tunic last year at Tavistock." He glanced down ruefully at his old white, stained and worn robe. "I think I had better get changed," he sighed.

His head felt as if it was about to fall from his shoulders. When he opened his eyes, everything was misted and befogged, as if he was looking through a badly finished glass window. Movement of any sort was agony; even blinking brought a stab of pain to his temples.

Gradually, as he recovered his senses, John realized

where he was. He was lying on the floor of his room, beside the fire he had been trying to build. He reached out a hand, and slowly, with infinite care, eased himself onto his belly. As he tried to lever himself up, simultaneous bolts like white-hot brands seared his head and leg. Gasping, he had to let himself flop to the ground, and passed out.

It was not until the sun was already up and shining in through the open door that he could take any interest in his surroundings again. From the light coming in, he could survey the room. It was clear that someone had ransacked the place. All his belongings were all over the floor, his trunk was opened, and his chairs and tables upset. It made him give a wry grin. "Too late, lads!" he whispered.

At last he could make a second attempt to move. He gradually forced himself into a position from which he could crawl, and inched his way toward the door, sweat beading his brow. It took all his strength to do so without screaming. It was ironic, he thought, that the only thing he had brought with him from Ireland was this: his stoicism.

Outside the door was his little rainbutt, and beside that his stool. He stared at them, teeth gritted. It seemed an immense distance, but he was determined to get there; he needed water, and he had to get into the daylight to inspect his wounds. The ground was hard, and each time his leg dragged over a pebble or scraped over a rough patch of dried mud, he bit his lip to keep from swearing.

It took the very last atom of his energy to hoist himself on to the stool. Then, before he looked at his leg, he forced himself to thrust his head under the freezing water. Coming up blowing and panting, the liquid streaming from his face, he felt quickly nauseous, and had to swallow hard to keep the bile at bay, but the feeling soon passed, and he could sink back on the stool with a grunt and a gasp.

Only then did he look down at his leg. The foot was twisted, and he couldn't bear to touch his knee, much less move it. When he gingerly touched his head, it felt as if someone had been beating it like a bolt of iron on an anvil. Both sides of his skull were bruised and swollen. Wincing and shaking with pain and reaction, he squinted at his gate: it hung open. Behind him was the storage shed where he kept his ale, and he felt his mouth water at the thought of a strong draft, but he rejected it as being beyond his power.

His leg was broken, near the knee. He stared at it grimly. His head felt as if it was being ruthlessly sawn in two, and the sensation wasn't helped by the occasional impression that his vision was doubling. He wanted to throw up, but couldn't afford the luxury; he must get help, go and see a surgeon or a monk, and get his leg mended. But to do that he must somehow get into town, and he couldn't crawl the whole way. If he lived down toward the center of town, he could simply call from his door—but if he had lived in the town itself, he wouldn't have been attacked: his screams would have been heard. Not that he'd managed to make much noise last night, he reminded himself glumly.

No, nobody was going to come up here. It wasn't on the beaten track, and if it was, nobody would be likely to spot him in his yard so far from the path.

John had been a soldier. He knew a little about fixing broken bones, and he eyed his ruined leg sourly for a while. The only way he was going to get help was if he could get himself down to the church to demand it. He took out his knife, doffed his jacket, and began to hack the cloth into strips.

* * *

When Baldwin entered his hall, he felt more than a little self-conscious. His new tunic was of a bright red hue, more colorful than anything he had possessed before, and he could see that Simon was startled to see him so resplendent.

The knight ignored his friend, instead walking to the quiet woman near the fire. She was clothed in a new tunic of bright red velvet, and as he surveyed it, he recognized the cloth. It was that which he had bought for her in Tavistock.

"My lady, I am flattered and honored by your gift."

If he sounded a littly stiffly formal, his face belied it. Jeanne smiled back at him, delighted to see how the color suited him. It was twelve months ago that she and Margaret had bought the cloth, and Jeanne had quickly made up the tunic when she returned home after that first meeting, but it had not seemed right, somehow, to merely send it to him with her compliments. She had wanted to see him wear it for the first time, and now, to be able to see how his face was softened by the color, and by his pleasure, she felt her heart swell with pride that she had achieved this on her own, with only her skill at needlework. "It is my pleasure, Sir Baldwin. I am delighted to see that it fits as well as I had hoped."

Margaret smiled, and as she felt her husband prepare to offer a humorous sally, shoved a warning arm through his.

"Do you recognize this cloth?" Jeanne asked.

"It is the material I bought you in Tavistock," he smiled.

She heard Emma cluck her tongue at her side, but ignored it. "Yes. I have not worn it until now. I wanted to put it on for the first time when you had your gift from me."

"Perhaps when you have finished admiring each other's attire, we can get down to Crediton and find this thief and murderer?" Simon suggested drily.

Baldwin threw him an irritated look, but Jeanne laughed out loud and pushed him toward the bailiff. "I think your other guest is keen to be off."

"What about some food first?"

Simon indicated a small satchel and wineskin. "It's ready! We can eat on our journey."

With a bad grace, Baldwin submitted, and soon the two men, with Edgar in their train, were on their way, the knight taking the leading position.

As they began the long, shallow descent from Cadbury toward the town, Simon took a deep gulp of wine. "Where to first?"

"The leper house. I want to speak to Ralph."

~ 18 ~

hen they arrived at the chapel's little gate, they found the monk already waiting, a stout cudgel in his hand.

"Sir Baldwin, I am so glad you could come, sir."

"Why? Has something happened?"

"Hadn't you heard? I assumed you must have. We had two men stoned last night—a recent inmate, and a travelling man. Both had rocks hurled at them; they could have been killed!"

Baldwin dropped from his horse and tied it to a branch. "Show me!" he instructed.

Behind him, Edgar sprang down easily enough, but Simon was less keen. He swung his leg over his rounsey's rump, and knotted the reins over another branch but he entered the compound unwillingly. He had never before been into a leper colony.

There were many laws to protect the public from lepers, and they all had one aim, to acknowledge God's punishment. Lepers were defiled, and it was the duty of society to exclude them. Now, walking into the chapel's grounds, Simon felt as if he was entering the very heart of pollution and decay. He could almost sense the vapor given off by the foul, diseased people as if it was reaching out to him, trying to grasp him in its chilly grip. It was perverse to go into a place of such hideous danger.

At his side he felt Edgar's presence, and was grateful for it. The servant, still more than his master, seemed to exude confidence and strength, and Simon kept close to him, as though a little of it could rub off on him—and as if there might be some prophylactic merit in numbers. For his part, he was fearful to the point of feeling sick—not merely queasy, but genuinely close to vomiting.

Ralph led them at a smart pace past the church, along a patch of lawn, which was rimed with hoar-frost, and into one of the little buildings.

Baldwin glanced in, and almost drew back at the smell. It was not only the stench of disease, but of unwashed bodies, dirty clothes, and filth. He had to swallow hard before he could steel himself to cross the threshold.

The brother moved confidently to a shadowed corner, but the knight had to pause again, this time to accustom his eyes to the darkness. It was as if the disgusting fumes were clogging all his senses, even his eyes, and blinding him. It was impossible to see anything at first. Then, thankfully, the monk struck a flame from flint and steel, and Baldwin could look about him.

It was merely a hovel. There was a hearth in the middle, and two straw-filled palliasses lay at either side. Ralph stood between the two, candle held high to illuminate his patients.

"Quivil!" Baldwin exclaimed.

"Sir Baldwin?"

The voice was strained, but it was not merely the hoarseness of the leprosy that made the voice feeble. Baldwin motioned, and Ralph held the light nearer. By it the knight saw the bruises, the clotted blood over the bridge of the nose, the long, ragged slash down one cheek where the flesh had been torn like cloth.

"Who *dared* do this?" Baldwin hissed.

"It was the good gentlefolk of this pleasant town," said another voice, and Baldwin turned and peered at the man on the other bed.

Thomas Rodde grimaced as the candle came closer, shutting his eyes against the glare.

"Why should they do this to you?"

"They fear us. That makes them hate us. And it only takes a couple of stupid comments about how a leper might have seduced a girl, for drunks to decide to take revenge."

"This was done by drunks, you say?"

"Oh yes. At least, I assume they were. They had an interesting vocabulary; not the sort of thing I'd expect sober men to use."

"Did you recognize them?"

Quivil spoke again. "Arthur, and Jack the smith . . ." The names were all familiar to Baldwin. None was a great troublemaker, but all were known to take their own action when the fancy took them, rather than troubling the officers of the law.

"Jack," he mused, then shot a glance at the other bed again. "You're not from this town, are you? Your accent is strange."

"No, sir. I hail from London originally, although have been travelling in the north of the country in recent years. I only came to this place a few weeks ago. Now begin to regret it."

"I cannot blame you," Baldwin smiled sympathetically. "It is not the kind of welcome I would appreciate either, if I was a newcomer. Have you caused insult to any man since you arrived?"

"Me?" Thomas Rodde was driven to laugh at such an

ınnocent question. When he spoke again, his voice had
ɔst all trace of humor, and his eyes were cold. "What
lo you think, Sir Knight? Look on me! I used to be a
omely enough man: hale, powerful and wealthy. Now?
'es—look on me! I am a shell, something for men and
vomen of all conditions to avoid, pityingly perhaps, but
vith revulsion. Look on me, Sir Knight! I insult all by
xisting!"

"I make no apology, friend, for all I am trying to do
discover who could have had reason to wound you,"
aldwin said soothingly. "You must know that I need to
sk questions to find out why this happened."

"You have been told who was responsible."

"And these men could have got it into their heads to
o this," agreed the knight, "but I always expect to find
ɔme other reason to explain *why*. Men do not suddenly
o mad and throw stones at others, no—not even at
:pers—without good cause, in my experience. Do you
now of any reason why these men should take it into
ıeir heads to assault you in the streets?"

Seeing that both lepers were silent, Ralph interjected,
I know why, Sir Baldwin."

The knight could see that the leper master had
vorked himself into an angry, bitter mood. His lips
vere pursed, his eyes unblinking. The hand that held
ıe candle didn't shake, but the other was working
:eadily, the middle finger clicking its nail against that of
ıe thumb to create an irritated percussion.

"Why, then, Brother?"

"Come with me!"

Ralph led the way out of the hovel and over the grass
ɔward the church. Opening the door of the chapel, he
ırust it open and strode inside, his shoes making a
range flapping noise as he passed over the cobbles.

Simon walked along behind Baldwin, wondering

what the monk could be about to show them. He felt a strange premonition that another dead man was at the heart of it, and his expectation seemed to be fulfilled when he came upon the aisle and saw the hearse before the altar. The simple metal frame, draped with its cheap black cloth, with the three candles in each of the triangular brackets at head and foot, obviously covered another dead body, and Simon took a deep swallow. He had seen enough dead men in his time, and almost all of them were the victims of violence, but he had never lost his squeamishness. It was different when the body was that of a man who had died in his sleep after a long and useful life, his family and friends at his bedside, the priest ready to give comfort to the passing spirit; then it was a natural, an acceptable event.

Here, in the chapel of St. Lawrence's, Simon knew that the body beneath the draped hearse would be that of a leper, someone who had lived out his last years in pain and suffering, always aware that those who had been his friends and relations now despised him for his appalling disease.

It was with unutterable relief that he realized the priest was not heading toward it. Instead Ralph turned, made his obeisance, and went out to a small chamber at the side. As Simon came closer, he could hear a strange sound. Approaching the door, he realized it was a subdued moaning that issued from within. At first the bailiff was fearful what he might discover inside, but as the monk shoved the door wide, he saw it was only a young woman.

Baldwin stopped. "Mary? Mary Cordwainer?"

"Yes, sir?"

Her eyes were red and swollen from weeping—that was the first thing Simon noticed about her. They appeared luminous in the gloom of the dark room, which was little more than a cupboard beside the altar, a kind of lean-to affair at the side of the church which was used as a storeroom for brushes and other essentials necessary to clean the place.

Ralph threw his arm toward her. "Ask her—ask Mary what was going on last night!"

"Mary? We have come from Edmund and his friend—you know that they were beaten? Can you tell us anything about it?"

The knight's voice, so calm and gentle, was enough to help her take control of herself. She took two deep breaths; each racked her frame, as if she was about to sob anew. She looked at her hands, seeing their cracked and dried skin, and held them over her eyes while a convulsive shudder shook her, and then let them fall.

She was exhausted. Knowing that her man was taken from her, that the life she had planned and prayed for was denied to her, was a hideous shock, but now to have to suffer so much more, when all she was trying to do was alleviate the anguish of others, was still worse. She had looked to her friends and neighbors to support her in her tribulation, and they had rejected her.

"Can you tell us?" Baldwin asked.

"Yes, sir. Yes, I am well now, thank you."

The knight studied her. He remembered her from before Quivil's illness as a bright, cheery girl, one who was given to playing pranks when she was still running about the streets with her hair unbraided, who had taken on a solemn steadiness when she was betrothed, as if it was a more fitting demeanor for a wife-to-be. Her face still looked as if it was better suited to laughing than crying, but all pleasure had been wiped from it, as if by a malignant cloth.

Mary stared past him to the bailiff in the doorway. "It was men in the town. I come here every day to help

Brother Ralph. There isn't much for me to do, but I wanted to help all I could. It was the only thing I could do for my poor Edmund, him being so low after his disease. Well, who wouldn't be low, knowing they've got this?" She waved a hand as if to indicate all the inmates and their disease.

"I've been coming since the day he was brought here, to dust and sweep, to help change the bandages of the sick men, and sometimes to sit up with the dying, like with the poor soul out there, Bernard, so poor Brother Ralph can get some rest."

"She has been a tower of strength to me," murmured Ralph.

"Poor Edmund had no one who could love him like I could," she asserted defensively. "Who else could help him in his last months or years? Not even his mother would come here to see him, but I dared, because how could God strike me down for helping the ill? And if He did, then I would go to my grave knowing I'd done all I could for another suffering creature, and I would go to join my Edmund in Heaven."

Baldwin nodded understandingly. He had a pleasant face, she thought. A little like the statue of Jesus by the altar. The attentive concentration in his face was attractive, and she felt her heart warming to him. Instinctively she felt she could trust him.

"Last night, the same as each day before, I left here at twilight to go home. I still live with my parents, sir, and it is a lengthy walk, so I try to leave before nightfall. It was when I got to the crossroads near the inn I realized I'd left my coat here. I ran back, but it meant that when I left the second time it was already dark, and as I went through the streets, some men called to me, thinking I might be about some other business."

Her face darkened as she recalled the two figures leer-ing and making suggestive gestures as they praised her strong, young body. A female out and about in the dark, they had said, must be after one thing and one thing only. One of them had shaken his purse before her, trying to tempt her into an alley with him. It was only when a passer-by had shouted that she worked daily at the leper camp that they had pulled away, disdaining her with curses as if she had invited their lechery.

It was only a short walk after that to where she had found Quivil and Rodde. The two were cowering by a wall, arms up to protect their heads from the stones, clods of earth, broken sticks and rubbish that were being hurled at them by the small crowd of jeering, swearing townspeople.

She had stood a moment, aghast, then run forward, beating with her bare hands at the men nearest, thrusting them from her path and kicking at all who refused to move. In a few seconds she had broken through the press, and was between the men and their prey. "What are you *doing*? Don't you know these men are defenseless?"

One of the men had given a scornful laugh. "You want to protect them? I didn't think whores took that much interest in their punters!"

"Who calls me whore?" she had spat, thinking it was one man speaking through his ale, but others had taken up the call. Although the lepers were safe now, the crowd was eager to attack another target. Mary saw that Edmund was slumped at the wall, blood dribbling from a gash in his cheek and another on his scalp, and the other leper was crouched at his side cleaning the wounds as best he could. "How dare you call me that!"

"I dare." It was Jack, the smith. He stood with his arms akimbo, meeting her gaze steadily. "You think we're all so stupid we don't realize what you're doing in the lazar house every day—well, we do! You say you nurse the men there, but how many do you service a day, eh?"

She had felt the blood rise to her face, the hot blood of injustice. That she could be accused of consorting with any man was foul, but to suggest that she was capable of throwing her body at the poor diseased souls of St. Lawrence's when all she was doing was looking after them because no one else would, stung her into retaliation. She said nothing, but remained where she was for a long period, then launched herself forward, fists bunched and ready to strike.

The smith laughed with contempt. As she came close, he grabbed her flailing hands and held her fast. "What do you think, lads? Is she worth taking?"

"Not now," another responded, jerking his head at the two lepers. "She's damaged!"

"Yeah!" Jack sneered, his breath reeking of alcohol as he surveyed her. "Go on, stay with your friends, wench." And with that he shoved hard. She stumbled, weeping tears of rage, tripped on a stone and fell at Rodde's feet. He shook his head in sympathy, but couldn't take her hand in front of the crowd. It was forbidden for a leper to touch a healthy person. When she looked again, all the men were dispersing.

As she came to the end of her tale, Baldwin patted her hand. "What then?"

"I was going to walk back here with Edmund and Rodde, but Rodde said I ought to go straight home. He said it wasn't good for me to come here any more, that I would be in danger, that the mob might attack me for lewd behavior, that they could burn me for heresy. He refused to let me help him, but sent me on my way."

"That showed some good sense . . . and some stupidity," Baldwin muttered. "What if you had been attacked again on the way home? He should have asked someone to escort you. Anyway, let us hope that this is an end to the violence. Mary, I am sorry. I will speak today to the smith and tell him plainly that if there's any other disturbance, he will be in the jail before he can pick up a stone to throw. As it is, I'll have him on a charge for slandering you and causing a riot. That should cost him several pretty pennies!"

"And what about poor Mary?" cried Ralph. "Go on, girl, tell the knight the rest. Tell him what happened when you arrived home!"

Mary's gaze dropped to her hands once again, and she allowed her face to fall into them. She wasn't weeping now, for she felt so exhausted with her crying that there was no energy left with which to fuel her grief. All she had was with her—there rolled up in her kerchief by the door. First she had lost her husband, but now she had lost everything else. It truly was too fabulous a disaster for her to fully comprehend.

"Sir, since last night, I have been trying to understand Jack and the others, and I had almost forgiven them, for any man might make a fool of himself after too much ale, but it is hard, so hard, after what they did . . ." Her eyes brimmed once more, and she had to sit quietly to bring herself under control. "Sir, my father wasn't home when I arrived. He often visits the inn at night. I was sitting with my mother when he returned. He had been accosted in the street by this man Jack and others, and they had told him that I was no better than a slut. They said I wasn't wanted in the town any more, and they would make me leave, and my family too."

"They dared to do this?" Baldwin growled, glancing at the monk.

"They said they would burn my parents out of the house unless I left, with us all inside it; they said there was no place in Crediton for a woman who consorted with lepers." She lifted her eyes to meet the knight's. "So all I have is here. I have left my home so that my parents and brothers and sisters can live in peace. What else could I do?"

"Enough, Mary," Baldwin said, and stood. His face was composed, but there was a tightness in his voice as he spoke. "This Jack will answer to me for what he has threatened. You need fear no more from him or from his friends. I will see to them—*now*!"

He swept from the room, pushing past Simon in his urgency, and it was not until he had reached the chapel's main door that the hurrying monk managed to catch up with him. "Sir Baldwin? Please, wait one minute."

"What, Brother Ralph?"

"Don't go and persecute one man for his stupidity! Wait until you can consider his case more calmly. There's no point in creating even more bad feeling in the town than already exists."

"I think there is. If a young woman like Mary can be forced from her home with nowhere to go, there's every need for these cretins to realize their fault!"

"I agree that she must be cared for, but don't go rushing at them like a bull at a gate. For one thing, I have to ask myself whether it would be sensible for her to stay in the town after this."

"Meaning?"

"All I mean is, she is so good a nurse, and so devoted to her new calling, that it might be better for her to leave the town anyway. If she remains here, she can only ever be a cause of strife. Wouldn't it be preferable that she should go somewhere else where she would be appreciated? I think she would be ideally suited for a life of prayer."

"You think she might go to a convent?"

"I think she might be happier there. She would be

fe from further comment from the uneducated, safe om slanders and lies, and could dedicate her life to lping others in a hospital."

"And the town would have its boil lanced." Baldwin rew a wrathful glower eastward, back toward the lumns of smoke over the hill. "And bigots would have cceeded in driving away a poor girl to no purpose."

"Better that than a hothead should fire her house and rn her and all her family."

"Better that one innocent should suffer than many?" ldwin muttered, his lip curled, but he gave a short d. "I despise your argument, Brother, but I find it mpelling. Yet I will still visit the smith and make my ews known. I'll not have him poisoning this town. ad I won't have lepers beaten in the streets, either."

~ 19 ~

s the sun climbed higher, and cast its ra into his yard, John had to close his ey against the glare. It was too painful, wi his head throbbing and pulsing in tir with his shattered leg.

After struggling for what felt like an age, he had nally got himself into some kind of shape. It had be hard, for to tie the old walking stick and besom hanc to his leg, he had needed to bend, and each time he d so, a fresh wave of nausea washed over him. Each tir he was forced to snap his eyes shut and keep absolute still for a few minutes, until the sensation passed, a each time he must open his eyes and continue.

One bandage he had reserved for his head. Where t club had struck the right of his skull, there was a gro ing lump, and there was a smaller one on the oppos side as well. He had to give a twisted grin as he tigh ened the band round his forehead, thinking that at lea the constriction hurt both sides of his skull equally; wouldn't be unbalanced when he tried to move.

He had found a staff, a good elm branch which had been saving to axe into kindling, and gripped hard. Gritting his teeth, he cautiously eased himself u

ard, the sweat breaking out at his forehead and chill-
ng his back under his shirt. It was cool enough without
is coat, and this moisture made him shudder as if he
ad the ague, but with set expression and firmly locked
w, he set the staff to the ground and took a step.

The grating of smashed bone almost made him faint.
lis headache returned, thudding as hard as if a man
as beating him again; his stomach roiled. The world
virled before his eyes, and he had to shut them, but
en all his concentration could focus on the exquisite
gony, and that was unendurable; he had to open them
gain.

Now his see-sawing vision steadied a little, and he
ould swallow heavily. Before he could lose his determi-
ation, he moved another step. This time he let out a
out of anguish as his foot caught on a stone and the
eling shot up his leg and into his heart. Eyes wide, he
ttered, the breath sobbing in his throat.

And he took another step.

aldwin set their pace back into town, and it was an
ngry canter. He had given Simon and Edgar no time to
lk to him, but had climbed onto his steed and moved
ff as soon as they had come to the gate, and the others
ad needed to hurry to keep him in view.

The knight was no fool, and had no intention of in-
rvening in the normal hurly-burly of Crediton's life,
ut this was something different. The town was gener-
lly among the quietest in the kingdom, and he knew
at other officials of the King looked upon him with a
rtain degree of jealousy for having not much to do;
ut if something like this wasn't nipped in the bud
uickly it could grow an evil fruit whose harvest would
e death. It was a miracle that the two lepers hadn't
een killed the night before, and still more that the girl

hadn't received more than verbal abuse. If such behav
ior was permitted to go unchecked, it could only resu
in violent disturbance, and it was Baldwin's duty to se
to it that no such thing happened.

They rode fast along the street scattering the peopl
until they came to the hall where Godfrey had died, an
here Baldwin slowed. He had a strange presentimen
and he turned his head to look at the hall. There were
few people in the garden, tending to the vegetables, an
behind them he saw Putthe standing in the doorway, n
longer wearing a bandage, but leaning against a doo
post as if he had a headache while in the broad dayligh

As Baldwin watched, he saw Putthe's mistress appea
The servant moved aside respectfully, and the knigh
noticed his slow and careful movement. His head wa
clearly still giving him pain. Then Baldwin found his a
tention taken by the woman at Putthe's side.

She stood happily, tugging on gloves while she kep
her eye on the gardeners. In the bright sunlight her ha
sparkled as if an ethereal fire was upon it. She notice
the knight and gave him a curt nod of her head, the
spun around and stalked back inside.

"Looks like she's on her way off for a ride, eh, Bald
win?" Simon said from his side.

"Yes. It does, doesn't it?" said Baldwin. "Simon, w
have been taken in by that woman."

"Taken in? What are you talking about?"

"Didn't you see her behavior just then?"

"She was haughty, no question, but so what?"

"I think you missed the most important issue. W
shall need to speak to her again."

And with that the knight clapped spurs to his hors
and rode off; if possible, in Simon's opinion, more an
grily than before. The mystified bailiff glanced at Edga
who gave a shrug as if to indicate that there were time

vhen he gave up trying to understand his master, and
hased after.

Cecily was in no good mood when she stalked out to the
tables. Her mare, which she had ordered to be ready
ialf an hour before, was not yet saddled, nor was the
tallion for her companion and chaperone, one of the
grooms.

Of course, she accepted that it would take time for
he normal routines to reassert themselves, but that was
io reason for simple tasks not to be carried out. It was
is though the servants were trying to be—she could
hink of no other way to put it—willfully incompetent.
She made her feelings clear to the head groom and
truck the stableboy holding her mare with her crop to
nake him hurry. The only way, she knew, was to make
ure that the staff all knew who was paying their wages
rom now on. Cecily was no longer the darling little
hild of the master, the pretty ornament who suffered so
nuch from her bullying father. She was the mistress of
he estates and all the money Godfrey had amassed.

The mare was led to her, the lad sullen as she climbed
ip the stone blocks and mounted. Looking coldly at the
oy rubbing his shoulder, she set off through the gates
nd into the road.

It wasn't that she was hard—she wasn't—but my
Lady Cecily of London was no fool. From now on she
nust shift for herself. She was of age, so she was safe
nough from interfering cretins who wanted to protect
ier from the world by uniting her to any man who
night show an interest, but Cecily knew that she was
bout to become known as the most eligible woman in
niddle Devon, and confidently expected to receive calls
rom various well- or less well-intentioned buffoons in
ight hose and smart tunics, all of them displaying qual-

ities such as a lady should require: money, horses, dogs farms, and access to the best society. Cecily's trouble was, she wanted none of them.

She was a shrewd woman. Brought up a pampered young girl in London, she knew the value of polite circles, and didn't esteem them highly. To her, a pretty husband with a good-looking leg in hose was as handy as a bucket with no base. She had no use for either.

No, Cecily knew her own worth, and she knew full well that she would soon become the source of intense speculation, but she must reject all offers. And to do that she must show an ability to see to her own affairs. Only by seeming strong could she remain free. She must make sure that the staff were all kept on their toes. That was the way to guarantee that she had a free hand to continue with her scheme. She couldn't fail to meet the requirements of the oath she had made to the stern-faced leper from the north country.

That thought made her eyes glisten, and her companion, noticing her wiping at them, called out anxiously "Mistress? Are you well?"

He was used to her fluctuating moods, and had been warned by old Putthe that she could change her temper more swiftly than a coursed hare could change direction, but he was unprepared for her fury.

"Of course I'm all right! Do you think I'm some weakly slut who can't cope with a little dust in her eye?"

He had thought she was thinking about her father. Until his death she had been so quiet always, so meek and obedient to the tyrant who was Godfrey, the stableman had assumed the tear was a sign of feminine sadness. Her biting contempt was as unexpected as it was cruel, when he had only been trying to offer his sympathy. He resolved to keep silent for the rest of their journey.

She rode out every day for her exercise, no matter what the weather, and her routine had only been changed on the day after her father's death. Now she insisted that she must carry on as before. The usual route was to avoid the town itself, and today the groom saw she was intending to keep to it. She led the way, turning right from the hall's entrance, and leading up the hill toward the woods at the top. This was the road that went past John of Irelaunde's place, and she glanced at it in some surprise. The gates were open.

Having ridden this way since before John had built his little place, she knew that he always kept his gates shut against the inquisitive. Not so today. As her mare took her closer, she saw that they stood wide open, and she stared in with interest. It was the first time she had been able to. She had almost gone past, when with a gasp she recognized what she had seen.

Wrenching her mare's head around, she rode in, and hurtled herself from the saddle, throwing herself at the little bundle of rags the stableman had already noticed and disregarded.

"Quick!" she screamed. "To the church! Ride as though the Devil's wish-hounds were at your heels! Bring a monk trained in nursing. Don't sit there gaping, fool! *Go!*"

They rode into the smith's yard at full tilt, and Baldwin's horse reared as he came to a halt. "Smith? Come out here, I want to talk to you!"

Simon, who knew most of the knight's moods, was surprised to hear him bellow in so strident a tone. To the bailiff, lepers were a source of disgust and loathing, and although they deserved sympathy, perhaps, and compassion as well, their repulsive appearance was reason enough, he felt, for them to be victimized. It wasn't due to any cruelty on his part. Simon was generally an easygoing man, comfortable with himself and his life, and he was happy to see others enjoy their own lives as best they might. He was not driven by an inane compulsion to bully those he didn't understand, but he was fearful of leprosy; not only because it might clutch him in its hideous grip, taking away his freedom and his health, but because it could similarly strike down his wife, or his precious daughter. That another might attack lepers as dangerous, he could not condone, but neither could he find it in his heart to condemn. Their feelings were simply a little more guided by hatred than his, which leaned rather toward pity.

The matter was not so difficult for Baldwin. He had an enduring revulsion of anything that smacked of victimization. His friends, the members of the Poor Fellow Soldiers of Christ and the Temple of Solomon—the Knights Templar—had been accused of heinous crimes by an avaricious French King who lusted after their property and money, and were hounded throughout France. Arrested, jailed, and convicted without an opportunity of defense, they had been guilty only of believing the word of the King and the Pope. Their faith and integrity led to their death in the fires.

That, Baldwin knew, was the result of intolerance mixed with the twin spices of repression and propaganda. He had seen it before. He was determined not to see it here.

"Smith! Come out!"

Simon dropped from his horse and passed the reins to Edgar. Striding to the door, he hammered on it with his fist. "It's strange he's not open yet," he noted. "You'd expect him to have the forge going by now."

As he spoke, there was the sound of a heavy bar being

lifted from its sockets. A moment later the doors swung open, and they found themselves faced with the smith.

Jack had evidently enjoyed his ale the night before. His eyes were red-rimmed, and his complexion, under its layer of charcoal dust and ashes, looked almost transparent. He shivered, although whether from the cold or a reaction to alcohol Baldwin wasn't sure. Blearily looking from one to the other, he wiped a hand over his mouth as if to remove a foul taste. "What is it?" he asked sullenly. "Can't a man take a rest without being woken?"

"Your appearance explains a little your behavior last night," Baldwin said harshly, and shoved the confused smith from his path. The others followed him inside.

"What's all this about?"

"Shut up! Last night you and your friends chose to attack a pair of lepers, and then you had the bad judgment to put the fear of God into a young woman whose only guilt was that she has devoted her time to caring for those who are worse off than herself. Today I hear you threatened her family."

"That's not true," Jack muttered. "Why'd I want to do that?"

"That is what *I* want to know, and the explanation had better be good."

Jack shrugged and walked to his forge, raking the ashes and clearing the old fire out. As he worked, setting out tinder and striking a spark from flint and knife-blade, he spoke as though he was talking to himself. "I don't see what cause there is for anyone to take upset at trying to get rid of the likes of them. Who wants lepers in the town? They're defiled by their disease, and they defile the town itself by being here. It's not like they're normal. They're marked out by God—they'd only get that if they were specially evil. They must have committed the most horrible sins."

"I doubt that's true," said Baldwin, and a certain tone in his voice made Simon glance at him.

It was clear to the bailiff that the knight was holding his anger at bay with only the greatest difficulty. It was natural, Simon thought, that his friend should wish to defend the girl—Mary had done nothing that merited the persecution she had received—but he felt at best ambivalent toward lepers. All he had heard said that they had been marked out by God for punishment, as the smith claimed, and their hideous deformities bore it out.

"No one can doubt it," said the smith, and bent to blow his tinder into flame. When he was satisfied, he set twigs about the little fire, and soon had a cheerful blaze. Only then did he surround it with charcoal, creating a small mountain, and throw himself on the bellows. Soon the cone was glowing red-hot, and the smith lifted the whole sack of coals and upended it, giving the bellows a couple of experimental squeezes to ensure the fire would catch, and then wiping his hands while he waited for the forge to build up its heat. "It'd be heresy to suggest otherwise."

"It would be heresy to throw them out of their own camp when God Himself caused them to be allowed to live here," said the knight. "Do you think yourself above God? If they are marked out by God for His own divine justice, you can have no right to execute *your* justice on them. It is not for you to decide who should live here, and who should not."

"I am a free man of Crediton. I have—"

"*No* right in this, smith!" Baldwin suddenly bellowed. He crossed the floor in a couple of steps and grabbed the smith by the neck of his linen shirt. Holding the man close to his face, the knight glared at him.

"You have no right to decide on divine or secular justice, understand? *I* speak for the King in this town, and Peter Clifford speaks for God. We don't need you sticking your nose where it doesn't belong! If you so much as speak to a leper in this town again, I will have you amerced for swearing; if I hear you have tried to harm them, I will have you thrown into jail; if a leper is harmed because of your vile and ridiculous slanders, I will have every ounce of pain reflected on your own body! Is that clear?"

The smith met his angry gaze resolutely. "And what if they kill us in the meantime? That's what they want, you know, to kill us all off so that they can take over our town. They're going to poison all the wells except their own."

"What?" the knight expostulated. "Are you so moronic that you believe there is a conspiracy of lepers to kill you off?"

"It's happening all over Europe, haven't you heard? The Jews have put them up to it. When they've killed us all, they'll be rewarded by the Jews, and then they'll take our daughters and wives for their own. It's down to the clean-living, God-fearing folk like us to stop them."

Baldwin stared deep into the eyes before him. There was no reason there, and he suddenly felt a gut churning disgust that was close to retching. "You cretin! You know nothing except what your bigotry wants to believe, no matter what the truth may be. You think they'll poison the wells with something that'll just kill off the menfolk but leave all the women all right? You're too stupid to take seriously!" Contemptuously, he threw the man from him.

Jack tripped on a bolt of iron and collapsed. Before he could rise, Baldwin was kneeling on his chest. As the smith made to get up, he stopped, and his eyes for the first time registered fear.

"Yes," hissed Baldwin quietly. "I have a dagger at your throat. It would take just a small push to shove it into your brain, if I could find something so small. You listen to me, you fool, and listen very carefully: you will not spread any more stories about lepers, and if you hear anybody else talking such rubbish, you'll tell them to stop. Is that clear? I will not have them made even more miserable because of a moron like you."

"Baldwin, you shouldn't hurt him," said Simon quietly. He had got to his feet, and now stood a short way from the two men.

The knight slowly released the smith, who lay still, his eyes glittering with rage. "You say you are 'God-fearing,' so go to Peter Clifford and ask him what God thinks of those who spread lies about others and incite the mob to murder. I will speak to him and tell him to expect you. But for now, don't forget I'll be listening to every rumor with a view to hearing what you've been saying, and if there's anything malicious about lepers, you'll suffer for it."

He shoved his dagger back in its sheath and left the room. Edgar hurried after him, but Simon paused a moment, staring down at the smith.

"He's mad," said Jack with disgust, bringing himself up to a sitting position and brushing dirt from his shirt.

Simon kicked his elbow, and the smith fell back, striking his head on the ground, and cursing.

"Mad he may be, but so help me, if I hear you've been slandering that sweet girl Mary," said Simon pleasantly, "I shall come back here and roast you over your own forge."

"You couldn't. You're an officer of the law yourself, Bailiff."

Simon gave him a lazy smile. "Don't try me, Jack.
he Keeper always sticks within the law. Me, I'm used
issuing my own justice. So listen carefully. If I hear
at Mary has been insulted or hurt by anything you do,
l be back here, and I'll impose my own vengeance on
u. You are to be congratulated. In a matter of a few
ort hours, you've managed to make two new enemies,
d both are officers, one of the King, one of the War-
n of the Stannaries. Don't make us have to return."

- 20 -

ecily mopped the sweat from John'
brow. He was deathly pale, and hi
breathing was irregular, panting one mo
ment and taking long, slow breaths th
next. His rudimentary first aid was unravelling. She ha
removed his headband already, and the splints he had s
carefully constructed and bound to his leg were loos
and coming free.

Hearing the mad rattle of hooves and iron on th
stones of the roadway, she was tempted to leave hir
and rush to the gate to urge the men on faster, but sh
swallowed hard and remained. The hand clutching a
her own was enough to convince her that she was c
more use here, holding onto the injured man, than ou
side getting in the way of the riders.

First through the gateway was her stableman, and h
was off his mount as soon as he was through it, leapin
to her side. Then the wagon came in at a gallop, and th
driver had to haul on the reins to stop the two beasts b
fore they compounded John's hurts.

"Mistress, let me help you up."

Cecily shook her head. She had no intention of lettin
go of the man's hand while John gripped it. A mon

ame to her side, and gently felt John's head before tudying his posture and coloring. "The diagnosis isn't ifficult, at any rate," he murmured. "It's the prognosis hat will be more complicated."

"How is he?"

"How?" He was an older monk, with a fringe of vhitening hair all round his head that only served to mphasize the lines of worry and confusion on his brow. Why, with a beating like this, it's hard to say. I should hink he's concussed, which means he would have been etter employed lying in his bed, rather than getting up o these antics. The only effect of his moving around vill be a severe headache."

"But his leg!"

"Yes. It's obvious he had to try to fetch help. The leg s in a dreadful state, but at least his pulse seems stable. ometimes you find that a man will slide away quickly vhen he has had a bad accident. The pneuma, the life orce which is manufactured in the heart from the air ollected in the lungs, and carried about the body with he blood until it—"

"Can you cure him?" snapped Cecily.

"Why yes—I suppose so. I think that—"

"Where will you cure him?"

"At the hospital attached to the church, of course, so—"

"So you should hold your lectures until he's installed here, shouldn't you?"

She quickly had the men take John's door off its inges, and they carefully lifted him onto it, suffering he lash of Cecily's tongue when she thought they might ave failed in any way or made him uncomfortable. oon John was on the back of the wagon, and Cecily ode in it with him, still holding his hand.

They set off down the hill, the driver standing war-y, talking to his two charges as they began the descent, for this was a steep hill in places, and he didn't want to be called to Cecily's attention for careless driving. As they went, Cecily was surprised to feel her hand squeezed by the injured Irishman. She looked down and smiled at him.

At that moment, with the sun above lighting her head like a halo, John of Irelaunde was blinded. "Have I died? Are you an angel?" he asked querulously. Before she could answer, the cart hit a stone and jolted, beating his bruised skull against the boarded walls. "Jesus' Blood!" he swore, and when he glanced upward again and saw her smile, he gave a pale grin in return. "Ah, Mistress Cecily. You must be an angel—almost the best angel I could have hoped to meet this morning. I hope you won't mind taking a message to my sweet girl?"

"Poor John. Was this all because of me?"

"Well now, I think it was, but don't speak of it to anyone, or *he* might be taken—and then all this would have been in vain. Just keep quiet!"

Simon rode slumped on his horse, grinning. "You must be losing your touch, Baldwin. This town used to be quite a calm and quiet place, and now you've got a nutter of a smith trying to rouse the rabble."

"You think it is because of me?"

Simon smiled at the knight and Baldwin gradually relaxed, even giving a self-conscious grin. "All right, so I am a little prickly. But that idiot got under my skin."

"It's not just him, it's the murder. We still appear to have little to go on."

"No. We know so much, but none of it makes any sense. For example, I am not sure why the smith was at Godfrey's house."

"You want to go back and ask him?"

"Thank you for the thought, Simon, but I don't think

: would be productive. Still, I wonder if there is any-
hing that could link the smith to Godfrey."

"He was ugly enough—do you think he might be the
iller?"

"Who, Jack?" Baldwin laughed. "Oh, who knows?
Ie's repellent, certainly, but I don't like to judge every-
ne by their outer appearance. That is what people like
ack are guilty of when they look at lepers. I don't want
› commit the same crime as them." Baldwin mused
uietly a moment. "The difficulty I have is, Godfrey
sed him on the afternoon he died . . ."

"Yes. For a horse that had cast a shoe."

"And they had kept the shoe so it could be refitted."

"A sign of real tightfistedness."

"True," said Baldwin, but there was a faraway look
ı his eye. "Many would have thrown the old shoe
way, surely, and had a new one made."

Simon put his head to one side, considering. "And
ıen come to the smithy to get a new one the right size."

"Precisely what I was thinking. If they had asked for
fresh one, it would have meant they would have had
› bring the horse here. But they kept the old one, and
ıat meant they could have the smith go to the house.
.ll he needed was a rasp, some nails and a hammer."

"But why should they want him there?"

"Let me finish: taking a horseshoe off is easy enough.
ll you have to do is lever it. It could well be that some-
ne wanted the smith out of here, so they took off the
ıoe and pretended that it had fallen off just so that
ıck would go to the housc."

"That's one explanation, Baldwin, but don't forget
ıere's another possibility. What if someone wanted the
nith *there*, at the house? It could easily have been done
› make sure that he was in Godfrey's hall."

"True, but *why*? Why would they want Jack there?

And again I come back to Putthe: he could have levered off the old horseshoe in order to give an excuse for Jack's presence at Godfrey's."

"You're thinking that they could both have been in-volved in the killing? But that doesn't make sense! Al they achieved in having Jack at the house was to make him a suspect. There was no witness to his departure no witness to his return, no gain for him whatever. Ef-fectively all he did was point to himself with a large sign saying, 'Look at me! I was there on the night Godfrey died!' It only served to bring him to our attention."

"Perhaps it also tied him to his accomplice? If he and Putthe were partners in this felony, perhaps Putthe didn't trust his confederate enough, and wanted to en sure that equal risk was enjoyed by both?" He threw his hands in the air with disgust. "It's no good, it's all guess work. All we really know is that this man was at the hal for some reason. Whether he was there for his own pur poses or for someone else's entirely we may neve know."

"There's another factor, though. What if the victim ization of the lepers has something to do with it?"

"What do you mean?"

"I'm not sure, but it seems an odd coincidence tha Jack should start fomenting trouble so soon after the murder. I assume this was new to you? You're not aware that there's been a load of trouble brewing over leper recently?"

Baldwin scratched his beard. "No, it was a complet shock to me. But before we go worrying at that idea let's go and speak to Putthe again. I'm not convinced he's told us all he knows. And while we're there, I want to talk to Mistress Cecily, too."

"You can't suspect her of killing her own father!"

"She's not told us the truth," Baldwin said. "I am cer-
ain she's lied."

"What about?"

"About being unconscious until she was woken in her
oom. I don't believe her."

"Sir Baldwin! Sir Baldwin, sir!"

The knight glanced up. Running toward them, his habit
railing, was a young novice monk. He came to a halt beore them, panting and red-faced from his exertion.

"Well? Do you have a message for me?"

"Sir, someone's tried to kill the Irishman, and my
Dean asks you to join him as soon as you can."

Simon and Baldwin exchanged a glance, and without
a word the two men set spurs to their horses and gal-
oped to Peter Clifford's hall.

Waking from a short and troubled sleep, Rodde grunted as
he rolled over. Immediately a cool, damp cloth was at his
orehead, and he smiled through his pain. "Thank you."

"It is nothing."

His eyes snapping open, Rodde stared up at Mary.
"What are you doing in here? What if the people in the
own hear?"

Rodde knew as well as she that it was forbidden for
any women other than wives or other relations to visit
epers in their cabins. "Women of easy fame" were sup-
osed to be excluded from the camp, because it was too
asy for gossip to start.

"It's all right. I'm here too," said Ralph. He was sit-
ing near the door, gazing out over the lawned space.
"Mary refused to let me continue to minister to you."

"You've done enough, Brother. You were here all night,
nd got little sleep. Rest now, and I'll see to these men."

"Sister, you have a great heart," said Ralph, and

rested his head against the doorpost. Soon he was asleep, his arms crossed over his chest.

Rodde could hear Quivil snoring in his corner. He spoke quietly. "You should still be careful, Mary."

"It's too late for that," she said, and while her hand soothed his brow with water, she told him what had happened.

"You mean they will make you leave your home?"

"They want me from the town, not just my home." He could feel her hand tremble, even though her voice was calm and steady. "But nobody will get hurt. I'll go."

Rodde's face hardened. "So they've won? The Keeper and the others will allow this to happen and won't do anything to stop it?"

"The Keeper was furious, but it's not his decision, it's mine. I want to help people who suffer, so I'll go to a convent. There I can do more good than I can here."

"Mary, you were named well, you are as good and kind as Christ's own mother. But this is unfair! That you should be driven from your home for caring for other people is an outrage."

"No, because it means I'll be going to do something worthwhile," she said serenely, dipping the cloth in the bowl once more.

Rodde rose to his feet. Setting his hat on his head, he took up his staff.

"You are leaving the camp?" she asked.

"Yes. I have something to see to in town. But remember this, Mary: while I live, you will not have to leave here. Trust me! The smith will not trouble you again, that I promise, and no matter what you decide to do the people of the town will not force you to leave or do anything you don't want to. This I swear!"

* * *

hen Baldwin and Simon entered the room, Clifford as standing by the fire, warming his hands. "I won-red how long it would take for you to get here."

"Peter, where is he?"

"In the infirmary. It was lucky he was brought here so omptly. Ah, Cecily, how is the patient?"

She walked to his side and stood warming her back. Ie is well enough for now, although I hate to think hat would have happened to him if I hadn't ridden st. To see him like that, lying in the mess of his yard—was dreadful!"

Baldwin studied her carefully. When she noticed his ention, she lifted her chin defiantly.

"You seem very affected by the Irishman's pain."

"Isn't it a Christian duty to feel sympathy for a poor low-creature?"

"One would have said the same about your father, rely?"

"I was very sad at his death," she protested.

"But you chose not to tell us the truth about what ppened. And you pretended to have been worse hurt an was the case."

"I don't know what you mean."

"I think you do. When we spoke to you, you said you re knocked out by a man who was hiding near the ndow, didn't you?"

"Yes."

"And at the time you were wearing your blue tunic."

"What of it?"

"Why did you lie to us?"

"I didn't!"

"Who were you speaking to?"

She stopped, her mouth open a short way. There was nething in her face which the knight couldn't recog-

nize, but it wasn't guilt, nor was it sadness. It was mo
a kind of wariness, as if she was trying to evalua
which near-truth would be most palatable.

"We know you were talking to somebody. Wh
was it?"

"Who says I was?" she demanded.

"That is not your concern! What *is*, however, is wh
might have killed your father."

She tried one last denial. "I told you what happene
As I was about to go to the window, the man leaped o
at me."

"That is *not* what happened! You were at the window-
I know that. Your tunic tore on a splinter." Her ey
narrowed, and he sighed. "You must tell us the trut
Otherwise the wrong man could be punished for yo
father's death. Already some are thinking it could ha
been John."

"But John had *nothing* to do with it! He didn't com
in until later."

"And what did you say to him?"

She hesitated—only a moment, but noticeably. "I w
unconscious."

"I don't believe you. You are lying."

She tossed her head angrily. "I hope you have som
justification for that assertion! It's a disgrace that
knight should thus berate a woman who's just lost h
father."

"She is right, Sir Baldwin," chided the mystified Cl
ford. "What possible cause do you have for making th
allegation?"

"*Look* at her, Peter!" Baldwin threw out a hand em
phatically. "Look at her! How many men have y
seen knocked unconscious? And how many of the
can move their heads so easily a couple of days late
This girl would have you believe she was out cold fo

od few hours, and in that time her father was killed, r servant Putthe was struck down, and she was car-d upstairs and placed in her bed, not waking until e following morning—*yet look at her!* She can fling r head back like that without even a twinge of pain. it credible?"

Simon and Clifford stared. The bailiff realized at last hat had been troubling the knight since passing her use. He remembered the scene with perfect clarity: tthe standing and wincing with the pain as he moved head, while she gave him a sharp nod of recognition. d yet she was supposed to have been unconscious for nger than he!

Cecily avoided their gaze. This meddlesome knight s ruining things. It was ridiculous that he should ve spotted her little deception because of such a trifle! ite composed, she asked, "And what do you intend do?"

"All I want is the truth, Mistress. What really hap-ned? Who were you speaking to?"

"Child, you must tell the knight all you know, for w else can the murderer be captured?"

"It is not my secret, Father. I can tell the knight thing."

"Cecily," said Baldwin, "it was your father who died. ur *father*! How can you protect his killer?"

She looked up at him then, and Baldwin saw the ked fury in her eyes. "You dare to talk to me of my her? The man who made my mother die, the man o broke up my family and kept me under so tight a n that I could do nothing without his approval?" She allowed hard, and forced herself to calm, unmaking fists she had unknowingly formed in her passion. "If ould help you, I would, but I will not tell you any re than I already have."

"Did he often beat you?"

"Beat me?" she repeated, staring at the knight. "Ho
did you guess?"

Baldwin took his seat at a stool near her. "Was it h
who punched you that night?"

Cecily stepped away from him. Her hand rose as if t
ward him off, and she gave a short gasp. "I could b
lieve you were the Devil himself!"

"So he did, then. And I believe it was because he sa
who you were talking to at the window. He was so e
raged that he dragged you from it and struck you dow
Your friend did what? leaped inside in a murdero
frenzy? Struck with all his might and killed Godfrey
protect you from any further attacks?"

"I'll say no more."

"Why? Because you love your suitor so much mo
than the father who had become hateful to you that yo
would happily see him escape justice?"

"There can be no justice for him," she said, and Bal
win was concerned to see that her eyes appeared to b
filling with tears.

He was careful to use a more gentle tone of voic
"But doesn't your father deserve justice?"

"He's gone. I have to think of the living."

"You have a duty as a daughter!"

"And I don't forget it!"

"Then who was it?" Simon demanded.

She ignored his outburst. "You have been dreamin
Keeper. There was no one. I went into the room, and
I came close to the window, someone sprang out and h
me. When I awoke, I was in my room, in my bed. Tha
all I know. And now, if you don't mind, I shall go hor
and change my clothes. I have some of that poor Iris
man's blood on my skirts."

Peter Clifford stared after her as she drifted from t

ɔm, then at Baldwin. "I cannot understand this. She
clares she doesn't forget her duty as a daughter, but
llfully continues in what you obviously think is a de-
ɔtion. Whom could she be protecting?"

"When we know that we'll have the killer," Baldwin
d pensively. He was still gazing after the girl, a slight
wn wrinkling his brow. Recalling why he was in the
an's hall, he faced Clifford. "Now, tell us what has
ppened to John. All we know is what your messenger
d us—that he was found badly beaten up, and
ought here in a cart."

"That's about it. He's taken several blows to the
ad, and his leg was broken below the knee. I think
ll be crippled for life, from the look of it. He com-
ins that he didn't see who did it, but then with his
ad so sorely bruised, I think he'd hardly remember if
had seen his attacker."

"Let's find out."

- 21 -

The tranter lay on a low mattress in t infirmary, a cheap russet cloth coveri him. A monk was helping him to a litt wine as the three entered, and w about to stand back when the Dean gestured for hi to carry on.

John had changed, Simon thought. Gone was t cheerful, happy-go-lucky salesman with the gift of ea patter and a winning smile. Now the fellow look shrivelled. His face had an ashen pallor, his eyes an u healthy glitter, and his lips were cracked and dry. Whe the red wine dribbled, it looked like blood.

His voice was weak. “Good day, gentlemen. I'd sta and bow, but you can see, I'm not at my best today.”

“John, how are you feeling?”

“Well now, Keeper, not to put too fine a point on and saving the presence of the two gentlemen in holy o ders here, I feel like shite. I don't recommend letti people use your head for practicing their aim with clu and sticks. It gives you the most unholy headache y can imagine.”

“And how's the leg?” asked Simon.

For answer, John flicked back the corner of the rou

anket. Simon winced at the sight of the blood soaking e fresh linen bandages.

It was the infirmarer who spoke, talking in a soft, ntle voice. "It's badly broken. The bones of the shin ere shattered. He must keep still for at least three onths, and then we might be lucky and find he hasn't st the use of it."

"I hope not, Brother," said John weakly. The brother ve him a smile, and John returned it. He was enor- ously grateful for the man's care, although he was still eling feeble. It was the first time John had needed to sit a surgery of any sort and he was not looking for- ard to the pain of having the bones reset. Just the ought of the man's determined, probing fingers trying poke shards of broken bone into place made him feel k. Swallowing hard, he turned to the knight and oke, his voice gruff with pain. He still had to wince d slit his eyes, even here in the relatively dark room.

"So are you here to ask me who did this? If so, I'm sorry say I don't know. I didn't get a good look at him."

"What actually happened, John?" prompted Bald- n. He had noticed that as John spoke, his eyes had ne to the Dean.

"I'd been out, and when I got back the fire was low, I bent down to blow some life into it. I suppose it was ıen I'd just got a flame that I realized something was ong. Maybe he couldn't see enough in there to be le to make sure of me, so he waited until I had pro- ced a little light for him, and then he struck. And *how* struck! Christ Jesus! Oh, sorry, Dean; sorry, other . . ."

"I think I should allow you a certain latitude, my n," said Clifford affably. "When you are well again I all give you a penance."

John shot him a suspicious look, and became more

cautious in his speech. "I saw the club. It was just an ordinary hazel or ash stick. The sort which is made of young sapling, where the stem grows a few feet. Th grip was a large ball, and that was what he hit me with I could see it coming, and . . . Well, there was no tim to move. It struck me, and I was down. Then I saw i rise again."

"You remember all this?" Baldwin probed. From hi experience of combat, he knew how often memorie could become confused or imagined after a vicious blo to the head.

John was definite. "Oh yes, Sir Baldwin. Make n mistake, I saw it! I'll never forget that sight as long as live."

"Is there anything you can think of which might explain why this was done to you?"

"No, Sir Baldwin. I've got no idea at all." The sunke eyes, rimmed with agony, turned to him with disingenuous conviction. "Why should anybody want to hurt me?

"I was wondering, after some of the rumors abo you and—um . . ." Baldwin glanced thoughtfully a Peter. It was not the kind of question he felt the Dea would be happy to hear. The Dean caught his glanc and grinned before tactfully muttering about his duti and walking from the room. Relieved, Baldwin continued, "What about a man? Someone who was married t a pretty young wife?"

"Sir Baldwin, there are many rumors about me, know, but I can assure you that this has nothing to d with any woman—at least, not that I know of."

"In that case, who could want to do this to you?"

"As to why they should want to, I have absolutely n idea."

"Come on, be honest with us. You say you saw th weapon clearly enough—you must have seen the man

"Ah, but if I tell you, what's to stop the fellow coming back and having another game of bat-and-ball with my head?"

There was an anxious look to him that the knight could understand. "As for that, what is to stop him doing so as soon as he hears you're not dead? From the look of your wounds, one would assume he was trying to kill. He may well return."

"You do have a point there," John said, trying to grin. He winced as another bolt of pain shot up from his knee.

"Why didn't you want to talk in front of the Dean?"

"Well, now—it's like you say: there are lots of rumors about me, and I don't want to see the good Dean being made to believe in them. The gossip about me isn't true."

"So who was it?"

"Matthew Coffyn."

"So it was because of your adultery with Martha Coffyn," said Baldwin sternly. "I have warned you before about your lechery. It's only surprising that no one got to you before this."

John sighed with unfeigned disgust. "I told you before, I have never committed adultery with Martha Coffyn."

"You enjoyed her favors whenever her husband was away," Baldwin accused roughly. "The whole town is full of gossip about it."

Slowly at first but soon with a kind of helpless despair, John began to laugh. "Jesus, Mary and all the angels, it's so daft. It's funny! Sir Knight, I've never touched Martha Coffyn. I don't like Martha Coffyn, and Martha Coffyn wouldn't so much as look at a fellow like me. She thinks herself as far above me as a beech tree above a daisy. Oh, Christ's Teeth!" And he burst out laughing again, moaning with pain between gales of mirth as his ribs and head complained. Calming himself, he at last gave a soft sigh. "No, Sir Baldwin. I never had anything to do with the lady. But I suppose if *you* believe it at least that explains why Coffyn decided to beat me like this."

"If you haven't why were you in Godfrey's yard the night he died?" demanded Simon.

His reply was a twisted grin. "I wouldn't lie, Bailiff. I never touched the lady. No, I was off seeing another girl."

"Who?" Baldwin pressed him.

"I can't tell you that, sir. Like I said, I can't betray her honor. Would you betray your own lady? Of course not. If I was to tell you, it could hurt her reputation, and I won't do that, but believe me when I swear that I've never committed adultery with Martha."

"Then who has?"

"It's not my secret, but if you want to know, go and ask Putthe."

Peter was waiting in his hall, surrounded by piles of paper. Since the arrival of the Bishop, who was now with the Dean's master, the precentor of the collegiate church, Clifford had been forced to dig out all of the accounts of the different outlying chapels and churches to help the Treasurer with his report to Stapledon. It was a relief to him to have another interruption when Baldwin and Simon walked in. "Did you get anywhere?"

The knight gave a distracted shrug. "He has given us a hint, but once more we are told to go and see someone else. Each time something happens here, we appear to be driven back to Godfrey's household. It's possible John is telling the truth, but that depends on how much another man has himself been deceived."

"I would find it hard to trust too much that John tells you," Clifford observed judicially. "We all know his background."

"I fear you might be doing him a disservice," Baldwin commented.

"So I may, but I have heard some stories about him . . ."

The bailiff grinned. "So have we all, but John just denied them most convincingly, and won't tell us who it is that he *has* been seeing."

"Yet he was in Godfrey's yard and saw the bodies, I understand?" Clifford was perplexed. He had also heard the rumors about John and Martha, but didn't want to prejudice Baldwin's investigation.

"That's right," Simon nodded. "And disappeared when Matthew Coffyn arrived."

"Well, that would be no surprise, if he knew that Coffyn could be searching for him." He sighed, passing a hand over his eyes. "It all seems so confused. And while we speculate, a murderer is loose. He might strike again."

"I would hope not," Baldwin said dryly. "It's my job to see he doesn't—and in any case, I have to believe that Godfrey was killed for some logical, comprehensible reason. In England people don't kill for no purpose; there is always a motive if one can only see it. But I have to win over Cecily and get her cooperation. I am sure she somehow holds the key to this whole mess."

"Why should someone attack John?" Peter wondered.

"I think we already know the answer to that question," said the knight. "Many of your congregation think that John has been carrying on an affair with Martha."

Peter blinked, then gave a sheepish grin. He should have realized that the knight would already have discovered something that was so readily discussed in the town. "So you *had* heard that? I must confess, I always thought it extremely unlikely. She thinks herself a great lady—that she might get involved with a tranter seems somehow incredible."

"John is certain that it was Coffyn who beat him."

Peter Clifford screwed up his face as he considered this. "Because Coffyn thought John had been committing adultery with his wife?"

Baldwin gave a shrug that showed his own confusion. "That is the logical conclusion. It's possible, but why should Coffyn think John was toying with his wife if he wasn't? He must surely have had some convincing evidence to make him take such drastic action."

"I would certainly hope so!" said the Dean faintly. He poured himself a large goblet of wine and drank it straight off. "We cannot have our town disturbed in this way—men wandering the streets at night, breaking into private homes and beating the occupants."

Baldwin shook his head. "There is nothing random in it, Peter. John was thoroughly thrashed for a reason, whether the reason was justified or not. In the same way Godfrey was not the victim of a wild and unthinking attack. He was murdered deliberately. This mystery has a simple explanation, if only we can find it."

"Yes," offered Simon gloomily. "And if we can get Cecily to tell us the truth."

At that moment the object of their thoughts was walking quickly up and down her hall, her hands clasped firmly at her breast as if in prayer.

It was ludicrous! There was no reason for *anyone* to attack John! Nobody had wanted to steal from him, and there was little to take if they had wanted to. No, she was sure that whoever had committed this hideous crime was motivated by some kind of desire for revenge, but for what? Had he unknowingly insulted someone? Or was it simply that someone in the town hated the Irish?

That was mad, though. Nobody could hate John. All who met him were forced to laugh at him, or with him. He was too inoffensive to make enemies. Yet her mind kept coming back to the fact that John's injuries were inflicted not to kill but to cause maximum pain, as if they were intended solely to punish him.

There was a scratching sound, and she spun around, startled.

In the garden, Thomas smiled dryly. She looked so like a fawn scared by the breaking twig under a hunter's foot. "It's all right, Cecily. I haven't come to rob you."

"Thomas! Oh, dear, dear Thomas! I wasn't sure you'd still come. Oh, your poor face! How are you?"

He leaned uncomfortably on his old ash staff. "A little the worse for wear," he admitted.

"I heard about what happened to you. The whole town seems to have gone mad."

"Why? What's happened?"

Quickly she told him about John, finishing, "And now the Keeper of the King's Peace realizes I've been lying. I think he guesses I know what happened to Father."

"But he can't! No one else saw anything."

"Sir Baldwin is very shrewd. He has eyes that are hard to fool. They seem to see right through any deceit."

Rodde sneered contemptuously and tilted his hat back on his head. "Let him try to convict a leper. A leper doesn't exist under the law."

"A leper can still burn. That's what they do to lepers found guilty in other parts, Thomas," she pointed out helplessly. "And they say that this knight is very determined once he's on the track of a felon."

He shrugged. "He must be very determined indeed if he intends to catch Godfrey's killer. He won't find it easy."

"Oh, why did we have to come here!" she burst out, and covered her face in her hands. "If we'd only stayed in London, you'd still be settled and resigned, and Father would be alive. Instead he's dead, and it's all my fault. If only I hadn't seen you and—"

"Hush, Cecily," he said more gently. Watching her through the window, he was tempted to pull off his rough, clumsy glove and give her the comfort she needed. But he couldn't. "It's not your fault. If anyone is to blame, I suppose it's me for trying to see you again. If I hadn't come here, if I hadn't brought my friend, if I hadn't spoken to you so often, then he might still be alive—but none of that is your responsibility."

"You cannot know how much I have missed you, Thomas."

"Nor you I, Cecily."

"How many years is it?"

He considered, as if the memory was difficult to trace. "Is it seven years? Or eight?"

"It's nine years since you left London. You always pretended not to remember dates!"

"What makes you think it's a pretense?"

She laughed then, not the constrained, miserable laugh he had heard so often recently, but the old belly-laugh she had used when he joked with her.

"It's good to hear you laugh again like that."

She smiled at the softness in his voice. "We have not so very much to laugh about, do we?"

"No," he agreed quietly. "We have very little to laugh about."

Jack drained his mug and belched, wincing at the sour taste. When he moved toward his barrel of ale, he knocked a hammer from his bench, and the iron rang on the flagstone, making him wince and groan.

It was the wine, he told himself. If it wasn't for that, he'd be fine. The inn's ale was of good quality, and never gave him a head like this. No, it was the fact that he had mixed his drinks: the ale at the smithy in the afternoon; wine at the inn, until William had left them; more ale at the inn; then ale at home after seeing Mary's father. His mouth tasted like the bottom of the forge's grate. There was a gritty texture on his teeth that he longed to sluice away with ale, and a bitter, near-vomiting taste at the back of his throat. His head was pounding so hard it felt like someone was using one of his own hammers on him.

He tilted the barrel to fill his mug and glowered when there wasn't enough, kicking the barrel from him. Sitting on a low stool, he closed his eyes a moment, keeping the bright sunlight from them.

The knight was a fool. Why should Jack listen to someone who couldn't even see the danger? Knights thought they were better than everyone else, just because they were born with money in their purses, but money didn't buy brains. Jack knew that he was fortunate. He had been born poor, and he'd had to learn how to make his own path in life the hard way, learning about people and his trade as he struggled to earn a living. That was something you'd never find a knight succeeding at, he thought as he grimly took a pull of his ale.

If he had enjoyed an easier life, Jack might have turned out very differently. He wasn't cruel by nature, and neither was he dim, but he had been marked out for a hard life, breathing in foul smoke from his charcoal all day, slaving bare-chested over red-hot bolts of steel and iron, pausing only long enough to slake his thirst with his barrel of ale. If he had been educated, if he had enjoyed intellectual debate with men who reasoned and appreciated his logic, he might have grown to understand that those who wore a different appearance were not necessarily different in their motivations.

But Jack had only the companionship of the tavern or inn, where his prejudices were reinforced by others who believed the same as him, and who were prone to embellish their tales to make them more easily swallowed when mixed with ale. And his brain was fogged by the fumes that rose each day from the glowing coals.

The heat of the smithy made him toss back the last of his ale; he peered into the empty mug, then across at the barrel, which lay gently rocking. There was nothing for it, he would have to buy a fresh one. He picked up the barrel and set it on his little handcart, pushing it before him as he made his way to the inn.

When he set off, he had no intention of going against the knight's instructions. The damn thug had appeared and threatened him, but that was the sort of behavior one expected from a metal-clad meat-head. All they were good for was beating up the innocent as they went about their daily business. Jack knew that, just as he knew that a foreigner, someone from a place five or six miles away, for example, was likely to be a troublemaker. Most of them only wanted to come to Crediton to steal or live off other men's work.

Yet while he walked, he found his bitter thoughts turning more and more toward the evil represented by the lepers. Why should the knight wish to protect them? As he mused, he was coming level with Godfrey's hall. There he saw a dark figure slip from the gate, and he gaped. It was that leper, the stranger from outside town, the one who had decided to come here to Crediton.

His two favorite grudges were linked by this single, hated figure. Not only was he a leper, he was also forign, begging money from the good people of the parish when he had done nothing to deserve it—he hadn't even been born in the town!

Jack was filled with a sudden hatred. This was the sort of scum that knight and his friend had tried to protect. A man completely undeserving of any charity, someone who should be hounded from the place. Unconsciously, Jack had slowed his pace to match that of the limping man before him, and now he consciously followed him.

~ 22 ~

t feels as if I am coming here every other hour at present," Baldwin muttered as he dropped from his horse.

"You are," Simon laughed.

They had collected Edgar from the Dean's buttery and now stood together outside Godfrey's hall. Baldwin glanced at the door, but musingly. Then, jerking his head for the others to follow, he led the way round the corner of the house to the back.

It was all quiet, though Baldwin could hear noise from without the yard, and he strode quickly over the cobbled area to the low building where the horses lived. Going down the row, he could find only two mares, the others were all stallions, geldings and other males. The first of them, a pleasant roan, stood quietly while he lifted each hoof, but there was no sign of one that had been recently reshod. The second was a calm bay. This too was happy to let him investigate her, and he paused at the second hoof. "Look!"

Simon bent to see. The hoof had new, almost undamaged nail heads, but the shoe itself was badly worn at the inside and front. "That should have been replaced with a new one," he said.

The knight nodded, thoughtfully setting the hoof own and patting the mare. Then he walked from the lace toward the large gates.

Standing just outside were a pair of carts, and as aldwin watched, a servant arrived with a bucket and egan wiping the clotted red mud from its wheels.

"Why do you do this out here and not in the yard?"

The man turned and gave him a disinterested glance. My lady has a bad headache. She said she wanted no oise out in the yard, but she wants these things leaned. Where would *you* do them?"

"Are you a stableman?" Baldwin asked, but this time e had the man's undivided attention. In his hand he pun a coin.

"Yes, sir."

"So you know all about your mistress' mare which rew a shoe on the day your master died?"

The man nodded, his bucket and cloth forgotten as he atched the little silver coin spin and curve in the air so rettily. He could almost hear it calling to him, de-anding a comfortable resting place in his purse.

"Was Godfrey mean with his horses?"

"No, he was always careful to make sure they were ell looked after, sir."

"Yet on this occasion he had a shoe replaced on his are's hoof. Why didn't he send the mare to the smithy or a new one?"

"Well, the mistress saw her mare had cast a shoe—she ointed it out to me when she was back from her ride—nd said it seemed a pity to have a new one made when e old one was fine."

"You mean she saw the shoe come off and went to tch it?" Simon asked disbelievingly. "Do you think at's normal?"

The servant gave him a long-suffering look, as if

nothing much that happened in his household would surprise him. "Her father could have an evil temper. Maybe she was nervous about causing extra expense."

"But you said he always saw his horses were well looked after?"

"That doesn't mean he'd appreciate seeing others frittering away his money on their own."

Baldwin nodded. "And your mistress might have been nervous about his response? Do you have good reason to suppose he'd treat her badly?"

"I haven't seen her being beaten, but we've all heard her weeping. Especially over the last few weeks."

"Had Godfrey been different, then, over that period? Had he treated everyone more harshly?"

"No, sir. Generally, he was better to us all." The servant was frowning, as if he was himself surprised by the recollection. "But the mistress has certainly been very upset. I assumed she was being beaten by her father. He could have a violent turn of mood on occasion."

"So you said. Very well, so Cecily asked you to go to the smith?"

"Yes, sir. Her mare lost the shoe on the morning that the master was killed. As soon as the mistress came home she asked me to fetch the smith, and tell him to get here for the afternoon. He said that was fine, but if the shoe needed replacing he'd have to take the mare back to the forge to make one. As it was, Mistress persuaded him not to bother and just to refit the old one and told him he could join Putthe in the buttery when he was done."

"You heard all this?" Baldwin pressed.

"Yes, I was there while they were looking at the mare. Mistress said he could carry on, and she went back inside."

"And this was early afternoon?"

"Yes, I guess so, by the time the smith got here."

"One thing," Simon asked frowningly. "Was the nith an especial friend of the bottler? Did Jack often rop in to meet with Putthe over a jar or two of ale?"

"Him?" the servant guffawed, dropping his cloth into e bucket and holding his chest with mirth. "You must e mad! Putthe friends with a smith? Look, Putthe is the ottler in a good hall. He gave his vow to the master for fe—and a man like Putthe takes that kind of oath seri- usly. You honestly think a fellow like him would be the omrade of a peasant who's managed to learn a trade? o, Putthe and Jack aren't friends. At best they'll pass e time of day, but no more than that."

"So why should Putthe be expected to entertain Jack the buttery with him?"

"You know how it is—the master or mistress tells the rvant who to meet and talk to. I daresay Putthe was ot pleased to be told to have a boorish fool like Jack in e room with him, but once he was told, what was he pposed to do?"

"I think it's time we went to speak to Putthe again," id Simon.

odde was unaware of the steps behind him. He had her things to consider. Apart from anything else, his p hurt as though the bone was chipped—a rock had ruck him there the night before, and it burned as if he d been branded. It was so painful, it overwhelmed all e other bruises and scrapes of his body, and caused his ow, limping gait.

It was not the pain that made him pensive and fur- wed his brow, it was Cecily's words. He had refused r, as he should, but she had been very determined, and wasn't sure she had listened to his condemnation of r idea. It would be mad for her to try to win a place in the leper camp—he couldn't permit it. He knew some women, especially the insanely religious, sometimes copied Christ and tended to the sick. The most fanatica would kiss a leper's sores, demonstrating their faith by their devotion to those whom God had chosen, but for Thomas Rodde the thought that Cecily should join the lepers was intolerable.

There was only one route for him, he felt, and he was now determined to take it. He must go from Crediton and find somewhere else to end his days. This place was no longer safe or peaceful. Since first seeing Cecily, it had become a place of horror—especially now her father had died because of him. Yet it was impossibl while his leg was so painful. He couldn't run away when running was impossible.

That night was branded on his soul. The way that Godfrey had rushed in, hauling his daughter from the window, punching her and sending her flying, befor turning to Rodde himself and holding up his hand to order him not to flee. Hearing his agonized shout, seeing the man's eyes turn upward until the white showed and slowly toppling forward like a felled tree.

And behind him, holding the heavy staff, the ma who had only wanted to protect Rodde, his friend Edmund Quivil.

Edgar pounded on the sun-darkened oak. There was call from within, and soon footsteps could be heard approaching. "I'm coming, I'm coming!"

It opened wide, and Putthe stood on the threshold His face, grim at the best of times, fell into a scowl when he saw who waited on the doorstep.

"May we come in?" asked Baldwin smoothly as he walked into the screens. "I think we can speak easiest in your buttery, don't you?"

Putthe gave a non-committal grunt and the knight led he way inside.

"Your head looks as if it's a bit better, Putthe," comnented Simon.

"Wish it felt it."

"Still giving you grief? I know head wounds can take ime."

"It hurts," he conceded with an ill grace.

"We aren't here to talk about your wound, however," aid Baldwin, sitting at Putthe's own stool and watching im speculatively. "We're here because of the odd way hat Jack happened to come along here on the afternoon Godfrey died."

Putthe was not made of such strong material as his nistress, he gave a start and shot a look at the night. He hadn't expected the blasted Keeper to ave realized how odd that little event was. When he poke, his tone was wary. "What do I know of that, Master? I'm the bottler, I don't know what goes on in he stableyard."

"So you know something was wrong, too. Either that r you suspect something—or someone. What was trange about calling Jack out like that?"

"How should I know?"

"I don't know how you should know, but you are bout to tell us. What struck you about having Jack alled up here that day? Was it the fact that Godfrey vould never normally stint on looking after his horses, nd the mare might just as well have been sent to the mithy? Or was it that Cecily herself appeared to have ome ulterior motive in it?"

"What sort of motive could my lady have had in askng the smith to come up here?" the bottler asked cornfully.

"That," said Simon, who had moved behind the bottler, "is what we wish to find out from you. What advantage was there, having the smith up here?"

"Because," Baldwin added smoothly, "there is always the other possibility: that it was *you* who arranged matters such that the smith came up here."

"Me?" the bottler squeaked. "What possible reason would *I* have to ask a slovenly fool like him to come up here?"

"To establish your alibi."

Putthe gaped. It felt as if a fist of ice had clenched around his bowels and he was aware of all the flesh on his back suddenly chilling with a frozen expectation. He was no fool. If a man could be accused of aiding or abetting in a murder, the justice was likely to be swift and predictable. The bottler considered his position quickly while the knight rested his chin on his cupped hand. Putthe had done all he could, but loyalty was one thing: the certainty of a noose was another.

"Sir," and now his tone had a persuasive certainty to it, "I swear before God and as I believe in the life to come, I had nothing to do with the death of my master. I didn't even know anything was going on. My Lady Cecily did ask that the smith should come here, but it was not with any malicious intent."

"Tell me all you know."

The bottler sighed and took his seat on a barrel. As an afterthought, he reached between his knees and poured himself a jug of ale. He seemed to have no intention of drinking, but held the drink as an aid to his concentration, much, Baldwin considered, as a knight might toy with a sword or dagger while he regaled an audience with a story.

"I told you before about the master finding John in the garden. It was true. And later the master told me about it. He thought it was quite funny, the way that he

ught the little Irishman. But now I have heard someing a little different. Now I am told that John never
d an affair with Martha Coffyn; the man who was
ing over to see her was not the Irishman, but my own
aster!"

Baldwin nodded slowly. "So each time Coffyn went
f on his travels, your master used to say he was going
t to keep an eye on things and protect the garden
om the hired thugs next door, whereas in reality he
as visiting Coffyn's wife?"

"That's it, sir. Every journey Coffyn made, he would
arn his partner, my master, so my master knew exactly
hen to go and see Martha."

"But why should Godfrey have invested in the busi-
ss in the first place? Oh, of course!"

"The last thing he wanted was for Coffyn's business
fail. That would have meant an end to the trips away.
, my master was happy to make sure that Master
offyn's business did well enough."

"What has this to do with the smith?" Simon de-
anded.

"Sir, my mistress had to have the mare's hoof fixed,
d she didn't want the master to find out about it, be-
use he was always berating her for the money she
asted. Not that it was fair. Mistress Cecily has always
en quite frugal. Still, that was why she asked Jack to
me here and refit the old shoe, to save money."

"It would have saved more if she had sent the mare
th the shoe down to the forge, and not asked the
ith to come up here," Baldwin commented.

"Jack doesn't charge for coming up here," Putthe cor-
cted him.

"But her father came in here and saw the smith," said
mon.

"She didn't know he would come in here. As it was,

it was so long after Jack had done her mare, it didn
matter. Master Godfrey thought the smith was her
socially."

Simon scratched at his head. "There's one thing w
still don't know, and that is what you promised to te
us: why did Cecily *want* the smith here?"

Putthe gave him a lugubrious stare. "I couldn't te
you for certain. That smith is a rather repellent charac
ter and isn't the sort of man I'd want to entertain in m
buttery usually, but the mistress asked me to look afte
him, and I was happy to."

"What did she actually say to you?" Baldwi
frowned.

"She just asked if I could fill him with ale once he'
finished playing about with the horse. In fact, I remem
ber she said she was sorry to ask me to do it, becaus
she knew Jack wasn't the most generous soul in th
town. She made some comment about how intolerar
he was."

Simon gazed blankly at him. " 'Intolerant?' Wha
would she have meant by that?"

"Jack can be a complete fool on occasion. Look at h
behavior with the lepers last night. There was no excus
for that. No excuse whatever."

Baldwin nodded, then he went perfectly still, starin
into the distance. After a few minutes his brow cleare
"Very well, Putthe. You've been very helpful. Let m
know if anything else occurs to you, won't you?" H
rose and stalked from the room.

In the screens, to Simon's surprise, he stopped an
peeped into the hall. When Simon went to his side, h
saw what the knight was staring at.

The maid, Alison, was at the cupboard, rearrangin
the pewter on the shelves. Simon's eyes opened wide a
he saw that the shelves had all been filled. On the to

as a pair of silver plates and a drinking horn; beneath
ere six pewter plates and a silver salt cellar shaped like
swan; below that was another row of six plates,
anked by two large flagons; on the lowest was a row
eight smaller plates. Simon gasped, but before he
uld speak, Baldwin put a finger to his lips, and led the
ay from the building.

ne sun was waning as Rodde reached the top of the
gh street, and he moved more slowly as the air cooled.
is hip held him back, for every step he took made it
he. Many years before, he had fallen from a ladder
d broken his shoulder, and this reminded him of that,
dull, throbbing pain that expanded when he put his
eight on it. It made him wonder whether he had actu-
ly broken something.

At the inn he paused. Cristine saw him patiently lean-
g on his staff and came out with a jug of ale. Giving
r a smile of sheer gratitude, he held out his bowl. It
as illegal for a leper to touch a jug or pot that could
used by a healthy person, but the girl poured straight
to his bowl, and he drank greedily.

Cristine filled the bowl again, and watched solici-
usly while he drained it a second time. There was no
ed for her to try to say anything; her kindness in giv-
g him ale to drink was itself enough. She couldn't
ink of anything to say to him in any case. Thomas
odde was not yet so hideously deformed as some of
e others, but the sores on his face were enough to
ake her want to keep her distance.

Finishing his drink, he gave her a slow bow and made
f back to the leper house. Cristine stood some while
atching him go, his staff tapping regularly at his side
hile he shuffled away. She was trying to imagine how
would have looked before he had been struck down.

In her mind's eye she straightened his back. Tha would surely add six inches or more to his height, sh realized, which would make him a tall man, possibly a most six feet. Then his hair, now so lank and besmeare with mud, still showed signs of its underlying tawn hue, a color which would make him stand out. His eye were unchanged, he hadn't yet lost his sight, and were peculiarly bright blue, while his flesh was bronzed fro exposure. He was just the sort of man she had alway fancied. The sort of man she might have chatted to i the tavern before he became scarred with leprosy.

She felt a shiver pass down her back. Someone walked over my grave, she thought, and crossed herse automatically.

"Hello, Cristine. Can you get this filled for me?"

"You've finished the barrel already? Jack, you mu have too much work if your thirst is that bad!"

"My thirst is bad enough, I reckon," he muttered, b his eyes were fixed on Rodde's back.

As Cristine watched, he made off after the leper, an when she called to him, "Hey, what about your ale?" h merely waved.

"I'll come and get it later."

His urgency made her hesitate, and her gaze move off toward the limping man.

- 23 -

Baldwin and Simon walked out to the street while Edgar unhitched their mounts and followed after them. In the roadway, Baldwin glanced at Simon.

"Interesting."

"Baffling! What on earth can it mean? Someone stole l the plate, and has now returned it?"

"No," Baldwin chuckled. "No, I think it's a great eal simpler than that. Simon, we are coming closer to solution to this problem." He bit his upper lip, suck-g at his moustache contemplatively. At last he gave a ight groan. "Enough speculation! Right, it is not a easant duty we must go and perform now, but it must e done. Are you ready?"

Simon immediately understood him. "As ready as one in be. I don't want to be involved in reminding a man ' his wife's infidelity, but we have to know the truth, on't we?"

Baldwin nodded sourly and marched through the gate to Coffyn's garden. He strode up to the front door id knocked loudly. Edgar joined them as they waited. oon they were in the hall, and here they saw William id his master sitting at the great table at the dais.

There was no one else in the room, which was some re lief to Baldwin.

He confronted the merchant. "You were responsibl for the beating given to John of Irelaunde last night. H is not dead, but he is sorely hurt, and you will be pay ing him compensation. If he desires to press charge against you, I will help him."

Throughout this little speech, Coffyn had remaine coolly silent. Now he spoke. "I don't know what make you think I was there, Sir Knight. I was in this hall al most all the night. My men were with me."

"You were seen and recognized by John."

"The man who was wounded? Perhaps his brai was addled. It can happen, you know, when a man i badly wounded about the head. He was wrong in thi case. I was here from a little after dark, and never wen out again. Why should I want to hurt a fellow I'v never met?"

Baldwin shook his head. "Good, but not goo enough. We know why you went to molest him."

Coffyn rallied well, Baldwin thought. He made great show of pouring wine and sipping it slowly, cor centrating all the while on Baldwin's face. "I'm not sur I know what you mean."

"You thought John was involved with your wife. Yo were hurt, naturally, and shocked too, I have no doub You had no idea who could have been responsible, bu it was easy to hazard a guess. Or maybe you didn't nee to—maybe you heard rumors of how John behavec and reasoned that there was no smoke without fire. I either case, it was you who went to John's house las night and waylaid him. You wanted to make sure tha John was given to understand that you wouldn't toler ate his flirtation."

"You're talking nonsense," said Coffyn, but his fac

ʼas pale, and Baldwin saw that the hand holding his oblet was shaking.

"I wish to speak to your wife," Baldwin stated luntly.

"That isn't possible."

"Matthew, this won't achieve anything. You can re-ıse me permission to talk to her if you want, but you eed to hear the truth as well. The man you beat last ight was not her lover. I have heard that from two peo-le today who ought to know. Why don't we ask your ʼife?"

"You have no right to demand it."

"No, I don't," Baldwin said reasonably. "But I hap-en to know that you are wrong in thinking John has nything to do with her. Of course you are hurt and ruck with grief by her adultery . . ."

Coffyn started and glowered.

". . . but that is no reason to attack the wrong man. ohn has had nothing to do with your wife."

"I won't believe it! He was seeing her every time I ent off to a fair or market."

"Someone was, but not John. John was seeing some-ody else."

"I heard him leaping from my roof and making off rough the garden."

"*It wasn't John.* Fetch your wife, and we'll see what e says."

"My wife is indisposed. She can see no one."

Baldwin leaned on the table so that his face was close the merchant's. "Matthew Coffyn, I cannot order our wife to make any statement which might incrimi-ate you. But if I can make you believe that John was nocent, I may prevent you having him beaten again. ease call your wife here."

With a bad grace, Coffyn surrendered. He waved a

hand at William, and the man-at-arms strolled from th room. There was quite a delay before he returned, wandering along behind the young wife of Matthew Coffyn

This was the first time Simon had seen Marth Coffyn since his move to Lydford. Then she had been a elegant young woman who had a tendency to put on little too much weight, but with her lively nature an sense of fun, she had never lacked popularity. Befor Coffyn had managed to ensnare her, she had attracted host of admirers not only from Crediton but from several miles away.

But the woman Simon now saw was not the same— not at least at first sight. She was still a little overweigh but her size only added to her voluptuous attraction emphasizing her heavy breasts, the sweep of her broa hips and the length of her legs. The difference lay in he manner and her face.

Her beautiful pale complexion, which in color had always reminded the bailiff of the finest clotted crea from Tavistock Abbey, was mottled and blotched wit red. Her eyes looked as though they were raw fro weeping, her nose shone, her lips were bloated wit sobbing, crimson as blood itself. Even her hair was unkempt and bedraggled, hardly contained in her wimpl

She stood before her husband, but her gaze never m his. Instead, she stared at Baldwin with a kind of arrogant disdain. "Well, husband? You wanted to see me— here I am! What do you want now you have witnesse my utter destruction? What more do you want of me?"

Coffyn sank down in his chair. "You're in error, m lady. It was this knight who wished to speak to yo Please answer him."

"My lady, I am sorry to have brought you dow here to ask you these questions, but I have to preve any more violence if I can, and you are the key. I kno our husband has been keeping you locked in your oom, but—"

"Keeping me locked in my room?" she demanded, yes flashing. "You think I would let him do that? He id no such thing, Keeper. Oh no, I chose to stay in my oom."

"Please, Martha," Coffyn groaned, putting a hand to is brow and shielding his eyes from the contempt in er own.

"Please, Martha!" she sneered. "He pleads with me ow, trying to stop me telling you what I know, while—"

"Martha, these men are here because yesterday I beat our lover to within a breath of his death," Coffyn said oldly. "They want you to tell me I was wrong and had he wrong man almost killed."

She gaped at him, before giving a wild laugh. To imon it sounded like the beginning of hysteria, and he vas about to move nearer her to offer some comfort vhen she held up her hand. "Don't approach me," she issed. "I am perfectly well, although it is a miracle in his household. So this absolute cretin had the monumental stupidity to try to have someone killed in an attempt to get him to leave me alone?"

"It was John of Irelaunde," Baldwin murmured.

"Him!" she spat contemptuously. "The pedlar? You *are* to think I would defile myself with a slovenly little hit like him?" Her voice became harsher. "You think I vould demean myself with a pathetic creature like that? How dare you?"

Simon was intrigued by her rage. It was entirely genuine, he was convinced of that, but he was staggered hat the woman could feel so degraded by the allegation. She felt no shame about her wanton adultery, but ould be appalled when her husband felt she would give erself to a lowly tranter.

Baldwin interrupted her protestations. His attention had been fixed on Coffyn, whose face had taken on the appearance of a man who had seen a ghost. His hand had fallen, and now he sat as though struck dumb with horror.

"Mistress Martha," Baldwin said. "I think you have said enough."

"Who was it, then?" Coffyn's voice was a whisper.

"Your friend, dear Matthew! Your favorite—your partner. Dearest Godfrey was my lover, and had been for months. You never guessed, because you were never here to see, but he was with me every night whenever you went away. He stole into my room each night, and he stole my heart when he left me."

"Why, Martha? All I ever wanted was to please you to make you comfortable. Why should you betray me in this way?"

"You're pathetic!" Her anger made her enunciation slow and deliberate. "You think you own me because of a contract, but you never bothered to satisfy me. You thought by buying me new jewels and robes you could hold my love—but you never realized that to hold my love, first you had to hold *me*! Why should I betray you you ask! Why should I remain loyal when that mean living the life of a celibate?"

She turned sharply, the long skirt sweeping over th rushes. "Sir Baldwin, I have answered your questions. hope my husband is not stupid enough to try to attack anyone else, but if he is keen to, perhaps the next man he springs on will do me the favor of sending my husband to Hell. I have no use for him."

With that parting shot, she marched haughtily from the room.

Matthew shivered and rested his head on his hands He had never before felt the vastness of his wife's con empt for him. It came as almost a physical blow to his tomach to see Martha behave in this way. He felt sickned, revolted by her absolute disgust for him.

"Matthew, do you accept your wife's word?" Baldvin asked softly.

"I believe her." The words came as if wrung from his ery soul. Matthew Coffyn shook his head. His future was lasted. There could be no hope of peace or renewed love n his marriage. Before her outburst there was still a hance, but now that chance was gone. Her words had corched his pride. It was impossible that she would ever e able to reciprocate his feelings. He had hoped that with is competitor out of the way, her love for him would eturn—instead, her loathing for him had increased.

"You accept that John of Irelaunde had nothing to do vith your wife's infidelity?"

"It seemed so obvious!" He held up his head appealngly to the knight. "Everyone knows of John's reputaon. As soon as I realized what was happening with my ife, I was convinced it had to be that little sod!"

"On the night Godfrey died, you were here looking or John, weren't you? You came home earlier than exected, and were searching for him in your home when ou heard Godfrey's scream."

"Yes. The time before when I'd been away, I returned te at night instead of the following morning, and alough Martha came fairly quickly to meet me, I heard omeone jumping from the roof and making off through e garden. Well, John lives out at the back of Godfrey's— thought it would be easy for him to clamber over Godey's wall and thence into my garden. It seemed so bvious that the little git was ravishing my wife, I hardly ave it a second thought."

"It took you a long time to decide to have him eaten," commented Simon.

"I intended catching him." The merchant turned his angry, unblinking eyes on the bailiff, worrying at a fingernail. "What would you have done? I had no real proof. That was why I invented this charade of a final trip away. I said I had to go to Exeter for a couple of days, but after a few hours at a tavern on the way, I came back. My men I sent into the garden to block any escape, while I ran upstairs. There was no sign of anyone, and my wife insisted she was alone, but I searched her chamber, and went through all the chests. There was no sign of him. I just thought John must have heard us in the street before we got here, and then made use of the same escape route as before, climbing through the window and leaping from the roof before making off."

"Whereas it never was John," Baldwin reminded him.

"No. Instead, when I ran next door to save my neighbor from being attacked, I was in truth trying to save the man who had been cuckolding me. Oh, my God!" he cried, and covered his face with his hands. "I have lost my wife, and now I'll be prosecuted for having my revenge on the wrong man! How could I have been so *stupid*!"

Baldwin sighed. "You may well find that an apology to John will prevent him from taking you to court. For my part, so long as you ensure that he is furnished with money while he recovers, I will not try to take matters further. This is all a ridiculous mess. In future, don't take the law into your own hands. If you are aggrieved, take your case to court and seek redress there."

"Redress, Sir Baldwin?" asked Coffyn, looking up at the knight blankly. "Redress for losing my wife? What redress could I expect for having had my life taken, for having my future wrested from my hands, for having my opportunities for wedded happiness stolen? What hope is there for me, Sir Baldwin?"

* * *

alph left the chapel. He could see the limping figure of odde making his way from the gate, heading back to is room. The brother wondered whether to have a talk ith him. Rodde was spending too much time outside e hospital for his liking; lepers were supposed to re- ain within their walls, devoting themselves to prayer, ot wandering the roads whenever it took their fancy. alph considered, but decided not to speak to him yet. odde and Quivil both appeared to need time to them- lves. If they were shown compassion, Ralph thought, ey might come to appreciate God's mercy, and find eir own salvation within the hospital grounds.

Having deliberated over this for a minute or two, alph was about to go to his little room when he heard oices at the gate. Tutting to himself at this interruption his routine, he turned to seek the source. His mouth ll open in astonishment.

"What is this?" he demanded.

"She wants to come in to see Rodde, the new one. I ld her she can't, but she won't listen."

"Lady, it's impossible. This is a leper hospital, some- here for men who have been inflicted by the disease. ou mustn't come in."

"Brother, I would like to speak with you."

"Very well," Ralph sighed. "Wait there, and I'll fetch cloak."

He signed to the gatekeeper to keep it closed and arched off to his room. His cloak was on top of his est, and he pulled it over his shoulders. The sun was ready dying in the west, and with its passing the armth of the day was rapidly fading.

"Here I am, madam. Now," he opened the gate and ssed out, "What is the matter? Why make such a fuss re?"

"You have an inmate here, a man called Rodde, I believe?"

"Why, yes. He came here a few weeks ago," Ralph said. He caught sight of the smith standing nearby and listening to her words with interest. Ralph frowned at him, and began to walk up the hill away from the town itself, circling the perimeter of the compound. "He came from somewhere in the north. Luckily his illness is not far progressed, and he has his own money, so he is little drain on the hospital's resources. But what is your interest in him?"

"I wish to see him in the hospital."

"I fear that isn't possible."

She smiled and reached for her purse.

"That's not the difficulty, Lady," Ralph declared hotly. He resolutely stuffed his hands into the sleeves of his robe as if to prevent their temptation. "I am afraid that the inmates are only allowed a certain kind of woman to visit them."

"A certain kind, Brother?" she asked softly with a raised eyebrow.

"Not *that* kind, Lady," he snapped, "*They* aren't permitted to cross the gate at all. No, the only women allowed in here are the relatives of inmates, and even then they are only allowed in during daylight so that nothing untoward can happen."

"You have that young girl in to help."

"You mean Mary? She's different—she's the housekeeper."

"I had thought that the housekeeper to a lazar house should be a woman of mature appearance, who couldn't be attractive to the inmates and tempt them to lascivious thoughts or acts; someone who should be known for good conversation, but little else."

Ralph shot her a look. "That's true," he admitted

'But when no one else will lift a finger to help these ɔoor souls, it's necessary to use whoever will volunteer."

"She docs look very young."

"Her age is not something that bothers me. More imɔortant is her keenness to provide comfort to the men n there." Realizing the equivocal nature of the phrase, ıe reddened, continuing hurriedly, "What I mean is, she ıelps to keep the chapel clean and tidy, and assists me n my duties such as they are. She has already indicated hat she might wish to go to a convent and offer her life o God."

"She is so young."

"She's old enough to love her God," he returned piously.

"But I should still like to come into the house to see Thomas."

"Mistress . . ."

"My name is Cecily."

"Well, Mistress Cecily, I am afraid you may not. It is ıot permitted."

"I know the rules well enough. Relations *can* go hrough your doors."

"Yes, mothers and sisters may." Ralph saw with relief hat they had almost returned to the gate of the hospial. Soon he would be able to leave this woman behind nd return to his work. Her next words halted him in ıis tracks.

"What about wives?"

He gaped. She raised an eyebrow and cocked her ead.

"I . . . but this is quite impossible!" he stammered.

"Am I so undesirable, Brother?" she murmured.

"You intentionally misinterpret my thoughts, Misress! It is still not possible for you to enter."

"But why? I thought that the wife of a man could not e separated from him."

He sighed. That was the drift of the law as it related to normal men and women, it was true, but a leper's wife was different. The leper, once consigned to his doom, had been declared dead. His will had been executed on his entrance to the leper house.

"If you were married to him," he tried to explain, "you are now legally his widow. You can have no claim on him, just as he can have no hold on you. You should find yourself a new man, someone who's untainted."

"Brother, I love him. Who are you to tell me I should leave him alone now? He is sick, and I can comfort him better than any other."

"But you have no rights with him any more. He is no longer your husband."

"Brother," she said coldly, and turned to face him. He could see the anger bubbling beneath her calm exterior. "He *is* my husband. Your church married us before God, and here, before God, I affirm my love for him. If he is to be nursed until his death, I, his wife, shall be at his side. I demand the right to join him in your hospital."

Jack watched the two argue with disgust. It was appalling! That a young woman, perfectly healthy and attractive, and wealthy enough as well, could actually want to go and stay with the perverts and sinners in the hospital was grossly offensive. A good, normal girl like Cecily should want to spend her time with strong, rich men. The smith couldn't quite consider himself a suitable mate for her, as the gulf in their status was too broad, but he was clear in his own mind that he was significantly better for her than any leper.

He marched back to the town. His abhorrence of what he had heard lent speed to his feet. It was only as he came to the eastern outskirts that he slowed, an idea striking him with sudden force.

It was impossible that any woman could want to ·eep with a leper. Such a thing was ridiculous, and yet ·ere in Crediton, two women, both of them attractive ·nough, appeared to want to do just that. Jack knew he ·asn't stupid: there must be some reason why these two ·anted to go into the hospital. Love he could discount. ·Ie couldn't believe that any woman could of her own ·ee will choose a diseased and defiled creature like a ·per as the focus of her love. There must be another ·ason.

The lepers themselves must be practicing some form ·f black art on the women of the town.

- 24 -

Simon took the hill from Crediton at a canter, Baldwin and Edgar at his side. It was a relief to be leaving the town behind them, and this was the first time in his life Simon had ever been glad to leave the town he knew so well.

He found himself considering this. The town itself hadn't changed that much, he thought. He had left it some four years ago when he was given the job of bailiff of Lydford Castle, and before then he had always looked on Crediton as a bustling large town, infinitely bigger than Sandford, the small village where he was born, but still somehow comforting. Yet now he was pleased to be leaving it.

In part, he thought, it had something to do with his growing used to the space of Dartmoor. The rolling moorland held a fascination for him. It looked as though it had been blighted in some powerful battle between God and the Devil, with its withered bushes, the curious trees by the stream called Wistman's Wood where the oaks grew stunted, none of them reaching a height of more than a few feet. And then there were the swamplands, from where issued the awful cries o onies and sheep as they struggled to free themselves om being sucked into the mire. It gave an impression f strength, of barren power, such as he had never felt efore.

In contrast, Crediton now made him feel a little austrophobic. It was so busy always, with people ushing about trying to make a living. On the moors, a ew men fought with the ground to make it yield up its ches, digging and smelting the tin and the lead, or cutng the peat, but their numbers were so small comared with Crediton that when he rode out he could nagine himself alone, with no other man for miles round. On the moors it was possible to ride for hours nd see no one. In Crediton a man could not avoid ther people.

But it was more than simply this, he told himself. rediton felt as if it had changed. The senseless murder f Godfrey had poisoned his feelings about the town ore than he would have expected.

Simon Puttock had seen enough dead men to know at he was not simply struck by the unfairness of a man sing his life, nor by the apparent pointlessness of Godey's end. No, it was more the fact that no one apeared to mourn Godfrey. His daughter, although she emonstrated the dutiful sadness of a child for her faer's death, was withholding things—of that Simon ow had no doubt. The man's servant, Putthe, who ould have been loyal even to death, had also kept ings to himself. In fact, the only person who appeared regret his loss was that strange woman Martha offyn, and she was only the man's mistress in an adulrous relationship.

"Thinking it all through again?" Baldwin asked.

"Was it that obvious?"

"Only when you sighed so loud! Godfrey's passing

would not seem to have caused anyone a great deal o
pain, would it?"

"That's just what I was thinking. The only real affec
tion for him came from Coffyn's wife, and that's hardl
a suitable love. I suppose it's hard to say it, but woul
anyone be happy to know that the only mourner at hi
funeral would be a slut?"

Baldwin threw him a curious look. "Probably not
but I suppose I'd be more glad to have even one whor
regret my passing than no one at all."

"I expect you're right," Simon agreed. "All I can sa
is, I thank God that I have a wife and daughter t
mourn me when I pass."

"Yes, you are lucky."

"Baldwin, I'm sorry. I know you crave the compan
of a wife."

The knight gave a dry grin. "There is no harm i
being proud of your wife, Simon. Any man could b
proud of a woman like Margaret. And the same is tru
for Edith. She is a daughter any man would be please
to call his own."

"Yes. I am fortunate," said Simon complacently. The
he pursed his lips and whistled, low and mournfully.

"All right, Simon. What is it?"

"What do you mean?" the bailiff asked.

"Why have you adopted that innocent demeanor
Why are you whistling like a slow wind soughin
through the trees? In short, spit it out, whatever it is!"

"Baldwin, I really don't know what you're on abou
All I was thinking was, what a pleasant woman Jeann
de Liddinstone is."

"Oh, good God!"

"She's good at sewing, too," Simon mused, casting a
approving eye over the knight's new tunic.

"Hmm. Yes, she was most kind to make it for me," id Baldwin, unconsciously fingering the embroidery at s neck.

"In fact, I should think you are a very lucky man," mon said judiciously.

"Simon . . ." Baldwin paused. It was hard to broach ch a topic even with his closest friend, especially when knew his servant was listening to every word. But lgar had been his servant for so many years, it would ve been unthinkable to send him away, and he knew his heart of hearts he could trust Simon completely. imon, what would you do in my position?"

"Me? I'd marry her tomorrow. If you really love her, mean, and certainly your expression when she apars seems to bear out that construction. Anyway, her nds are good, she's beautiful, and her needlework is cellent."

"You know that's not what I mean."

"Oh well, if you're asking the best way to prose . . ."

"Simon, do you intend to be the most exasperating an alive, or is it just a skill you were born with? I ean, how in God's name can I get rid of that damned rgon who masquerades as a maid? What can I do out Emma?"

"Ah, now there you have me. I've never had that speic problem before myself. I'll tell you who you should k about her, though, and that is Meg."

"Your wife?"

"She has thrown out more useless staff than anyone se I know of. If she can't help you, no one can."

"I shall speak to her." With this determination, Baldn settled to staring at the road ahead. They had rdly come halfway yet, and he shook his shoulders to

settle his cloak more evenly, pulling at the trailing en
until it came over his chest and kept the wind out.

"Baldwin, who *do* you think might have done th
murder?"

The knight sat silently for some while, and Simon a
most thought he hadn't heard. He was about to ask th
question again when the knight began speaking quietl
and ruminatively.

"I know who I don't think it is: Cecily. To me it seem
highly improbable that she committed the crime, eve
though I am quite convinced she lied to us about th
events of the evening. That makes me wonder why sh
should want to lie. The only logical assumption has t
be that she is trying to protect someone—but we don
know whom.

"Then again there is that dreadful little tranter. Joh
could have tried to rob the place—in fact, that was m
first thought, that he might be a drawlatch, and th
robbery went sadly wrong when he was found—bu
that is not the case. The goods are back, so there was n
theft."

"Isn't it possible that someone broke in to steal th
plate and was found out? Maybe that's why. It's a
back, because someone went to fetch it back?"

"If that was the case, why keep it secret? They'd ca
the constable to fetch it for them, and to see that th
drawlatch was arrested."

"Unless they wanted to take their own revenge. The
might have thought it more suitable."

Baldwin considered this. "You mean that John *wa*
the thief, and was beaten for his felony, rather than fo
his assumed adultery? If Coffyn hadn't admitted his a
tack, I'd be tempted by that as a theory. But the fact i
Coffyn confessed to having him beaten. Thus we are le
with why someone should steal the plate only to retur

. In which case, why was it removed at all? Why *do* ᴇople move their plate?"

"They'll take it out if there's a fire," Simon mused.

"There was no fire," pointed out the knight.

"Well, people pack it up when they are going to avel."

"There was no sign that Godfrey was about to leave, as there?" Baldwin frowned suddenly. "Unless . . ."

Simon waited, but the knight sat silently, and at last e bailiff burst out, "You had the nerve to accuse *me* of ing frustrating! 'Unless' what?"

"I was thinking—people take their most valuable ings with them when they travel, and leave anything at they can't take with them in safekeeping."

"So?"

"So—perhaps someone took Godfrey's silver and oked after it. There was no theft because it is all back ere now. Godfrey wasn't going away, there was no e, but perhaps someone felt the plate could be at risk it was allowed to stay where it was, so it was put in a fe place."

"Why should it be safe now, when it wasn't before?" mon demanded, mystified.

"Clearly it was unsafe when the whole household as unconscious. Now members of the house are fine ice more, it is safe to return it."

Simon shook his head, "What of the other suspects, en? You've only considered Cecily and John."

"Who else? Putthe I cannot understand. I would be ore suspicious of him if he had not been struck down mself. Since he was, I can't see how he could have en involved."

"There's his friend, Jack the smith."

"Except even the stablelad said Putthe couldn't stand e smith. I would need to see some kind of proof that

they regularly met before I could see them as conspira
tors. No, I find it hard to accept that Putthe could hav
killed his master and then Jack knocked him out. Wha
would be the point? Jack can't even have robbed th
place—the stuffs all back on the sideboard now."

"Coffyn said he came in from the front, too, so h
should have seen Jack running away if he'd been there.

"Whoever was there obviously made off through th
garden at the back. That in itself tells us nothing. Jac
could have come back, committed his acts, and then ru
off through the back."

"True enough. And we still have the question of th
mysterious stranger at the window. Someone wit
whom Cecily spoke, and presumably a man since Jac
heard a man and a woman."

"Yes, and since his identity is being kept from us, he
naturally very suspicious." Baldwin nodded. "I shoul
like to question Cecily more about him—or them, if w
believe John. Surely the two he saw must be the sam
That is something we shall have to do tomorrow."

"Fine. In the meantime, let's hurry back to you
house. This wind is cutting through to my bones!"

Baldwin laughed, and glanced about him. "Anoth
mile or so, not more. Come on!"

Moving at a fast trot, they soon warmed themselve
The land was peaceful as they passed. Smoke rose fro
cottage fires, only to be dissipated by the gentle breez
As night fell, Simon found himself looking up at th
stars more—his horse would follow Baldwin's witho
needing guidance. Already the sky was blue-black, wit
a sprinkling of white stars standing out distinctly, lik
flour shaken finely over a dark cloth. A solitary clou
floated above him, as fine as a feather of silver. Woul
a feather float on the air if it was made of silver? I
wondered. Could any other metals float if they we

arefully constructed to the same dimensions as a eather?

The thought made him give a wry grin at his own oolishness. Metal was metal! Metal was heavy, and ouldn't float, neither on air nor water. The idea was idiculous. Just because you made something look like omething else, just because you changed its outward ppearance, didn't mean you changed its essence . . .

He jolted along for some moments lost in thought. ppearances, he thought, could be deceptive.

Inevitably his thoughts turned to Coffyn. The man ad thought his wife was enjoying an affair with the ishman, and all because the evidence appeared to support that view. Yet in reality the culprit was his neighor, an unscrupulous character who was prepared not nly to cuckold him, but was also quite possibly willing spread the rumor that it was John who was guilty, hich had at last led to John's brutal beating at the ands of the jealous husband.

And suddenly Simon had a strange idea.

the leper camp, Ralph saw to the wounded Quivil. he man was shaken, but his injuries from the stoning ere mending nicely, and Ralph was confident that he ould be up and about, perfectly well, within a few ays. Getting up from the leper's bedside, he forced his sts into the small of his back and stretched. He was nding that seeing to the needs of his inmates was becoming painful. It was easy to see why those of his colagues who spent their days tending to the sick were rone to aches and pains in their backs, he felt. It came om constantly bending over their charges.

Edmund Quivil was snoring peacefully enough, and alph could hear the church bells tolling from the other de of the town. He moved to the door and wrapped

his robe about him more tightly as he saw how cold i
was. Shivering, he threw more logs on the fire befor
pulling the thick curtain over the doorway and walkin
quickly to the chapel.

Inside he found a couple of the more devout leper
waiting, and with them he went through the mass. Ther
was always so much to be done, but this was the offic
he most enjoyed. The candles flickered as they cast thei
soft light, glinting on metal and paintwork, remindin
him of his duties: to tend to those souls whom most ha
already assumed to be consigned to damnation.

It was with a light heart that he left the little chape
He was always more contented leaving than going in
the small chamber was filled with the love of God. It
pictures of Christ and His mother seemed almost t
glow with adoration. The very walls were constructe
of kindness and generosity. Its atmosphere of incens
and dirty clothing was to Ralph the very essence of wor
ship, for the two smells demonstrated the love of ma
for God, and Christ's love of the sick and the dyin
There couldn't be a better place to worship God, he fel
than from inside the chapel of a lazar house.

The ground crunched underfoot. Since he had walke
inside the chapel, the frost had dusted the grass, and h
inhaled the crisp air with satisfaction. It tasted clean i
his mouth, like a fresh mountain spring. Outside hi
own door, he snuffed the air happily and sighed wit
pleasure.

He knew many of his friends and fellow-brothe
thought he was insane to want to look after the leper
that was partly why he was here, because at the electio
for the post there was no one else who wanted the jo
But Ralph was convinced it was the best way for him t
serve God. This was surely the best way too to sav

ouls, and that was the sacred duty of all who wore the
onsure. They were God's own army, whose only task
vas to save mankind in the eternal battle.

Something caught his attention, but he was only
ware of it as a niggling irritation at first, something
which interrupted the flow of his thoughts. It was like a
iece of carpentry where the workman has been forced
o leave off his task when he has all but finished. The
ast little unfinished part is an annoyance. This was sim-
ar; it was a tiny part of his normal scenery that was
vrong. He looked over the whole encampment, but
othing appeared out of place. Toward the town he
ould see nothing wrong—until he realized that there
vas a glow, just over the brow of the hill, where he had
ever seen one before. It appeared to waver in the night
ir, and the sight made him frown.

He walked toward the gate. From here he had a good
iew of the road, and he stared eastward, trying to
ierce the gloom, but it wasn't possible. In the end he
vas about to return to his room and seek a good night's
eep, when he saw them.

From the town came what looked like a solid mass of
nen. They approached inexorably, some carrying burn-
ng torches, clad in a malevolent silence that was more
ntimidating than if they had been chanting slogans or
houting.

He fell back from the gate, his guts churning. The
igns were all too easy to recognize; this was an attack.
e had heard of the murders in France from a traveller
hen he lived in Houndeslow. There, he had heard, a
hole number of lepers had been captured and burned
ive, on the pretext that they had been involved in poi-
oning wells. It was nonsensical, of course. The lepers
epended on the alms of the healthy—if they killed their

neighbors, they would be killing themselves—but that hadn't persuaded the peasants who wanted to extirpate the "sinners."

His glance roved up and down the camp. He had no choice but to defend the place, but *how*?

- 25 -

imon was a little in front of the other two when they arrived at the stableyard. It was already dark, and there were no torches lighted. Baldwin bellowed for his ooms as he passed through the gates.

The bailiff was impatient to get to the fire. His horse anced, hooves pounding at the packed earth, and non hunched his shoulders to keep his neck warm. ldwin kicked his feet free of the stirrups, and leaped wn, stumbling and almost falling. Seeing this, Simon ve a short laugh.

"Very funny!" Baldwin growled.

"This is how you do it," said Simon, and swung his over his horse's neck. As he did so, his mount lifted head, catching the bailiff's foot. Simon found his leg ing higher and higher. He had no reins to hold, his t were free of the stirrups, and suddenly he found nself falling, eyes wide in surprise. He hit the ground th an unpleasant squelch, his ears filled with the de-hted, mocking laughter of his friend.

Margaret set aside her tapestry as the two men lked in. She smiled and welcomed Baldwin, but then

froze at the sight of her husband. “Simon, what *ha*
you done?” she wailed.

“He was showing off, Margaret!” was Baldwin’s un
sympathetic contribution.

“I just had an accident in the yard,” said Simon, an
yawned.

“You must go and change.”

Baldwin could see her point. Simon was smothered i
mud and straw. An old pile of rubbish and hay had bro
ken his fall, but he was liberally bespattered with brigh
red mud.

“Meg, I can’t. I’m exhausted. Maybe in a while, whe
I’ve had a chance to warm up a bit.”

Hearing voices, Jeanne walked in and stood on th
dais. She returned Baldwin’s smile. “I was wonderin
whether you were coming home again today. It is ver
late.”

“We have had an interesting day,” Baldwin sai
crossing the room and taking her hand courteously t
lead her to the fire. Jeanne listened while he explaine
all that had happened to them.

“We’re no nearer discovering Godfrey’s killer,” Simo
added sourly as Baldwin finished.

“Oh, I can’t be so negative, Simon. We may not hav
solved the murder, but at least we appear to have solve
a theft without knowing it, and we have averted the vi
timization of the lepers!”

At the gate once more, Ralph would have laughed t
hear his words. He held a heavy staff of oak, one whic
he was sure would do good service if he was able to h
someone with it. The monk was untroubled with th
concept of fighting to defend his inmates. It was the na
ural duty of a religious man to protect his floc
whether the man was a bishop leading the people of h

ity, his sword in his hand, against barbarians, or the naster of a leper house defending his sufferers.

"They don't look as if they're going to stop, Brother."

Ralph glanced to his side. Thomas Rodde stood there, his hat tilted forward as he peered forward through slited eyes at the approaching horde. The leper wore his loves, and his strong staff was in his hands, but he tood like an old man, bent at waist and shoulder.

Rodde was no fool. He counted the men, and gave up when he reached twenty. That number of strong and ealthy folk could overrun the camp in a matter of mintes. There were only the few lepers here, and of them e and Quivil, even after their ordeal of the night beore, were still the most healthy. The best thing for him o do, he knew, would be to run quickly. He had little trength, but this rabble of townspeople was here to vict the lepers. They wouldn't, if he knew the English t all, be remotely bothered about chasing their prey. heir objective was to see the lepers away from Credion. What happened after that would be someone else's roblem.

"Brother, wouldn't it be best for us all to leave?" he aggested.

"Leave *here*? This is our home! It's where we belong. low can we go? And where to?"

Rodde met his look resolutely. He was not suggesting coward's route, but a sensible retreat in the face of verwhelming odds. "In that case, let me suggest that ou should send for the constable, and also for the Preentor or Dean of the church. We'll need all the help we an get."

aldwin washed his hands and settled back in his chair. le had a delightful sense of warmth sitting here before is fire. The presence of guests had persuaded him to partake of some strong wine, and it flowed through his veins like fire. He had not drunk enough yet to feel the soporific effect, but it had certainly heightened other senses. To his mind, Jeanne appeared to be devastatingly beautiful.

She glanced in his direction every now and again. Seeing him sitting there so calm and contented made her feel curiously relaxed. It was an odd sensation, this feeling of well-being—she refused to put it stronger than that—that she felt while near him. He exuded an air of stability and honor. It felt as if, when he walked into a room, that room suddenly took on a fresh splendor, and it was down to his self-effacing, gentle personality.

Jeanne still had no idea of his past in the service of the Knights Templar. She had no idea of his involvement with the Order, but she was aware of the latent anger that lurked within him, constantly searching for injustice and oppression. This harder side to his character lent a subtle charm to his generally calm demeanor.

Studying him now, as he stared at the fire, the contours of his face softened by the glow of the flames, she was taken by a sudden desire. She could see his confusion, that he was still mulling over the killing in the town, and it made her want to fold him into a strong embrace and shield him from the world outside. He was vulnerable. She knew his air of cold rationality was a mask to conceal his defenselessness against a world he only partly understood and mostly disliked. He was a man composed of opposites: he was the Keeper of the King's Peace, yet he doubted any man's absolute guilt he was a knight, yet he felt sympathy for villeins; he was a landowner, yet he shared the profit of the land with the people who farmed it for him. All in all, he was a curious mixture.

She felt the attraction to the man of action, which he

doubtedly was, as well as to the cautious, but gener-
s and kind man who looked after his peasants. There
s no denying the fact that he was good-looking. To
nne's eye he was almost perfect. Even the scar, the
und of some old battle that marred his cheek, was
ractive, a reminder that this was not some picture
t a real flesh-and-blood man. She smiled, and found
self once more considering how well she would fit
o this hall, with these servants, with this man. Bald-
n would probably find it harder than her, she
essed. She had been married, had lived with a man;
dwin had never married. He was a bachelor, and at
er forty, must be set in his ways. But the thought
n't frighten Jeanne. It wasn't her wish to change
n—if she changed him, he wouldn't be the man she
ired. No, she wanted him just as he was, and if liv-
with him entailed her having to alter her lifestyle a
le, then so be it.

Yes, she thought. Her decision was already made for
. She would become a married woman again.

Simon grunted and stretched out his legs. The fire
s blazing merrily, and the cloak at his back prevented
draft from troubling him. He had already put events
Crediton from his mind, and was now only looking
ward to a good meal and his bed. Casting a glance at
wife, he tried to catch her eye, tempted to suggest
t they might go to their room early for some hori-
ntal exercise to build up an appetite, but she was
king away, watching Baldwin.

uddenly she turned to Simon, and held out her hand.
ntly, she led him from the room. Surprised, but by
means unwilling, he followed her.

eanne felt her heart pound as she realized they were
ne. It was obvious why Margaret had taken her hus-
d out, and Jeanne realized that now, at any mo-

ment, Baldwin must ask her again for her hand. To h
delight, not unmixed with fear, she saw the knight ta
in the empty seats, and face her. He smiled, she
turned it; he rose to his feet, and she did likewise;
held out his hands to her, and she raised her own b
fore moving to him.

And there was a furious barking, a scream, a shou
and Edgar ran in.

"God's Teeth! What the hell's the matter this time
Baldwin roared.

Jack stood a short distance in front, a torch burning
one hand, a long-bladed knife in the other. He w
elated. It had taken no time to win Arthur's suppo
and once they'd spoken to a few others at the in
they'd soon gathered a following. The men they'd
cruited were all horrified to hear that a second wom
had been perverted by the lepers. How long would it
before all the young women were ensnared? Jack h
asked rhetorically.

"Out of the way, Brother. They're none of them w
come here anymore, we want them all to go. You ca
stop us!"

Ralph set his feet firmly and glared at the men. "H
many of you are there? Such a lot of brave folk you a
All of you here to eject five or six ill people. And wh
would you have them go? Would you throw them
to die on the moors? How do you think God wou
react to that?"

"God?" Jack sneered. "God has pointed them
with this disease—it's our duty as God-fearing men
support Him in His punishment. They don't dese
alms, they deserve death!"

"That is blasphemy! You believe Christ would su
port victimizing these poor souls? Didn't He sa

ızarus? Didn't He wash the feet of lepers? How dare ›u suggest you have God's sanction!"

"Enough of this! You twist my words, Brother. Stand ide, or we'll move you ourselves."

"I will not move. Here I stand, to defend my poor in- ates. They suffer to remind you of the purgatory to ›me, and you *dare* to threaten them, and me? I will not ove."

"Then we'll shift you ourselves, monk."

Jack thrust the knife in his belt and nodded to an- her man.

Ralph was aware of the murmuring of the lepers be- nd him. One man was sobbing, and from the sound was sure it was Quivil: he shouldn't be up, the onk thought distractedly, but he had other things to ncern him. The others were talking in a hushed, ıxious tone that showed their terror. All had heard of e murders in France. Their worry lent strength to the onk. His fingers tightened on the stave, and he raised like a pike. "Don't try to come in. I will not let you ıss!"

"You, little priest?" cried Jack, laughing. "And how you propose to stop us? Eh?"

Suddenly Ralph was joined by two men. One, snivel- ıg, he recognized as Quivil. The other was Rodde. Both rried their strong staffs, and both stood determinedly.

Rodde pointed with his staff. "You, smith, are break- g the law. You have incited the people to mutiny, and u will be punished. Any man who passes the gate ıen the leper master has refused permission will be ar- sted and punished. If any one of you tries to kill or in- re a leper, you will have to answer to the Keeper."

"You can't accuse someone of killing a dead man."

"I breathe; I eat; I drink; I piss; I shit—just the same you do. If any of you doubt I am alive, you can argue the matter with the Keeper of the King's Peace and th Dean of the church. You'll need to be very convincin to persuade them, though, I reckon!"

His words and his easy manner made a few in th crowd laugh, and Jack was enraged to be thus thwarte "You're a leper," he shouted. "You have no rights. you think you have, go somewhere where they'll sup port you. You'll not stay here."

"I'm ill, you fool. I am dying—but so are you. Wit you, your death may come tomorrow, while mine will b in four or five years, if God spares me, but we'll both en up in the ground. And what then? I wonder where Go would send a man who rouses the town to murder."

"You're not even a local man! Why should we starv ourselves to feed your useless belly, eh? Go on! Leav our town. You're not welcome here."

"No one will cross this gate," stated Ralph firml "These men are here under my protection, and und the protection of the Church. You have no rights her smith. Go home."

"Yes, go home."

Jack turned to find himself face to face with the Dea and Bishop Stapledon.

Peter Clifford was bristling with anger. "How *da* you march out here to the Church's land and threaten brother in his holy work? How *dare* you rouse the mo to violence? This is outrageous behavior even for a fo like you. You are arrested, smith. Put down the knife

Over the priest's shoulder the smith could see that h small army was dwindling as people realized the cons quences of being discovered could be dire—and expe sive. "We have the right to see God's will done," declared.

"Not here, my son," said Stapledon calmly. "I a your Bishop. You have no rights here. This is a hospit r the sick and dying. Every wound you see on these en is given to them by God Himself to serve as a sign you. Your actions tonight are an insult to Him."

"I don't believe you! They're evil—they've managed win over two of our women already, and they'll not happy till they've won all the others. They shouldn't allowed to stay on, they should be evicted!" Jack outed, glaring from one to another. Suddenly he atched the knife from his belt. Spinning, he rushed at e gate.

"Jack, stop!" bellowed Clifford, but the running man ped over the gate and pelted toward Quivil.

The leper was overcome with shock to see the madned smith heading for him. With his mouth hanging en, he lifted the stave in his hand, and Rodde moved help him, but even as Thomas saw the oaken stick int to the smith, he saw it fall. "Edmund, no!"

It was over in an instant. No one there missed the ok of fear disappear, to be replaced by one of gratide. They all saw Quivil drop his sole weapon of dense, saw the faint smile that passed over his face, and vaguely surprised expression that succeeded it as the ife slipped in up to the hilt in his chest.

"No!" Rodde screamed, swinging his staff. It cracked o Jack's head above the ear, and he slumped to the ound at Quivil's feet, leaving the dagger buried in the er's body. "Edmund! How could you?"

Rodde caught at Quivil as he began to topple.

Edmund felt light-headed. Suddenly his knees weren't ong enough to hold him, and he was thankful for his end's arms. He could feel Rodde carefully easing him wn to a sitting position.

"Why didn't you defend yourself? You could have hit n and kept him away!"

Ralph went over to the fallen smith. Jack was lying

face down, and as the monk tried to pull him over, h
felt a horrible stickiness on the man's shoulder. Bendin
he saw that the back of his head was crushed, an
Ralph gave a low sighing groan for Jack's folly befo
muttering a quick prayer.

He stood and put a hand on the weeping lepe
shoulder. Rodde's hat had fallen from his head, and h
tousled hair hung loose, obscuring his face. Gently th
monk took Rodde's hands away and lowered Quivil
the ground before closing the sightless eyes.

Baldwin ran out with his servant, leaving the quiet
fuming Jeanne in the hall. Out near the kitchen
found Emma, sobbing hysterically and holding her ar

"It was the hound, your blasted hound! You shou
have killed it when I said; you should have killed it. I
mad! Look at me, look at my poor hand, and all b
cause I was trying to stroke it!"

"Edgar, what happened?"

The servant shook his head sadly. "I am sorry, sir, b
she says Uther went for her. She tried to be friendly wi
him, and when she made to stroke him, he bit her."

Baldwin looked at her skeptically. "Where did
bite you?"

"Here! Look!" she wailed, holding out her hand.

There on her wrist, Baldwin could see the toothmar
by the light of the moon. Blood was drawn on tw
gashes where the canines had gouged the skin, but th
were not the deep wounds of a savaged limb—they we
no worse than Baldwin himself had received when e
joying a tussle with the dog. Teeth like Uther's would
vastly more harm than this. "Is that all?"

"All? What more proof do you need, you unnatu
fellow! That dog is vicious, it's a brute. What do y

ean by asking if that's all! What more do you need? A
ɔrpse?"

The knight eyed her with frustration. That she was
ared he didn't doubt, but to say that Uther was in any
ay ferocious was ludicrous. "Look, Emma, perhaps
e should go indoors and get your wounds seen to."

"Why, so you can try to persuade me I imagined this?
ɔok: *blood!* The dog must be killed. *Now!*"

"Where is he?"

Edgar answered. "Hugh took him back to your
ɔom, sir."

"Sir Baldwin?"

"What now? Oh, sorry, Hugh. What can I do for you?"

In answer, Hugh said nothing, but pushed past Emma
a bush by the wall. He stared for a moment, then
ached in, and brought out a long stick. Passing it to
ıldwin, he stood and stared at Emma with his arms
lded.

The knight studied it, and glanced helplessly at the
ıpassive servant. "Well?"

"That's why Uther bit her. She kept stabbing him with
I saw her from the window."

One end of the stick had been sharpened to a point.
ıldwin tested it on his finger as he surveyed the maid.
s this true?"

"The hound attacked me. He's mad and vicious."

"Is it true you baited him?"

"Answer him, Emma."

Baldwin turned to find Jeanne at his side. She was
atching her maid with an expression of contempt.
Did you make the dog try to bite you?"

"No, I only had the stick to defend myself."

Baldwin broke the stick in half and threw it away.
That dog is less cruel than most humans, and you tried

to beat him into betraying his nature. You did so t
make him appear dangerous so that you could get hi
destroyed. You are less humane than he is."

"Emma, you are released from my service. I will n
give you a home when I return to Liddinstone. Yo
must find somewhere else to live," said Jeanne coldl
then she spun on her heel and went back into the ha
Baldwin walked after her.

"Madam, I am sorry if my hound has been the cau
of your losing your maid."

"Can you believe that I would want you to have yo
best dog killed because of a foolish woman who mi
treats him?"

"No, of course not. And I don't think I could suff
her to live with me, either."

She shot him a look. Baldwin was smiling broadl
his happiness a mixture of delight at the removal
the block from his path, and new-found confidenc
Now he was certain of her answer. He held out h
hands to her again. "Come, I think we were about
talk of something important when your maid inte
rupted us."

"Yes, Baldwin?" she said, and walked into his arm

It was unfortunate that Hugh had thought Uth
should be freed from his confinement. More so, th
Uther felt left out when he saw his master kissing a
embracing Jeanne. So it wasn't surprising that
jumped up at them, although he *was* surprised at t
way his master shouted at him.

Simon and his wife knew nothing of the scene. Upstai
in their room, Simon threw a tunic at his wife. She w
still naked on the bed, languidly running her han
through her long blonde hair.

"You should get dressed," he grinned.

"It was you who delayed the process," she retorted, reading the green velvet tunic beside her over the tch where he had been lying only a few moments be-re. "If you hadn't decided to attack me as soon as we t up here, I'd be ready now."

"My apologies, Lady. In future I'll leave you to dress one."

"I don't think so," she chuckled, rising from the mat-ss and pulling a shift over her head. Simon watched r as she clothed herself, smiling to himself. When she as ready, and he had pulled on his hose, shirt, and tunic, held out his hand and they left the room together.

Simon was filled with expectation. He knew only well how much Baldwin wanted a wife, a woman o could comfort him and provide him with chil-en, and his friend had selected the widow. All Simon ped was that she would accept him and be the lady longed for.

He walked down to the screens. The way was cur-ned. Margaret paused, her grip on his hand tighten-. "Do you think they've agreed?"

"That's in their hands."

He smiled, but she could see his confusion: he wanted go in and hear good news, but he wasn't sure that he uld.

"Come, my love," she murmured, her mouth at his . "The anticipation is killing me."

With a resolute movement, Simon swept the curtain de and they walked in. In front of the fire sat Jeanne. ldwin was nowhere to be seen. Jeanne rose elegantly they approached. "I think Baldwin will be back ortly."

"He left you here?" Simon asked.

Jeanne caught the note of enquiry in his voice, a
her eyebrow rose. "His dog came in here and jumped
at us," she said, and lifted her arm. There, beneath h
arm, were two massive muddy footprints. "Baldwin
seeing to him."

Simon shook his head. So his friend had failed.
soon as he had tried to persuade Jeanne to marry hi
the blasted dog had ruined things again.

"Uther has already caused the removal of Em
from my service," Jeanne continued, seating herself.
fear Baldwin was rather angry with the dog. I ca
imagine why."

Her words made Simon grit his teeth. She was be
so cold and unresponsive, yet Simon was convinced s
knew perfectly well that Baldwin wanted to have her
his wife, and she must also be aware that he adored
dogs—especially "Chopsie." "It is a shame," he s
quietly. "I hope Baldwin will not do anything hasty w
Uther."

" 'Hasty?' Oh, I don't think his treatment of the br
would be at all hasty."

Just then there was a clap from behind them. Sim
spun around to see his friend walking in, wiping
hands on a towel as if cleaning them of dirt—or, Sim
thought, blood.

"Simon! Margaret! Are you ready to eat?"

The bailiff couldn't stop himself glancing at Jean
Baldwin saw the look, and raised his eyebrows. She
turned his glance, innocently widening her eyes.

"I told them you were seeing to Uther," she sa
"Have you done it?"

"Baldwin, you haven't had him killed, have yo
Margaret demanded.

"No," said Baldwin.

"But . . . Then what were you doing?" Simon stamme

The knight laughed out loud. "I don't want him leap-
; all over me while I am celebrating! Simon, Mar-
ret, meet the lady who will be my wife! Jeanne de
ldinstone has accepted me, providing I keep the brute
ay from her while she is in her best tunic."

- 26 -

imon and the cheerful knight rode in
Crediton in the middle of the mornin
They went straight to the Dean's hou
and it was here that they heard about t
near riot. Baldwin immediately insisted on riding out
the leper camp to ensure that all was now well. Th
found Ralph morosely wandering about the grassed ar

"Brother Ralph, I came to offer you my apologies
last night."

"Sir Baldwin, that is very good of you. And I
pleased to see you too, Simon. Yes, it was a dread
shock."

"And two dead?"

"Yes. Edmund Quivil died immediately. He nev
spoke again. The other, the smith, was soon dead
well. His skull was crushed when another tried to st
him killing poor Edmund."

"I shall have to see Edmund's parents," Baldwin mu
mured, shaking his head. "What a ridiculous was
though. If only Jack had been sensible."

"Do you want to see the bodies?"

"Where are they?"

"I have them in the chapel. I thought they might

ll wait there until the Coroner could view them. We n't want them out in the open to rot."

"Er, quite so."

He and Simon studied the corpses. The knight was ocked to see how skinny Quivil had become.

"He lost his appetite as soon as he was diagnosed, d the weight fell off him while he was here," Ralph plained.

"And you say that the other man who died had his ad stoved in?"

"Yes. Quivil's friend here, Thomas Rodde, tried to e him, but the blow had already been struck."

"I was too late."

Baldwin turned to see Rodde approaching. Although s was the lepers' own chapel, Rodde obeyed the rules standing some three yards from the others, sadly eye- the cold body. "He could have defended himself if d wanted."

"He turned the other cheek, Thomas," said the monk etly. "He behaved as a good Christian should."

"But he didn't need to."

"I think he had lost the will to live. Everything he nted as most dear was taken from him."

"Yes. Even his woman was to go to be a nun."

"Mary chose that route for herself," Ralph pointed quietly.

"And you will not allow my wife in to be with me?"

"Your wife?" Baldwin asked.

Ralph nodded. "This man is the husband of the man you know as Cecily."

Simon gave a gasp. "So it was *you* she was talking to the night her father was killed!"

Thomas Rodde gave a slight grin. "It appears you ow much about my business, sir. But yes, I was re."

“Come outside and let us talk,” said Baldwin. “W
have much to ask you.”

They walked out into the bright but chilly sunlig
and stood near the gate where two had died the nig
before. Rodde shook his head when his eye caught
glimpse of a reddish-brown smudge on the grass.

“He was a good friend to you?” asked Baldw
noticing his expression.

“Yes. He was brought here the day I arrived. Th
night he was attacked by other inmates, and I sav
him. He was my friend from that moment.”

“It's no surprise he decided to let Jack kill him, the
said Simon. “If the poor bastard was hounded in h
by his peers, and bullied outside by the townsfolk.”

“No,” agreed Rodde. “Yet I wish he'd let his illn
take its course. There was no need for him to die.
could have had plenty of enjoyment in the years he h
to come. I would have shown him how.”

“You have yourself been ill for many years?” Baldv
asked.

“Yes, sir. I was struck down when I was alm
twenty. My father was another goldsmith in Lond
and we lived close to Godfrey and my wife.” There w
a defiance in his voice, as if daring Baldwin to deny t
he, a leper, could still be married. Seeing no dispute
the knight's eye, he continued. “We grew up togetl
living almost next door. It was only natural that
should marry.”

“What sort of a man was Godfrey?”

“Him?” Rodde blew out his cheeks as he consider
“He was a good, generous man in those days. It w
only more recently that he changed, or so I understa
As soon as I was denounced for this—” he waved
hand at his face “—he became quite hysterical.

ife, Cecily's mother, was horror-struck, and I think
st her mind. Because of that she was run over by a cart
d died. That, I think, was what made Godfrey snap.
ntil then, he had tried to help me and Cecily. He had
und a good place for me in a leper hospital, and pro-
ded the place with alms and money, and allowed Ce-
y to come and visit me, but when his wife died, he
as embittered. He blamed me for his wife's death, and
extension he blamed Cecily herself."

"Was that why he came here?"

"No. I saw what effect he was having on my wife,
d rather than ruining her life, I persuaded my leper
aster to release me, and took myself off to the north.
vanted to leave her to find a new man. She wouldn't
it while I still lived there, but I felt sure that once I'd
ne she'd discover someone else. Some time after I left,
nich was a good nine years ago, Godfrey brought Ce-
y down here."

"Why did he come here? It's a strange place for a
ndon goldsmith to come to."

"Cecily wouldn't forget me. She is a loyal woman.
ith me gone, he came to blame Cecily even more for
r mother's death. I think he needed someone to hold
sponsible, and she was an easy target: it was her de-
ion to marry me, and thus she was at least partly
volved in her mother's death. Cecily wanted to re-
ain in London near her memories of our life to-
ther, and I think it was to punish her that he
cided to move. He said he wanted to take her away
om the disease and corruption of the city, but I don't
lieve that. Mind you, it may be that he was also
rvous I would return. He had no wish to be con-
onted by me again."

"And you did come back."

"It wasn't my intention. I spent many years living i
the north, and hated every moment. It was cold, and th
chilly rain seeped into my soul, but even that wouldn
have made me come back to the south where I migh
upset my Cecily. No, it was the raid. The Scots were in
volved in one of their periodic attacks and flooded ove
the border. My lazar house happened to be in their path
The priest and I were lucky, we weren't there at th
time—we tended to walk when we could—and when w
got back, the place was razed to the ground. All tha
was left was smoke and ash."

"So you came down here?"

"Not at first, no. I went back home, to Londo
There I found that Godfrey and Cecily had left. A ma
in the town told me they had come this way, althoug
he thought it was Exeter."

"And you found them here?"

"By luck, yes. While I was in Exeter I hung aroun
the goldsmiths' streets and overheard some men talkin
They were actually discussing the loans made to Coffyn
but one of them mentioned Godfrey. When someon
spoke of a retired goldsmith from London who had
beautiful daughter, and whose name was Godfrey,
wasn't hard to guess that my search was ended."

"And what did you intend?" Simon burst out. "Di
you mean to hold your wife to her vows and force h
to go with you?"

Rodde glowered at him. "Do I seem so unfeelin
You, a healthy man, can afford to be arrogant, but
you loved your own wife as I do, you'd know that
bring her down to my level would be the most besti
act! No, I didn't mean to take her away, although if
had wanted to, I would have been within my rights. A
I wanted to do was see her and reassure myself that sh
was all right. I never meant her to see me, for I kne

ıat would unsettle her, but I did want to see her again, ıst the once, before I die. Is it wrong to love a woman › much?"

"Of course not," said Baldwin soothingly. "But she ıd see you, didn't she?"

"I was a fool. I'd hardly got here when I saw her. ıe didn't recognize me—how could she when I wore l this stuff? But then one day she walked over to give ıe money. I tried to hide my face from her, but she cognized me somehow, gave me her whole purse. She ıld me to come and see her. We couldn't talk in the reet, but she promised to contrive that all the ser-ınts would be out of the house at a certain time so we ıuld talk."

"And Godfrey as well, of course."

"Yes. Cecily trusted Alison, but none of the others. ny of them might have told Godfrey."

"Including Putthe?"

Thomas Rodde grinned. "Cecily knew *he'd* tell God-ey, so she decided to make sure he was busy."

"And she was sure she could arrange for her father to : out?"

"She had to do nothing. She knew whenever Matthew offyn was away, her father would visit Mrs. Coffyn. ll I had to do was find out when Matthew's next jour-ıy was. Godfrey wouldn't miss his chance of seeing artha. I agreed to see Cecily as soon as Coffyn went ı his next journey."

"And that was the night Godfrey died?"

"Yes, sir. I stood outside the window, but Cecily was nvinced we had plenty of time, and asked me inside. ıe'd got rid of all the servants, and there was no ıance we'd be seen together. Quivil was with me, and e asked him in too. Well, we weren't there above a w minutes, when we heard a row from Coffyn's

house. I suppose we were too busy with our ow
thoughts and didn't connect the noises with Godfrey
but suddenly there he was, chortling merrily to himself
He saw me and stopped dead in his tracks. Edmund ha
ducked behind the door, and Godfrey didn't see him.

"He gave a bellow, grabbed Cecily, and punched he
in the face. I was furious, and was going to attack him
Godfrey held up his hand, said was I trying to ruin he
as well, or something. Edmund thought he was going t
attack me, so he . . ."

"Edmund clobbered him with his staff, just as yo
last night felled Jack the smith."

"Yes. Then there were steps, and in came Putthe. H
saw his master and mistress and gave a squeak of hi
own. Edmund didn't know better, and he was panick
ing, so he knocked Putthe down as well."

"What then?"

"Well, I made sure Cecily was all right; she was a
that mattered to me. Her face was bloody, but sh
seemed fit enough. I was with her by the window,
never even really looked at Godfrey. Why should I, afte
what he did to my wife? In any case, I thought he wa
merely unconscious. It was Cecily who told us to fle
We nipped out through the window, because we coul
already hear noises from the garden as Coffyn's me
searched for Godfrey. It was only the next day we hear
he was dead.

"Once outside we hurried off, but soon heard step
coming after us. We didn't know who it could be, an
after what had happened, we didn't want to get caugh
in Godfrey's grounds, so we hid, not far from John
wall. Well, it was John himself, and he saw us, I sup
pose. He was as startled as us, because he ran back to
ward Cecily's house. I'd heard enough about him t

loubt this Irishman, and thinking of poor Cecily all
lone with only her maid to protect her, I followed after
im. When I went to the window, I saw him at Cecily's
ide, making sure she was all right, while Alison stood
ear. It was obvious that John was not threatening the
vomen in any way. It was enough for me, and I left the
lace. I collected Edmund and we walked up to the back
f the garden—there's a section of wall there that's easy
o climb if you know it. We got back into the street and
nade our way to the camp."

"What of the silver?" asked Simon. "We know it was
one on the night Godfrey died, but it reappeared
ater."

"You'll have to speak to my wife about that," Rodde
rinned.

"So we've sought a murderer, when in reality it was
n accident," mused Baldwin.

"Edmund didn't mean to kill him; the lad was no
nurderer. When he heard Godfrey was dead, he was as
orrified as me."

"I see. Well, I want to know what happened to the
late, so I will go and see your wife now, but I thank
ou for your candor."

"There's no point in protecting Edmund now, is
here?" Rodde said sadly. "He's already gone to a
igher court than yours, Keeper."

"Hmm. Just one quick question—how long did you
ay you've had leprosy?"

The surprised man answered him, and Baldwin nodded, but with a puzzled expression.

Cecily sat in her small solar and eyed the knight suspiciously when the two men entered. "And what do you
vant this time? How often must you pester me?"

"Mistress, I apologize if we are disturbing you, but we have been talking to your husband and he suggested that you could help us with one last point."

"Thomas has told you all?" she asked, eyes round with shock.

Baldwin realized she hadn't heard about the two deaths the night before. He explained what had happened, and told her he knew Quivil had killed her father.

In response, her eyes filled with tears, and she turned away from them. After sniffing and wiping at her face, she exclaimed: "It's a huge relief! Oh, my God! It's as if I have been released from a curse: unable to admit what I knew, having to hide the man who killed my father, trying to keep calm to protect my husband! Perhaps it's odd that I should be pleased to hear that Edmund is dead—well, I am not happy at his death. But it is wonderful to know that at last I can tell the truth."

She slumped back in her seat as if exhausted, closing her eyes a moment. When she had recovered herself a little, aided by a strong draft of wine administered by her maid, she began to speak, and her tale was identical to Rodde's.

"It was a terrible shock to see him here after so long a separation," she confessed. "I had almost assumed the worst, that the disease had taken its hold on him, or even that he had died. Seeing him in Crediton was like seeing a man raised from the dead."

"You were conscious when the two left?"

"Yes. And thankfully, I could save our plate."

"That was what I was keenest to hear about," Baldwin smiled.

"You noticed it had gone, didn't you? You were very quick to see that. Well, it wasn't stolen. All that happened was, when Thomas and Edmund had gone, my maid came down and walked into the room. She screamed as soon as she saw us all lying on the ground. I called her over and told her I was all right, but while we spoke, John came in at full pelt."

"What was he doing there?"

"Visiting my maid."

"*She* was the woman John of Irelaunde was seeing! *That* explains a lot!"

"They had been meeting regularly for some weeks. I saw no harm in it, so I didn't stop them. John convinced me that he wasn't merely taking advantage of a young and impressionable girl."

"So that evening, John ran in, thinking something was wrong with his woman."

"Yes. I can't think he was anxious on my own account! He came in, and went straight to Alison. When he saw me, though, he came to my side. I told him to shove as much of the plate as possible into a sack."

"Why?"

"Father was down; I was hurt, though not badly; but he was unconscious and the other servants all away. There was no one to protect our silver, the best in Crediton, worth more than the plate in Exeter Cathedral! And you know as well as I how many outlaws there are—men who'd break down a door for a loaf of bread, let alone a king's ransom in silver!"

"If you had asked John to remain there, he could have looked after it for you."

"I couldn't! You know the reputation John has in the town. He's looked on as a conman and thief—how would people react to finding him in my house with two men knocked out and me feeble with a bloody mouth?"

"You could have stood up for him," Baldwin said reasonably.

"Sir Baldwin, I felt horrible—sick, weak, with a mas-

sive headache. I was in a terrible state of shock an
needed my bed. If I went up, and people came in an
found John, he'd be carted off before anyone woul
bother to speak to me. And while he was gone, anybod
could have come in and taken all the plate. No, I felt i
best that the more costly items should be hidden until
knew they could be protected."

"So John bundled up the plate and made his wa
home?"

"He wasn't going to originally. I only asked him t
put it all into a sack and take it up to my room, but the
we heard Coffyn and his men approaching."

Baldwin closed his eyes. "Let me just get this right,
he said. "Your father shouted, and was struck dowr
then Putthe ran in, and lastly John arrived. John wa
never left alone in here?"

"No. I was here all the time. I felt too weak to stand.

"We know that your father returned home because c
the arrival of Coffyn's men. So in the time it took fo
Godfrey to come back and be knocked down, in th
time it took for John to come in and find you, that wa
how long Coffyn and his men were running aroun
opening all the cupboards and searching the garder
Once they had finished, they came round here."

"That's right. As soon as we heard their steps ap
proaching the door, I told John to go in case he migh
be hurt. He wasn't sure about it, and he wasn't please
to leave my maid and me alone, but we insisted, and lu
cidly he went. I asked him to take the silver with hin
and he agreed. In the meantime I sent my maid out an
told her to listen at the door."

"But why? You were about to be safe, with Coffy
here."

She gave him a half-apologetic glance. "That may b

o, but at the time all I knew was that a man who was lesperate for money, who had borrowed money from ny father, was on his way. What would he do when he ound all the household's plate undefended?"

"You thought *Coffyn* could have tried to steal it?"

"He needs money."

"But for all you knew, your father was only uncon- cious, and Putthe could have woken at any moment. Vhy should Coffyn steal from you?"

"Sir Baldwin, I had noticed that whenever Coffyn ame here, he always used to look longingly at the late. Now, if someone was hard up for money and ney were to walk into a room in which the house- wner and his servant were knocked down, wouldn't ou wonder what they might do? As it was, when he ame into the room, I saw his gaze fly to the cup- oard. It didn't take him long to see the plate was one. Only then did he come to me and see how I was. Ie called my maid in, and ordered his man to help er take me upstairs. Once I was in my chamber, he ent for Tanner."

Simon was frowning with confusion. "But all we've eard suggests that Coffyn is wealthy now. I thought his ioney problems were over."

"Over?" Cecily laughed. "No, Matthew Coffyn owed iy father a small fortune. Oh, he may have been able keep up his lifestyle, but only with my father's assis- ince. I don't know what he'll do now."

"When did John bring back all the plate?" Baldwin sked.

"The night he was attacked. He was returning from elivering the plate here when he was taken, poor evil!"

Simon nodded. "And the horseshoe? You asked Jack

up here that night because you didn't want such a leper
hater to see Thomas in the street?"

"That's right—how did you guess? Jack loathed th
sight of lepers. The last thing I wanted was for Thoma
to be attacked, or for rumors of his visit to be bruite
abroad. Either would spell disaster. At the same time
allowed me to ensure that Putthe was out of the wa
as well."

"What about Putthe?" asked Baldwin. "He seems t
have been confused almost all the time. On the nigh
your father died, he hinted that John must have stole
the plate, then that the smith was involved—was tha
because you told him to confuse us?"

"Putthe can be a fool on occasion. Don't forget h
knew nothing about the plate being given to John fo
protection. All he knew was, I was seeing someone, an
then he noticed John in the yard just before he saw u
in the hall. He knew of John's reputation—wh
doesn't?—and when you told him the plate was gone
he leapt to the wrong conclusion."

"But the second time he more or less implied that th
smith must be guilty."

"By then he had been told how John had taken th
plate and looked after it. He had also been told off b
Alison, who left him in no doubt why John was visiting
Putthe was confused. He knew Jack and didn't tru
him. Who else should he think could be guilty?"

"I see," Baldwin said, and stood. "And now, I thin
we should leave you alone. You should be resting afte
so much excitement."

She smiled wistfully. "Yes, it's been a mad time. Fir
seeing my husband again, then my father dying by poo
Quivil's hand. My whole life appears to have changed i
a matter of days. But I can't let Thomas disappea
again."

"He may decide to go and leave you to begin a new ife," Simon pointed out.

"I cannot let him. Who else will be willing to take are of him?"

"Quite," said Baldwin, but he said it with a distracted ir, and he avoided her eyes.

- 27 -

n the street, Baldwin turned his moun toward the Dean's house. There th knight and his friend went through t John's room. John was happy enough t confirm the true events of the evening of Godfrey' death, but Simon noticed once more that Baldwin ap peared to be listening with only half an ear. His atten tion was elsewhere.

To Simon this was no surprise. Baldwin was be trothed, and the knight had plenty to consider. All th bailiff knew was that it was a relief Emma wouldn't b able to poison the marriage. Some women got so at tached to their maids that the possibility of discardin them was intolerable. Simon himself felt pretty muc the same about his own servant, Hugh. The man wa morose, sullen, and gloomy. He was slow, and often ir effectual. Yet he was a part of Simon's household, an life without him was unthinkable.

But it was also quite clear that a man like Baldwi who prized his hounds almost above all else, woul loathe the sight of someone who had tried to tease hi favorite into attacking, purely so that the dog must b destroyed. Simon shook his head. It was hard for him t nderstand, because he always felt dogs were just like ny other animal—he didn't like seeing them beaten or toned in the street, even if mangy and flea-ridden mutts ad to be killed—but they weren't something to get parcicularly fond of; they were just guards, and they earned heir food and drink by protecting their master. The ailiff would never have risked the hand of his wife beause of a blasted hound!

"Before you accuse me of fornication, Sir Baldwin, I hould tell you that Alison has already agreed to narry me."

"That is good to hear," Baldwin said. "Especially ince I know the hardship you endured in Ireland."

"It was a long time ago. It's time I found a life again."

"One thing I don't understand yet is why you told us nere were two men in Godfrey's garden, and that they nade you turn back to the house," Baldwin frowned as e and Simon sat on a bench near the Irishman's bed.

John grinned. "I knew very little at the time. Alison adn't told me about her mistress' husband, so I simply old you the truth. I didn't realize Mistress Cecily would ant to protect the men who had killed her father—hy should I? All I knew was, someone had attacked ne place and for all I knew the two men out near my all could have been them."

"That clears it all up," said Baldwin.

"I only hope this leg will clear up as quickly as your nystery has, Sir Baldwin," John muttered glumly.

"The monks here are as good as any in the realm," aldwin grinned. "And you have a new life to look forard to. I am sure your wife-to-be will visit you often assist your recovery."

The knight stood, smiling reassuringly down at the ounded man, and the bailiff also rose to his feet.

As Simon observed his friend, he mused over the

knight's affection for his dog. It led him to anothe thought. The incident with the dog was false; it had bee manufactured by the maid. If her deception hadn't bee witnessed by Hugh, Uther would probably (Simon stil wasn't convinced that Baldwin could have seen the brut killed) be dead, and Emma would be cock-a-hoop. H was reminded of his reflection the previous day as he rod back to Baldwin's house: appearances could be deceptive

"My God!"

His startled expostulation made Baldwin glance up momentarily brought out of his glum reflections "What?"

"That leper, Quivil! What did he look like?"

"Simon, what are you on about?"

"He was wasted, wasn't he? You recall his arms? Lik sticks. Ralph told us he had lost his appetite since learn ing of his disease, didn't he?"

"So?"

"Could a man in so weak a condition have crushe Godfrey's skull like that?"

Baldwin stared. Before he could speak, John inter rupted them.

"There is one thing I didn't understand, gentlemer While I was with Cecily, I really didn't think Godfre was dead. I mean, as a soldier, I've seen enough me who're dead or about to be, but Godfrey didn't look i He was just lying there as if he was asleep, you know?

Now Baldwin met Simon's gaze and nodded slowl "When you were attacked, John, why did you thin your home was ransacked?"

"Oh, because they were hoping to find the plat That's what I thought then, and I still think so now."

"But you couldn't tell us?"

"Mistress Cecily wanted to keep things quiet abou that night. It was her secret, not mine."

Simon took hold of his friend's arm. "Just as Coffyn ept his wife's secret! He wanted to keep things quiet bout her," he said urgently.

"What are you getting at, Simon?"

"Baldwin, for some time, according to Coffyn, he has aspected that his wife has been having an affair—and et he did little or nothing about it until now! Is it credle? Any man would take the revenge he took on John ere as soon as he realized what was going on!"

John stared from one to the other. "But nothing as!" he protested.

"Not with you, no. That was why Coffyn didn't atck you," Simon said, and sighed as he caught sight of s friend's expression. "Come on, Baldwin. We both now what happened, don't we?"

The knight rose, and was about to leave the room hen the infirmarer nursing John came back into the oom. Baldwin hesitated, then grabbed him and mutred to him. Simon thought the monk looked surprised be manhandled like that, but the bailiff saw him own, head on one side while he listened, then he gave vo sharp nods of agreement, and before he went to hn, Simon heard him say, "Yes, I will. It would be sy to check, as you say."

"Good. Now, come along Simon," Baldwin called ver his shoulder as he ran from the room.

he door was ajar, and Baldwin pushed it wide and enred the passage. He exchanged a glance with Simon. he house was silent. On every other occasion when ey had walked in, there had been a guard at the door, rvants rattling pots and pans, soldiers shouting or ughing as they played merrils or dice, yet now there as nothing.

They walked along the screens, Simon finding his

hand wandering to his sword-hilt in the darkened pas
sage. There were no candles in the sconces, no ope
door at the far end, and the light spilled out from th
hall itself. With the absence of noise, it was oddly ir
timidating, and Simon found he was unwilling to ste
into the pool of brightness.

Baldwin felt a similar tension. He was anxious to pre
vent another killing. It was a relief when he recognize
his quarry in the hall.

The room was almost empty. William sat on a benc
near the wall, swinging his legs idly, and his master wa
seated near the fire. The place seemed unnaturally quie

"I was about to find you to confess."

"You may do so now. It might help."

"It will," Coffyn said with conviction. He was
shrivelled hulk, a pallid reflection of his former self. A
he spoke, he had a knuckle resting on his chin as if i
preparation to chew the nails again should the pressu
become too much. "I have nothing to live for now. M
men have gone because they know I have no coin to pa
them with. My wife has left me. I think she's gone to h
brother in Exeter. My work is finished because sh
cleared out my strongbox before she went. I have notl
ing left. God has ruined me, and yet I don't know why

Baldwin sat opposite him, fixing the merchant with
serious, but compassionate stare. He waved briefly
William, who appeared to understand, and went
fetch wine for them. "God would not have been please
with your behavior, Matthew," Baldwin murmured.

"Eh? How dare you say that! Of course He would
the other stated scornfully. "I destroyed a man who wa
breaking one of His commandments. 'Thou shalt n
commit adultery,' remember? God would have bee
pleased with my efforts. And all I did with the lepe
was to fulfill His aim of punishing them."

Baldwin accepted a warmed mug of wine from Villiam, who walked to stand close to his master, al-hough whether to support Coffyn or to hold him, the night wasn't sure.

"When did you first realize Godfrey had seduced our wife?" asked Baldwin.

Coffyn shot him a black look before studying his ails. "You think *he* seduced *her*? That's charitable, Sir Baldwin. Personally I'd hesitate to jump to that conclu-ion. No matter! I never guessed he was interested in her ntil my last journey on business. Before that, we had ever got on particularly well. Suddenly, about four nonths ago, he began to take an interest in my work. As soon as he heard that things were becoming tough, e offered me some help.

"Now it seems so obvious. It was at just the same ime as Martha started preening herself. As she de-nanded new clothes and trinkets to show off her eauty, my neighbor offered me money. But the more I orrowed, the more he demanded in interest, and the nore my wife wanted tunics and jewels. I never thought e would cuckold me, just as I never thought she would lisgrace herself."

"When did you know for certain?"

"I'd heard something in the street about John with ny wife. People used to go quiet when they saw me, and ome pointed and laughed, but I knew she'd not de-nean herself to that extent. She's not the kind to want ender embraces from a miserable peasant like him. No, realized who was sleeping with her when I came home arly one day and heard him leaping from my roof. ome of my men were in the front garden, so whoever t was must have escaped through the back, and that neant whoever it was had got away over the fence into Godfrey's land. It made me start to wonder about Godfrey. When I went away the next time, the night Godfrey died, I had a man stationed out here. He went to the hall and asked for Godfrey, on the pretext that I wanted to check on a loan from him. But Godfrey wasn't there. That was when I knew for certain."

"So you came home, you searched your house, and while you did so, you heard his cry."

"I heard him shout, yes, but I didn't realize it was him at the time. My man was here, and told me Godfrey wasn't in his hall, so I searched my house. I was convinced he was here somewhere."

"But when you went to his house?"

"I ran round there to confront him, not save the bastard! The place was in a mess. Cecily was apparently coming round, and her maid came downstairs as I walked in. William here was with me. I told him to carry Cecily to her chamber, and while they were gone Godfrey began to groan.

"I was angry. Furious! That's my only excuse. As soon as he started making a noise, a red rage overcame me. I wouldn't have done it otherwise; I couldn't have."

"You hit him with what—a stick?"

In answer Coffyn jerked his head at the fire. "It was a blackthorn cudgel. I used to carry it with me all the time, but when I saw what I'd done, I couldn't keep it. The ball of the handle was smothered in gore, and I couldn't bear to use it again, so I broke it over my knee and threw it into Godfrey's fire."

"While your man went off to fetch the constable?"

"Yes. Just as a good citizen should. And when he arrived, I told him I'd found Godfrey already dead while the other two were merely wounded. And I walked home."

He broke off and glowered at the knight. "I don't regret it, Sir Baldwin. Godfrey was an evil, moneyıbbing bastard. He shafted me in business, and then ıfted my wife as well. It wasn't that he made me a ɔl, I could cope with that happily enough. No, it was ıt he took everything I had—money, marriage, every-ng! I killed him with as little compunction as I would ve killed a beetle."

"And what of John?"

"John of Irelaunde?" Coffyn glanced up uncompre-ndingly. "That shady little bugger? What of him?"

"He was innocent of any involvement with your wife, : you were happy to let others circulate the rumor ıt he had enjoyed an affair with her . . ."

"That was the reputation hc had cultivated for him-f, Sir Knight."

"But you were happy to go to his house and beat him, rely to deflect attention from yourself, weren't you? u knew perfectly well he had nothing to do with your fe's infidelity when you gave him that savage clubbing."

Simon let his hand fall on his friend's shoulder. Bald-n's voice had taken on a cold precision as the anger gan to overtake him. Feeling Simon's hand, the knight ɔk a deep breath and forced himself to relax a little.

Coffyn sat shaking his head, nibbling hard at a tiny ed of thumbnail. "I had to make sure you thought I s convinced of his guilt. If I did nothing about the Irish-ın, you might have realized I knew about Godfrey."

"Yes. That was why you were so careful to let him see u. It was important that he should be able to swear ıt you were his attacker." Baldwin stood, and his ice dropped. "Well, Matthew Coffyn, you have made ull confession, but it only serves to highlight your ilt. You were prepared to almost kill John without tification; to steal your neighbor's plate; and to com-t murder. There is only one penalty for all that—the ɔe!"

* * *

Ralph had finished tidying his chapel when Mary e-
tered. She walked quietly to the body at the hearse ar
stood there, shaking her head with grief.

"Mary, I am so very sorry."

"He had such a little life."

"But he has a great life now," he reminded her.

"I am grateful for that."

He could hear the doubt in her voice. "Mary, dor
believe what the uneducated say about lepers: Edmur
wasn't evil. He was certainly not a great sinner, for
followed Christ's teaching. He turned the other chee
he allowed another to kill him without using his ow
weapon in defense. He died refusing to protect himse
from another's attack. Christ would revere young E
mund as a friend."

"I am glad for that," she said quietly.

Her tears appeared to be a relief to her. Ral
thought her sadness looked overwhelming, but her ey
held gratitude too, as if in the midst of her misery s
was glad to have known her man. "What will you
now?" he asked.

"With Jack gone, I don't think anyone else will ma
my life too difficult, but I haven't changed my mind."

"You will go to the convent?"

"Yes. The Bishop has promised to find me a positi
with one of the convents in his diocese. I will spend n
time praying for Edmund and helping others who a
sick. After my treatment recently I feel I can understa
the suffering of others. Maybe I can help them."

"I will pray for you."

"Thank you, Brother. That would mean much to me

She closed her eyes and knelt before the altar, a
Ralph quietly left her. Outside the clear weather a
peared to be breaking at last, and heavy gray clou

ere hanging almost motionless in the air. He took in
e view for a while, tugging his robes tighter around
s body against the bitter wind.

Seeing a figure near the gate, Ralph frowned quickly,
en strolled over to him. "Thomas?"

"It is no good, Brother. My mind is made up. After
hat has happened here, I think I would always be a render of the attack, and that can't be good for the
mp or for the town."

"And you fear that you'll cause her more hurt?"

"What can I offer her? She's still young. Let her be-
me a widow once more. If she tries to stay with me,
e will be devoting her life to suffering. It's not right."

"I think you are right. And I wish you godspeed, my
end."

"Thank you."

Ralph noticed that a monk was walking toward them.
wasn't the almoner, for Ralph would have recognized
s bent back and slightly shuffling gait. This man
alked with a spring in his step. As he came closer, he
iled Ralph. "Brother, may I speak to you a moment?"

Shrugging, Ralph joined him at the gate. Rodde
aited patiently, his attention fixed on the town's
noke in the distance. When he was called, he was sur-
ised, but he ambled over willingly enough, although
e suppressed excitement in Ralph's voice made him
ary.

"Thomas, this brother would like to have a word
th you."

argaret walked slowly with Jeanne through the
ight's orchard. The clouds overhead tried to cast a
oomy atmosphere over the area, but Margaret
uldn't sense it. She was still filled with delight over the
ws of the night before.

"When will you arrange the celebration?"

Jeanne giggled. "I don't know! Perhaps early in t
New Year. I would like to wed in springtime. It seen
best to marry when the flowers are springing up and t
leaves are bright and fresh. A new year for beginning
new life—it seems appropriate, doesn't it?"

"Most appropriate! And I will look forward to it."

"So will I. He is a good man."

"He is," Margaret smiled. "You have won the hea
of a kind and noble gentleman."

"I am glad you think so too. It would be horrible
find myself attached to another man like my first hu
band," Jeanne said with a shudder.

Margaret put her arm round her friend's should
"You can forget your past now. Baldwin will be a goo
husband for you."

They were coming close to the house again, and in t
doorway they saw Hugh helping Wat to bring in woo
The dour servant nodded to his mistress, before she
herding the boy inside.

"Is that man always so miserable?" Jeanne whispere

"Oh yes," Margaret laughed. "He was born with a so
apple in his mouth and the flavor has never left him!"

They went through into the house and along t
screens. In the hall Wat was tending to the fire und
Hugh's supervision. Hugh rolled his eyes at his mistre
as the women passed the doorway.

"I think when you are the lady of this house you
need to take that boy under your wing," Margaret mu
mured, trying not to grin.

Jeanne caught the boy's glance and gave him a wink. H
instantly reddened to have been noticed by his maste
lady, and bent to his task with renewed vigor. His evide
embarrassment made Jeanne hurry to the door and out
the open air, where her laughter couldn't upset him.

But as they came out into the sunlight, her attention as caught by the low cloud of dust on the road. "Is at them? They've not been very long, if it is."

Margaret nodded, shielding her eyes from a sudden ısh of sunlight that burst from between the clouds. Yes. It's Baldwin and Simon."

The knight could see the two women standing waitg at the door, and instead of riding through to the staeyard as normal, he cantered along the roadway and ined in before them.

"Is there anything the matter?" asked Margaret.

"Nothing," replied the knight. "In fact, all is very ell indeed. A murderer is in jail. Let's get inside and e'll tell you what we've done today."

The fire was hissing and crackling merrily, the wine as warmed and spiced, sitting in pewter jugs on the arth, the cold meats had been brought out with bread, d the four made a good meal while Baldwin and mon told their ladies of their morning's discoveries.

"But why," said Jeanne, a slight frown wrinkling her ow, "why did Coffyn kill him then? Surely he could ve killed Godfrey at any time?"

"Yes," said Baldwin, "but at any other time he ouldn't have had his enemy totally at his mercy. There something about seeing a weak foe that does someing to a certain type of man. I think Coffyn is of that nd. He met with Godfrey regularly, and probably ssed the time of day with him, always having that gue, niggling doubt worrying at him, but never found e courage to strike at him, or even simply accuse him his face."

"Many men would have waited until they could find m with the woman and killed in hot blood," said argaret.

"And that was what he planned, I think. A surprise

return, followed by a hideous slaughter. But althoug
his blood was up, he couldn't find his quarry. It was on
when he remembered he had heard a shout from h
neighbor's house that he realized Godfrey must have g
home, and that was when he rushed next door. Ar
when he found that the man he hated was completely
his power, he couldn't stop himself. All alone in th
room with the man he loathed, and no one to preve
him taking his revenge. No constraints, no restrictions-
and best of all, everyone would assume, as they did, th
it was a tragic mistake, that the first blow had been t
one to kill Godfrey."

"Even the leper Quivil thought his blow had kill
him," mused Simon.

"I wonder whether his servant was persuade
though," said Baldwin.

Margaret paused with a morsel of meat at her mout
"Why?"

"He has the look of a man-at-arms. Even John n
ticed Godfrey didn't appear dead, and John had on
very limited experience of warfare. William, Coffy
guard, seems much more experienced. I think he mu
have known Godfrey wasn't dead when they first got
the hall."

"True," said Jeanne. "But just thinking Godfrey ha
died after they arrived wouldn't mean he'd automa
cally assume his master had murdered him. He'd pro
ably only think Godfrey had suffered some sort
collapse."

Baldwin shook his head. "I think it's more than th
Jeanne. He must have realized his master's stick was mis
ing; I suspect he noticed Godfrey's wound was wor
than when he first arrived. I expect he'd never admit
but I think he knew perfectly well who was guilty."

"Which leads us on to the other leper," said Ma

ıret. "He is the man I am most sorry for. And how his ›or wife must feel! What a love she must have for her an, that she can still adore him when he is so deously disfigured."

Baldwin grinned and took a sip of wine. "That is the her thing. Thomas Rodde is not actually very revolt-g. Oh, he's got lots of sores, and he looks a bit of a ess, but what can you expect from someone who lives a lazar house?"

"But to think what he will become! And this Cecily ill wants to stay with him and tend to him. She must ıve great courage."

"I think she has to be one of the most loyal women ıaginable," said Simon frankly. "Don't look at me like at, Meg! There's no point denying the fact that most omen would desert their spouse if he developed that sease. Yet this woman wants to make sure she doesn't se him again, and she appears to be utterly determined ı that score."

"And now, thanks to God, I think they may be able live together," said Baldwin.

Jeanne stared at him. "You mean the leper master has ;reed to let her live with him?"

"I fear not. Brother Ralph is quite determined too, in s own way."

"So they will leave the town together? That's a ame. But maybe it's for the best. There are so many d memories for them both in Crediton."

Baldwin let both arms fall to the table, and shook ith laughter. "No, Jeanne! That's not it!"

It was Simon who explained, while the knight chor-:d. "You see, this odious knight of yours has travelled ıdely. He has been to the Holy Land, and while he was ere, he saw many lepers. But there are different kinds skin disease."

"There are two forms of leprosy," said Baldwi
"*Morphea alba* and *morphea nigra*. It is hard to t
them apart, but if you prick the skin with a needle—

"Baldwin!" Margaret wailed, pushing her trench
from her.

He gave her a grin of apology. "Let it be said, the
that there is an easy enough test, but *morphea alba*
curable. It is not the true leprosy, for that would k
even a strong man in less than eight years, and we
know what an old leper looks like. Yet this man told r
that he had carried his disease for over nine years
ready. It struck me that his illness couldn't be the bla
morphew."

Jeanne stared. "You mean all the time the poor fellc
has been living in leper camps he has been free of t
disease?"

"Exactly. He is no more a leper than I am. And so
I think I should be able to have him declared clean
the Dean. As soon as that happens, he'll be free to ta
up his life again. And so will Cecily."

"So the murderer is arrested, the leper will be cure
and all ends well," said Jeanne.

"Apart from poor Quivil," said Margaret. "He we
to his death thinking he had murdered a man—in fa
it was probably *why* he allowed himself to be killed.
he had felt innocent, surely he would have defend
himself."

Baldwin eyed her thoughtfully. "Perhaps," he sa
"But then, how can we tell? It was undoubtedly a b
ter death for him than the slow and lingering one fa
was holding for him, and for that I am sure he w
grateful. Especially since he died without defendi
himself, just as Christ taught. That must be some sola
to his soul."

They had all but finished their meal, and Edgar nc

released the mastiff. Uther bounded in joyfully, running pell-mell for his master, and sat at his feet panting, a long dribble of saliva hanging from one jowl.

"And you helped us get to the truth, Chops," said Simon.

Baldwin stroked the broad head, ruffling the short fur. Uther panted up at him, mouth gaping in a broad smile. Then he twitched round, his great paw lifted, and he scratched at his ear. Baldwin watched, paralyzed with horror as the long stream of dribble rose, curved, performed a short, sinuous dance, and finally flicked off, climbing upward before the knight's face, seeming to get ever closer.

Edgar, out in the buttery with Hugh, was sitting on a barrel and chatting when they heard the roar. He half-rose, then shrugged and sat back again.

"What was that?" asked the mystified Hugh.

"From the sound," said Edgar, taking a reflective pull of his ale, "I think my master is debating whether to ask Emma to stay."

If you enjoyed
THE LEPER'S RETURN,
turn the page to explore
the first five books in the intriguing
Knights Templar Mystery Series
from Michael Jecks

—

THE LAST TEMPLAR
THE MERCHANT'S PARTNER
A MOORLAND HANGING
THE CREDITON KILLINGS
THE ABBOT'S GIBBET

*In **THE LAST TEMPLAR**, Simon Puttock has just been appointed bailiff of Lydford Castle, when he's called to a village where a charred body has been found in a burned-out cottage. Unaccustomed to violence in this peaceful area, Simon assumes it's an accidental death—but his partner, Sir Baldwin Furnshill, quickly convinces him that the victim had been killed before the fire began!*

/hen Tanner and the others arrived, the constable was ırprised to find the monk and the bailiff sitting by the de of the road in front of a small fire. The monk rose nmediately and ran to greet them, his nervous features 'acking with an expression of desperate relief, and hen Tanner caught a glimpse of the bailiff he began to ıderstand why he was grateful for the new arrivals. imon did not move. He sat still and quiet with his oak wrapped tightly around him as he stared into the re. Tanner dismounted and walked over to him.

"Thank God you've arrived! We were wondering hether you'd all wait for morning before coming and e didn't want to stay here alone all night," said the onk, breathlessly, as Tanner walked to the bailiff. he constable nodded absently and continued on, leavg the monk to welcome the others.

"Bailiff? What's wrong, bailiff?"

Simon could only slowly bring his eyes up from the re. After the horror in the woods he felt more tired an he had ever been in his life before. The nervous

energy and the anger that had kept him going throug
the woods had drained him, and the horror of the sigh
in the clearing and his mad rush back to the road ha
finished the job. Now as he looked up he seemed to th
constable to have aged by twenty years since the after
noon; his face was gaunt and pale and his eyes glittere
as if he was in a fever, and Tanner crouched quickl
beside him, his face full of concern. Simon hardl
seemed to notice him. Almost as if he wanted not t
see the constable, he turned his gaze back to the fir
and stared vacantly into the flames.

"Bailiff? What's happened?" said the constable i
shocked amazement.

"We got here just before dark," Simon said quietl
"We found it easily enough. David—that's the monk—
he found it quite quickly. The tracks were clear, goin
off into the woods over there." He pointed briefly wit
his chin to the opposite side of the road and returned t
his solitary stare, talking softly and calmly while th
constable frowned at him in anxious concern. "I tol
David to wait here for you and I went in alone. I mu
have been going for over an hour when I found a sma
clearing. One horse at least had been kept there; the
was a fresh pile of shit where it had been tied."

Simon looked up suddenly and the constable felt th
pain in the bailiff's eyes as they searched his face for
moment before returning to their introspective study
the flames. "The abbot was not far away. I carried on an
found him. He had been tied up—tied to a tree. Someon
had gathered up a load of twigs and branches and pile
them underneath him." Tanner saw him shudder once, i
voluntarily, but then his voice continued calmly. "The
set light to them and burned the abbot to death."

*In **THE MERCHANT'S PARTNER**, the mutilated body of a midwife and healer is discovered one wintry morning, and at first it appears that a lack of clues will render the crime unsolvable. Soon suspicion falls on a local youth. But Sir Baldwin has doubts about the boy's guilt, and enlists Simon in a hunt for the real murderer. And the truth, which lies beneath layers of jealousy, suspicion, and hatred, could prove fatal to anyone who disturbs it.*

Six miles to the south the Bourc was glancing up through the trees as he rode, retreating into his cloak in the bitter cold. On either side the trees rose stolidly impervious to the weather, but high above he could catch occasional glimpses of the stars, shining as tiny pinpricks of light which flared and were hidden like sparks from a fire. They glittered briefly before being smothered by the ghostly clouds rushing by, clouds that made him frown with wary anxiety. They raced by as if fearful of the weather that he knew must chase hard on their heels.

Hearing hooves, he stopped and stared ahead cautiously. It was late to be traveling. Soon he saw a man riding toward him. Showing his teeth in a short grin, he nodded. The other man, dressed warm and dark for hunting, nodded back and hurried on. The Bourc smiled ruefully to himself. He was muddy from splashing through puddles, and he knew he was hardly a sight to inspire confidence in a stranger. At a sudden thought he turned, and saw that the man was staring back with frank interest. The Bourc smiled ruefully as he kicked his horse and ambled off toward Wefford.

He had travelled far enough tonight. At the first clearing that looked hopeful, he pulled off the road. Through the trees he could see a cabin, a simple affair of rough-hewn logs. Part of the roof was gone, and it was in a sorry state, but for all that it was a refuge from the worst of the wind. He led the horses inside and saw to them before starting a fire.

Chewing at some dried meat, he considered his options. His business was finished now, so there was nothing to keep him here. The sooner he could get home the better. If he continued this way, heading to the west and retracing the route he had taken from the coast, he should arrive within a couple of days, but it would surely take a lot longer than necessary. The journey west to Oakhampton and then south was quite out of his way, working its way round the perimeter of the moors. It would be more direct and quicker to cut straight south, over the moors to the sea that way.

It was still dark the next morning, Wednesday, when, over to the south of Furnshill, Samuel Cottey harnessed his old mule to the wagon and prepared for his journey, cursing in the deep blackness before dawn as his already numbed fingers struggled with the rough brass and leather fittings, pulling hard at the thick leather straps.

"Sorry, my love," he muttered as he occasionally caught a flap of skin in the buckles, making the old animal snort and stamp. "Not long, now. We'll soon have you done."

All set, he stood back and surveyed his work, rubbing the bandage on his arm that covered the long

sh. It was a week ago now that the branch had
opped from the tree he was felling and slashed the
sh of his arm like a sword, but, thanks to God, the
d woman's poultices seemed to be working and it
as healing. Sighing, he stretched and then walked
ck to the cottage, stamping his feet to get the feeling
return to cold toes. Inside the smoky room, he
armed himself by the fire in the clay hearth in the
iddle, smiling crookedly from the side of his mouth,
 lips pale and thin in the square, ruddy face under
 hatch of gray hair. Sarah, his daughter, smiled back
to his light brown eyes as she handed his mug full of
armed beer to him and watched carefully as he
ained it, smacking his lips and wiping his hand over
s mouth, then burping appreciatively. Giving her a
ick grin, he passed back the mug.

"That's good," he said, then kissed her cheek briefly.
e back soon as I can—I'll try to be home before
rk, anyway."

When she nodded, he left, stomping quickly to the
agon and clambering aboard, whistling for his dog.
ter a quick wave, he snapped the reins and began to
ake his way from Wefford to Crediton, the dog bark-
g excitedly behind.

As he left the light from the open doorway behind,
s mind turned back to their problems. This last year
d been the hardest he had known, especially since
s brother had been killed by the trial bastons, down
 to the south on the moors. Now the family relied on
n alone to keep both farms going. His sister-in-law
as right when she said that the two families could not
e on either holding: both were too small to support
em all, and neither could be expanded without a deal
 work, hacking down the trees that fringed them. No,
 only way to continue was by keeping both going.

But how to do that? There was only him, his daugh
ter Sarah, and his brother's son Paul. There was to
much work for them, now that they had to try to kee
both properties working. Maybe they should do
Sarah suggested, and buy more pigs. At least the
could often feed themselves; they did not need grai
like cows.

The sun was lighting the eastern sky as he rattle
and squeaked his way down the track into the villag
head down, chin on his chest and shoulders hunched i
an effort to keep the bitter cold from his vulnerabl
neck. Samuel had been a farmer for many years, and h
was used to the cruelty of the wind and the freezin
snow that attacked the land every winter, but th
weather got worse with each passing year. Glancin
up, he saw the sky was lighted with a vivid angry re
and sighed. The sharpness of the air, the streamers
mist from his mouth, and the red sky could only mea
one thing: snow was on its way at last.

Passing the inn on his left, he glanced at it wi
longing, already wishing he could stop and warm him
self before the great fire in the hall but, shuddering ar
shivering, he carried on, rubbing at his arm every no
and again. Beyond was the turn he needed, and h
made off to the right, toward Crediton, where h
brother's farm lay, between the town itself and San
ford. He had to collect their chickens and take the
into the market. Paul was still too young to be allowe
to go to market on his own.

It was hard, he thought, sighing again. If only
Judith had lived longer. But his wife had succumbed
the pestilence that followed on the tail of the rain th
killed off the harvest two years ago.

The trees suddenly seemed to crowd in around hir
their thick trunks looming menacingly from the th

ist that still lay heavy on the ground, almost appear-
g to be free of the earth, as if they could move and
alk if they wished. It was this feeling that made him
iver again, peering up at the branches overhead.
om somewhere deep in the trees came the screech of
bird, then some rooks called overhead, sounding
range and unnatural.

All he could hear was the clattering and squeaking
the wagon, with the occasional dull, deadened
ump as the iron-shod wheels struck stones or fell into
les, and it felt impossible that any noise could be
ard over the row he made, but still he caught the
unds of the waking forest, and his eyes flitted here
d there nervously, as if fearing what he might see.

Then, all at once, he was out of it. The track led up-
ard here, to a small hill where the woods had been
eared, and he drew a deep breath of relief, blowing it
t in a long feather of misted air. The feelings of
ead left him, and he squirmed on the board that made
s seat, telling himself he was a fool to be fearful of
ises in the woods.

Cold-blooded murder has transformed Simon's official obligation into something horrid—and he will need the assistance of his friend, Sir Baldwin, to draw a criminal out.

*In **A MOORLAND HANGING**, justice must be served even if their search exposes extortion and foul corruption, and killers willing, even eager, to shed more blood.*

—

"They are certainly very curious. All the branche point in the same direction—had you noticed that?"

"It's as if they're pointing to something, isn't i There are rumors I've heard . . ."

"Yes?"

"Well, you remember the stories, don't you? Abo the Devil and his pack of wish-hounds baying after lo souls? This is where those stories come from, Baldwi out here on the moors. They say that the wish-houn are heard here when the winds blow hard."

Baldwin gave him a sour stare. "I suppose you thir the hounds come here to piss on the trees? Diabolic hounds peeing on the branches kill them off, and th makes the oaks die on one side? Really, Simon, I—"

"No, of course not," said Simon, hastily holding u a hand to stem the knight's ironic flow. "But I know wouldn't want to stay here after dark."

"No, I can see why," said Baldwin reflectively, ga ing at the trees. The atmosphere was oppressive, I thought, and it was easy to understand how peop

uld imagine the worst of such a place, especially if
: wind howled among the boughs as night fell. Bald-
n did not believe in old wives' tales himself, but it
is natural for anyone to be affected by the menacing
wer of a place like this.

"The people here think there's some kind of strange-
ss about it," Simon continued. "Maybe that's where
: names come from. Round here, 'wisht' means un-
nny, or weird. Certainly these trees look it."

"Yes, they do. But I think these trees grow this way
· some mundane reason. Wish-hounds!" His voice
trayed his amusement, and the bailiff shot him a sus-
:ious glance.

Another mile southward, after they had breasted an-
ner hill, Baldwin at last understood why Simon had
ought him this way. He reined in his horse and stared.

"This is what I wanted you to see, Baldwin. Wel-
me to the tin mines of Dartmoor!", Simon announced
they came to a halt.

Baldwin found himself staring at a wide encamp-
:nt on a plain surrounded by low hills, the whole un-
irked by wall or fence. Dotted here and there stood
iall, gray turf and stone cottages. One, larger than the
iers and set in their midst, gave off a thick plume of
oke which straggled in the slight breeze. The broad
:a was pitted and scarred with holes and trenches.
rough the middle trailed a narrow but fast-flowing
eam, from which sprang several man-made rivulets,
d there was a large dam over to their right. Other
ts were fed by this, tailing off into the distance, and
ldwin guessed that they led to other workings.

"With all these houses, there must be many men
re," said Baldwin, eyeing the area speculatively.

"An army. Over a hundred in this camp alone,"
non agreed, and kicked his horse on.

They had only traveled a short way when they saw
pair of men at the outskirts of the vill, and Sim
smiled with sardonic amusement at their reaction—
was all too typical of the attitude of miners out he
that they should be suspicious of strangers. O
pointed in their direction before running off, while t
other man grasped what looked like a pick and fac
them resolutely. By the time the bailiff and his frie
had come closer, there was a group waiting for the
looking like trained soldiers to Baldwin's military ey
The man who had run for help had returned, joined
a thickset character who looked as if he was in charg

The town of Crediton is awaiting an important guest, the Bishop of Exeter. Unfortunately, a local band of mercenaries has been stirring up trouble in the town, and Bailiff Simon Puttock and his partner, Sir Baldwin Furnshill, are put in charge of keeping order for the visit of the town's esteemed guest. But when the bishop's welcome dinner is disrupted by a robbery, and a young girl is discovered murdered, ***THE CREDITON KILLINGS*** *have begun, and Simon and Baldwin must identify the killer before their own lives are put at risk . . .*

—

nd who are these, I wonder?" he murmured.

"Who?" Adam asked, his train of thought broken. rning, he could see at last the source of the noise he d heard earlier.

Coming down the road toward them was a group of en, but these were no ordinary travellers, and Adam t himself stiffen. They *were* soldiers.

Out in front were two riders on tired-looking but rdy ponies. Both wore quilted jacks, stained and thy from long use, over green tunics. One had on a sinet with the visor tilted up, and held a lance in s hand, while the other wore a long-bladed knife e a short sword. Both stared at the two men by the ad, and the helmeted one winked at Adam before ssing.

Behind them came another, seated on a massive ck stallion which gleamed as if it had been oiled as

it passed among the pools of daylight. It was this m
who immediately caught Peter's eye.

He was huge, at least six feet tall, and his demear
showed he was used to commanding men. It was the
in his self-awareness and stillness, in the way
scarcely glanced at the strangers by the side of t
road, but rode on, his frown fixed ahead as if searchi
out new battles. His tunic showed the effects of da
on the road, but was made of expensive cloth and b
no device to show his allegiance. Crediton w
renowned for its wool, and Peter, like most men fr
the town, could recognize quality material. This ma
was very good. Light, soft, and fine woven, under
layer of dust it was the fresh crimson of a good, fu
bodied wine. Whoever the man was, he must surely
wealthy.

Adam's glance fell on the men behind. Three m
were on horseback, but behind were at least anot
twenty, and wagons trailed along in the rear. He co
not help cringing away. Warrior bands were too unp
dictable for his liking.

As the stallion came level with him, Peter Cliff
stepped forward. "Good morning, sir. Peace be with yo

The little column of men and horses stopped, a
there was silence for a moment. Then the man's he
snapped to Clifford and stared at him unblinking
The priest smiled, but his face slowly froze under t
intense gaze of the pale gray eyes. They were wide-
in the square face, and held no compassion, only c
tempt. Unnerved, the priest nearly retreated under th
sullen scrutiny. He had no idea what he had said
cause so much offense. As he opened his mouth
speak further, the knight spat at his feet.

"There, *Priest*!" he said. "So much for your peac

"I meant no insult, sir, it was merely a greeting—

"No insult?" he thundered, and his horse stamped and blew as if it too felt the depth of the slight. This time Clifford could not help himself taking a quick step back. Adam felt a prickle of cold fear wash his back as, suddenly, the man leaned down until his elbow rested on the horse's withers, and he looked back at the men on foot. " 'No insult,' the little priest says. 'No insult,' " he sneered, and faced Clifford again. "Do you think we are friars, Priest? Do we look like monks? Or maybe you think we're weavers and millers looking for a new market. We are *soldiers,* man! We fight for our living. We don't want peace! In peacetime we starve. We want *war*! The pox on your peace!"

It is 1319. Tavistock's fair has drawn merchants to Devon from all of England and beyond. Keeping the streets clean and the locals in order is no easy task, since the influx of visitors and their money puts temptations in the way of cut-purses and other villains.

But in ***THE ABBOT'S GIBBET*** *no one expects a murder, and the town butcher is stunned when he comes across a headless corpse! Sir Baldwin Furnshill and Bailiff Simon Puttock have just arrived in town as guests of Abbot Robert Champeaux when the body is found. When the Abbot asks Baldwin and Simon to investigate, they can hardly refuse. But with an unidentifiable victim, their task won't be an easy one.*

—

Of all the roads he'd travelled since the murders, this one, with the unwanted memories insinuating themselves into his mind, felt the most ominous.

The trees met overhead, their branches intermingling to shut out the light and creating a cavern twilight beneath. Here in the gloom lay the road. In the oppressive, muggy heat of late August, the horses' hooves and harnesses sounded dull. Soft grass underfoot deadened the tramping feet. The rumble of the wagon wheels, the squeaking of the axles and chains, the hollow rattle of pans knocking together, all sounded dead to him, as if he was riding on in a dream in which the pictures were distinct but all noise had been killed. Many years ago this envi ronment had given him peace. Now it represented only danger.

As the track began to rise, he could remember that last journey as distinctly as if it had been last week, not years ago. It felt as if the road was taking him back to his past, and it was with a mixture of fear and hope that he jolted along. Both struggled to overcome him, but he kept his face expressionless. His fellow travellers could not guess at his emotions.

It was nearly twenty years ago, he recalled. Yet after so long, the smells and sounds were still familiar. This was the place of his birth. These were the smells of his childhood: herbs, peat fires, the tang of cattle in their yards, the musky stench of humans. Even the reek from the midden was oddly poignant.

Now, over the creaking and thundering of the wagons, he could hear other noises. There was hammering and shouting, the rasp of saws through wood, and echoing thuds as axes sliced into boughs. They were the noises of his youth, the cacophony of business as could be heard in any thriving borough, but in these surroundings they gave him a feeling of release, as if he was at last being freed from his isolation.